W9-CJP-352

1

STRAIGHT OUT OF LEWIS

CARROLL'S

TRASH CAN

A JONATHAN TOLLHAUSLER ADVENTURE [*]

BY

MICHAEL J. RUMPF

---

[*] Book 1 in the How Did We Get Here? Series

THIS BOOK IS

LOVINGLY

DEDICATED TO

EVERYONE OUT

THERE WHO EVER

ATTENDED COLLEGE.

WHAT DID *YOU*

LEARN?

Let's take a trip on memory's ship
Back to the bygone days
Sail to the old village school house
Anchor outside the school door
Look in and see
There's you and there's me
A couple of kids once more

School days, school days
Dear old golden rule days
Readin' and 'ritin' and 'rithmetic
Taught to the tune of the hickory stick
You were my queen in calico
I was your bashful barefoot beau
And you wrote on my slate
"I love you, so"
When we were a couple of kids

'Member the hill
Nellie Darling
And the oak tree
That grew on its brow
They've built forty storeys
Upon that old hill
And the oak's an old chestnut now
'Member the meadows
So green, dear
So fragrant with clover and maize
Into new city lots
And preferred business plots
They've cut them up
Since those days *

_____

*1Lyrics from School Days, School Days
Music by Gus Edwards; Lyrics by Will D. Cobb, 1907

SEPTEMBER 7 OCTOBER17 NOVEMBER 2 NOVEMBER 30 DECEMBER 30
SEPTEMBER 7 OCTOBER17 NOVEMBER 2 NOVEMBER 30 DECEMBER 30
SEPTEMBER 7 OCTOBER17 NOVEMBER 2 NOVEMBER 30 DECEMBER 30
SEPTEMBER 7 OCTOBER17 NOVEMBER 2 NOVEMBER 30 DECEMBER 30
SEPTEMBER 7 OCTOBER17 NOVEMBER 2 NOVEMBER 30 DECEMBER 30
SEPTEMBER 7 OCTOBER17 NOVEMBER 2 NOVEMBER 30 DECEMBER 30
SEPTEMBER 7 OCTOBER17 NOVEMBER 2 NOVEMBER 30 DECEMBER 30
SEPTEMBER 7 OCTOBER17 NOVEMBER 2 NOVEMBER 30 DECEMBER 30
SEPTEMBER 7 OCTOBER17 NOVEMBER 2 NOVEMBER 30 DECEMBER 30
SEPTEMBER 7 OCTOBER17 NOVEMBER 2 NOVEMBER 30 DECEMBER 30
SEPTEMBER 7 OCTOBER17 NOVEMBER 2 NOVEMBER 30 DECEMBER 30
SEPTEMBER 7 OCTOBER17 NOVEMBER 2 NOVEMBER 30 DECEMBER 30
SEPTEMBER 7 OCTOBER17 NOVEMBER 2 NOVEMBER 30 DECEMBER 30
SEPTEMBER 7 OCTOBER17 NOVEMBER 2 NOVEMBER 30 DECEMBER 30
SEPTEMBER 7 OCTOBER17 NOVEMBER 2 NOVEMBER 30 DECEMBER 30
SEPTEMBER 7 OCTOBER17 NOVEMBER 2 NOVEMBER 30 DECEMBER 30
SEPTEMBER 7 OCTOBER17 NOVEMBER 2 NOVEMBER 30 DECEMBER 30
SEPTEMBER 7 OCTOBER17 NOVEMBER 2 NOVEMBER 30 DECEMBER 30
SEPTEMBER 7 OCTOBER17 NOVEMBER 2 NOVEMBER 30 DECEMBER 30
SEPTEMBER 7 OCTOBER17 NOVEMBER 2 NOVEMBER 30 DECEMBER 30
SEPTEMBER 7 OCTOBER17 NOVEMBER 2 NOVEMBER 30 DECEMBER 30
SEPTEMBER 7 OCTOBER17 NOVEMBER 2 NOVEMBER 30 DECEMBER 30
SEPTEMBER 7 OCTOBER17 NOVEMBER 2 NOVEMBER 30 DECEMBER 30
SEPTEMBER 7 OCTOBER17 NOVEMBER 2 NOVEMBER 30 DECEMBER 30

September 7, 1983:
"That's a very interesting name."

SEPTEMBER 7 OCTOBER17 NOVEMBER 2 NOVEMBER 30 DECEMBER 30
SEPTEMBER 7 OCTOBER17 NOVEMBER 2 NOVEMBER 30 DECEMBER 30
SEPTEMBER 7 OCTOBER17 NOVEMBER 2 NOVEMBER 30 DECEMBER 30
SEPTEMBER 7 OCTOBER17 NOVEMBER 2 NOVEMBER 30 DECEMBER 30
SEPTEMBER 7 OCTOBER17 NOVEMBER 2 NOVEMBER 30 DECEMBER 30
SEPTEMBER 7 OCTOBER17 NOVEMBER 2 NOVEMBER 30 DECEMBER 30
SEPTEMBER 7 OCTOBER17 NOVEMBER 2 NOVEMBER 30 DECEMBER 30
SEPTEMBER 7 OCTOBER17 NOVEMBER 2 NOVEMBER 30 DECEMBER 30
SEPTEMBER 7 OCTOBER17 NOVEMBER 2 NOVEMBER 30 DECEMBER 30
SEPTEMBER 7 OCTOBER17 NOVEMBER 2 NOVEMBER 30 DECEMBER 30
SEPTEMBER 7 OCTOBER17 NOVEMBER 2 NOVEMBER 30 DECEMBER 30
SEPTEMBER 7 OCTOBER17 NOVEMBER 2 NOVEMBER 30 DECEMBER 30
SEPTEMBER 7 OCTOBER17 NOVEMBER 2 NOVEMBER 30 DECEMBER 30
SEPTEMBER 7 OCTOBER17 NOVEMBER 2 NOVEMBER 30 DECEMBER 30
SEPTEMBER 7 OCTOBER17 NOVEMBER 2 NOVEMBER 30 DECEMBER 30
SEPTEMBER 7 OCTOBER17 NOVEMBER 2 NOVEMBER 30 DECEMBER 30
SEPTEMBER 7 OCTOBER17 NOVEMBER 2 NOVEMBER 30 DECEMBER 30
SEPTEMBER 7 OCTOBER17 NOVEMBER 2 NOVEMBER 30 DECEMBER 30
SEPTEMBER 7 OCTOBER17 NOVEMBER 2 NOVEMBER 30 DECEMBER 30
SEPTEMBER 7 OCTOBER17 NOVEMBER 2 NOVEMBER 30 DECEMBER 30

1

That morning, the semester officially began for him when his teacher, Anne Hathaway, promptly arrived at 8:40. Carefully packed into a tailored blue business suit, she strolled to her desk, gently placed her gray brief case down, and began distributing a syllabus to the class.

His attention slowly drifted away as the aroma of freshly brewed coffee wafted passed, and then his stomach growled. He watched with envy as the student across the aisle from him happily sipped away at a large green and white container of coffee and wished he had had the foresight to buy a cup.

He prayed for a short class.

In a calm, firm voice, Ms. Hathaway explained the course objectives for **SPEECH** 101, and after going over her one page syllabus, announced that everyone was going to stand up and give their first speech of the semester.

"Nothing complicated," she assured them. "What you'll do is stand up and introduce yourselves to the class. This way we can get acquainted, and I'll get an idea of where we all stand. And please, tell us anything else you might think is relevant or would like to share about yourself with the rest of the class. An introduction doesn't have to be just your name and Major. It can be so much more."

He squeezed his eyes shut and vowed to pray next time with greater conviction.

Thirty minutes later, he was still in the middle of row 6, but now he was frowning. Ms. Hathaway was seated at the front of the room, wearing a very interested expression, and in the back, a burly fellow by the name of Gus Wills was busy expounding upon the benefits of joining the ROTC.

He assumed this was what a speech class was supposed to be. Of course, he hadn't really signed up for SPEECH 101 because he wanted to learn how to make a speech. He had taken this class because it was supposed to be easy. *Everyone* had recommended it to him. "Do the small amount of work the teacher expects," they had told him, "and you should be able to sleepwalk out of there with an A."

He liked the idea of sleepwalking through a class, and could always use another A on his transcripts. He could use a lot more.

But he really didn't like easy classes. In his mind, they were a charade, a sham, a cheat of education. Take this class, do the work prescribed on the syllabus, and you get an A. Return with the aforementioned items and you were set. That wasn't education. That was a grocery list. Still, he didn't have to wrestle with his conscience too long, and there he was in a guaranteed Vaseline course (You just slide on through.).

He sighed. He wanted to be far away from this classroom and its ugly polished tiles. He'd already read the syllabus and the graffiti on his desk twice, and there wasn't much else left to do.

He knew he could always listen to his classmates, but he'd noticed how most of them had been saying the same damned things over and over again; all of it dull, superfluous nonsense even they found tedious. Of course, he had to admit, there were some exceptions.

"My name is Frank Brosius, but I like being called Tad."

11

Ms. Hathaway nodded. "Class, this is?"

"Tad," they replied, some people mumbling and others shifting in their seats.

"My Major is Business Administration. I want to go far with it, you know, become a manager or something, you know, something lasting and secure." Tad straightened the collar of his polo shirt. "Part time I work for this accounting firm. I make good money, and they've told me they'll gladly hire me after I graduate. I'll probably take them up on their offer, but I'm going to keep looking, just in case something better comes along. I drive a Honda Accord, and I think graduate school might not be a bad idea, especially since it could increase my earning potential."

Now, he understood confident students, but some spoke as if they'd already seen their lives played out. They had made their plans and there would be no deviations. It was crazy. He was never that certain about anything, especially his future.

He surveyed the people around him. A pretty girl was seated to his right, and he wondered what it would be like to speak with her. He imagined talking to her at the end of class and inviting her over to the cafeteria for a cup of coffee. It'd be great, he decided with a smirk, but he knew it would never happen.

Jonathan hadn't had much luck in this area in the past. Usually when he tried to strike up a conversation with a woman he didn't know, his voice would either become three octaves higher (Due to nerves) or he would mumble incoherently (Also due to nerves) and those few times he could speak naturally, he would inevitably say something stupid (Due to gender).

At the moment, a short girl with green and red-tinted hair was standing. "....my real name is Barbara, but I'd prefer it if you'd call me Norn..."

He sighed again. If he had trouble speaking to one stranger, what was he going to do when it came time to talk to an entire room full of them?

Jonathan would have liked to dismiss what was going on as just boring routine (Everyone had to do this the first day of classes.), but he had to admit it was also a little intimidating. Well, it was more than a little intimidating. It was downright frightening, and his gut was alive with a gallon-of-adrenaline-wildly-coursing-through-my-veins quiver. It was a flutter that only reminded him he wasn't comfortable doing this. What *would* he say?

To be clear--for those of you who might be skimming this on a crowded bus--Jonathan was terribly insecure, introverted and self-conscious. Consequently, he wasn't at all happy about the situation, and felt more and more nauseous as his turn approached.

It was going to be soon.

The first person in his row stood up.

He felt butterflies in his stomach.

The next person took the floor, and the butterflies suddenly turned into bats with huge, leathery wings. The bats were replaced by jet airliners as the girl in front of him began to stand. Then she was sitting down, and he was convinced he was going to vomit, two space shuttles blasting fiery liquid oxygen into his belly.

He stood up and looked around. The teacher was smiling, patient and attentive, waiting for him to start, and he glanced over his shoulder, as if maybe he wasn't next.

"Next," Anne Hathaway said helpfully.

He knew he would have to say something. What did everyone else start with? "I'm Jonathan Tollhausler."

"And what would you like us to call you?"

She had been asking everyone this, but he didn't particularly care how he was addressed. He'd answer to just about anything, even hand gestures. However, he wasn't quite sure how to politely impart this information to the class. "Uh, Jonathan or Jon's fine with me."

"All right Jonathan or Jon. Class, this is?"

"Jonathan or Jon."

They smiled, and Jonathan smiled back. It was a welcome bit of humor, and had brought practically everyone back to consciousness.

However, the moment didn't last very long, and once again, everyone was waiting for him to proceed. It was quiet, Tollhausler reflected, a little *too* quiet. He was scared and feeling slightly dizzy. Then he remembered something very important: He was crazy.

"Ms. Hathaway, ladies and gentlemen, the babe in the back with the tattoo." He smiled. "When my forebears landed on Plymouth Rock, they couldn't possibly have imagined that all their hard work would one day make it possible for one of their ancestors to stand up in a classroom, in a major university, and talk about all their hard work. On the contrary, I'm sure that if they had, they would have gotten right back on the boat, turned around and gone home."

He started walking down the aisle. "So here I am at Rudyard University, just happy to be here, and I don't care what rumors the newspapers might spread, this time I'm going to stay.

"I've been a Communications Major for two years, but I've been at Rudyard for three." He leaned against the teacher's desk. "I was an English Major my first year, but since I don't really like hearing myself talk, I don't think I'd be a very good teacher. I also found out I'd be much more unemployable as a Communications Major.

"But I'm not worried about my future, there's always a convenience store hiring some place. Why with my credentials, I could start selling jerky and rolling papers to wandering drunks and psychopaths tomorrow. Ah, the power of a college education."

Tollhausler smiled at a girl to his right. "My main goal is to graduate, hopefully before the turn of the century, but I don't want to rush anything. In the mean time, I'll sit around here, accumulating credits, waiting for my calling in life to call. Like a very rich girl with very poor eyesight."

He started back to his desk. "I don't drive a Honda Accord or any other car for that matter. I don't even have a license. I did take the driver's test, but the state trooper failed me after I backed over him with my car. Welllll, I might not drive, but at least I don't work."

Tollhausler thought for a moment. "I wouldn't be a good student, and a good student wouldn't be me, and I lived happily ever after." He bowed and sat down.

Nobody was really sure what *that* was all about, so they remained quiet, and turned to their instructor for guidance. Unfortunately, Ms. Hathaway was also confused, but had been teaching long enough to understand the importance of appearing to understand everything. She slowly looked up from her notes. "Well, that was, er, very interesting. Thank you Jonathan or Jon. Next?"

A very placid, blonde-haired and blue-eyed fellow stood up. He was wearing a red flannel shirt. He then proceeded to tell the class about his God and why he was a Religion Major. He displayed a small bible for everyone, and mentioned that he was also minoring in Accounting.

Tollhausler guessed it might have been a bit premature, but he couldn't *wait* for the end of the semester.

2

"paullawrence."

"Um." A student over by the window slowly raised his hand. "Paul Lawrence?"

Nathan Buckles glanced up from his desk. He had his arms crossed and a pipe firmly clamped between his teeth. He nodded.

"Here," Paul Lawrence replied.

"patriciamatthews."

Buckles' throat had gone dry halfway through the F's, and he'd been mumbling for the last five minutes.

"Er...here," Patricia answered uncertainly.

"richardmead."

No answer.

"Richard Mead?"

Nothing.

Nathan Buckles was reading off the third revised list he'd received that day, and wondered if he had the right one. He hated reading down apocryphal rosters of alphabetized names, especially the first week of the semester. It was one of the few things he disliked about being a teacher, besides compiling test scores. One corner of his crowded office had been devoted to an uneven pile of people he could not remember or had never seen, and they would probably remain there, forsaken, long after he and Rudyard had parted ways.

Buckles cleared his throat. "Richard Mead?"

"Here."

Buckles watched Richard Mead enter. There was an asterisk next to his name. "Mr. Mead," Buckles said, "Do you have your Drop/Add Slip?"

Mead smiled. "I sure do."

Buckles accepted a pink slip from Mead, and extended his right arm. He was positive he didn't need the glasses his doctor had prescribed for him the week before, and attempted reading the rectangular sheet. "Mr. Mead."

"Yes?"

"I can't make out this signature at the bottom. What's your advisor's name?"

"Oh…uh…Jonathan Tollhausler."

"Is he new at Rudyard?"

"Why...yes." Mead looked away. "He told me he'd be very surprised if you'd ever seen his name before."

"Oh."

"Or if you'd ever see it again," Mead said under his breath.

Buckles laid the folded pink form on top of other pink forms, and hoped Mead wouldn't be making a habit of arriving late for class. Tardy students broke the flow of his lectures, and Buckles wouldn't stand for that. If it happens again, Buckles thought, I'll have to inform Mr. Mead of my displeasure. Folding his arms, Buckles went back to taking roll.

"Amy Metterling."

"Present."

Slipping his jacket over the back of his desk, Mead sat down, and took a closer look at the close-mouthed, pipe-smoking Buckles. The man was obviously in his late fifties, and below his thinning gray hair were two narrow eyes. They matched his gray suit. Buckles didn't seem to move all that much either. Looks like a live one, Mead thought.

Glancing right, he suddenly decided to stare. She looks like a live one too, was his next thought, as he took in the student seated across the aisle from him. She was listening closely for her name, and Mead looked up into her big brown eyes and smiled.

The young woman adjusted her sleeve, grimaced, and looked away. He's cute, she thought to herself, impressed. He hadn't even broken eye contact with her when she had frowned. Glimpsing left, she noticed he was still ogling her, and was flattered.

18

Mead started undressing her with his eyes, but got stuck on one of her zippers. The shirt she was wearing had four. In Richard's defense, it should be noted that this young lady was indeed very pretty, did have a good body and, more importantly, knew that, which is why his tactics were such a success. Other guys had noticed her and tried catching her eye, but none had forged ahead after her initial rebuff. They had simply retreated. Mead's gaze did not waver. It had only gotten more intense. It might work out, she decided, and smiled back.

"Nancy Pritchards."

"Here."

Buckles had observed this interaction from the front of the room, and was certain he had never seen such effrontery in all his life. Mr. Mead was being very forward, and the girl wasn't entirely blameless either. Buckles didn't like that sort of thing going on in his classroom, and made a mental note of keeping an eye on this Richard Mead for the rest of the semester.

"Holly Rake."

The girl next to Mead sat up straight. "Present."

Mead bowed his head to Holly.

He was experiencing that most savage and primal of emotions: Lust. It was a fleeting and unsatisfying desire, he knew, bordering close to masturbation because its only goal was the completion of an unfeeling mechanical act. However, after hours and hours of self-examination, Mead also knew he could live with that.

"Thomas Sanstrom."

"Yo."

"Audrey Thomas."

No answer.

"Audrey Thomas?"

They could hear people talking out in the hallway.

"Audrey Thomas?"

Nope, no Audrey Thomas. Clicking his pen into action, Buckles checked another name off of another list and sighed. He was glad that was over, and slowly stood up. He went round to the front of his desk, squinting, and removed his pipe. Buckles didn't mind teaching, but he wouldn't mind retiring either.

"This is Economics 251, so if you didn't register for it you're probably in the wrong place." He waited a couple of seconds. "I'm Nathan Buckles, and I'll be teaching it."

Big deal, Mead brooded. He wanted to be alone with Holly, to get to know her and fondle her lovely little body, that wasn't so little in all the right places. Mead didn't understand why Buckles couldn't just hand out a syllabus and dismiss them. Nobody expects a lecture on the first day of the semester, he thought petulantly. Nobody needs one. He believed that all anybody wanted to do on the first day of class was hang out and see who was still there at Rudyard.

Holly gave Mead a look that, among other things, brought the word sensuous booming through his imagination. In the background, Buckles was going on about something or other, but Mead just wanted to see Holly's thighs. Call me crazy, Mead mused, but I don't care about economics of any sort, especially when it's a required course. Mead was positive Holly had required thighs. He had to meet her.

"...and econometrics will become more prevalent as the course progresses. We'll be using specific mathematical equations to visualize certain economic relationships, and how they affect one another, especially during certain political climates…"

Mead knew he didn't give a damn. He hated required courses. The teachers were either gung-ho or slack, and inevitably passed everyone anyway because they didn't want to hold anyone back. Besides, the University was continually informing the faculty that they needed the space. The incredibly stupid might not pass the first time around, but even they would pass the second time.

Mead was incredibly stupid. He wasn't slow mentally, but he was taking this course a second time. The previous semester, he had cut too many classes, failed too many quizzes, and turned a hastily written term paper in too late. He could have passed, he could have made up the work, but he had done nothing. Sometimes he felt very foolish.

"…and there is a workbook for the course. The book store said it'll be in in about a week, so it probably won't be here till October."

Buckles filled the air with a puff of smoke. "And don't let this talk of equations make you nervous. We'll still be dealing with the basic principles and theories you learned from Economics 50 to 200. It'll be a tough semester, but you'll get your money's worth."

Mead coughed. He knew any teacher who promised you your money's worth was going to be a bastard when it came to class attendance and papers. Buckles' variety of teacher never missed a class day. What was worse, his kind would always teach past that point students were willing to listen. Nathan Buckles' sort would finish the lesson they had planned for that day, find they had thirty minutes left to go and move on to something else.

21

Buckles' type wouldn't actually finish what they'd started in that time, but they just didn't seem capable of reconciling themselves to an early dismissal. All a student could do in those situations was sit there and try to listen. Usually, their eyes would glaze over. Mead's solution was to doodle in the margins of his notebook.

Buckles relit his pipe. "It's going to be an interesting semester, and I hope you'll all find it enlightening." He exhaled a jet of smoke. "I also hope that the female portion of this class works just as hard as the male portion." He glanced in Holly's direction. "I know some of you are here looking for husbands, but don't waste all your time trying to meet fellows who are Pre-Med or Pre-Law." He glanced at Mead. "Try to learn something. What if you get divorced one day?" Buckles' thin lips curled up at the edges. "It pains me that some of my students are simply here to get engaged. Most women shouldn't even attend college. They just take their diplomas, get married and move off to the suburbs. The only time they even refer to their college educations is when they correct their children for saying ain't.

"They could spend their evenings attending bars and get the same things they want now. I honestly think most women should re-think what they're doing."

A hand shot up and hovered at the back of the room.

Buckles removed his pipe. "Yes?"

"Pardon me." A young woman stood up, her haunting blue eyes shining brightly. "But would you mind it very much if I told you to eat..."

The person in front of Mead suddenly sat up straight, scraping his desk along the floor, causing Rich to miss the next word, but the rest of the class had heard it loud and clear.

"....and die?!" She walked to the front of the tense, silent class, crumpled up Mead's drop/Add form, and threw it in Buckles' poker face. She slammed the door.

"It would appear I'm in danger of being incorrect about my theory on why girls attend college." Buckles returned the pipe to his mouth. "Let's hope I am a little more accurate when it comes to Economics."

Buckles didn't say it, but class was over.

3

Standing there, with the sun peeking over his shoulder and the sound of beeping cars in his ears, Professor Robert A. Tenchman, positive now he shouldn't have bolted down that last cup of coffee, could do little else but come to the conclusion that he was having one of *those* days.

First, he couldn't find his notes for the big lecture he was supposed to give that morning--his secretary had left them in his mailbox--and then, after locating them, he had discovered a rather curt note from the department chairman, Andrew Wuthers, alerting him to the fact that he had somehow forgotten the department meeting scheduled for the day before.

Tenchman winced as he recalled the memo. It's tone was cool, very cool, and the good professor knew it would only be a matter of time before he was called on to the carpet before his superior.

He wouldn't have minded any of this, his misplaced notes, incurring Andrew Wuthers' wrath, or the fact that he had been running late ever since he had set foot out of bed that morning, except for the fact that he was now standing on 2nd Street with a flat tire. Two lanes of rush hour traffic were senselessly speeding past him to the south, and for some reason, he found the sight incredibly irritating.

"Damn it," he muttered, and then bit his lip. He wondered how long he had been doing *that*.

When riled, Tenchman would often, unconsciously, begin to swear, much the same way a nervous person might absently chew on a pen or tap their foot in the middle of a crisis, and he hoped that he hadn't been doing it for very long. After all, he didn't want to offend anyone. Still, he felt that if ever there was a time he should be allowed to curse, this was it.

Tenchman *hated* changing flat tires.

In fact, he probably dreaded that more than any other task he could think of in the entire known world. Grumbling, he walked to the back of his maroon Buick Skylark, shoved a key into the lock and sighed. "*Gee*-zus."

He eased open the trunk, and started rummaging through the oily contents for a jack. However, after several minutes had passed, he realized that it didn't really matter whether he found one or not. There was no spare tire. "*Damn. It.*" He had left it propped up against the wall of his garage back home in Elmer, New Jersey. "*God damn it,*" he hissed. "*To hell!*"

This sudden outburst surprised Esther Glowbody, a secretary in the Comptroller's Office, and her eyes quickly lighted upon the nametag hanging from the breast pocket of Tenchman's jacket. As he had feared, she did not appreciate that kind of language coming from anyone, let alone a teacher--he was obviously a teacher--and she carefully memorized the handwritten name centered below the machine-printed **HELLO, MY NAME IS** on his chest. She was going to report Tenchman's appalling conduct to someone in authority. The man was obviously crazy.

Tenchman punched the side of his car, and wondered what he was going to do next. Here it was, the opening day of the Fall Semester, and it looked as if he was going to miss his first lecture. He was a featured speaker at a special seminar the university was conducting on current movie trends at a center city theater and he had been looking forward to it for some time.

Frowning, Tenchman looked up and down the street. Sleepy students, some clutching paper cups and others gripping soda cans, were quietly making their way on to the Rudyard Campus through a gate in the distance. That was where Tenchman spotted the phone booth.

Perspiring and lightly panting, Tenchman closed the scratched, graffiti-marked door and reached into his pocket for a quarter. Unfortunately, the good professor wasn't very happy with what he found: one dime, two overcrowded key rings and a fragile assortment of pocket lint—which he promptly brushed away. He also had a folded dollar bill.

It was while he was considering making a collect call that he saw somebody outside the booth. "Pardon me," he croaked at a short guy in a gray cap.

"Yeah?"

"By any chance could you lend me fifteen cents?"

The smile the passerby was wearing disappeared. "Heyyy," he growled, "why don't you get a job, you bum?!"

Tenchman's mouth fell open. "I do have a job. I teach here at the university."

"Well they must not pay you very much if you're out here bumming change."

Tenchman charged out of the booth. "See here—"

The other fellow held up a hand. "Whoa, whoa, don't blow a gasket." He switched the case in his left hand to his right. "It's just that I make it a policy never to loan money to strangers. Or anyone else for that matter."

Tenchman looked down the street. "My God, perhaps the most important call of the week, and I don't have the money." His eyes searched the street. "Where can I get change?"

"I've got change."

"What?"

"Sure." He set down his bag. "Whaddya' got?"

"A dollar bill."

"I got change for a dollar."

"Great." Tenchman stuffed a hand in his pocket. "Funny, how something like this always happens at the worst possible moment." He produced the dollar. "Here."

The guy in the hat dumped a bunch of coins into Tenchman's palm and took the dollar.

"Thank you very much." Tenchman tightened his fingers around the shifting change. "And what's your name?"

He paused. "Why?"

"I want to know who I have to thank for saving me."

"Oh." The other person looked away. "I'm...uh..." He adjusted his cap. "....I'm Jonathan Tollhausler."

Tenchman shook his hand. "Tollhausler? That's a very interesting name."

A laugh escaped from his benefactor. "No it isn't."

Tenchman was confused. "Er, yes, well, thanks once again Mr. Tollhausler. You've saved a very important seminar." Tenchman patted him on the shoulder. "I'm slated to lecture this morning on film genre and its inevitable cohesion." He took a step back. "The students at the seminar will be very grateful."

Picking up a small suitcase, the person identifying himself as Jonathan Tollhausler smirked. "Yeah, well, I guess you'd know better about that than I would."

Back in the booth, Tenchman dumped the coins on to the ledge. One nickel, two dimes, three Canadian pennies and a nonnegotiable coin commemorating Washington's crossing of the Delaware stared back at him. Yanking the folding door aside, Tenchman ran on to the pavement, but the crook in the cap had vanished. Tenchman fumed, but this time, he wasn't at all concerned about the heated volley of invective he was about to unleash into the air. He knew it wasn't going to help matters any, but he also knew it wouldn't hurt them all that much either.

4

They were sitting together on a warped wooden bench, a gift from the Graduating Class of 1979, and had just finished saying all there was to say about their six month relationship. A quiet had descended, and spaced squares of reflected sunlight were slowly crawling towards them along the ground.

Joann was wearing trendy shades, the latest summer fashion and a popular hairstyle. Her appearance was immaculate, and she resembled one of those gaunt models one generally sees in chic magazine ads. At the moment, her face was held in a moody frown that was supposedly deep in thought.

Michael was attired just as fashionably. He was wearing a colorful pair of shorts that glowed in the bright morning sun, and a green polo shirt.

He sighed, and Joann put a slim arm around his shoulders. "We've got to be mature about this," she counseled, and Michael nodded. "I guess you're right."

He was playing with a covered tennis racket. "We have tried to make it work these last couple of months. A goodbye now would only help us both."

She confirmed his statement by removing her sunglasses and displaying two moist eyes. "We're going to have to. We've got to realize that a clean break is the best thing. If we would continue seeing each other, we'd only hinder each other's emotional progress. We've got to be grown up about this. You know that I feel for you…"

He returned her sad puppy eyes. "And I feel for you."

"….and you feel for me. But we can't let these feelings bias our decisions. We're not objective. Sure, we're still friends, but if we linger together—"

Somebody ran past. "Augh!"

Michael and Joann stared after the woman who had just run by.

A bag full of books bounced behind her, and a purse was slapping against her left thigh. Then she spun around.

A short fellow with a crazy smile and a guitar case charged past.

"Ernie! Stop it! Ernieeee!" She ran.

Ernie dropped his case on the trampled grass, and was on her in a matter of seconds.

"Ernie! Stop!" She turned around in his arms. "Ernie, you are nuts!"

He smiled and shrugged his shoulders.

She laughed, panting, and leaned against him. "You're always chasing me. Why are you always chasing me?"

"Because *you* never chase *me*."

"*You* never give me a chance."

"I'm very busy." He pushed his curly black hair out of his face. "I can't waste time. Besides, what if I outrun you?"

"Let me worry about that." They laughed and then they kissed.

Joann and Michael regarded the happy couple coolly, and then looked at one another. They turned away.

"A good relationship is hard to find," Joann announced. She slipped her sunglasses back on. "We can't afford to be illogical. We've got to use our intelligence and act rationally. Relationships are for mature, thinking people."

Susan adjusted the school bag on her shoulder, and Ernie kissed her again. He leaned back and tugged at the strap. The heavy bag slid down the length of her arm. "Ernie." She moved the bag to her left shoulder, and his hand brushed the blue band of the bag aside once more. It fell. "Ernie Turpin," Susan snapped. "I can't believe you did that."

He looked into her eyes and smiled, embarrassed, as if he didn't know how he could have done such a terrible thing. He replaced the bag on her right shoulder, and she tried to act flustered.

"Thank you." He flicked the purse string from her other shoulder. "Ohhhh," she groaned. Then she laughed. "Get away from me!"

Ernie attempted skimming the bag from her shoulder a third time. "Ernieeee!" Susan ducked and flung the heavy school bag at him. He caught it in the chest, and plummeted to the ground.

Kneeling beside him, she punched him. "You can be soooo annoying sometimes."

He nodded with a grin and rolled to his side.

She pecked him on the cheek. "Very, very annoying."

"Yeah."

Susan took a deep breath, relaxing, and stroked his soft black hair. "So why do I still feel like going away with you for a little while at this hour of the morning?"

He kissed her hand. "Because I play a mean guitar and have a nice smile?"

"I thought it was because you have a nice guitar and a mean smile?"

Ernie shrugged. Then he reached up and shrugged her shoulders.

Susan laughed. "You are nuts."

Joann stood up. "I guess it's time I got over to the bookstore and picked up the books for my classes."

"Yeah," Michael agreed. He checked the time on his watch. "I should grab some books too. While I have the money."

Neither one looked back.

5

Humming, Jonathan Tollhausler hurried down the stairs in Tremble Hall. His speech class finally over—after what had seemed like a hundred years—he couldn't wait to get outside.

The campus was steadily waking up, and the quiet of the morning was giving way to people's laughter and shouts of greeting. Favorite hangouts, the benches around Pfaehler Library and the outdoor tables in Bailey Square, were already bursting with chattering students, and Tollhausler smiled as he traveled through the crowded streets. He might not have liked the classes, but he dearly loved the first day of the semester.

Two converging cliques had settled on the front steps of Rudyard's Student Center, and Tollhausler filed between them, certain he didn't belong on either side. To his right, tanned students with sweaters tied around their necks discussed chic summer resorts, and to his left, students, clad entirely in black, with chains wrapped around their jackboots were talking about the latest metal band. He rolled his eyes.

At the top of the crumbling steps, Tollhausler passed a trio of would-be rock stars. Two were wrestling a large amplifier across the landing, and one was unwinding a pile of tangled cords. They were taking turns hooting at passing women, and the rocker with the wires realized it was his turn. He expertly whistled, in key, at a girl wearing pink heels, and Tollhausler frowned disapprovingly. Animals, he thought--until he happened to take a closer look at the woman, and then he whistled too. She was gorgeous.

Entering the Student Center, Tollhausler paused behind a tall, muscular guy stalled in front of him.

Unending streams of visitors were coursing through the lobby around huddles of students, teachers and administrators, sometimes drawing people along or dropping them off, and only lost their momentum towards the center of the room. That was where a group of long, folding tables had been installed by the university's many committees and organizations. They were trolling for new members.

The person ahead still hadn't budged, and Tollhausler looked over one of the guy's massive shoulders. "What? Is there a toll?"

Stepping aside, the strong man glared down at him, and Tollhausler saw what was blocking the way: a breathtaking blonde with the nicest green eyes. She was frowning, but her expression lightened at the sight of Tollhausler.

"Never mind, I'll ask him."

"What?" The weight lifter couldn't believe the girl preferred speaking with Tollhausler to him, and before stomping off, he flexed twice.

She stepped closer. "I was wondering," she hesitantly began.

Tollhausler couldn't believe his good fortune. "Yes?"

"Do you know where Brady Hall is?"

All she needed was directions. Of course that's all she needed. Why else would someone like *her* speak to someone like *him*?! Tollhausler frowned. "Never heard of it."

"Oh." Now she was disappointed. "All right. Thanks." She turned away.

"Wait a minute. Why couldn't you ask the barbell boy that?"

"He was more interested in getting my phone number."

Tollhausler wanted to do the same. "Men. Hunh?"

She didn't pick up on his facetious tone. "Then I saw you, and you looked...safe."

"Ohhh," he groaned. "You shouldn't say things like that to people you don't even know."

She realized how what she had just said must have sounded, and tried to go back. "I didn't mean..."

"Of course you did." Tollhausler crossed his arms. "And ordinarily I would storm off, but I like being seen with attractive women. So remember, I'm only using you. Prepare to be cast aside like a soiled tissue."

Actually seeing him for the first time, she smiled. "Really."

"I thought you should know where we stand." He waited a beat. "This is the Student Center."

"All I meant was, I knew I could ask you something and not have to give you my number."

Tollhausler had to agree with her on that. He never started conversations with women he didn't know, let alone ask them for their phone numbers, which is why he was lonely.

"Maybe that guy just wanted your number so he could call you when he located Brady Hall."

She smiled. "I don't think so."

"I guess I shouldn't call then."

"Wellll…"

"All right, I'll send you a postcard."

The girl raised a lovely wrist, or at least it was to him, and checked her watch. "I'm sorry, but I don't have the time."

"Why, did your watch stop?"

She laughed and he looked away. She wondered why she wanted to stay, and he couldn't understand why he was being so bold. Tollhausler knew it wouldn't last.

"Did you ask about Brady Hall at the information desk?"

"Not yet."

Rudyard University's Student Assistance desk was right around the corner from the fire tower, and surrounded by shelves and shelves of free flyers and informative brochures. Above it, a huge friendly sign welcomed everyone to Rudyard, and a student in a yellow Rudyard shirt was seated at the counter. The guide stopped reading a worn paperback when she noticed Tollhausler approaching.

Nancy Saunders smiled. "Can I help you?"

Tollhausler's companion nodded. "Could you tell me where Brady Hall is?"

The smile drooped. "No, I'm afraid I can't."

The girl looked at Tollhausler, and he looked at Nancy. "Come again?"

"You see, I've called Registration, Security and even one of the Deans, but no one seems to know." Nancy shook her head. "I don't know who I should call next." She pouted. "To tell you the truth, I've never even heard of Brady Hall, and I've been at Rudyard almost four years now."

"I've been here two, and I haven't either," the green-eyed girl said with a frown. "I thought I knew the campus pretty well."

"Maybe you could ask around in the cafeteria."

"Where's that again?"

Nancy and Tollhausler pointed.

It was twenty feet away, and easy to spot. Between its double doors, a small rack of newspapers was on fire, and tendrils of black smoke were gently climbing the wall.

Nancy scowled. "That's a darned shame. Some people think it's so funny ruining a good thing for everyone else. Burning the first edition of this semester's Rudyard Chronicle."

Tollhausler nodded. "What a crime. Why if not for the Rudyard Chronicle, I wouldn't know what a good newspaper was." He grinned. "It's any other paper."

A fire extinguisher coughed in the silence.

"There isn't much more I can tell you," Nancy said, giving Tollhausler a reproving look, "except that everyone thinks Brady Hall's somewhere on the other side of campus. By the parking areas."

35

The girl nodded and adjusted the purse on her arm.

"And even if it's not, maybe someone there'll know about it." Nancy shrugged. "I'm sorry I couldn't be more help. Good luck."

"Thanks."

Her green eyes settled on Tollhausler, and she smiled. "Thanks for your help too."

Tollhausler felt like a million bucks. "It was nothing."

"I just hope you don't have a class in Brady Hall." She walked off.

"Ohhh I don't know." Tollhausler followed her. He'd decided to ask her out. "If you can't find the building then you don't have to go to the class. That's great."

"I guess."

They left the Student Center and walked down the steps.

Tollhausler was set on asking her for a date. However, a lump the size of New Jersey had taken up residency in his windpipe and all he could do was smile nonsensically. He needed more time. "Maybe…" He swallowed, trying to dislodge the Garden State from his trachea. "….we could talk to somebody in the Bursar's Office. They might know where Brady Hall is."

Checking the time, she shook her head. "I can't. I'm going to be late."

"But you don't even know where you're going."

"I'll find it." She hurried off. He's cute, she thought, wishing she had had a little more time to spend with him, but knew she had to get to class—wherever that was.

Tollhausler watched her go. "Oh well, at least you tried." He headed back to the Student center. "You failed miserably, but at least you tried."

Inside, music was playing from within a large circle of people standing across from the information desk. Having no other choice, Tollhausler joined the circle, headed for the cafeteria, and was forced to stop behind a petite woman in the front row. She was listing to the right because of the size of the purse hanging from her right shoulder, and he couldn't get passed.

He wouldn't have been able to proceed anyway because there was a six-foot robot standing in the middle of the circle.

It observed the throng of people through two, calm lenses set in the middle of a spherical head. The head turned on the shoulders of a V-shaped torso, and its cylindrical arms thinned into two black claws at its sides.

"Ohhh, my," an overweight student standing on tip toes said.

A narrow rectangular tray surrounded it at the waist and below the tray, legs, in the shape of an inverted V, stretched down to a flat base lined with silver and black grooves.

"Ahhh," a girl in a blue jersey cooed.

The robot was broadcasting the music Tollhausler had heard from a speaker in its chest, and started rolling back and forth to the beat on three wheels.

"Wow," somebody declared over Tollhausler's shoulder.

He was impressed. When he had first seen the crowd, he had assumed it would be for the usual Rudyard diversion, like an annoying mime in a Rudyard shirt performing the type of antics mimes are disliked for around the globe or the pep squad, but the robot was certainly a welcome change. Just as pointless, he thought, But nevertheless a welcome change.

The song slowly faded, and a voice came from the speaker in the robot's chest. "Hi there. I'm Rodney the Robot, and I'd like to welcome everyone here to Rudyard University." The machine started circling. "I'm here courtesy of the Activities Counsel to say hello to the incoming freshmen." Its orbit increased, and it passed closer and closer to the smiling people. "I'd also like to greet all those students returning to Rudyard for another term.

"The university and the Activities Counsel both wish everyone the best of luck this fall and hope we'll all have a healthy, happy semester." The computer swung around once more, and stopped in front of a student with red and blue hair. "And what's your name?"

"Bud."

"Nice hair Bud. Now I know why robots don't have any."

Surprised, the audience laughed.

More music played from the robot, and Rodney once again made several passes before the troop of people. Decelerating, he wheeled across the floor and spun to an abrupt halt. The music grew faint, and mesmerized, a woman in front watched as Rodney raised its claw towards her silver purse.

"Nice bag," the robot gurgled. "Can I have it?"

Its owner smiled. "No."

Rodney pulled the bag away, and the woman grabbed her purse. They started a tug-of-war.

"Please? It matches my outfit better than yours." The robot shook back and forth. "What do you need it for anyway? I'm the one who doesn't have any pockets."

The audience giggled as the two struggled.

"I tell you what, I'll give you back your purse, but could you loan me a couple of dollars? I run on more than batteries."

She wasn't amused anymore. "Le' go." She yanked the bag away, and the robot almost tipped forward.

It fell back. "Sayyyyy, don't go away mad—like a human. Go away cool—like a robot." It glided along the tiled floor. "Reeeeeal smooooooooooth!"

Most everybody there was eating it up.

Richard Mead tapped Tollhausler on the shoulder. "Hey Toll, some fun, eh? Look, technology can be just as annoying as people."

"As if we didn't already know that." Tollhausler stepped to the right. "I thought you'd be in the cafeteria by now."

Mead shook his head. "No, I've got class till 10:30. And teachers hate it when you leave early, especially on the first day."

"Have you seen Mennon?"

"No, but you know him. He'll probably be selling coupon books all morning."

"And running from security all afternoon."

Rodney gyrated over to a striking red head to Tollhausler and Mead's right. "And what's your name?"

"Sally."

"You're very pretty Sally."

She blushed. "Thanks."

39

"Not as pretty as a soda machine, but what do I know, I'm only a robot."

Everyone chuckled, and Rodney moved in on Sally. It raised a curved arm. "Would you like to hold my hand?"

She did, and the plastic man backed away with her into the circle. Sally was smiling, but looked a little uncomfortable.

"Would you like to dance?"

She nodded.

"Then jump on."

"Okay," she said, and carefully stepped on to Rodney's base.

Rodney lifted its left arm, and she rested her right hand on it. Sally carefully placed her other arm on Rodney's waist.

"Ready Sally?"

"Yes Rodney."

"Here we go."

A waltz started playing from Rodney's speaker, and the mechanical man began wheeling about in time to the music. The audience, especially the female segment, thought that was great.

Tollhausler sneered. He envied the ease with which Rodney had spoken to Sally and regretted not having had the right words to ask the girl with the green eyes out. He thought she had liked him, but knew there was no way of telling now. Mad at himself, he mumbled, "Oh to be a robot."

"This is the most amazing thing I've ever seen," somebody blubbered, and Tollhausler rolled his eyes. "He'd do great at a club."

"Most robots do," observed Mead. "But at least there's one glimmer of hope."

"What's that?"

"Maybe Rodney gets dull after its 30-day trial period ends. Just like everybody else."

"We can only hope. Let's get out of here."

Approaching the cafeteria, Tollhausler noticed a gleam in Mead's eyes. "You look extremely happy this morning for a Business Major with no future."

"Tollhausler, I just got the number of a beautiful woman."

"Is that all?"

"Is that all?!" Mead frowned. "What do you mean 'Is that all?' Do *you* have the telephone number of a beautiful woman?"

"Of course. But she told me if I ever use it she'll call the police."

They entered the cafeteria.

6

Usually, Sheila Dougherty hated paying her tuition because lines at Rudyard always seemed to go on forever. No matter when she arrived or whichever strategy she employed, she constantly found herself propped up against a wall, staring down a student-filled corridor. Admittedly, the wait hadn't been bad that morning, she had already caught sight of the Bursar's Office after only thirty minutes, and, except for the guy by the elevators, she was satisfied.

He had shown up wearing a black t-shirt with the word "Streetwise" printed across it and a gray cap minutes before, and appeared to be in a very good mood. Sheila assumed it was because he wasn't trapped in line like everybody else. However, it wasn't his disposition she was having trouble with so much as his whistling. He had been doing it since he'd arrived, and he kept missing all the high notes. Then, to Sheila's relief, the shrill tune ended, and she looked over to see what had happened.

Raising a blue and white paper cup to his lips, he caught sight of her, lowered the cup and smiled. It wasn't perfect, his nose had once been broken and his face contorted as the corners of his mouth were raised, but Sheila thought it was very warm. She would have returned the smile if the eyes above weren't inspecting her so, and she turned her attention back to the ragged stretch of students ahead.

He enjoyed her reaction, and considered striking up a conversation with her, or any of the other attractive women standing on line, but knew he didn't have the time. There was work to be done. He finished the coffee Robert Tenchman had paid for, and crumpled the blue and white container up.

As the reader may have already guessed, his name was not Jonathan Tollhausler.

It was John D. Mennon.

Mennon tossed his cup into a round white trash can and reached for the small bag at his feet. It was a suitcase with folding legs on one side and a Rudyard University bumper sticker on the other. He started down the hall.

The queue led into the Bursar's Office through two wide doors, and at the moment, a short, tired looking man was holding the right door open with his arched back. Eyes glazed over with frustration watched as Mennon passed, and Johnny smiled

42

sympathetically. College might not teach you much, he thought, But by the time you graduate, you certainly know how to stand in line.

He peered into the Bursar's Office through the other door. It was jam-packed with people, and the front of the mile—long procession snaked around the center of the room three times. There weren't enough cashiers.

"As usual," he mumbled to himself.

Seemingly oblivious of the swollen serpentine of people five feet away, the cashiers performed their repetitive accounting with discernible apathy, and Mennon wondered if the bulletproof glass lining the counter was to shield them from gun-wielding robbers or disgruntled students.

He spotted a sign to his left:

RUDYARD UNIVERSITY ACTIVITIES BOOK
STATION #1
PLEASE SHOW PAID RECEIPT

After concluding their business with the bursar, students would stop at a chipped table under the sign, and hand their receipts over to an elderly woman seated beside it. She would glance at their yellow slips, type on a dented computer terminal to her right, and a bored student in a red running suit would hand out a small yellow and white book. Rows and rows of the books were piled on the floor beside her.

Mennon started whistling. That's what he was there for: the stacks and stacks of paperbacked books. He wasn't interested in what they purported to be. No, he just wanted to get his hands on as many of them as he could carry. It's a scam, he admitted, Like any other scam, but still just as sweet. He smiled a crooked smile.

"Mennon," a gentleman in a yellow painter's cap snapped. "Didn't I tell you something bad was going to happen if I ever laid eyes on you again?"

"Yeah," Mennon said over his shoulder, the small books still dancing in his head, "but as threats go, it was a little vague, so I forgot all about it."

The people on line immediately directed their attention to the gentlemen by the doors, just in case the discussion turned violent all of a sudden and they had to make a break for it.

"You won't forget this." The guy in the painter's cap pointed at Mennon. "Know what I mean?"

Mennon turned away from the door. "All right, all right, give me your sister's phone number already."

"Hah."

"How you been Gerald?"

"Not bad. How's about yourself?"

They shook hands.

"I was doin' pretty good until this whole school thing started up again."

A stunning woman with perfect skin gracefully exited the Bursar's Office, and Mennon recognized her running suit. She was the same woman who had been handing out Activities Books inside.

"Hey Terri. You look a lot different when you aren't bored out of your skull."

She rolled her eyes. "Uh. Johnny, I feel like I've been handing those books out for a month."

Gerald put his arm around her. "Well you're done now."

They went down the hall and entered the fire tower.

Mennon shifted his bag to his other hand. "Either of you pay your tuition yet?"

Terri nodded. "Last week. To avoid having to stand in line like some dumbies I could mention."

"Okay. You were right, I was wrong." Gerald absently waved an Activities Book in his other hand. "I should have gone with you last week." He shook his head. "Thirty-five minutes in line, and all I got was this stupid Activities Book."

Mennon tried not to stare. "I saw." He motioned over his shoulder with a thumb.

"Only three cashiers."

"The day everyone's tuition is due," Terri reported with a frown. "You'd think they would know by now how busy they're going to be."

"You know Rudyard," Mennon said with a grin. "It was either hire more cashiers or football coaches, and word on the street says a university this size can't get by with less than twenty coaches."

Gerald slapped his Activities book against his thigh. "Yeah, well, one of these days, we're going to get organized and tell Rudyard what it can do with its lines."

They stopped at the bottom of the steps, and Terri threw her arms around him. "Ooooh, lighten up lover." She pulled him close. "If standing in line is the worst thing you have to put up with this morning, you're doing fine."

"Mmmm."

"Let's change the subject. Do you think you're band'll play here again this semester Johnny?"

"Which one?"

"The one that played last spring." Gerald pointed at Mennon. "You know, the name of the band on your shirt?"

"Ohhhh Streetwise," Mennon said, as if he hadn't heard the name in twenty years, "I don't think so." He set his suitcase down. "We sort of broke up."

Terri was surprised. "Aw, that's too bad. I really liked you guys."

Gerald nodded. "What happened?"

"Well, you know bands." Mennon knelt down and unfolded a pair of metal legs from the bag. "The drummer said I didn't know which direction the music should go, and I told him maybe not, but I knew where he could go, and then things got nasty."

"It was a bitter split."

Mennon pulled another pair of legs into place. "After I punched him in the stomach it was."

Gerald smirked, and Terri shook her head.

"But that's show biz." Mennon unscrewed the bottom of one leg, and slid out a smaller leg. "I got a band together the very next week." He extended the other legs the very same way.

"Great," Terri said. "And what's the name of that band?"

"Well, actually…" He stood the case up. "….we didn't stay together long enough to decide on one."

Terri gave Gerald a knowing look, and Mennon grinned because he knew people with knowing looks didn't know anything at all.

Gerald smiled. "Same old Mennon. You still hangin' out with Ernie Turpin?"

"I just spoke with him this morning." Johnny popped the clasps on his case. "I asked him for a ride to school, and he said he didn't have a car. Which, when you come to think of it, is really his problem, not mine."

"Are you still seeing that nice girl we met last Spring?"

"Which one?"

"You know, um…" Terri thought for a second. "I want to say her name was Angela. But for some reason I think it might have been Suzanne. She was that pretty red head who was there in the cafeteria every time we stopped by."

Puzzled, Mennon rubbed his neck. Then he snapped his fingers. "Ohhhh, sure, sure. I was dating Angela, the blonde, at the beginning of last semester. Suzanne, the red head, was the one Angela caught me with in the library after midterms."

Gerald chuckled. "You got the same luck with women that you do with bands."

"Yeah." Mennon gloated. "It's a good life."

"Uh-hunh." Terri tugged on Gerald 's wrist and read his watch. "I'm going to grab a soda. Before my next class."

Gerald nodded. "Sure."

Johnny winked. "Got a minute G?"

"Sure." He looked at Terri. "I'll be right out."

She nodded and went over to the exit. "See you Johnny."

"See you Terri." She pushed through the exit.

"Say." Mennon pointed at Gerald's coupon book. "You want to sell that?"

"This?" Gerald was surprised. "How much?"

"Five bucks."

"A fin? For this? Sure." Gerald tossed it to him.

"I didn't want to ask in front of Terri. Her working for the university and all." He handed over five singles.

"Terri? I doubt if she'd mind." Gerald slid the money into his pocket. "She's real sweet. Besides, what are you going to do with it anyway?"

"Ohhhh. nothing illegal."

Gerald started for the exit. "Well if you're going to use it to hold up a liquor store, could you please wipe my prints off it first?"

"Will do."

Gerald put a hand on the door. "Heard anything about the strike?"

"Not much. I hear the guards are pretty unhappy."

"The guards?!" Gerald clicked his tongue. "I've been hearing about how the teachers are gonna' go out."

"Really?" Mennon was surprised. "I haven't heard about that. I been hangin' out in all the wrong places."

"The guards are going on strike? Geeez, who's next, the students?"

Mennon laughed. "There'll be nothing but picket lines down here."

Gerald sighed. "It's going to be a real interesting semester."

"It always is. Thanks for the book."

7

Mennon pulled a sign from his bag. He taped it on the case right above his Rudyard University bumper sticker, and placed Gerald's Activities Book inside. The hard part was now over. He had gotten the first book. He would have had two if he had paid his tuition, but he never did that the first week of school. The lines were too long.

Footsteps echoed in the tower overhead, and Sheila Dougherty came walking into view. She had finally paid her tuition and looked relieved. Descending, she noticed the two-inch letters on Mennon's sign.

WILL BUY ANY? ACTIVITIES BOOK FOR $5!

She glanced up at him, and he smiled.

"Hello again."

She thought he looked even more insufferable up close.

"Hi."

"Want to sell your Activities Book?"

Sheila shrugged. "I don't know."

"You think you're gonna' use it?"

She looked thoughtful, but not that thoughtful.

He winked. "Look, I'm gonna' give you five dollars for it. Did you use it last semester?"

"It doesn't matter." She ran her thumb across its cover. "I paid forty dollars for it. You're only offering me five."

"That's all its worth to me." He lit a cigarette, and blew smoke out of the side of his mouth. "Besides, is anybody else around here willing to pay more?"

"The university says the coupons in there are worth over two hundred dollars."

He tapped his cigarette. "You'll save that much if you use them all, but most of them are for shops outside the city." Mennon paged through Gerald's coupon book. "Do you shop outside the city much?"

She took a closer look at the tops of her sneakers. "No."

He laughed. "Then I guess you aren't going to save all that money."

Sheila was getting annoyed, especially since she knew he was right. "Yes, but maybe I'll use enough coupons to get my forty dollars back."

"Okay," Mennon agreed, "maybe you will. How many coupons did you use last semester?"

She looked away. "I used one."

Smoke breezed through his lips.

"I got into a movie with it."

"So why not sell me your book?" He pulled a five dollar bill out of his pocket and laid it flat on the top of his case. "No, I'm not promising you a ten percent discount at some boutique in Dresher, Pennsylvania, but I am giving you five American dollars. That might only be an eighth of what the book cost you, but it's also the only guaranteed return you're going to see from it."

Sheila grimaced. "It just doesn't sound right."

"Like charging every student on campus forty dollars for a book they're never going to use?"

Sheila handed Mennon her Activities Book.

"Thank you." He handed her the money.

"Heyyyyy." Mennon pulled a small bottle of amber liquid from his case. "While I've got you here. You want to buy some perfume?" He opened it and placed a drop on his wrist. "Mmmm. Very pretty."

"No thank you."

Mennon capped the bottle and lowered it out of sight. "How about some men's cologne?" He raised his arm again.

"That's the same bottle!"

"Hey, both are made by the same company." He sniffed at the bottle's neck. "Mmmmm. Very rugged."

"I'll pass." The bottle disappeared and a rack of thin bracelets glowed before her.

"Jewelry? I got plen'y of nice stuff."

Sheila shook her head. "No, really—"

"Pure gold." Mennon separated a bracelet from the rest. "Twenty karat. And because I like you, I'll sell it at the low, low price of ten dollars."

"I don't want anything." She leaned closer. "I just want to know why you're buying up coupon books."

He leaned forward. "You know who I am?"

"Why no."

"I'm Johnny Mennon."

"And?" She waited for him to explain.

"You want to go out with me?"

Stunned, the only thing she could think of to say was, "No."

"You got a sister?"

51

"No."

"Well maybe your mother isn't too old."

Sheila cringed at the thought, and staggered towards the exit in a daze.

He dropped his cigarette and stepped on it. "Like I'm going to tell her what I'm up to." He smiled at the security guard standing on the landing below. "What am I, an idiot?"

Then it hit him: *There was a security guard standing on the landing below.* The guard did not look happy either. He stared up at Johnny, motionless except for his chewing. His jaw would drop, audibly clicking his gum in the quiet stairwell, swivel clockwise and snap right back into place.

Johnny tried not to stare, but he could feel the cop's eyes on him. He dropped Sheila's book into the suitcase and carefully shut the bag. He was glad he'd finished his sales pitch before the guard had arrived. At least he hoped he had finished his sales pitch before the guard had arrived. While Mennon might have stood firm in his belief that he wasn't doing anything wrong, he also knew that, as defenses go, blind faith generally doesn't stand up very well in a court of law. Hence the suspended sentence he had received while still a junior in high school.

"Oh doorman," a familiar voice boomed, "call me a cab."

The guard turned.

"Don't just stand there. You're supposed to say, 'All right, you're a cab.'" Jonathan Tollhausler passed the officer and bounced up the steps.

Mennon smiled with relief. "Heyyyy Tollhausler. I've been looking all over for you."

52

Tollhausler was skeptical. "Really?"

"Well no." Mennon clicked his bag shut "But I don't think you were looking for me either."

"It's just my luck that I found you anyway."

He upended his case and shortened a metal leg. "What are you doin' here?"

"I came over to pay my tuition. But I can't since Rudyard lost my check from the government." Tollhausler scowled. "Again."

Mennon chuckled. "They lose your check every semester. Why is it always such a surprise?"

"I don't know. I thought the odds were in my favor that Rudyard would be able to find my check at least once while I was enrolled here."

"Hey, odds like that are incalculable."

"Thanks Einstein. I bet you'd be a lot less stoic about it if it was your aid they were messing up."

"What can I say, they haven't yet." Mennon grinned. "I'm a lucky guy. You're not."

"Uh-huh."

"That just means you've gotta' work harder."

"I'd rather play the lottery."

"Funny you should mention that." Mennon folded the legs closed on his bag. "Turpin and me have a proposal for you."

"I'm sorry, but I'm a little too young to be married. Especially to two guys."

"That's all right." Mennon took out a cigarette. "We're expecting a long engagement."

"Well I know my father's always had his heart set on giving me away. Lucky mom was always there to stop him."

Mennon flicked a red lighter into life. "There's something you should know."

"About my mother?"

"No." He lit his cigarette." About my band."

"Yes?"

"My band's about to buy a new sound system."

"Gosh, thanks for telling me Johnny." Tollhausler adjusted his glasses. "That isn't the sort of thing I'd want to hear from a stranger."

Mennon exhaled a little smoke. "The thing is, Ernie and me have been asking all our friends to chip in. To help us out with the cost."

"Do you and Ernie have that many friends?"

"Not since we started asking them for money."

"Well Johnny, have no fear." He patted him on the shoulder. "I'll always be there for you. No matter how much money you have to borrow from other people. In fact, while you're at it, grab a little for me."

"That's just it Toll. This whole thing got Ernie and me thinking about you."

"That's the scariest thing I've heard all day. The last time you guys thought of me was back in high school, and I wound up playing football in the middle of a thunder storm."

"Heyyyyy, this situation isn't anything like that one. And besides, you bet on my team just like everybody else that day. It isn't my fault we ran out of players, and a couple of us had to play."

"Uh-hunh."

"I can't believe you're still angry about that." Mennon laughed. "Tollhausler, you don't *need* thirty-two teeth. I lost a couple that day myself."

"Yeah, after our side found out you were betting on the other team."

"Those guys were great athletes." Mennon took a drag from his cigarette. "You guys weren't. I cleaned up."

"Especially after you handed over our play book."

Mennon brushed off his knee. "They were great athletes, but they were dumb. If you're gonna' bet, you gotta' play to the percentages."

"I'm just sorry our guys dragged you through the mud after they beat you up."

"Sure. It was your idea and you felt guilty about it."

Tollhausler nodded. "I'm just glad they didn't listen to my other suggestion."

"You were not the first person that day who yelled 'Hang him from the highest tree,'" corrected Mennon. "It was Ernie." Then he suddenly thought of something. "Sayyyy, you don't think those guys would have really hung me, do you?"

"I don't know," Tollhausler said. "But if the only tree in the neighborhood hadn't been struck by lightning, the both of us might not be standing here right now."

"Sore losers. Everywhere I go, sore losers."

"By the way Mennon, not that I dislike reminiscing about my carefree high school days, but how did we get on this subject?"

"I was telling you how me and Turpin wanted to borrow some money from you."

"Oh yeah." Tollhausler went over to the exit. "See you around."

Mennon grabbed his suitcase, winked at the guard and ran. He caught up with Tollhausler halfway down the block.

"Hey wait a minute. I know you got some money tucked away, and I was wondering if you'd untuck some for us."

Tollhausler shook his head. "I'm sorry, but—"

"You know, for me and Turpin, your best friends in the entire known world."

Tollhausler stopped. "Mennon, when you say we're best friends, do I detect a hint of sarcasm in your voice?"

"Only when I tell other people."

"Oh well, that's all right then."

"I don't want to rush you or anything…" Mennon looked at his watch. "….but I need an answer quick. If you're not gonna' help, than I'm going to have to hurry off and make some new friends."

"With your winning personality, I'm sure you'll have no problem whatsoever." Tollhausler had an idea. "Say, why don't you just get a job?"

Mennon shook his head. "I thought about that, but it only made me dizzy."

"I'd like to see that."

"It'll cost you."

Tollhausler sighed. "How much?"

"Any amount would be appreciated."

"What, like twenty bucks?"

Mennon shook his head. "Higher."

"Fifty?"

"How about a hundred?"

"A hundred?!" Tollhausler yelped.

Mennon grabbed Tollhausler's hand and shook it. "Deal!"

"That's a lot of money Mennon." Tollhausler watched a car go by. "I hope you appreciate it."

"Oh, I do." Mennon pulled a ledger from out of his back pocket, opened it and then closed it.

"You didn't write anything down."

"That's all right." Mennon returned the book to his pocket. "I already had you penciled in for a hundred."

"It felt more like I was penned in."

Mennon smirked. "Either way, I swear you'll eventually get all your money back."

"Promise?"

"I promise that you'll eventually get your money back."

Tollhausler turned to a passing student. "Why don't I like the way he keeps saying eventually?!"

8

Rudyard's Student Assistance Desk was still open for business, and a tanned fellow in a white turtleneck had a question.

"If I want a table this term so I can sell something here in the lobby, who do I have to speak to?"

Nancy Saunders lowered a singed copy of the Rudyard chronicle, and smiled. "I'm not sure."

"Well, is there a particular person around here I should talk to or is there an office somewhere else I need to go to?"

Nancy's brown eyes slid left as she thought for a second. "There used to be somebody upstairs, I think." She frowned. "But they moved his office."

A hand crawled over the edge of the U-shaped counter, and began rummaging through the leaflets and circulars there.

Expecting Nancy to react, the guy in the turtleneck waited, but she was still deep in thought.

A pool schedule glided off the counter.

Wondering if anyone else was seeing this, he surveyed the area. To his left, students were hanging up posters for upcoming campus events, and to his right, a new audience was enjoying Rodney the Robot's floorshow.

"This might help." Nancy lifted a small book with a faded Rudyard insignia on the cover from under the counter. "It has phone numbers for every department on campus."

"Do you think I should talk to someone who already has a table?"

The pool schedule reappeared, and three fingers swept a pamphlet entitled Safe Sex from view.

"No, the university assigns those tables to its own groups the first day of the semester, and all they have to do is show up." She looked back under the counter. "What you're talking about is a little different. Maybe I have--"

There was a tearing sound, and Nancy looked up. "What are you doing?"

"Nothing." He stepped back from the desk.

Nancy obviously didn't believe him.

"Really, I'm not doing anything." He considered saying something about the hand, but didn't think Nancy would believe him. "Except waiting for you to answer a simple question."

Nancy hooked a strand of brown hair behind her ear. "There's really no need to take that tone of voice with me."

The hand returned, and started dragging the phone book towards the edge.

"What?" He couldn't believe that Nancy was missing this.

She stared back. "I'm here to answer people's questions, not to be abused."

"But…"

"Maybe you *should* talk to one of the people around the corner." She had a very intense gaze. "You seem to be in a hurry, and I'm just not moving fast enough."

"Student Assistance my ass," was his parting line, and the departmental phone book slammed to the floor just as he was stomping away.

Nancy leaned in the direction the book had fallen, and a grinning Ernie Turpin popped up in front of her.

"Oh!" Nancy yelped.

Turpin handed her the phone book, and studied the fliers and advertisements stacked in front of him.

"You…" Nancy gulped. "….frightened me."

He nodded in total agreement.

"Can I help you?"

Turpin shook his head and grabbed a blue flyer. He skimmed its dry, patronizing sentences, realized it wasn't what he wanted, and crushed it into a ball. He tossed it over his shoulder.

"Oh my," Nancy said. She stared at where the paper had landed. "Are you *sure* there isn't anything I can help you with?"

Turpin stepped into the booth.

Nancy wondered if she should call security, but was curious about what he was looking for.

Ernie picked up a textbook, a remnant of the previous semester, and blew off a layer of dust. He sneezed. Then he found a box of blank paper, and removed a couple of sheets. It was the whitest paper he had ever seen, and he immediately tore up the glowing pages and threw them into the air. He giggled because the falling paper reminded him of falling snow.

That was why Nancy hadn't noticed the woman standing in front of her. She had been too busy watching the paper fall to the floor.

"Could you tell me where Brady Hall is?"

Nancy shook her head in defeat. "No, I'm afraid I can't."

Turpin found what he had been looking for: a Directory of Classes, and paged through it. Nancy had already launched into her explanation of the many things she had done that morning in order to locate the mystery building, and she was just about to finish when Ernie closed the directory with a victorious look on his face.

"....so they didn't know either. Nobody on campus knows where it is."

"I do."

Nancy and the girl turned.

"Where," Nancy said slowly, "is Brady Hall?"

"On this very campus." Ernie exited the booth, and posed a little too dramatically beside it. "Under our very noses."

He felt just like his hero Sherlock Holmes. "Brady Hall is Templeton Hall."

"How do you figure that," Nancy asked.

"I supposedly have a class in Brady Hall today, and it's a religion course." He gripped his chin with one hand and placed the other in his pocket. "But, there doesn't seem to be any Brady Hall. At least, not on this particular campus." He started pacing. "Quite a conundrum. However, there is no problem so difficult that it can not be solved by focused ratiocination."

"By what?"

"Now historically, most religion classes have been taught in Templeton Hall because that is where the Religion Department is located." He continued his pacing back and forth. "Correct?"

They nodded.

"So when I failed to locate Brady Hall in this semester's Directory of Classes, I looked for Templeton Hall, just in case. Is it on the list?"

Nancy read down the building index. "No."

"Ergo Brady Hall must be Templeton Hall. Neither is on the list, but both must exist. Q.E.D."

"You're a pretty smart fellow," the girl said. "I won't have any trouble finding Brady Hall now. Thanks." She headed off to class, and Nancy started to bubble. "You don't know what you've done! Thank you so much. No one came close to figuring this out, except you."

Turpin smiled humbly.

"Everybody's been going crazy around here trying to find it. You're a genius." Nancy grabbed the phone and started dialing.

His work there done, Ernie picked up his guitar case and headed for the cafeteria. He was very proud.

Suddenly, Ernie found himself face to molded plastic face with Rodney the robot. Rodney had spun out into the crowd and nearly collided with him, and Ernie had hopped up on Rodney's base at the last second.

"Make way for the wheels of progress," Rodney warned, "or get crushed beneath."

Ernie frowned, and knocked on Rodney's head.

"Ouch," the robot said, and the people around them laughed.

Ernie stepped down, and found the way blocked by a gleaming claw.

"No," the robot purred, "don't go yet."

Turpin glanced at the claw, and noticed the amused spectators beyond.

"What's your name," Rodney inquired, and Ernie stuck out his tongue and ducked under Rodney's arm.

The robot whirled, and, its audience cheering, it gave chase. "Hey human, I was talking to you."

Turpin ignored Rodney, and, gears grinding, the robot accelerated right into the back of Ernie's guitar case. "I asked you what your name is. Don't you know?"

Ernie slowly turned, a very strange expression on his face, and he placed his guitar on the ground.

"Cat got your tongue?"

Turpin pushed the robot.

"Hey," Rodney complained and wobbled to a stop.

Turpin grinned and next shoved Rodney with two hands.

"All right," the robot sputtered. "You don't have to tell me your name."

Turpin grinned. He brought his left foot down on the robot's grooved base and propelled Rodney and himself forward with a thrust of his right foot.

The spectators gave them plenty of room.

"Help!" Rodney brayed.

Turpin spied the doorway he'd been aiming for and straightened out his course.

"Stop him," Rodney begged. "This isn't part of the show!"

Ernie jumped off, and Rodney plummeted, backwards, down the stairs in the fire tower.

The audience rushed passed Ernie, yelling, but he could still hear something hollow thumping down the steps. Then somebody screamed. This was followed by a resounding crash.

Ernie couldn't help but smile. He *loved* technology.

9

Tollhausler still couldn't believe he had been unable to keep the girl with the green eyes from walking out of his life, and absently frowned as he navigated his coffee through the wide lobby of Bronowski Hall. He regretted the lost opportunity, and wished he had at least gotten the woman's name. He could never understand how women he didn't know always succeeded in rendering him speechless before they even spoke. No matter how much he psyched himself up or calmed himself down, he was helpless in these situations.

Then Jonathan remembered: he was very shy. He didn't consider himself attractive, which made him self-conscious, and he didn't want to come on too strong with a woman and be a nuisance, like he had seen Mennon frequently do, so he always held back. Tollhausler suspected he needed a little guidance. Or a lot. He wasn't quite sure.

What *would* the girl say after he had asked her out anyway? There was always the possibility she would say no, which after all his mental exertion would devastate him, but there was also the possibility she would say yes, and that was equally frightening.

He didn't drive, so he would have to explain that, and if the girl had a car, well, that would further complicate matters. Should she pick him up or should they meet at the theater or restaurant? Where would they go afterwards, he wondered, and what would happen at the end of the evening?

Tollhausler tried to foresee every eventuality, so he would be prepared, come what may, but by the time he had finished worrying about rejection (Number one on the list), his lack of a driver's license and thirty other things, the woman he wanted to speak to was gone. He sometimes wished he were someone else.

Withdrawing from his reverie with a sip of hot, sweet coffee, Tollhausler discovered himself at the back of a line. At the front, a scowling man in an ugly yellow jacket was standing between two security guards. He was holding a large clipboard in his small hands and asking students their names.

Tollhausler was unaware of any controversy surrounding his next class, and was reasonably certain that if there had been, the armed guards would have been mentioned somewhere in the course description. He slid a yellow and white square of paper from his back pocket, and stuffed a finger into one of its folds. Balancing his coffee while opening his roster, he made sure Aesthetics and Creativity was indeed meeting in room number nine.

COURSE	INSTRUCT	BUILD	RM#			C.H.
INTRO TO SPEECH	HATHAWAY	TREMB	207	8:30	MWF	3.00
AESTHET & CREAT	MANTELOS	BRONO	9	10:30	MW	4.00
CREATIVE WRITIN	STARER	BRADY	108	13:30	MW	4.00
FILM THEORY	BENSON	SANDE	306	9:30	TTH	4.00
BROADCAST HIST	VON STEI	NELSO	801	13:30	TTH	4.00

"Swell," he mumbled, replacing his class schedule, "another Rudyard line."

Minutes later, Robert Tenchman glanced up from his clipboard. "Name?"

"Jonathan Tollhausler."

The security guards immediately reacted, and Tollhausler suddenly found himself pinned between them.

He was horrified. "Hey! You spilled my coffee."

Twisting Tollhausler's arms behind him, the guards clicked something around his wrists.

"Don't struggle and everything will be all right," one guard advised.

"For you or for me?"

The second guard leaned forward. "Aren't you gonna' tell us how this is all a terrible mistake?"

"All right." Tollhausler cleared his throat. "This is all a terrible mistake." He turned to the guard. "How was that?"

"Perfect."

"Thanks. What should I say next?"

"Shut up."

"No, that isn't very good." He looked at the other guard. "How about you tall, dark & angry? Got any ideas?"

The guard glowered. "Is this the creep Professor Tenchman?"

"No Sergeant Buck, I'm afraid he isn't."

This gave both security guards a jolt. Pointing a thumb at Tollhausler, Tenchman frowned. "I don't know what this student's up to, but he is *not* Jonathan Tollhausler."

"That's funny, these are his pants."

"Did you actually think you would get away with this?" Tenchman sneered. "You don't even *look* like Jonathan Tollhausler."

"I know," Tollhausler agreed. "I don't get enough sun."

"Quips aren't going to get you out of this one, son," Tenchman replied. He stepped over a puddle of coffee. "The university has definite guidelines about how to deal with insubordinate students."

"Where do they stand on volleyball?" Tollhausler smiled. "I love that game."

A tall, distinguished gentleman made his way through the growing crowd to Sergeant Buck. "I'm Lyle G. Adams, and I teach Constitutional History in this building. What's going on here?"

"I'm not sure," Tollhausler answered, "but I think the library's started cracking down on students with overdue books."

Buck removed Tollhausler's wallet, and a condom fell out. Tollhausler rolled his eyes, and Buck reached down and picked the blue and white packet off the ground.

"Be careful with that," Tollhausler demanded. "It's an antique."

Stuffing it back inside, Sergeant Buck spotted a Rudyard I.D. "Here's what I was looking for." There was an atrocious picture of Tollhausler affixed to the lower left-hand corner, and Buck's eyes moodily settled on Tenchman. "Give me your key Will."

Will handed it over.

Adams' nostrils flared. "Are you telling me you've just detained the *wrong* person?"

"We never actually placed him under arrest," Will explained.

Tollhausler nodded. "They just handcuffed me in front of all these people."

The crowd was startled by the revelation, and started to mutter. Sergeant Buck handed Tollhausler's identification to Tenchman. "His name really is Jonathan Tollhausler."

Tenchman frowned at the small laminated card. "Son of a…"

"I'm horrified." Adams moved between Tenchman and Tollhausler. "Simply horrified. Taking the wrong person into custody! Without, apparently, even checking your facts. You owe this student an apology." Adams patted Jonathan on the shoulder. "If you want to bring these three up before the university's Student

Relations Board, I would be glad to serve as a witness. This is ghastly!"

Tenchman glared down the hall. "See here, this is no simple mistake. I was swindled out of money earlier by a real sharp operator, and he gave me this boy's name."

"So you hunted this poor fellow down instead."

"Well…" Tenchman stared at the floor. "….there's only one Tollhausler registered here at Rudyard."

"And you wonder why there aren't more," Tollhausler exclaimed. "We know when we're not wanted." Both metal bands slipped away, and Tollhausler rubbed his wrists.

"I thought I had the larcenous cad."

Adams frowned. "Why on earth would you give any credence to what an obvious thief had told you? Seldom do they give out their real names."

Tenchman pulled his glasses off and rubbed his eye. "You see…"

The students began to disperse, and Buck returned Tollhausler's wallet. Tenchman handed him his I.D.

Tollhausler took it. "Isn't that a rotten picture?"

Professor Adam frowned. "Jonathan, we can't allow this incident to go unnoticed. Students are losing ground each and every day, and clearly your rights have been violated." Adams regarded Tenchman coolly. "We can't have certain people on this campus using security as their own private army."

Tenchman noticed the security guards had slipped away and bit his lip. "Mr. Tollhausler, you have to understand, I've had a very difficult morning. Please forgive my rather hasty—"

"Oh sure." Tollhausler crossed his arms. "Now you want mercy. Here I am, a victim of your short-sighted accusations, unable to raise my head in polite society." For some reason, he liked the sound of that. "An outcast sleeping by day and traveling by night. How am I ever going to meet a respectable woman?" He shook his head. "They always seem to be riding in sports cars. How am I going to compete with those guys?"

"Now Mr. Tollhausler," Tenchman said in a reserved voice. He was fighting the urge to scream at the top of his lungs. "We need your help. Do you know why anyone would be giving your name out like this?"

"Not really. Did you give them any indication that you were going to fly off the handle and drop a pair of security guards on me?"

"I did not fly off—"

"Because maybe one of my friends wouldn't have given you my name if they had known that."

Tenchman was incredulous. "Would a friend do something like this to another friend?"

"Of course. That's what being friends is all about. Having someone to abuse on a daily basis." Tollhausler slipped his wallet back into his pocket. "What did this guy look like anyway?"

"The person who robbed me was *smiling*."

"For shame! A happy thief!"

"And he was carrying this rather odd kind of suitcase." Tenchman pictured it in his mind. "With folding legs."

"No wonder you had us confused. My legs fold too." He bit his knuckle. "Oh, I rue the day I was given knees."

Tenchman glared. "He was also wearing a gray cap."

"Gray cap and a suitcase?"

Adams crossed his arms. "So why didn't you give this description to the police?"

Tenchman frowned. "To tell you the truth, I thought that having his name was all we really needed."

"Well, you were wrong."

"See here," Tenchman said firmly, jabbing an index finger into the other teacher's chest, "if you think I'm unaware of the gravity of this situation, you're very much mistaken."

Tollhausler shook his left wrist. "There's a lot of that going around."

Tenchman grimaced. "What really bothers me about all this is that I'm positive the fellow was a student, and he clearly knew I was a teacher. Nevertheless, he went ahead and took my money anyway. As if it made very little difference to him that I had dedicated my life to teaching others."

"Now, now, don't look at it like that," reassured Tollhausler. "I'm sure it makes very little difference to lots of people that you've dedicated your life to teaching."

"How dare you!"

Adams sighed. "Please, try and remember this boy's been needlessly handcuffed in front of his peers, and sometimes an accusation is more harmful than any conviction. It's only natural that he exhibit some hostility." Adams looked at Tollhausler. "Now Jonathan, what do you think should be done in order to remedy this situation? We certainly can not change what happened, but what do you need in order to return your focus to the school day and not harbor a grudge about the last fifteen minutes? Do you want to bring Professor Tenchman up on charges?"

Tenchman bit his bottom lip. He couldn't believe Adams was offering this as an option.

"I could," Tollhausler said. "But to be honest, I believe we are overlooking something here. Something much more important than basic human dignity." He pointed to an approaching janitor. "Who's gonna' replace the coffee you jerks spilled all over the floor?!"

Tenchman shuddered. "What?"

"That coffee cost me sixty cents." Tollhausler glared at Tenchman. "It would probably cost you sixty cents too. Either way, it's gone. And coffee doesn't grow on trees you know. Or am I thinking of rutabagas?" He shrugged. "Either way, that rutabaga juice cost me sixty-cents."

Adams shook his head. "Tenchman, you don't know how fortunate you are. All this little episode is going to cost you is the price of a cup of coffee. Pretty reasonable considering the circumstances."

"Buy him coffee?!" Tenchman was outraged. He was also very cheap. "But I've already lost money today. This is black mail."

"Restitution," Adams corrected. "Besides, if he has you up before the board, the student press will undoubtedly pick up the story, and depending on how slow the next couple of days are news-wise, the story could actually turn up in the local papers. Rudyard could very well be compelled to take action should the story get too widely reported." Adams studied Tenchman. "By the way, how much did that fellow take from you this morning?"

Tenchman's eyes widened.

Tollhausler held out his hand. "Sixty cents makes it all go away."

Tenchman produced his wallet as if he were removing a major organ. He peered inside. "Do you have change? The smallest I've got is a five dollar bill."

"I've just raised the price of my settlement. I think you should buy me lunch too."

"What?!"

Adams shook his head. "Tenchman, are you mad? Just hand it over. It's the least you can do."

Tenchman's jaw tightened and he reluctantly relinquished the bill.

"It isn't always easy doing the right thing, but it is every citizen's duty." Adams checked his pocket watch. "Dash it all. I'm late for class." He started down the hall. "I hope you've learned something here today Professor."

Tenchman returned his wallet to his back pocket. "So you really have no clue as to who the con man was who cheated me."

"I'm sorry, I'd like to help, but I have to get to class. I haven't been sleeping well lately, and I really need the rest."

10

"....the wrong people in the wrong place. They don't belong here, and it isn't like they're fooling anyone. They aren't even trying." He was leaning against a pay phone in the basement of Brady Hall, and his body was rakishly curved like a parenthesis.

"I went to the Student Assistance Desk, and the girl didn't have a clue about where the building was."

It was unusually bright in the wide corridor, and the glare prompted him to don a pair of sunglasses. "Yeah, you'd think that if there was one thing she should know, it's that." He smoothed the collar of his pale shirt. "Yeah, I'm there now. No thanks to her."

The lights above started flickering on and off, and he raised his sunglasses and rested them on the top of his head. He studied the ceiling.

"How did I find it?"

The lights stopped flashing and the intense glow returned.

He lowered his shades. "This bunch of students were walking across the quad announcing to everyone how they knew where Brady Hall was."

The hall went dark.

"What the—"

A network of emergency lights went on, in the hallways, the classrooms and the stairways, suffusing the dark interior with an odd orange light, and then the square fixtures above sputtered into life.

"The lights just went out." He stared up. "Yeah, everything went completely black. I guess..." He chuckled. "....Rudyard forgot to pay its electric bill."

"Chugga chugga chugga chugga…"

He turned his head in the direction of the sound.

"….woo woooooooo."

He fixed Ernie Turpin with a disapproving look.

Three white coffee containers lined the top of Ernie's guitar case. "Chuff chuff, chuff chuff." Ernie stopped when he noticed he was getting stared at and quickly bowed his head. He passed the guy on the phone without making another sound.

"Did you hear that Donny?" The guy turned toward the pay phone. "The people down here are crazy."

"Woo wooooooooooooo," Turpin exclaimed from behind, taking the guy completely by surprise, and giggled. The guy had dropped the phone.

It had been a good day so far, and he couldn't remember having had a better time. He had even managed to see Susan once again, and made plans with her for the following night. Ernie started humming.

He breezed into room number thirteen, and glided towards the back. The other eleven people, seated in the chairs at the front, had been talking, but couldn't ignore the beaming Turpin. He plopped his coffee cups along the edge of the last desk in the second row, and dropped his guitar. He removed a dripping, plastic lid, sat down and began guzzling coffee.

Exchanging amused expressions, the others turned away. Then the room's lights flickered off a second time, and a box on the wall cast a pair of orange beams across the classroom. It was quiet, except for the sound of footsteps, and then something or someone loomed up in the doorway. "I guess Rudyard must have forgotten to pay its electric bill this month," the shadow purred. The fluorescent bulbs overhead suddenly fluttered back into life, and a lone figure, shrouded entirely in black, entered the room. "Good morning."

Their twelve faces froze. He didn't look like a student. Above the gray-streaked beard that covered his tanned face, a pair of shiny brown eyes bulged. His muscular hands were equally weathered, and gripped around an ungainly black schoolbag. He padded over to an imitation wood desk, and slid the bag to the center. Examining the class, he noticed Turpin seated at the back. "Wouldn't you like to sit with the rest of us?" Ernie politely declined by frantically shaking his head.

"Oh." The teacher gave Ernie a second look, and walked from behind the desk. "I'm Robert Sterbebett, and this is Death 345." He placed a hand on his bag. "I don't much care for the name myself, but that's how it's been listed since the mid-seventies."

The class was attentive, and Sterbebett continued. "I hope you'll all find this course worthwhile, and maybe even a little enjoyable. "He grinned. "I know it doesn't deal with the happiest of subjects." Turpin didn't smile along with the rest of the class. Sterbebett gave him the heebie-jeebies.

Sterbebett unzipped his bag, and pulled out a class list. He scanned the sheet, and, taking a quick count of the people there, nodded. He set it down. "I'm always intrigued by the wide variety of majors this class attracts. Even though it's small, there are over five different majors here. Oh sure, as expected, some of you are nursing majors and pre-med, but there are also English Majors, History Majors, a Biology Major, one of you is Pre-Law, we even have a Music Major. And the one question that I always ask is, why do so many different people take what promises to be such a dismal course?"

Turpin didn't have to think about it for too long. He was there for the distribution credits.

"The university must offer it for some reason. There are easier courses."

Uncovering his second cup, Turpin had to agree. However, months before, Rudyard had graciously informed him, via his advisor, Abigail Jennings, that his quota of "less demanding" courses had already been filled; like it or not, his academic career would have to take a much more serious turn.

"There's a very simple explanation for why you're all here." Sterbebett folded his hands together. "Maybe there's some sort of subconscious yearning or even a conscious one, but the bottom line is, we all want to understand death. No matter what people may say, we're all afraid of it. Because, like it or not, we are *all* going to die."

Sterbebett pointed to the student closest to him. "You're going to die." He nodded to the slim woman seated behind her. "And you're going to die." He gestured at the students seated across from them. "And you're going to die."

The room was quiet, and Ernie wasn't as interested in his coffee as he was before. When he had first arrived, he had felt great, but, thanks to Sterbebett, he wasn't feeling that way now.

"It's the great equalizer. No matter how old you are, who you are or how much money you make, you're going to die." Ernie wished Sterbebett would stop saying that. "What's that old saying? The only two things you can count on in life are death and taxes?" He straightened the ponytail at the back of his neck. "Well, there are some people who have found a way around paying taxes, but even they won't be able to avoid death.

"Death is the one constant in our lives." He crossed his arms. "How do I know? Well, for one thing, this class doesn't really change all that much. The material grows as we learn more and more about people and death, but the basic points remain the same. Other courses are reviewed by their departments every semester, and their material is constantly being updated. Shifts in emphasis and new developments in the world can render a course obsolete in a matter of months."

He pulled a bottle of orange juice from his bag. "For instance..."He shook the bottle, and peeled off its silver cap. "....over in the Communications Department right now, they're busy replacing all their film equipment with video cameras." He took a sip and laid the bottle down. "You see video's much cheaper to work with than film, and each new technology forces the department to rethink its curriculum. Then there are those discoveries which have the ability of negating facts we took to be true for centuries..."

Ernie quietly sipped his coffee. Shoved, face first, like this into his impending mortality, he had become, predictably, somewhat reflective, and was considering what Sterbebett had said. His conclusion: they were all wasting their time--not to mention a good deal of the government's money—if their diplomas only came, at best, with a limited warranty.

"....the way of the world. We're constantly in motion. Think about how different your life is from what it was two years ago or even a year. We aren't what we once were. And by the end of the century, everything will have changed. But the one thing that will make the journey, the one thing that in the year 1999 will be the same as it was back in 1899, is death."

Sterbebett swallowed more juice. "You can postpone it, sure. All you have to do is diet, exercise and eat right, and visit your doctor twice a year. It's tough, and in the end, won't make a bit of difference, but some people think those couple extra years are worth it.

"Then again, good health is no guarantee of longevity." He rested the bottle against his thigh. "Even the healthiest body is prone to disease." He snickered. "Did you know, that for all its advances, medical science has never wiped out a single disease? They know how most diseases work, how they can and can't treat you for them, but they don't know how to get rid of them. Cancer still kills. Children still suffer. And all the medical profession can do is ask us to wait."

Ernie was very sad now.

"On top of all those diseases, we also have to worry about crime. Exercise can't prevent you from turning up in the wrong place at the wrong time. Pick up a newspaper any day, and you'll find out how terribly we treat one another. And sometimes for nothing more than a couple of bucks."

Turpin realized how vulnerable they all were.

Sterbebett finished his juice. "What's the point of all this? That we are all going to die. All of us. No matter what we do, who we pray to, or who we love or hate." He squeezed the bottle flat. "Take drugs? Take a lot more. You jog? Keep running. You're going to die and no one can save you. We're all alone in our mortality. Doctors die, nurses die. Even priests and rabbis die. Nothing survives except death."

Everyone in the room appeared to be holding their breaths. Sterbebett walked deeper into the rows of desks. "I'm going to die," he said. "You're going to die," he said to the student to his left. "And you're going to die," he intoned, and pointed at Ernie.

Turpin's mouth dropped open.

"A

U

G

H

H

H

H

H

H

H!!!"

11

Every semester, most people were incredulous when they first discovered how far back the twin lines for the Registrar's Office actually went. "It can't be" was the phrase most commonly overheard when people were trudging along the hallway or down the steps in search of the line's end.

What happened when they finally arrived there depended solely on their basic outlook on life. Some people would become forlorn as they stared at the line ahead, unprepared for the tedious pilgrimage before them, while others would grit their teeth, more or less resigned to their lot. Quite a few of them would simply curse, and stomp off.

This day being no different from the first day of any other semester, the tail-end of the lines were already pushing across Dennison Hall's polished marble lobby and threatening, at any moment, to push out into the street.

After studying both lines for several seconds, one well-scrubbed fellow approached the end of what appeared to be the shorter of the two, and tapped the woman there on the shoulder. "Which office are you going to?" he asked, as if he suspected she was standing in the wrong line.

She speared him with her eyes. "The Registrar's."

"I see." His suspicions confirmed, he adjusted his glasses and smartly checked the watch on his left wrist. "I'll be right back."

Grateful for the bulletin, she nodded. "I won't move a muscle until after you return."

He stopped beside the exit.

ACTIVITIES BOOK STATION # 7

! !

ACTIVITIES BOOK -- $40.00

A woman with a heavy cloth bag was wrestling four bills free from a leopard-spotted wallet, and she handed them across the small table. She collected an Activities Book and rushed off.

"I'm glad Rudyard's finally doing it this way," he said, and pulled out a denim wallet. "I always thought it was stupid, making us pay for the coupon book along with our tuition. It saves time buying it separately."

The fellow in the yellow Rudyard shirt smiled. Then he pushed back the gray cap on his head. "Say, what's your name?"

The guy straightened up. "Phil Tendon. Why?"

"I's funny." Johnny Mennon took a pair of twenties from Phil, and handed over an Activities Book. "You look just like a guy I know."

"Really?" Phil tried acting interested. "Who?"

"Jonathan Tollhausler."

Phil's features constricted. He had obviously heard the name before. "Well first of all, I want you to know that I've never even met the guy, so if you want me to tell him how you're going to punch his lights out the next time you see him, I can't." He exhaled. "And no, we're not, to my knowledge, related in any way. I don't know why or how we look so much alike, but it's not through blood..."

Whew, Johnny thought. For a brief moment there, he had been considering returning Tendon's money--in the event that he happened to be a cousin or distant relative of Tollhausler's.

Fortunately though, Phil had just as big a mouth as Tollhausler, so there wasn't any danger of that now.

"…and if you're a good friend of his, than I'm sure you and I aren't going to get along either."

Mennon laughed. "You look a lot more like him when you're angry."

"Oh I've had enough of this."

"So what are you standing around for?"

"I was waiting for a receipt." Tendon adjusted his glasses. "I *assume* I get a receipt."

"Sure, sure."

Upon closer examination, Johnny noticed some subtle differences between the two. Besides his dressing a little more upscale than Tollhausler, Phil had that hurried look about him a lot of people confuse with success.

Mennon picked up a red rubber stamp, and slammed it from an inkpad on to a yellow page in a generic receipt book. He tore the page free. "Here you go. Paid in full."

Phil folded it neatly, and slipped it into his jacket. "Thank you." He memorized the name on Mennon's ID badge, and rushed out of the building.

Johnny was grateful for Phil's quick exit, as well as those of the seven previous students he had sold coupon books to. Haste played a very important part in this con. He withdrew his ledger from his pocket, and slid a pen off the table. Closing one eye, he added some figures together in his head, and scribbled something on to one of the book's lined pages. He filed Tendon's money away and smiled. "That sound system's gettin' closer and closer."

He slid his accounts book into a back pocket, and took a deep breath. He hoped he didn't appear too attentive. He knew boredom was the key to impersonating any Rudyard employee, no matter how high or low on the organizational chart; he was equally certain that no one would accept him as part of the university without it. He usually didn't say too much either, relying more on a basic system of grunts and hand gestures to communicate, and to complete the picture, he had moved his gray cap to the back of his head so people could easily spot his apathy from up to twenty feet away.

The lines were now approaching the building's front doors, and more students were coming in every minute. Then a gentleman carrying a trombone saw some people he thought he knew further up the line, and, hoping he could join them, charged forward. "Yo Alicia!"

A series of collisions was inevitable in such close quarters, especially with a trombone case added to the mix, and several people slammed into Mennon's table.

Steadying the woman who had latched on to his right arm, Johnny smiled. "Whaddya' know. Dreams *do* come true."

She had large brown eyes, but they weren't on him. They were scowling after the leaping youth who had just bowled into her. "Oh," she said, glancing at where she had landed, "Sorry." She let go and backed away. "Are you all right Mariko?"

The woman she was with had been propelled in Mennon's direction as well. "Yes Hillary, quite."

"You're one pretty girl Hillary."

Hillary slid the watch that had ended up on her forearm back to her wrist, and brooded while she read the sign on Mennon's table. "Thank you."

"You're a knockout too Mariko."

"Ohhhh…" Mariko grinned shyly and turned away. "….noooo."

"Yes you are."

Hillary grimaced and read Mennon's ID. "don't bother Bradley. Bradley?" She had a problem with that, but wasn't quite sure why. "Mariko hasn't been at Rudyard long and doesn't speak English very well."

"Like the rest of the Freshman Class."

Hillary's eyes narrowed. "So she doesn't fully comprehend what you're saying. Or what you're after for that matter."

"I don't know. Look at that smile. She knows I like her plenty."

Hillary studied her charge. Mariko was clearly captivated by Mennon's attention. "I guess she does at that, but don't you think you should stick to whoever it is you're seeing at the moment?"

"How do you know I'm seeing anybody?"

"Ohhhh, I know guys like you. I bet you're seeing lots of people."

"Mom said shop around."

"Well I wouldn't expect any major purchases today."

Mennon pulled down his hat. "Come on, I just said she was good lookin' . I wasn't proposing or anything. Besides, I said you were pretty too. I just thought it's something you ladies can't hear enough of."

"Guys around here are so innocent," Hillary observed. "Next time, keep it to yourself."

"Okay, okay." Mennon smiled. "Now why don't you give me your phone number?"

Hillary nudged Mariko forward. "Because I'm not. That's why."

"You want mine?"

Hillary laughed. "Do you ask out every girl you meet?"

"Hey, one day I'm gonna' ask out the woman I'm gonna' marry."

"Her and her friend."

"That's just in case my fiancée can't fulfill the responsibilities of her title."

"Ugh." Hillary directed Mariko away.

"Say, if anybody asks," Mennon called after them, "tell 'em *you* rejected *me*."

A low burst of static immediately caught Johnny's attention, and a security guard slowly made his way through the rows of people.

Mennon figured the tall uniformed guard was about twenty-seven, and his patient stride told him the guy had been doing this for a couple of years. Mennon considered that a point in his favor. The more experienced the guard, the less strict they were, Mennon always said.

The policeman lowered the volume on his radio. "Annoying women?"

"Yeahhhhhhhh, but what am I gonna' do? I've gotta' go out with somebody."

The guard surveyed the busy lobby. "Shouldn't you be in class?"

As discreetly as he could, Mennon moved in the direction of the nearest exit. "Ah, they don't do anything the first week of class. I'll go next week."

The officer tipped his head to the right, perusing Mennon's ID. "You're not a very good student, are you Mr. Winthrop."

Mennon grinned sheepishly. "Well no. This school thing's more of a hobby for me right now…" Mennon squinted at the guard's nameplate. "….Sergeant Quimby."

Quimby placed a hand on his holster. "Are you allowed to set up here?"

"Sure." Johnny pulled the table a little closer. He still had the exit in view. "I'm workin' for the university."

Quimby shook his head. "There are only four places on campus where students can pick up their Activities Books, and no one has to pay for them. All they have to do is present their paid tuition bill or an updated ID."

"Oh dear." Johnny furrowed his brow. "Did they change things around here on me again and forget to tell me?"

Quimby took Mennon's sign in hand. "You wouldn't be conning students out of their money, would you?"

Johnny scratched under his chin. "Now who would do something like that and still be able to sleep at night?"

"I don't know, but you look pretty well rested."

86

Mennon crossed his arms. "Okay, I get it. I think you got something to say to me."

"You're right. Especially if you're doing what I think you're doing."

Johnny tried to match the guard's stern tone. "Heyyy, what're you trying to say?"

"That you're a crook."

He relaxed. "Ah, better people than you have accused me of stuff over the years and they never proved a thing." He shrugged. "Not that much anyway."

"I'm sorry…" Quimby rounded the table. "….but you're going to have to come with me."

Mennon went the other way. "Awww, I'm not that cute am I?"

"Don't get smart." He grabbed Mennon by the arm.

"Okay, I'll get stupid." Johnny pulled away. "Where do you usually go?"

The sergeant's walkie-talkie interrupted him in mid-lunge, and he drew it to his mouth. "This is number nineteen."

Mennon folded his case shut.

Crackling reports followed, and Quimby glared at Mennon. "Can't you send somebody else? I've got a situation developing here myself." He didn't like the answer. "All right, on my way. Over." He flicked a switch and hung the radio on his belt. "There's a disturbance over in Brady Hall that's more important than you." He started off. "But I'm going to come back. Don't let me catch you here again."

"Don't worry." Johnny waved. "I won't let you catch me."

Quimby suddenly stopped, causing Mennon to pick up his case. "You know where Brady Hall is?"

"Heyyyyyyyyy," Mennon growled. "I'm no squealer."

"Damn it!" Sergeant Quimby ran out the door.

12

It was peaceful in the narrow green enclave, a farewell gift from the graduating class of 1975, so when the cigarette butt ricocheted off the statue's forehead, it did so with a light plink.

The bust, an exact likeness of Edmund Dennison, one of the co-founders of Rudyard University, was no easy target either. Nestled among the many branches surrounding it, the modern sculpture was barely visible amongst the bright pink flowers and purple blossoms, except for its haunting gray eyes and the finely—chiseled forehead above. Occasionally, someone would take the time to wonder how Dennison had wound up on this part of the campus behind all the camouflage in the first place.

She was not one of them.

Seated across the courtyard, she had one leg curled against her body, and the other was swinging back and forth under her in an agitated manner. A wayward ant, wandering along the top of the stone bench, climbed on to the sneaker by her thigh, and she flicked it away with the same ferocity she had directed at her cigarette. She wasn't in a particularly good mood.

Glowering at the world around her, she lit another cigarette. She had spent the better part of the morning searching for Brady Hall, and along the way had spoken to most of the campus: security guards, the girl at the information desk, students she knew, students she didn't know, the people who worked on the food trucks, a homeless man and even that nice guy at the Student Center. Unfortunately, no one had been able to help her, and she had missed her class. The entire incident was ablaze in her mind, and it made her feel incompetent; also furious. She expelled a jet of smoke.

Distracted by a light rustling in an angular bush to her left, she decided it was either a very large squirrel or a clumsy mugger. Both foraging creatures, she reflected, and clutched her purse to her side.

The top of someone's head emerged from the bush. "Did you ever find Brady Hall?"

She carefully lowered her leg to the ground. "What?"

"I said," Tollhausler stated, raising his chin above a jagged sprig, "'Did you ever find Brady Hall?'"

She immediately recognized him and relaxed. "No."

"Oh." Tollhausler disappeared under the leaves.

It was quiet again, and she moved over to where he had disappeared. "You know," she announced, "I thought you were weird before, but now I'm convinced." She tried spotting him on the other side of the shrub.

"Could I ask you another question?" Tollhausler's head was now jutting out of the bush to her right, and she took a step back. "Is everything all right? You look a little upset."

"That's because I am."

"Uh hunh." He tilted his head. "Did someone leave you high and dry?"

She shook her head.

"What, someone left you low and wet?"

She shook her head once more.

"Come now, your last class couldn't have been that bad."

"Oh, my last class was fine." She hung the cigarette from her bottom lip. "It's the one that I couldn't find that's got me so angry." She strolled back to the bench. "I never found Brady Hall." She sat down. "I was all over today," she complained, "but I just couldn't find it." The cigarette burned in her hand as she exhaled. "It didn't matter who I spoke to either. Nobody knew where Brady Hall was. It's so frustrating. I spoke to security guards, teachers…"

It was obvious to Tollhausler that she was taking this all far too seriously and he decided to interrupt. "Please, you don't have to continue with your sad, heartbreaking tale." He sat down next to her. "You see, I too know suffering." He leaned closer. "Wanna' see my scar?"

She smirked. "No."

He stood up, insulted, and skimmed between the overlapping branches of two wilted bushes. "Fine. I don't want to see yours either."

"You're crazy."

He reappeared. "No, just a little hurt." He sniffed. "No matter how much work I put into it, nobody ever wants to see my scar." He ran off.

"I'm having the strangest day." She smoked quietly for a bit. "I can't believe Rudyard has a building on campus no one ever heard of."

"It doesn't," Tollhausler replied. "Rudyard changed the name of Templeton Hall to Brady Hall in August."

"What?!" She jumped up and circled the bushes.

Tollhausler clambered up a tall cyclone fence. "Please don't kill the messenger. He has to work till three."

"Why didn't you tell me that before?"

"That I have to work till three?"

"No." She got hold of herself. "Why didn't you tell me about Brady Hall?"

"I didn't know." He leaned away from the fence and inspected his surroundings. "You know, this is a mighty pretty spot. It's a shame the campus has to surround it."

"How could they do something like that?"

"Yeah, Rudyard wasn't satisfied raising tuition, firing teachers and jettisoning courses." He dropped to the grass below. "Now it's going to change the names of the buildings around. It isn't going to stop until we all go away."

She threw her cigarette down, relieved, and crushed it out. "That's great though. Now I'll be able to find my class."

"You have my condolences."

"No, that's a good thing." She smiled. "I want to thank you."

It suddenly occurred to her how much fun it was spending time with him. He was a lunatic, sure, but things seemed better with him around. The feeling was very exhilarating, and she wondered what it would be like if she got to know him better. She stared at the ground. "I don't even know your name."

"Oh that's all right. Lots of people don't know my name. Why some days, even I can't remember it."

"Is today a good day?"

Tollhausler grinned. "Yes."

She looked into his eyes and extended her hand. "I'm Diane Curzewski."

He took her hand and gently shook it. It was very warm. "I'm J.R.R. Tollhausler."

They stood there for a moment, looking at one another, and then Diane pulled a leaf from his hair. "What does the J stand for?"

"Jerk."

"Were you named after your father?"

"That's what Mom tells me."

She giggled, and Tollhausler blushed.

"What else does the J stand for?"

"Oh lots of things. Haven't you ever seen a dictionary? J has its own section."

She bowed her head. "I'm sorry. I'm only a sophomore."

"Oh well, that explains it."

They both exchanged smiles, and suddenly became aware of the fact that they were still holding hands. There was some more blushing, and then they let go of each other. Tollhausler vanished behind a misshapen shrub, and Diane returned to the bench.

She opened her purse and removed a crumpled cigarette pack. Peering through the torn hole on top, she saw how many were left, and gracefully slid one out. She then folded the pack up in a pile of tissues, and placed a rubber band around them.

"What are you doing?" Tollhausler leaned against the back of the bench.

Diane, embarrassed, shrugged. "Well, um, I don't want anyone to know I smoke."

"Oh." Tollhausler frowned. "You know that cigarette you're holding is a dead giveaway."

"I don't want my *parents* to know."

"Ohhhhhhhhh." He still didn't understand. "How old are you?"

"Nineteen." Diane shoved the tissue-wrapped cigarettes into her purse, and pulled out a pack of matches. "Look, I'm just not comfortable with them knowing about my smoking right now. I'm not sure what they'd think, so I keep everything out of sight. It's as simple as that."

Tollhausler snickered.

"Ohhhh look—"

He was gone from the back of the bench.

Diane couldn't believe she had let that slip. She was certain it wasn't the sort of thing a person divulges to someone they desperately want to impress, and yanked a match loose from the book in her hand. "What are you doing here, anyway?" She scraped a match into life. "Or do you usually lurk in the bushes around here this time of day?"

"No, the lurking's much better on the other side of campus. Near the Science Building. But I usually stop by here at least once a semester to make sure the ugliest statue on campus is still here. I'm very sentimental."

She breathed out some smoke as she waved the match back and forth in the air. "Ugly? I like it."

"It's a head mounted on a block. No shoulders, no neck, no collar. Just Edmund Dennison's head. It looks like a hunting trophy."

"It's a nice monument."

"You're just saying that because it's buried under all that foliage. From behind, it looks like something growing out of a melon patch."

She studied it. "It's just a little memorial."

"Very little."

Diane laughed. "I *knew* you were going to say that."

"Well don't let it get around. It'd disappoint my fans."

"Oh, sorry." She sat back and sighed. "Why did you really stop by?"

"I usually shoot passed here on my way to the Student Center." He glanced through the cyclone fence into the adjoining parking lot. "I was coming from Brady Hall. The professor scheduled to teach my one-thirty class quit today." He glowered. "Of course, it took the university twenty minutes to get somebody to tell us that." He removed his glasses and rubbed his eye. "Now I'm down to twelve credits."

"You could add another class."

"Yeah, there's nothing like standing around in line for seven hours just so I can add a class."

"What's your Major?"

"Communications."

Diane sat up. "Mine too."

Tollhausler was equally surprised. "Really?"

They stared into space for a couple of seconds, and then Diane asked him a very funny question. At least it was to him. "Aren't you worried you won't graduate on time?"

Tollhausler stuck his head over the hedge. "On time for what?"

"Ohhh," she said. "I see."

She thought she knew his type, and Tollhausler smiled. It was obvious she didn't have a clue. However, he suspected she liked him anyway, and he decided he would have to act fast. He took a deep breath and broke cover.

"You know, if we went out, I probably wouldn't let you pay for a thing."

"Er...um..." Diane looked away. She had forgotten something.

"Oh all right. If you insist, you can buy." Tollhausler began pacing. "After all, this *is* the eighties."

"....thanks, but..."

"What, don't you want to be seen with me in public?"

"....I'm sort of seeing someone."

"Ohhhh." He sat down. "You don't even want to be seen with me in private."

"I'm sorry. I've been going with him for some time."

"Well I'm sorry you've been going with him for some time too." Tollhausler rolled his eyes. He wasn't particularly thrilled with her answer, but he was glad he had finally found the courage to ask the question. He hopped up and parted the big branches of a large bush. "If you should change your mind though, I'll be around."

"I hope so J.R.R. Tollhausler." Her hand shot out, and he took it. They released one another, and Tollhausler disappeared behind the waving branches. However, Diane knew, this time, he was gone.

13

It really wasn't a brutal robbery.

The mugger deftly leapt from beside the gate of parking lot # 5, grabbed a tall, gray-haired gentleman by the lapels of his blue pinstriped suit and shoved him up against a dented red Chevy. Approaching his victim, he flicked a knife into the air from his back pocket, and brandished it so there would be no misunderstanding. It was quite a professional display.

The mugger's quarry, Associate Professor Elliot Richards, could only stand there with his arms at his sides. He couldn't understand how he hadn't dropped the briefcase in his left hand, but he wished he had because right now it felt as if it weighed a thousand pounds.

"Give me your wallet!"

The luckless teacher realized it was going to take a minute or so. He had forgotten where he had put it.

Satisfied with their patrol of parking lot #3, Sergeant Larry Brooks and his partner were leisurely walking towards lot #4. Neither one of them was talking at the moment.

His partner was wholly absorbed by the task of dunking a tea bag in hot water, striving for just the right strength, and Brooks was quiet because he had somehow forgotten the other guard's name. To be fair, it wasn't exactly an easy one to remember, and they had only been teamed up now for two hours, but it still bothered Brooks. The new guy had sprung for the coffee.

Here was his chance. The other guard had stopped on the sidewalk and turned, and Brooks had an unobstructed view of his nameplate. He carefully stole a glance at the name, J. Krystichelinsky was printed there in white, easy-to-read capital letters, and he committed it, all five syllables, to memory. He hoped.

Oblivious of Brooks' scrutiny, Krystichelinsky continued his ministrations. The tea still wasn't dark enough. "How's your coffee sarge?"

"Fine Krystichelinsky."

A polished red car went speeding by right then. "____ing rent-a-cops," someone shouted from the window.

Both officers spilled their beverages, and glared in the direction of the speeding car. They promptly memorized the auto's year, make and license number, and the face of the loud mouth grinning back at them. They wouldn't forget him.

Brooks fingered his coffee-soaked tie, and Krystichelinsky held his shirt away from his body where his tea had splashed. It seemed dark enough now.

The stickup man had waited long enough. "Come on! Come on!"

Professor Richards was almost apologetic as he dipped into the watch pocket of his pants, hoping he might find a folded bill or two there, and for a second, his index finger and thumb seemed stuck in the narrow pouch. He couldn't believe it, and, hoping he could catch someone's attention, he yelled. "Help!"

The mugger pinned him up against the car, freeing his hand. "Stupid, stupid, stupid."

"Perhaps—"

"Shut up," the robber yelled in Richards' ear. "And give me your money!"

Suddenly, they were no longer alone.

"Pardon me," Tollhausler said. "I couldn't help overhearing that someone over here needed help, er, over here." Tollhausler didn't like the sound of that, but he continued anyway. "So which one of you guys needs it?"

The guy with the knife blinked.

"Come on, come on, I ain't got all day." Tollhausler glared at the thief. "I hope it isn't you. Imagine, a big strong mugger like yourself needing help with an old guy like this. And you with a knife. You ought to be ashamed of yourself."

The bandit's eyes flashed from Richards to Tollhausler and back again, and he waved the knife in the space between them. "Get out of here," he ordered, "or I'll rob you too!"

Tollhausler appeared doubtful. "I'm sorry, but that knife isn't big enough for the both of us."

"All right. I want your wallet too!"

"I couldn't do that. My little cousin made it for me in summer camp. Just before he ran into that beehive. I don't know how long it's going to be until he's well enough to go back and sew me another one."

"*I am serious man.*"

"If you were serious you'd be wearing a mask. Which would be a great improvement."

The crook lunged.

However, the previous exchange had provided Professor Richards with enough of a respite that he was finally able to remember where his wallet was: buried somewhere at the bottom of his briefcase under several bulky textbooks, a half a dozen pens and a yellow legal pad. He swung the hefty valise into the charging mugger's head, and his attacker was suddenly lying on the ground, face down.

"Say thanks." Tollhausler shook the trembling Richards' hand. "But if you'd have thought of that earlier, there wouldn't have been any need for this brief encounter."

"Thank the heavens you came along when you did! I didn't know what to do." Richards pumped Jonathan's hand. "Thank goodness you weren't afraid to get involved. How can I ever thank you?"

"Give me your wallet."

Richards chuckled. "Humble too, I see. I can see I was very fortunate that you were the person who stumbled upon this scene and not somebody else."

"Welllll, I always get my lamb."

"I couldn't believe what was happening." Richards was experiencing an adrenaline rush. "I was going to my car, the blue one over there, and this cad jumped out of nowhere, pushed me and tried to rob me. It was if I was watching the whole thing happen from far away." He sighed, and studied the motionless heap on the ground. "I guess we'd better find a security guard fast."

Tollhausler nodded. "I know just where to look too."

"Where?"

"In the cafeteria. They're probably over there right now. Picking up girls and donuts."

Krystichelinsky and Brooks saw Richards waving at them from across the street.

"Over there, a robber," he breathlessly announced. He led them over to the parking lot. "I suppose we'll have more guards than we really need once that young man returns."

Krystichelinsky surveyed the area. "Someone else was here?"

"Why yes." Richards followed the guards over to the unconscious mugger. "The student who thwarted the robbery."

The two guards crouched next to the guy laid out on the ground, rolled him over and tilted back his head to stop his nose from bleeding.

Krystichelinsky studied the smeared face. "Isn't that...?"

Brooks nodded. "Yep. He's a regular."

Richards shook his head. "He had the biggest knife I've ever seen." He held two index fingers a foot apart. "Yay big. Then a student appeared from out of nowhere..."

Sergeant Brooks stood up, and Krystichelinsky did the same.

"....and while this brute was distracted, I cuffed him with my case."

Brooks pulled out a pen and pad, and recorded the time. "We'd like you to wait for us at Petrie Hall." He knew Richards was a teacher. "In the Guard Station. We'll be there as soon as we can get a van over here." He wrote something else, and closed his note pad. "We'll need a statement, and so will the police."

Richards straightened his tie. "Whatever you need officer." He walked to the gate and stopped. "I guess this is one fellow who won't be breaking the law again."

"Yes sir." Brooks watched Richards leave, and then leaned against a dented green coupe. He hit a button on his walkie-talkie, and the crackle of static grew louder in the quiet parking lot. He requested a van, why and returned the radio to his belt.

Krystichelinsky shook his head. "That creep in the car, and now a teacher clobbers a crook. I guess this wouldn't be a good time to go on strike."

"Mmmmmmm." Brooks crossed his arms. "I doubt if a strike'd do us much good right now anyway."

Krystichelinsky took three steps, and reached under a small station wagon. He picked up the mugger's knife and folded it closed. "Don't you think a walk-out would get somebody's attention down here?"

The third member of their party groaned.

"Maybe if it looked like we were actually going to do it. Right now, whenever we talk about it, it sounds more like an empty threat. Just another bargaining tool."

"So you don't think it'll force the university to talk to us."

"Not really." Brooks looked at the suspect. "You said it yourself. The university doesn't need us. It just needs security guards. If the teachers walk out, like they've been threatening to do for the past year, then Rudyard will have to sit down and negotiate. If we go…" He adjusted the holster on his hip. "….class

101

is still in session. They don't have to bargain with us. Remember, all we are to them is rent-a-cops. The university can always rent them somewhere else."

"But wouldn't a strike complicate things for Rudyard? The university's had a pretty rough year employee-wise."

"But we're not teachers. Garibaldi will do a couple of interviews and make it sound like we're being greedy, like he always does when anyone around here starts making noises about money. Then everyone'll forget about us, and the story'll wind up buried at the back of the newspaper."

Krystichelinsky was puzzled. "You'd think Rudyard would work a little harder to keep us happy. After all, we protect this place."

"They're more concerned about protecting their money." Brooks watched the robber stir. "Did you see how they laid those teachers off in the spring? And they supposedly *need* them. Do you think they're going to lose any sleep over us?"

His partner was crestfallen. "Doesn't the university care about anyone?"

The reclining man shifted slightly. Then his eyes popped open.

"Only in the brochures Officer Krystichelinsky. Only in the brochures."

14

His classes for the first day finally ended, Richard Mead had once again returned to the Student Center, and was standing in the cafeteria. Stalled in the middle of a short line, he appeared preoccupied with something, so much so that the security guard directly behind him had to point out that the line was moving.

"Oh." Mead blindly stepped forward, and absently shook the orange juice container in his right hand. This sent several chunks of ice and drops of condensation flying into the air.

"Yo," a burly passerby in a striped shirt complained.

Mead winced. "Sorry." He switched the plastic container to his other hand, and wiped his free hand on his thigh.

Ahead, the lone cashier started grumbling from atop her red stool that she was out of nickels, and various sounds of discontent rippled down the length of the line.

Shifting his weight to one leg, Mead exhaled, and disappeared under the blanket of his previous thoughts. He still wasn't exactly sure what had happened or even when, but some time over the past year, he had begun to notice how uninspiring his courses were. He missed the excitement of his first semester at Rudyard, and realized he was bored. Now, at the start of his junior year, all he wanted to do was move on to something else, something different.

The sentiment reminded him of some of his previous relationships, and he was suddenly struck by how similar the situations were. Time and time again, he found himself losing interest in the women he was courting, and rather than prolong the agony, he would drop them, whether the relationship consisted of three weeks or three months. Still, he hadn't made any plans to split from Rudyard yet. Then again, he hadn't planned on losing his last girlfriend either. Like most accidents, it had simply happened. The name Julie rang loud and clear in his mind, and, preoccupied, he vigorously shook his orange juice.

"Hey," whined a young woman in a gray sweat suit.

"I am *so* sorry." He transferred the juice to his other hand. Whenever anyone asked, Rich would freely admit that his last relationship had probably collapsed under the weight of something he had done. He was always quick to remind himself, however, that Julie was the one who had issued the ultimatum, not him. "If you don't want to be in a long-term relationship, than just tell me and you'll never have to see me again."

Rich had been taken off guard by such tough talk, and he had been forced to go off by himself and reflect on what he wanted. Unfortunately, Julie had run into him, several days later, in the middle of his soul-searching. Him, and the rather tall Dance Major he had chosen as a guide.

"Do you mind," the cashier hissed. She ran a hand down her cheek.

"Huh?" Mead had shaken his juice again. "Oh. Sorry." He dropped some coins into her hand, and quickly moved along.

Yanked back to the cafeteria like this a third time, Rich tried to shake off his mood. He attributed the depressing nature of his thoughts to a mid-afternoon funk, and, observing some of the other people there, guessed he wasn't alone. Then he saw Julie's smiling face one more time, and flicked another barrage of condensation into the air.

"What the--?"

Mead rolled his eyes. "*Damn* it."

"Richard?"

He stopped in his tracks, and studied the young woman who had spoken his name. She was seated beside another woman, and they both looked familiar. He dug through the names and faces of the last year, and connected them up. Mead set his drink down on their table.

"Karen, right?"

Her friend nodded. "Great. Now who am I?"

Mead stared at the shorthaired blonde. "Don't you know?"

"I was hoping you could tell me."

"All right, I'm sure I've seen you somewhere before." He placed a finger to his lips. "Is your name…Wilma?"

"No," she said around a straw. She was drinking from a can of soda.

"Yes, but Wilma's a very nice name. Don't you think?"

"No."

"Well I do. It's quite versatile. If it was your name, than people could call you Wil for short. Or 'Ma. Wouldn't that be great?"

"No." She smiled at Karen.

"Both would be very sporty nicknames."

"Unh uh."

"Okay." He about-faced, took three steps and turned back. "Give me a hint. Were you ever on the FBI's Ten Most Wanted List?"

"Noooooo."

He landed next to the table with a single hop. "This is obviously taking much longer than I expected. Do you mind if I join you ladies?" He pulled out a chair. "Got it." He pointed at her. "Brenda, right?"

The woman across the table grimaced. "Not even close."

"Good. Brenda isn't half as nice a name as Wilma. Then again, what is?" He bit his lip. "Is your name Sandy Smythe-Jones?"

Both women crinkled up their noses at that one.

Mead hit the table. "I wish it was Rita. That was the name of my first love. My greatest love." He stared off dreamily. "Why oh why did she have to run off with that senator?" Mead convulsed with fake tears. "Sure he had money and power and a great car, but..." He looked up. "Come to think of it, *I* should have gone with him too."

Karen's friend clicked her tongue. "My name is—"

"Tina, I'm expressing my inner most feelings here. Dya' mind?!"

Karen smiled and Tina laughed.

"I didn't think you'd remember me. I figured you'd only remember Karen."

Mead simpered. "You are two ladies I would never forget."

"Well we did meet a long time ago," Tina explained.

Karen nodded. "You were with *those guys*."

Having been in the same class with Karen the previous spring, Mead had made the mistake of introducing himself in the company of Messieurs Mennon and Turpin, and, if memory served him right, it hadn't gone very well. If he had had any doubts, his suspicions were confirmed the way the words "those guys" contorted Karen's narrow face. Her grimace also gave ample warning that when referring to Turpine and Mennon, he should only do so in a derogatory fashion.

Mead didn't really want to be a party to such an ignoble act, but he knew the boys wouldn't mind. The four of them had a standing rule: if one of them could benefit from the positive or negative actions of the others, then they should always do so, especially when it came to women.

"You don't still go around with them, do you?"

"Sure."

"Why?" Tina demanded. "They think they're so cute. And that one guy kept asking me out."

"Mennon," informed Richard. He tried to appear sympathetic. "And I know what you mean. They're very immature." He peeled a silver foil cover from his juice. "It's just that we've known each other since grade school and I feel sorry for them." He had decided to try his boyhood chums alibi on them. "They don't take anything seriously, and they're frightened at the thought of being sensitive." He sipped some juice and swallowed. "They can be a major pain sometimes. But someone's got to look out for them."

"That's so nice," Karen said, and Tina agreed.

Mead was glad they thought so. "I try not to get mad at them, but at times, they can be pretty annoying."

"At times?" Karen shook her head. "I should think it would be tough all the time." She had bright eyes and her sweeping black hair was impeccably brushed. She nudged Tina. "Can you imagine?" "He's just too loyal."

"Mennon can get out of hand, but Turpin's crazy. Why there were these two cheerleaders once…" Richard immediately stopped himself. He had suddenly realized that Karen and Tina might not appreciate the story half as much as a guy would. "….ahem." He picked up his juice, and dropped the story along with his grin. He had another sip. "Er, I'm no angel either. I've done stuff that wasn't nice too."

"I can't imagine you being as bad as they were," Karen asserted.

"Well, I don't know," he concluded. "But I do get a little tired of making excuses for them all the time. I don't go to certain parties because the people who invite me tell me not to bring them."

His audience was very sympathetic, and Karen squeezed his arm. "That's very nice of you."

He looked away. "I guess." He usually waited a couple of seconds at this point, so the woman would get the impression he was sensitive.

Karen patted his hand.

It was time for him to strike. "It occurs to me," he said, "that I never got your phone number."

"You think you can help him out with that Karen?"

Karen's blue ballpoint pen traced seven digits across a small, yellow napkin, and Mead gracefully slid it off the table and made it disappear. They beamed at one another.

Then they were interrupted by a loud gurgling sound. Tina and Karen slowly revolved in their chairs, as if they were about to be swallowed whole by a wild animal.

"Well fancy meeting Richard Mead here on a bright summer's day," Tollhausler declared in a heavy Irish brogue. He took another sip from his large coffee with cream and sugar, and gargled some more.

"Another one of your interesting friends," Tina said coldly, and Rich smiled.

He clumsily introduced everyone.

"Hello," Karen said tightly.

"Hi," Tina intoned with a hint of disdain. She could tell immediately that she wasn't going to get along with Tollhausler. He reminded her of Rich's other difficult friends.

"Pleased to meet you." Tollhausler lowered himself into the chair next to Mead, and wondered what the problem was.

Mead smiled at Karen. "And how was your day Jon?"

Tollhausler replayed the day in his mind, running through his tedious classes, his confrontation with Robert Tenchman and his failed attempt at securing a date. He had already forgotten about the mugger. "About the usual. And yours?"

"Great."

Tollhausler opened his roster. "I wonder what's in store for me tomorrow."

Mead wondered how he was going to get Karen alone. "Me too."

"Do you want to see my roster?"

Rich frowned back.

"Richard," Karen said, "how did he know you'd be here?"

"We meet here all the time."

"Before class?" He nodded. "And after class."

"Sometimes even during class," Tollhausler quipped. He was trying to smooth out his wrinkled class schedule.

"You don't cut class often, do you Richard?"

"Well—"

"Not at all." Tollhausler looked up. "Why he's so studious, he even attends classes he hasn't signed up for. Last spring, for instance, he religiously attended a dance class…"

"Tollhausler."

"….with a gorgeous—"

"*Tollhausler*," he stated more firmly. "You really don't have to tell them about that."

"Don't you want these ladies to know what a conscientious student you are? As opposed to a rotten one, like me?"

Tina was annoyed. "Then why do you even bother coming here if you aren't going to go to class?"

Rich had to admit that this was indeed an interesting opening to a conversation; always provocative. He had heard the question posed from time to time whenever someone felt that their classmates weren't living up to the standards he or she had set for themselves as students. However, he wasn't quite sure how Tollhausler would react. Tollhausler didn't have any mixed emotions about cutting class nor did he care about what other people thought of the practice.

Mead regarded Tollhausler with a smirk, and Jonathan smiled at Rich. Then it became obvious that they were both waiting for the other to come up with a good, if not clever, retort to Tina's question. However, it was equally obvious that one would not be forthcoming any time soon, and, disappointed, they both turned away.

Tollhausler slid an arm on the table and cradled his chin in the palm of his hand. "Damned if I know. Why do you come here?"

And then Tina told him.

Boy did she tell him.

Despite that, they still managed to pass the next couple of minutes quite amicably, Tina graciously sharing her thoughts with them about what she thought other people should do with their lives. Eventually though, Tollhausler, true to form, ruined everything--him and his big mouth—and Tina was suddenly jumping up from the table.

Karen joined her. "*You.*" She pressed the palms of her hands flat on the tabletop and scowled at Tollhausler. "You, and those other two guys think you're so funny. Running around here like the Three Stooges--"

"Marx Brothers," corrected Tollhausler.

"Whoever." She pushed up from the table. "I'm glad Richard isn't part of your troupe. He puts up with you court jesters because he feels sorry for you, but I don't. You're just a bunch of jerks. You don't belong here. And you'll find out how unfunny you are the moment you take this act of yours out on the road." She looked at Mead. "We're leaving."

He got to his feet. "All right Karen."

"*Good* bye." Her eyes seemed to be saying something, but he didn't know what. She crossed her arms. "Aren't you coming?"

He thought it was a little early in the relationship for Karen to be demanding that he choose between her and an old friend.

"No." He tried to look stern. "I'm going to stay here and have a word with Mr. Tollhausler."

Karen was not pleased. "Maybe we'll talk later."

"Yeah." Mead watched the two enraged women storm off. They hurried out the doors, and, having held out as long as he could, Rich burst into laughter.

"I only date men with beards," Tollhausler repeated, mimicking Tina. "*Gee*-zus."

Mead coughed and took a deep breath. "Do you think I should go after them? Karen really didn't think I should stay here with you."

"I'd rather not say. There might be children present."

Mead sat down.

"How do you do it?" Tollhausler asked. "You escape unscathed while Mennon and me get blamed for everything."

"Timing and Luck Toll." Mead drained the rest of his orange juice. "Besides, my mouth isn't half as big as yours."

"Yeah, well, that only means you can't speak as much truth."

Rich frowned. "Oh puh-leeze."

Tollhausler crossed his arms, pouting, and couldn't understand why he always felt he had to have the last word. It certainly wasn't smart, and after a while, as he often did when reviewing his social skills, he decided that Turpin was the smartest one of them all. Ernie didn't say much, even when annoyed, whereas the rest of them were too vocal, and always at the most inappropriate times. The incident with Tina bore him out on that. Had he been a little more flexible, a little quicker on his toes, he could have easily hurdled her little comment about dating hirsute men. He knew from watching other people with women, especially Mennon, that sometimes persistence was the key to winning dates. Persistence, he thought to himself, And when all else fails, money.

15

An annoyed Ernie Turpin entered the cafeteria.

Two seconds later, the person who was annoying him appeared.

"She didn't leave on account of something I said," Johnny Mennon called after him, "did she?"

Turpin shrugged.

"She did leave without answering my question though," noted Mennon. "But she wouldn't have left because of that, would she?"

Ernie kept walking.

"All I did was ask her if she had a sister."

Tollhausler and Mead threw their legs up as Turpin and Mennon bowled their cases under the table.

"Why would she get angry about that," Mennon wondered. "It's not like I was asking her something personal."

Turpin sat down, and Mennon took the seat next to him.

Johnny pushed his gray hat to the back of his head. "Besides, she doesn't even have a sister. If she did, then she'd have something to get mad about. But since she doesn't, I don't see why she'd get so upset." He leaned to the left and reached into his pocket. "Sure, maybe if I did go out with her sister, and pulled a fast one, then maybe she would have something to get angry about, but she doesn't, I didn't, so it couldn't have been anything I did." He slapped a tattered red and white paper box on to the table.

"You know, I don't know what you two are talking about," Tollhausler admitted, moving his crumpled cup aside, "and I'd like to keep it that way if you don't mind."

A ten of clubs bounced off his glasses.

"And how was your day Johnny?"

"Not bad. Sales were good." He dealt three more cards. "But Ernie didn't have such a good day. He says he might quit school."

Another card glided to Tollhausler.

"Funny you should mention that. We were talking about the same thing a little earlier."

Mead shook his head. "This is *not* good. We should not be reconsidering school the first day of the semester."

"That's true," Tollhausler agreed. "We should do it at the end of the semester. Like everybody else."

Turpin shuffled his cards. " I don't belong in college." He set his cards down. "But then, I don't think any of us does."

"What are you talking about?" Mennon kept dealing. "You see the way some of these girls dress?"

Turpin squeezed his earlobe. "I didn't come here to meet women. I came here to learn."

Tollhausler stared at his cards. "I've seen your grades." He moved a card. "You're better off with the women."

Mennon flipped a card over in the center of the table, and set the deck alongside it. "Ernie says after he drops out, he's gonna' go off and do a lot of crazy stuff."

Mead reviewed his cards. "Like what?"

"Maybe I'll take up skydiving," he proposed. "Or learn how to fly. Things that make you feel alive."

"Ahhh, that ain't no plan." Mennon arranged his cards. "And why? Because some teacher says you're gonna' die."

Mead studied the cards in his left hand. "Gosh Ernie, what'd you do?"

"Nothing. We were sitting there, minding our own business, when the teacher strolled in, smiled and told us we were all going to die."

"Well, it's certainly not as upbeat as most of the speeches you hear on the first day of classes," Tollhausler confirmed, "but it certainly got your attention. What is it, an Accounting class?"

"It's a Death and Dying class," Turpin explained. "But there isn't much point to all this if we're going to die. Four years out of your life for college—"

Tollhausler tapped his cards on the table. "Don't you mean five or six?"

"Okay, five or six years out of your life for college, and what do you have to show for it? Nothing. Nothing but a lot of wasted time."

Tollhausler looked at Mennon. "Isn't he supposed to be the quiet one?"

"Well today he's the deep one."

Mead lowered his cards to the table. "So you think you might make better use of your time by spending it in airplanes."

115

"At least it'd be doing something. Instead of sitting around here waiting for my teachers to say something important."

Mennon picked up a King of Spades. "Then why not quit school and get a job?"

"That wouldn't solve anything." Ernie balanced a card on his index finger. "I'd still have the same problem, only somewhere else. Having a job doesn't make your life any more meaningful."

"Well what *do* you want to do then?"

With a flick of his hand, Turpin made the card disappear. "I don't know Tollhausler. Something important."

"Like what?"

"I'm not sure. I just think it should be important." He pulled the missing card from behind his ear. "And I want to help people."

Tollhausler rolled his eyes. "Well now we're getting somewhere."

Mead held up his cards. "Listen, before you do anything, why not take a couple days off and think about it? Grab Susan and go lay in a meadow somewhere. And after that, if you still want to go skydiving, go ahead. But pay me back that five dollars you owe me first." He frowned at his cards. "What are we playing again?"

Mennon clicked his tongue. "Gin. What do you think we're playing? You got seven cards, the deck and a face card in the middle of the table. What does it *look* like we're playing? Blackjack?"

"We could have been playing rummy. I was checking, all right crabby-pants?"

116

"We're trying to decide what Turpin should do with the rest of his life, and you want to know what we're playing?"

"Sor-reeeeeeee. I thought that once he finished his whining he'd get off his butt and figure it out for himself."

"Now now boys," Tollhausler interrupted, "Pisper shame on you. Acting like a couple of children. There'll be no fighting at this table until I start losing."

Mead grabbed a card from the pile, thought for a second, and then returned it.

Turpine moodily did the same.

Mennon didn't. He was too busy leering at a passing woman. "Say, look at the beautiful shape her mind is in."

Turpin, Tollhausler and Mead watched as she leisurely made her way over to a crowded table at the back of the cafeteria. It was populated by a band of overly muscular men, who didn't seem to have any necks.

Tollhausler adjusted his glasses. "Why don't we know any women like that?"

"I do," Mennon bragged.

Mead laughed. "He knows plenty of women without necks."

It was while this silly volley of words was bouncing from one side of the table to the other that a smile slowly bloomed across Ernie's drooping face.

The young woman's languid passage had stirred his thoughts in the opposite direction from where they were originally headed, setting off a lightning-fast round of free association. Ultimately, Ernie concluded that he wasn't as doomed as he had first suspected. Yes, he was going to die, but, God willing, not for a good long time. For now, he was alive, very alive, and jumping out of a plane wasn't the only way to make a person feel that way. He slammed a card down on to the table with a flourish.

Mennon noticed. "Hey Ernie, I told Tollhausler about them speakers and he's gonna' give us a hun-nert bucks."

This made Turpin even happier, and he stood up and shook Tollhausler's hand.

"It was nothing," Tollhausler told Mead. "And at fifty percent interest, I think it's quite a deal."

Turpin shoved him off the chair.

Mennon and Mead jumped up.

"You all right Toll?" Mennon asked.

"I want my money back."

Mennon examined Tollhausler's cards. "Sorry, no refunds."

16

"Hey look, it's Donna," Ernie enthusiastically announced, and returned a wave to a girl in the distance.

Tollhausler stood up. "Who?"

Mennon set down Tollhausler's cards. "I don't know, but he sure is glad to see her."

Ernie started towards her. "You know, Donna with the parrot—"

"Oh yeah." Tollhausler snatched his cards off the table, and glared at Mennon. "Nothing you can use?"

Johnny shook his head. "Nah."

Tollhausler fell back into his seat. "I remember her. Donna from freshman year. The one with no mind."

Mead frowned. "Tollhausler, they don't all have to have minds."

"Don't you need something to talk about in the dark afterwards?"

Mennon discarded a Queen of Hearts. "Not if they have a TV."

"Oh, well, I never thought of that." Tollhausler retrieved it. "*Pig.*"

"So I'm not particularly choosy. Like some people I could mention."

Tollhausler laid down a card. "I am not choosy. Wanting to be with someone who I can talk to does not make me choosy."

"Yeah…" Mead picked up a card. "….but you don't always have to discuss Kafka afterwards either."

"Point taken, but I would still want to talk to the girl, right? Still have to like her, right?"

"You like a lot of girls we know around here."

"And they would appear to like me, Rich, but they don't seem interested in going out with me."

"One *can* only carry friendship so far."

Mennon nodded. "I once carried it as far as Atlanta."

"Who carried it back," Mead asked.

"Nobody." Mennon picked up a card. "It was all gone by then."

"One woman," Tollhausler mused. "That's all I need."

Mead leaned back. "You'll get yourself a girl Toll."

119

"Mead's right," Mennon agreed. "You might have to inflate her and supply your own batteries, but you'll find one." He revealed his cards. "Gin."

Tollhausler threw down his cards. "He's cheating."

Mead sat forward. "How do you know?"

"Because I'm cheating and he's still winning."

"Ohhhhhh."

Tollhausler gathered the cards together in a stack, shuffled them and handed them to Mennon to cut. Tollhausler then tossed a card to Mead with his right, then shot one to Ernie, and, lastly, set one down in front of Mennon. "Let's see how you do with me dealing."

Mennon glanced at his card. "I'll do fine. I kept some of the cards from the last hand."

"Oh."

"Say Toll, have you ever considered moving out?"

"Of the cafeteria? Never."

"No, out of your house." Tollhausler looked at Mead, who was suddenly very fascinated with the cards in his hand. "No Johnny, as a matter of fact I haven't. However, my parents do occasionally bring the subject up. Actually, every time I come home. I keep telling them I have no where to go, but they refuse to believe me."

Mennon nodded. "I'm going to move out."

"What made you decide that?"

"My parents." He changed the order of the cards in his hand. "Last night they told me they wanted me out of the house."

"That'd do it." Tollhausler placed his cards flat on the table. "Johnny, why did your parents ask you to leave?"

"I had some friends over last night."

"What? Did you invite someone they didn't like?"

"No." Mennon scratched his ear. "There were some guys from the band, their girlfriends and some of their friends. Oh yeah, and some cops."

"Were the cops invited?"

"Sure. The neighbors asked them to stop by."

Preparing himself for what was coming next, Tollhausler closed one eye. "And then?"

"Not much." Mennon pulled his cap down. "A brief exchange of gunfire, but that wasn't really my fault."

Tollhausler closed his other eye. "No, no, I suppose it wasn't. And now you have to get out."

"My parents are pretty mad."

Tollhausler opened his eyes. "Well give them some time," he advised, "they'll change their minds."

"If I give them too much time they're going to change the locks."

Tollhausler glanced at Mead, who appeared to be memorizing his cards, and back at Mennon. "Johnny, do you think they'll throw you out for one stupid mistake? You said it yourself, it wasn't your fault." He lowered his voice. "It wasn't, right?"

"I swear."

"Do you really think they'll throw you out because of a small gun battle?"

"Well they haven't so far, but there's always a first time, you know."

Tollhausler sat back. "Personally, I'm not so sure about moving out."

"Afraid of being on your own?"

"No." He looked at Mennon. "I'm afraid of winding up in the same place with you."

"Don't worry." Mennon laughed. "You'll be in good company. Turpin and Mead'll be there too."

Tollhausler understood why Mead had been so quiet. "Gee, it sounds like it's going to be pretty crowded."

"Hey, with all of us," Mennon said optimistically, "we could probably afford to rent a house."

"Wait a minute, earlier I said I'd give you a hundred dollars for speakers, and now you've got me paying rent. Where am I getting all this money?"

Mennon smiled. "You could rob a bank."

Ernie returned, and he could tell by the atmosphere, and the expression on Tollhausler's face, what they were talking about.

"Or you could sell drugs," Mead suggested.

Ernie nodded with encouragement.

Mennon cleared his throat. "You could even get a job."

Tollhausler picked through his cards. "I said—"

"I heard you the first time!" Tollhausler jumped up. "I just can't decide which of the three is worse."

"Look," Mennon said firmly, "I know it sounds like a big sacrifice, but that's only because you've never done it before."

Tollhausler frowned. "That sounds like something they tell sacrificial virgins on their way up the side of the volcano."

"Tollhausler, don't you trust me?"

"What a silly question Johnny. Of course not."

Mennon was stunned. "Why not?"

"How about all the times you conned me in the past?"

"I did not con you. I simply offered you deals that benefited more than one party."

"And you were always one of them." Tollhausler put a leg up on his chair. "Which reminds me. Some teacher was waiting for me outside one of my classes this morning. He said that some guy in a gray cap had ripped him off, and as a parting gesture, gave him my name."

"What?" Mennon sprang to his feet. "That jerk! I only got seventy-five cents out of him too." He shook his head. "Imagine," he said to Ernie and Rich, "hunting someone down for a lousy six bits. Whew. But you never know with people. That's why I didn't give him my real name."

Tollhausler rolled his eyes. "Good thinking."

"Hey, if I'd have taken any more money than that, I wouldn't have given him your name. I would have given him Ernie's."

"And you wonder why people don't trust you."

Mennon threw up his hands. "If you're gonna' hold a grudge..."

"Hold a grudge?!" Tollhausler snorted. "When it comes to you, I'll embrace it lovingly."

"All right, all right," Mennon growled. "Then talk to Mead or Turpin about this then." He started pacing back and forth.

"Why? Ernie has three brothers and two sisters. He'd move into a subway tunnel if it meant a little more privacy."

"Okay. Then tell me Mead doesn't know what he's doing. That he's making a mistake."

"Mead doesn't know what he's doing. And he's making a mistake."

"Ugh! How can you say that?"

Tollhausler grinned. "It suddenly came to me." He looked at Mead. "So what do you think?"

"That it's time I moved out."

Tollhausler got the feeling the others had been talking about this for some time. "Where are we going to find a house at this time of the year?"

"My Uncle Stan said he would help us." Tollhausler grimaced.

"The same Uncle Stan who wanted to manage Mennon's band?"

Mead nodded.

"The same guy who Mennon said was a black hearted goblin who would sell his own mother if the money was right? We're going to trust him?!" He stared at Mennon. "What makes you think this guy would drop a sandbag on his own mother but not cheat his own nephew?"

No one had an answer for Tollhausler, and he suddenly felt rotten. They were apparently very excited about the idea. He poked at his cards on the table. "Besides, imagine living with Mennon."

Mennon cheered up. "That doesn't take much imagination."

"That's good," Tollhausler said with a sneer. "Rich doesn't have that much to begin with."

Mead smiled. "Look, I just think it's about time to get away from my parents. Time for a little responsibility. Time to grow up."

"Time to throw up." Tollhausler removed his glasses and rubbed his eyes. "We'll be living with Mennon, various members of his band, and from time to time, the police and the FBI will be stopping by to make sure we're all okay. Jail will be our home away from home. And once they place us in the Federal Witness Relocation Program, we won't have to worry about paying rent."

Mead smiled. "Johnny wouldn't let anything like that happen."

Tollhausler stared at Mennon. "Would he?"

"Heyyy, we haven't even moved out yet. I see no reason to make any promises at this time."

Tollhausler nodded. "I knew you were going to say something like that."

"See," Mennon chuckled, "already you can depend on me."

SEPTEMBER 7 OCTOBER17 NOVEMBER 2 NOVEMBER 30 DECEMBER 30
SEPTEMBER 7 OCTOBER17 NOVEMBER 2 NOVEMBER 30 DECEMBER 30
SEPTEMBER 7 OCTOBER17 NOVEMBER 2 NOVEMBER 30 DECEMBER 30
SEPTEMBER 7 OCTOBER17 NOVEMBER 2 NOVEMBER 30 DECEMBER 30
SEPTEMBER 7 OCTOBER17 NOVEMBER 2 NOVEMBER 30 DECEMBER 30
SEPTEMBER 7 OCTOBER17 NOVEMBER 2 NOVEMBER 30 DECEMBER 30
SEPTEMBER 7 OCTOBER17 NOVEMBER 2 NOVEMBER 30 DECEMBER 30
SEPTEMBER 7 OCTOBER17 NOVEMBER 2 NOVEMBER 30 DECEMBER 30
SEPTEMBER 7 OCTOBER17 NOVEMBER 2 NOVEMBER 30 DECEMBER 30
SEPTEMBER 7 OCTOBER17 NOVEMBER 2 NOVEMBER 30 DECEMBER 30
SEPTEMBER 7 OCTOBER17 NOVEMBER 2 NOVEMBER 30 DECEMBER 30
SEPTEMBER 7 OCTOBER17 NOVEMBER 2 NOVEMBER 30 DECEMBER 30
SEPTEMBER 7 OCTOBER17 NOVEMBER 2 NOVEMBER 30 DECEMBER 30
SEPTEMBER 7 OCTOBER17 NOVEMBER 2 NOVEMBER 30 DECEMBER 30
SEPTEMBER 7 OCTOBER17 NOVEMBER 2 NOVEMBER 30 DECEMBER 30
SEPTEMBER 7 OCTOBER17 NOVEMBER 2 NOVEMBER 30 DECEMBER 30
SEPTEMBER 7 OCTOBER17 NOVEMBER 2 NOVEMBER 30 DECEMBER 30
SEPTEMBER 7 OCTOBER17 NOVEMBER 2 NOVEMBER 30 DECEMBER 30
SEPTEMBER 7 OCTOBER17 NOVEMBER 2 NOVEMBER 30 DECEMBER 30
SEPTEMBER 7 OCTOBER17 NOVEMBER 2 NOVEMBER 30 DECEMBER 30
SEPTEMBER 7 OCTOBER17 NOVEMBER 2 NOVEMBER 30 DECEMBER 30
SEPTEMBER 7 OCTOBER17 NOVEMBER 2 NOVEMBER 30 DECEMBER 30
SEPTEMBER 7 OCTOBER17 NOVEMBER 2 NOVEMBER 30 DECEMBER 30
SEPTEMBER 7 OCTOBER17 NOVEMBER 2 NOVEMBER 30 DECEMBER 30
SEPTEMBER 7 OCTOBER17 NOVEMBER 2 NOVEMBER 30 DECEMBER 30

OCTOBER 17, 1983:
"….UP TO YOUR OLD TRICKS AGAIN."

SEPTEMBER 7 OCTOBER17 NOVEMBER 2 NOVEMBER 30 DECEMBER 30
SEPTEMBER 7 OCTOBER17 NOVEMBER 2 NOVEMBER 30 DECEMBER 30
SEPTEMBER 7 OCTOBER17 NOVEMBER 2 NOVEMBER 30 DECEMBER 30
SEPTEMBER 7 OCTOBER17 NOVEMBER 2 NOVEMBER 30 DECEMBER 30
SEPTEMBER 7 OCTOBER17 NOVEMBER 2 NOVEMBER 30 DECEMBER 30
SEPTEMBER 7 OCTOBER17 NOVEMBER 2 NOVEMBER 30 DECEMBER 30
SEPTEMBER 7 OCTOBER17 NOVEMBER 2 NOVEMBER 30 DECEMBER 30
SEPTEMBER 7 OCTOBER17 NOVEMBER 2 NOVEMBER 30 DECEMBER 30
SEPTEMBER 7 OCTOBER17 NOVEMBER 2 NOVEMBER 30 DECEMBER 30
SEPTEMBER 7 OCTOBER17 NOVEMBER 2 NOVEMBER 30 DECEMBER 30
SEPTEMBER 7 OCTOBER17 NOVEMBER 2 NOVEMBER 30 DECEMBER 30
SEPTEMBER 7 OCTOBER17 NOVEMBER 2 NOVEMBER 30 DECEMBER 30
SEPTEMBER 7 OCTOBER17 NOVEMBER 2 NOVEMBER 30 DECEMBER 30
SEPTEMBER 7 OCTOBER17 NOVEMBER 2 NOVEMBER 30 DECEMBER 30
SEPTEMBER 7 OCTOBER17 NOVEMBER 2 NOVEMBER 30 DECEMBER 30
SEPTEMBER 7 OCTOBER17 NOVEMBER 2 NOVEMBER 30 DECEMBER 30
SEPTEMBER 7 OCTOBER17 NOVEMBER 2 NOVEMBER 30 DECEMBER 30
SEPTEMBER 7 OCTOBER17 NOVEMBER 2 NOVEMBER 30 DECEMBER 30
SEPTEMBER 7 OCTOBER17 NOVEMBER 2 NOVEMBER 30 DECEMBER 30
SEPTEMBER 7 OCTOBER17 NOVEMBER 2 NOVEMBER 30 DECEMBER 30
SEPTEMBER 7 OCTOBER17 NOVEMBER 2 NOVEMBER 30 DECEMBER 30

1

It was a bleak, gray morning, and flocks of tattered litter and brittle leaves were being driven across campus by an unrelenting wind. The swooping air was swarming with September's debris, and people traveling the streets had to periodically stop and duck in order to avoid a face full of leaves.

One such gust touched down outside Lemmon Hall, swooshing mercilessly along the crowded sidewalk, and, sending every loose bit of trash and detritus into the air, smacked into a nearby building.

Nathan Buckles happened to be standing on the opposite side of the window where this collision had taken place, and was drawn to the formless collection of swirling trash to his left. He was speaking rather lackadaisically about inflation, and he watched as the dried leaves and crumpled paper danced round and round. They fell away from the double glass as quickly as they had appeared, and Buckles slowly turned his attention back to the topic at hand: cost—push inflation. He estimated that since he had begun teaching at Rudyard, he had spoken, give or take a class, about it at least six hundred times. He hoped it had not been in vain.

A teacher could never be sure, he knew, and he looked out at the class. The young men and women appeared to be following along with what he was saying, but their unaffected expressions told him they were only half-listening. Whatever he had to say about cost-push inflation was fine, it would seem, with them. They obviously couldn't have cared less.

Cost-push inflation, the reader may be interested to know was not particularly high on Professor Buckles' list of interesting subjects either, but he still had to cover it. He just wished his students could show a touch more interest. After all, they had only to listen to it once this semester. He, however, had already talked about it *six hundred* times, and Lord knew how many more times he would before he retired. He peered at the gold watch he was wearing. It wasn't even nine o'clock yet.

"And this is where the Federal Reserve comes in." He took a deep breath. "During a recession, you all know the Federal Reserve increases the money supply, thereby stimulating growth.

"But at the moment, our dear President believes the country isn't experiencing one. Believe it or not, he says, as they will do, everything's fine, thanks to his groundbreaking economic policies. So if the Federal Reserve increases the money supply during a recession, what do you think it would do during an excellent economic age like the one we're experiencing right now?" "It would decrease the supply." "Exactly, in order to curtail inflation the Fed decreases the nation's money supply in prosperous times."

A portion of the class jotted this down, while at the back of the room, people were busy asking the person directly in front to please repeat Buckles' last statement.

Richard Mead hadn't bothered.

He wasn't particularly interested in playing Economics 251 Whisper down the Lane, and hadn't been for some time now. Having already taken the course once, he had decided to confine himself mainly to reading the course's textbook. Something he hadn't done the first time around. He believed it was more practical. For one thing, he didn't have to strain too much in order to understand what it had to say, and while the text was almost as dry as Buckles' lectures, it possessed certain qualities the mumbling man in the gray suit did not: Mead could slam it shut at any given moment, throw it as far away as he wished or even shove it out a window if he so desired. He couldn't do any of those things with his teacher. Lemmon Hall was a climate-controlled building and the windows didn't open.

He started drawing a three-dimensional block in the margin of his notebook, and glanced across the aisle at Holly. She was hard at work, valiantly struggling to decipher Buckles' indistinguishable murmurs, and Mead slowly edged his desk along the smudged floor.

He placed a hand to his mouth. "Listen, if you can't go out tonight, how about Friday?"

She shook her head. "I have to work on a paper. It's due next week."

"Well, could I at least drive you home after class? I want to talk."

"No you don't," Holly whispered. "Every time I get in your car, all you want to do is make out. It's all you ever want to do."

He found the observation amusing, but tried not to let it show. "That is *not* the only thing I ever want to do."

Holly smirked. "I don't know..." She turned her attention back to Buckles. "What'd he say?" She laid her pen down. "Besides, don't you have to look at a house after school?"

He clicked his tongue. "Oh yeah. Damn. You want to come with?"

130

"No."

"You used to love traveling around with me and the guys."

"I still do. Don't I come to the cafeteria all the time?"

"Not lately." Baffled, Mead sat back. He looked down at his notebook, and noticed the word Saturday written in the left hand margin followed by three question marks. "Say, you were writing a term paper last weekend too."

"Richard, I'm in college. That's what college students do."

"But we haven't gone out in weeks," he pointed out, glancing towards the front of the room, "I would like to see you outside this classroom, you know."

She wrote something down. "Soon."

Suddenly, all the pieces fell together with a loud click, and Rich understood. "You're seeing someone else."

Holly stared at Buckles as if she hadn't heard what Richard had just said. However, she realized she couldn't sit there like that forever. Turning to him, she attempted a smile, but instead of being reassuring, all it did was confirm his suspicions. Rich groaned, and Holly patted him on the shoulder. "I think you'd like him. He's very nice."

Mead rolled his eyes. "What a relief."

"Do you want me to lie about it?"

He slumped down in his desk. "No. Yes. Maybe." Rich painfully nudged his desk back to where he had started.

He was never very comfortable receiving news of this sort, even though he had distributed his fair share on many an awkward occasion. He believed at a time like this, the only thing a

131

person could do, the only mature thing, was to stare at the floor and sulk. What did she see in that other guy anyway?

He suddenly felt very hurt, and glared at her. He didn't think she should be seeing other guys while she was also seeing him--and with her course load yet. Then he got angry with himself for feeling that way. In the beginning, they had both agreed there would be no attachments.

Rich only wished he didn't like her so much. She was invading his thoughts more and more frequently, and sometimes when he was with other women. Here I am, he ruminated with a frown, Trapped in another dull semester, and believe it or not— yeah right—in another doomed relationship. He blamed himself for the situation, and wished he could start all over again.

"Damn," he grumbled, and rubbed the back of his neck. He hoped this was not an indication of how the day was going to proceed.

"Mr. Mead, could you please tell us what the income elasticity of demand is, and provide us with the necessary formula for its determination?"

Surprised, Mead looked up. He would have never guessed that Buckles could project his voice like that, and sat forward. Then he cursed.

Buckles was standing at the front of the room with his hands thrust deep into his gray pockets. "I'm sorry Mr. Mead, I didn't quite catch that."

"Ohh, I haven't said anything yet. I was clearing my throat."

Some people began paging through their textbooks in search of the formula, just in case Mead confessed his ignorance and Buckles was forced to cast about somewhere else for the answer, while others, well-versed in the principles of classroom dynamics, were busy looking through their notes, up at the ceiling and out the window, anywhere that is, except at their teacher. They knew returning a teacher's gaze in situations like this was as dangerous as a deer staring into the headlights of an oncoming vehicle: it was fatal. No matter how fast the teacher was moving.

The corners of Buckles' mouth rose slightly. "Mr. Mead, the income elasticity of demand, please."

"The income elasticity of demand," Richard said doubtfully, as if maybe he suspected Buckles was making it up, "yes." He sat up straight. "Isn't that…isn't that the percentage change in the quantity of the good purchased, say widgets for example, due to a one percent change in the income?"

The teacher's eyes widened. "Why yes, Mr. Mead." He crossed his arms. "And the formula?"

"The percentage change in quantity bought divided by the change in income." He snapped his fingers. "The percentage change in income, I mean."

"Very good." Buckles was impressed, along with the rest of the class, and took a step backwards. "Now, with our ability to quantify this shift in sales…" His voice became muffled as he headed for the blackboard.

The woman to Rich's left tilted her head and smiled. "How did you know the answer to that?"

Rich knew repeating the same economics course would have to pay off somehow. "How did I…?" He made a face. "I thought *everybody* knew the answer to that one."

She smiled. "Right."

Holly was struggling to follow Buckles' discourse, bringing everything he had spoken about thus far together, but found herself distracted by Rich. She couldn't believe he was flirting with another woman right in front of her. He was obviously trying to make her jealous.

Worst of all, it was working.

Buckles stopped talking for an instant, and during the pause, Holly could overhear Richard saying the words "Friday night."

Incensed, she slammed her book shut and stood up.

"I didn't hear a bell, did you?" Rich looked over. "Or is there a fire drill scheduled for today?"

"Look Dick," Holly hissed, "why don't you mind your own business and go back to talking to your new friend?"

"You'd like her. She's very nice."

The heavy Economics book sailed past Mead's head, and crash-landed on the desk behind.

Professor Buckles approached. "Here here, what goes on?"

Mead handed Holly her book. "Sir, this woman is deranged."

"What," Buckles and Holly asked simultaneously.

"Seriously deranged. I'm glad she doesn't own a hunting rifle. Poor kid's carrying a torch for me, but my studies are far more important to me than any meaningless tryst."

"*Carry a torch?*" Holly laughed. "If anybody's crazy around here, it's you."

"I would say the jury's still out on both of you." Buckles' eyes moved between Holly and Rich. "I would also appreciate it if you could act with a little more decorum in my classroom and keep your little lover's quarrel outside."

"Lover's quarrel?!" Holly hugged her book to her chest. "Love's got nothing to do with this. He's just a sore loser."

"I'm not the one who threw the book."

"No, you're the one who threw that redhead in my face."

"In your-? I was only *talking* to her."

Buckles grimaced, and Mead held up a hand." About a very complex Economics problem."

Holly held the book tighter. "It was the way you were doing it."

"I told you she wasn't well," Mead said to Buckles. "She's obsessed with me. No doubt tormented by my good looks and ready wit."

"No doubt." Buckles took a step back. "I would like you both to leave class early today, and use the time to work things out. Whatever happens between you is no concern of mine, but I never want the class to have to witness another confrontation like this again. If it should, you will both be thrown out. Understood?"

"Yes sir," Holly said tightly.

"Sorry." Mead got up. "It's this power I have over women. I'm just trying to be nice, but they always want more."

"Yes Mr. Mead. Now let's make our way out of the classroom, and I hope you'll be able to work out whatever differences you two might have."

Richard and Holly gathered up their things, sneaking peeks at one another, and the door hadn't closed behind them before people started talking about what had happened.

Buckles cleared his throat and sat on the edge of his desk. "So we see that the ways of the heart, like the Economy, are a series of checks and balances. One member withdraws something, and the other's interest flags. Suddenly, a young man and woman have to replace what has been lost or reinvest in someone else. The only problem being that this recovery sometimes takes months, or even years, and some people find the waiting excruciating. They want a quick fix. However, in love, as in the Economy, there are no quick fixes."

The class seemed a little confused, and a hand tentatively appeared in the air.

"Yes Mr. Lawrence?"

"Mr. Buckles, we aren't going to be tested on this, are we?"

Buckles smiled. "One day Mr. Lawrence. One day."

2

Diagrams had been scrawled across every last inch of the three chalkboards, so when the gentleman in the expensive sweater turned to add yet another one, he had to reach for an eraser. He pushed it across the green board with one long stroke, and pulled it back in the opposite direction.

"….and as Ruben says, under these circumstances, we select certain data over other information." He traced a lopsided rectangle on the chalk-smeared board in the middle, and wrote an S in it. "Even something as simple as deciding which stranger to ask for directions on a street corner requires a very elaborate sequence of information processing on our part. A complicated process which takes the brain only seconds to perform." He drew a sphere and placed an R in it. "The speed at which this is accomplished makes it very easy for us to dismiss this as anything more than making a quick inquiry. However, this is not the case." He connected the figures with a line, and stepped away from the board.

"For instance, say you see someone on campus, and you pause to speak with them." He smartly clapped the chalk dust from his hands. "You have already done quite a lot. First, you had to identify a single face from an unending stream of other faces, had to match that face up with the information stored in your memory so you could assign a history to that face. And you had to stop."

"Next, you then had to recall the necessary data for the impending interchange. Once this has all been done, depending on your relationship with that person, you will unconsciously record the other information in the environment: the weather, who the person's with, which direction they're headed, how they're dressed, how many other people are on the street etc. It's the selective nature of information processing. This can be broken down into several steps…"

Diane Curzewski was seated in the fourth row of the large auditorium, and she grimaced as the teacher, Professor Georges Melange, returned to the board to sketch out yet another diagram.

Diane absolutely *hated* Georges Melange.

She was not captivated by his cool, calculating eyes the way some of her classmates were nor did she find his fish-like mouth sensuous. Most of all, she detested the way he taught.

He had been breezing through the course's four textbooks (Two hardback and two paperback) since the first week of classes, and she found his habit of leapfrogging from one book to the next in his lectures maddening. No matter how much she read or ignored her other classes, she was never able to keep up.

Her classmates frequently voiced similar complaints, and she couldn't help thinking that Melange was doing it on purpose. It was as if he didn't understand the course's many theories and communications models any more than they did, but knew that if he glossed over them fast enough, nobody would notice.

"….because the meaning of the verbal message is not stamped on the face of the words themselves. As Mortenson points out, receivers have a way of attaching meaning to verbal cues that invariably reflect the unique dynamics of their own intuitive logic. Meanings result as much from psychological orientation as from any conventional interpretation. In other words, even the simplest of statements can be the most complex."

Crossing her arms, Diane tilted her head to the side, and read the watch on her left wrist. She immediately thought of her boyfriend, Gus. It wasn't difficult. Gus had been on her mind since the night before. His ROTC class was climbing down Roberts Hall in twenty minutes, and he had told her the previous afternoon how much he wanted her to be there. Having already seen the drill once, she had diplomatically explained how she might not be able to attend, especially since she couldn't afford to fall behind in Melange's class.

Gus' response, as expected, was to sulk. However, before locking himself away behind a shaded mask of dejection, he had paused long enough to remind Diane of her priorities. He knew he wasn't at the top of the list, her parents obviously had a lock on that envious position, but he figured he must have at least placed somewhere in the top five. With that said, he didn't think he needed to say anything more. Diane, however, did.

They had been going out now for almost a year, and like most relationships, he wasn't half as nice as he used to be and she wasn't half as oblivious of his shortcomings. She didn't mind, really, she knew how things never stayed the same between people, except Gus had started telling her what to do and how to think. Apparently, he had grown tired of waiting for her to come round to his way of thinking, and wanted her to be someone else.

Diane didn't obsess too much about who she needed to be in order to please Gus simply because she didn't get the impression that he had spent a single moment worrying about who he needed to be for her. Whenever she discussed her rocky relationship with her girlfriend, she theorized it was simply a phase (Not the first, as a matter of fact) they were going through, and assumed it would pass. In the meantime, she tried to appease Gus when she could.

Which was why she was sitting in this Psychology of Communications class. Gus had had her change her schedule around several times because he felt it was important that they eat lunch together every day. Gus thought that was an important part of a relationship. Diane believed that there was more to love than sharing a meal, especially when one of the people involved devoted a good deal of that sacred mealtime to talking with his ROTC buddies about the Army.

Dr. Melange was now drawing stick figures on the board. "....distinct types of information are conveyed by the head and body, and what we're going to do is create a situation of stress or tension, thereby increasing the probability of stimulating an affect display. The more frequent the interruptions, personal attacks and unkind criticism, the more likely it is that our subjects will react unequivocally in an emotional manner.

"So for the next hour or so, I'm going to bring in two or three subjects, and ask them a series of seemingly dull questions about themselves. Then I'll take issue with some of them. Since I've told them we're conducting a simple experiment, this line of questioning will take them off guard. It should confuse them, and they'll experience a certain amount of discomfort. If not anger.

"Either way, we shall be able to elicit a response, and hopefully have a proof of Ekman's Theory: That body movement and facial expression can be reliably matched with verbal statements, and that distinct types of information can be gleaned from the head and body."

Melange started down a set of steps. "I would also remind everyone to watch each subject carefully. Write down your observations. In particular, as the experiment proceeds, note shifting body movement and verbal responses. And for our next class, summarize each interview and include your own observations. Parenthetically, this experiment will be a lot easier to run than the one we did last week--with the hand buzzer--thanks to my authoritarian role here." Melange walked over to a green door, opened it and leaned into a small room.

Diane checked her watch. Gus' drill was going to start very soon, but she obviously couldn't miss what was about to happen next.

Somebody bounced past Melange and took the stage. Diane sat forward, and didn't notice she had dropped her pen.

"Josh, that's Phil Tendon," somebody said behind her.

"Get out of here," Josh replied. "What would he be doing here?"

"I don't know, but that's him."

Diane frowned. She felt sure it was J.R.R. Tollhausler.

Melange moved two chairs to the front of the platform. "Class, this is Subject 1017A."

Subject 1017A waved. "Greetings racing fans." He adjusted his glasses. "By the way, would you mind calling me Subject X-2641-Q?"

Melange picked a clipboard up from his desk. "And why is that?"

"It makes it sound more like I'm participating in an experiment in a science fiction story."

Dr. Melange was confused. "Why would—"

"An experiment that will go terribly wrong. Transforming me into a *flesh-eating mutant!*"

"All right." Melange could use 1017A's interest in science fiction a little later in the experiment. "Class, please note that Subject 1017A would like to be called, uh, X-2641..." He looked at the subject.

"Q."

"Ah, yes, Subject X-2641-Q." Melange wrote that down, and slid the one chair away from the other. "Please take a seat."

X-2641-Q slowly circled the chairs. One was red, the other blue, and after careful examination, he sat on the blue one.

Melange sat next to him.

141

"Is that it?"

Melange frowned. "We haven't even started yet."

"Ohhh." X-2641-Q sat back. "You mean the chair thing wasn't the experiment?"

"Not at all."

"I just thought I'd ask." Subject X-2641-Q looked out at the gallery, and back at Melange. "Why do you think I picked the blue chair over the red one?"

Melange was arranging his papers on the clipboard. "I'm sure I don't know."

X-2641-Q folded his arms. "Well I'm sure you don't know either, but I thought I'd give you a shot anyway."

As this volley concluded, Diane felt sure that she knew the real identity of Subject X-2641-Q, and smiled. It *was* J.R.R. Tollhausler. She hadn't seen him since that first day of classes, but had often wondered what had happened to him. Which always surprised her. She couldn't understand why, out of all the guys she had met that semester, someone like him would still be on her mind.

X-2641-Q leaned back. "By the way, Doc, are you a strict Freudian or a Neo-Jungian?"

Melange clicked his pen. "Neo-Jungian."

"I thought so," the subject bragged. "You look Jung for your age."

Melange froze for an instant, and X-2641-Q smirked. "You know, I used to know a girl who read practically everything Carl Jung wrote."

The teacher studied his watch. "Really?"

"She had an irrational fear of sea serpents." He grinned. "She suffered from hydra phobia."

Diane groaned.

Melange wrote down the time. "Please, we've wasted enough time as it is."

"I've suspected that myself for some time now." He patted Melange on the knee. "Must be pretty rough for someone *your age* to finally realize something like that though."

Melange stared back. "Please, may we begin?"

"All right." X-2641-Q sat up straight and folded his hands in his lap. "Let's start with American History."

Melange tapped his pen on his clipboard. "You're not here to answer questions about American History."

"Well I hope you aren't going to ask me about geography. When it comes to Eastern Europe, I'm lost."

"Please, you'll be able to answer these questions." Melange held his pen in readiness. "Now, question one. What kind of music do you like?"

"I guess you would say I like rock." X-2641-Q turned his body so he could rest an elbow on the back of the chair. "Although I did play bassoon in high school."

Writing, Melange nodded. "And why did you give it up?"

"Oh, I didn't give it up. They wrestled it away from me."

"I see." Melange made a note.

"Question two. Who is your favorite singer or musical group?"

"The Beatles."

Diane loved the Beatles.

"Good." Melange enthusiastically recorded this answer. He was confident that, after one or two more, he would be able to launch his attack. "Question three. What is your favorite sports team?"

"I don't have one. There are no professional volleyball teams."

Melange scratched behind an ear. "You mean you don't have a favorite hometown team? Football or baseball...?"

"I don't like any of them." X-2641-Q reached into his pocket. "They're all overpaid babies." He unwrapped a stick of gum. "You shouldn't like them either. They get paid a lot more money then you do, and only have to play seven months out of the year."

"Yes," Melange began, "but—"

"Oh sure," Subject X-2641-Q popped the gum in his mouth, "you don't work all year round either, but you have a much more demanding job." He crushed the gum wrapper. "Still, you don't do half as much as a garbage man. Of course, they take home a lot more money than you do as well. Everybody gets paid more than you. Where did you go wrong?"

"Subject X--" Melange said flatly.

"Picked the wrong major when you were in college I bet."

"I—"

"It's all right. All you teachers did. Isn't that why you were gonna' go on strike a couple of weeks ago?"

"I'd rather not go into that right now, subject X-26...er, I'd rather not go into that."

"Sure you don't, but what about me? I had plans you know. Big plans. If you teachers went on strike, I was going to sleep all day and stay out all night. It was going to be great." X-2641-Q shook his head. "But you never did. I went ahead and stayed out late anyway, but I've missed a lot of classes thanks to you guys."

"Subject X-2641-Q."

The subject scowled. "I hope you're happy."

"I don't see—"

"If you people say you're going to strike, then don't you think you should go out on strike? What do you teachers want to do anyway, *teach* all your lives?!"

Melange sniffed. "I would like to remind you that there is a class in session right now."

"Oh I'm so sorry." He seemed genuinely surprised and looked around. "Where?"

Professor Melange laid the clipboard flat on his leg. "Look, if you don't think this is important…"

"Sorry Doc," interrupted X-2641-Q, "but there are people starving in the world, and you're in here asking me about football teams. How do you sleep?"

Melange stood up. "If you aren't going to take this experiment seriously—"

The subject also got to his feet. "I am taking this experiment seriously. It's you I'm having trouble with." He grabbed Melange's notes. "But I don't entirely blame you." He flipped up the first page. "I think I might have something to do with it as well." He handed back the clipboard.

"Yes, well—"

"What?!" X-2641-Q was outraged. "Aren't you going to admit you're partially to blame as well?!" He jumped up on the chair. "You know it takes *two* people to make a bad marriage. Three to make a good one. And four to paint a house." He scanned the auditorium. "By the way, why do so many gorgeous women take psychology courses? Are you all crazy?" He stepped down off the chair. "Or did I just answer my own question?"

Melange was still at a loss for words. "Subject X-2641-Q."

"Sure, you talk now."

"I—"

"But who would listen?"

"I would appreciate it if—"

"I'd only *depreciate* it." He hopped back up on the chair. "And now I'd like to share a dream with the class."

"What?"

"A couple of weeks ago, I had a dream, and in it, for some reason, I was wearing a red bra."

Melange grimaced. "Then what happened?"

"Nothing, I woke up."

"I see."

"So what did it mean?"

"Subject X-26, er…"

"41-Q."

"Yes. That description doesn't really give us much to go on."

X-2641-Q got down off the chair. "Wasn't wearing the bra enough?"

"Well there's a lot more to analyzing a dream than being told the dream's contents."

"Yes, I know." X-2641-Q started pacing back and forth. "I had a lot of questions myself. Like where did I get the bra, why was I wearing it and how much did it cost? Being a healthy red-blooded American male—or a facsimile thereof—I was devastated by the implications of the whole thing. Oh the shame of waking up after a dream like that. Was this my subconscious' way of telling me I should trade in my girlie magazines for men's fashion magazines? Or was I turning into a cross-dressing communist?" He stopped pacing. "Oh, the countless hours I spent worrying." He looked out at the class. "I know they were countless because I tried counting them and lost count." He slumped back into the blue chair. "The whole thing made me very insecure. And since it had been practically twelve hours since I had last felt that way, I was in quite a pickle. In fact, that was another dream I had." He stood up on the chair again. "I dreamt I was a pickle…"

Melange winced. "Subject X…"

"….bobbing back and forth in a sea of brine. Gherkins as far as the eye could see—"

"….2641-Q, please, what did you do about the dream with the bra? Did you talk to anybody about it?"

"I tried to console myself with that old line of Sigmund Freud's, 'Sometimes a cigar's just a cigar,' but that didn't really help much. After all, a red bra's always a red bra. So I fell to my knees and prayed for guidance. Two hours later, my legs were asleep and apparently so was God. So I figured the next best thing was to consult a priest. God always works in mysterious ways, and why any man would want to be a priest is certainly a mystery to me."

"And what did he say?"

"Well…" He dropped to the floor. "….first he wanted to know when I had been to church last, and I told him."

"Then what did he say?"

"That I should be ashamed of myself. Then he told me to leave."

Melange closed his eyes. "Subject X…."

"And they wonder why I cancelled my subscription to their religion."

"….we haven't accomplished a thing."

He hopped back up on the chair. "Nobody cares about that. What does the dream mean?"

"That would depend." Melange sat down. "Have you ever thought about wearing women's clothing before?"

"Noooooo." X-2641-Q's eyes narrowed. "Have you?"

"What I mean, is," Melange said, "have you ever wondered how you would look in women's clothing?"

"Why?! You think I'd look better?"

"No, not at all—"

"You think I'd look worse?!"

Melange pushed himself out of the chair. "Subject X, you don't want to know what the dream means at all. All you're interested in is standing around and making jokes. I don't know which is worse."

"The feedback I've gotten so far leads me to believe that the part about standing around and making jokes is the problem."

Melange stomped his foot. "That's all very well, but we have to move on. You've already cost us too much time."

"Well all right then," X-2641-Q said, "why don't you ask me another stupid question?"

"I think I would like another subject."

"Well you don't seem to be doing so hot with Psychology."

"Thank you Subject X-2641-Q." He placed a hand in his pocket. "For your time." He handed the subject some money.

"Five dollars," X-2641-Q noted. "I was told I would get ten."

"That was before you ruined the experiment."

He put his hands on his hips. "The teacher across the hall gives me ten dollars whenever I trash *his* experiments."

"That will be all."

"Welllllllll," Subject X-2641-Q growled. "All right." He walked down the steps and turned. "And I hope you realize I'm leaving because I want to, not because you asked. Although that *did* have something to do with it." He went to the door and paused. "Call us when you get there, but don't be surprised if the phone is off the hook." He snapped his fingers, and left.

Diane started shoving her books into a bulky green bag, and awkwardly slid out of her desk.

The woman seated next to her smiled. "Going to see your boyfriend's drill?"

"Yes," Diane lied. She had no intention of sitting through Gus' maneuver a second time. What she really wanted to do was catch up to Subject X-2641-Q.

3

Like most annoying sounds, the high-pitched whistling seemed to be everywhere in the narrow fire tower, and the culprit, John D. Mennon, blew even louder once he noticed it was reverberating around the landings above. Johnny paused to listen, and nudged the medium-sized amplifier he was carrying higher with his knee. He had been trudging around campus with it for the last forty minutes, and the wide box was a lot heavier than it looked.

At least, that was the conclusion Johnny came to seconds later after it had skidded down his leg on to his foot. He painfully slid his shoe out from under the wheeled cabinet, and limped over to the railing. He steadied himself against it and flexed the toes of his aching foot. "*Maaaaaaaan.*"

Directing his gaze away from the speaker, he carefully massaged the front of his running shoe, and placed his foot down. An almost straight line of mud ran along the bottom of his pant leg across his sneaker, and he angrily brushed it away with the back of his hand. "I had to roll it across that field." He rubbed the top of his shoe with a thumb. "Only patch of mud for miles, and I had to find it."

The impulse to kick the amplifier down the stairs passed as soon as the throbbing in his foot had subsided, and he returned to the amp. "What a day."

He dreaded having to haul it up to the next landing by himself, and wished he could have taken it up in the building's elevator instead. Remembering why he couldn't, he laughed, and carefully took the speaker in his arms. He had to keep out of sight-

-if he knew what was good for him—but, like the speaker, he embraced the elevator idea anyway. It would have made the next four stories go by so much easier.

Perspiration began to dot his forehead as he struggled up the next flight of steps, but by then his thoughts were already somewhere else. His band was playing in a contest that evening, and as the leader, he had to organize their transportation. First, of course, he would have to determine if everyone in the band was still speaking with one another.

Some weeks, depending on the phase of the moon and the earth's proximity to the sun, the drummer, Seth, would be fighting with the bass player, Chuck, due to some offhanded comment made the week before, and Seth would refuse to ride with Chuck in the same car. Chuck's auto was the biggest and held the most equipment, but Seth wasn't going to let that sway his decision about avoiding close quarters with the nefarious bass player.

Seth could have caught a ride with the rhythm guitar player, Paul, except that Seth (Drums) and Paul (Rhythm guitar) were *perpetually* at odds with one another due to an imagined slight that had occurred the summer before. Consequently, Mennon would have to drop off Turpin's equipment at Chuck's (Bass), so that he could cram Seth's drum kit, along with his own stuff, into the back of his mother's station wagon. Mennon and Turpin never fought about the music or the jobs, they had been playing together far too long for that, but part of each night was generally spent listening to Seth (Jerk) railing on about either one of those things.

He propped the amp up on his knee, and changed his grip on it. He knew he would also have to call everyone and remind them to bring what they needed for the show. Some of the other guys were constantly forgetting things, like cables, microphones and snare drums, and Mennon, with Turpin's aid, would be forced to improvise some solution on the spot. He wondered if it was like this with other bands, and guessed that it was. That was why so many of them were always breaking up.

Waddling up on to the next landing, he began poring over the dozens of songs his band had been practicing the last four months. He wanted to start the night off strong, but not too strong, and he needed an amazing finish as well. Johnny had been playing in bars since the tender age of sixteen, and knew how crucial a structured play list was. No matter how good the band, a set of songs assembled with little or no thought could either bore an audience or lose them entirely. However, a great set could take the night for even the worst band.

Increasing his pressure around the box in his arms, Mennon decided he wasn't going to choose the final number just yet. He trusted that something would occur to him during the course of the evening, and relaxed--for about two seconds.

It suddenly struck him that he had asked someone to go with him, but he couldn't remember her name.

4

Johnny might have had a better chance of slipping into class unnoticed, even with the large black speaker in tow, if he hadn't shoved the door to the classroom so hard.

He watched in surprise as it glided over the tile floor without a sound. Then the doorknob crashed into the round, plastic guard on the wall with a loud thud.

His teacher turned with the rest of the class, and Mennon wheeled the speaker into the room. **PROPERTY OF THE US ARMY** was printed across the cabinet's left side, and **RUDYARD UNIVERSITY ROTC** was written on the right.

Mennon quickly shut the door. "Sorry I'm late." He pushed the speaker over to an empty desk. "But I had to hide in that bush for ten minutes."

Lyle G. Adams hooked a thumb in his blue pinstripe vest, and checked the time on his pocket watch. "How did I know you were going to join us today Mr. Mennon? *And so early*. Why, class only started *twenty* minutes ago."

"Heyyy," Mennon replied, "you try carrying this thing across campus in that wind, and see if you make it anywhere on time."

"What *was* I thinking," Adams purred. He hated irresponsible students, and couldn't imagine what he had done to deserve Mennon. "And to what do we owe this signal honor? Are you here because you're afraid you've already missed too many classes this semester or because the weather today is lousy?"

"Aww, you're not even close." Mennon took off a green bomber jacket, and hung it on the back of the desk. "You see, I borrowed this second rate, banged up equipment from some Army guys over by Roberts Hall, and wouldn't you know it, the next thing I knew, they wanted it back."

Adams crossed his arms. "Didn't everyone in the unit know it was on loan?"

"As soon as it was gone they did." Johnny wiped his forehead with the back of his wrist. "Anyway, I needed a place to hide, and I asked myself, where could I go where no one would find me? And I thought and I thought, and you know what? The answer was suddenly right there in front of me." Mennon sat down. "Hardly anybody would figure they'd be able to find me here in class."

Adams found Mennon's logic impeccable. "It'd certainly be the last place I'd look for you."

"See? I couldn't believe how simple it was." He pulled the amp closer and leaned an elbow on it. "And *that's* why I'm here today."

"Thank you Mr. Mennon for that rather lengthy explanation." Adams moved back to his desk, and started paging through a dilapidated book. "Now, where was I?"

"How should I know? I just got here."

Adams frowned. "I wasn't talking to you Mr. Mennon. I was speaking to the people who have been here since the beginning of the class."

"Well when are you gonna' talk to me?"

"As soon as you give me the chance."

"Okay." Mennon reached over to the desk across from him. Someone had left a copy of that day's Rudyard Chronicle there.

"Now," Adams intoned, "I was reading from the speech Benjamin Franklin gave at the Constitutional Convention of 1787." He found his place in the book, and sat on the desk. "' In these sentiments, sir, I agree to this Constitution with all its faults, if they are such because I think a general government necessary

154

for us, and there is no form of government but what may be a blessing to the people if well-administered for a course of...course of..."'

The whistling was subtle, but off-key enough for Adams to notice it. He lowered his book. "Mr. Mennon, do you have to whistle while I'm talking?"

"Well I can't whistle while *I'm* talking."

Adams set the book down. "Mr. Mennon, why do you feel compelled to do old vaudeville routines in this class?"

Mennon lowered his paper. " 'Cause I think, deep down, people miss 'em."

"You do know that midterms are dangerously close now, right?"

"If you say so."

"How do you think you're going to do?"

"That depends."

"On how much you study?"

"Nahhh." Mennon folded the paper closed. "On how close I sit to that smart guy who always answers your questions."

Adams frowned. "So you're going to cheat."

"I don't like calling it that."

"But it *is* cheating."

"Sure," Mennon replied, "but I still don't like calling it that."

Adams exhaled. "Mr. Mennon, why do you even bother going to school?"

"Well, I tell you," he responded, "that's a funny thing."

Adams already regretted having posed the question.

155

Johnny stood up, and sat on the speaker. "My friends and me, we've been askin' ourselves the same question since the first week of classes. You know, why should we stay in college? Are we cut out for this stuff? Should we take a semester off or quit completely? And you know what? I'm *sick of talkin' about it*! I mean you either stay in college or you don't. That's all there is to it."

"Then why are your friends having so much trouble deciding?"

"I guess deep down, they're afraid. It's a pretty frightening thing to walk away from college, especially after so many people kept telling us we had to go."

"And where do you stand on all this?"

"Me?" Mennon took off his cap and ran a hand through his damp hair. "I'm a systems man myself. And if goin' to college will get me ahead in the system, then that's fine with me. At least until it starts getting in the way of the really important stuff."

"And what, pray tell, do you consider important?"

"Well..." He placed his cap on the back of his head. "....first there's my band. Second, I've been trying to set up a small recording studio in my friend Ernie's basement. Of course, lately, I've been spendin' more time looking for a place to live, so I guess the studio dropped to third." A name and a face suddenly emerged from behind the labyrinthine maze of Mennon's thoughts. "And Tracy." He snapped his fingers. "*Tracy*. She's important too. Especially tonight."

Adams felt a little lost. "But if you think you're going to stay in college, why doesn't it show up somewhere on that list of yours?"

"It does," Mennon replied unconvincingly. "But what's most important is always shiftin' for me. Like right now, I gotta' get a bunch of speakers together for tonight because of Tar."

Adams felt the room spin. "What?"

"Tar's this guy I know, and he came by my house yesterday. He told me that if I let him make a couple of adjustments to my sound equipment, he could boost my band's sound a hundred percent."

"And did he?"

"I've never heard an explosion that loud in my life."

Adams' eyes snapped shut.

"Blew out my basement window," Mennon added. "Strange how life is. One minute you have a relatively new sound system, the next, you have a worthless pile of smoking junk." He shook his head. "'Course, I blame myself. Anybody who listens to a guy named Tar deserves whatever they get."

"And now you have to replace your speakers."

"Sure. Because, wouldn't you know it, tonight we're supposed to play in a band contest. Talk about bad timing. So now I've gotta' run aroun' town and find enough equipment so my band can make it. Because keeping my band going is more important to me than college, the Constitution or that term paper I didn't finish for my next class all put together."

"Then why do you even bother coming here? It sounds to me as if your band takes up a lot more of your time than your classes do, and you obviously *like* the music business, despite its many drawbacks." Adams returned to his desk. "I think you've found exactly what it is you want to do with *your* life. You don't

157

need Rudyard at all. Why not drop out and save us all a lot of trouble?"

"Boy, if I had a dollar every time I heard *that* from a teacher, I could retire." He stood up. "Hey Professor Adams, you want to give me a dollar?"

"Mr. Mennon, your dropping out would be worth much more to me than a dollar."

"All right then, let the bidding begin."

"Mr. Mennon, I am not giving you *any* money."

Johnny sat down at his desk. "Then I guess this is where I'm going to have to stay."

(Several classes later, after another run-in with Mennon, Professor Adams would ask himself why, in the name of all that was holy, he hadn't just given Mennon the dollar in an effort to get rid of him.)

5

Eight blocks away and seven stories up, standing in a lush, state-of-the-art office--just the place you'd expect to find the person ultimately responsible for a spread like this--Ralph Garibaldi, the President of Rudyard University, was standing beside a scale model of the Rudyard University campus. He was holding aloft a small, cathedral-like building from the campus.

Robert Falconbruder, his guest for the afternoon, was frowning. "Biddle Hall?"

"Yes."

"Your plan involves tearing down Biddle Hall?"

"Yes," Ralph said with confidence.

Falconbruder stared thoughtfully at his cigar. "Ralph," he began, "correct me if I'm wrong, but isn't that the oldest building on campus?"

"Yes Bob, I believe it is."

"We just held a ceremony celebrating its hundredth year last July, didn't we?"

Ralph set the building down. "I know what you're going to say. The Board would never allow us to do such a thing."

Falconbruder took a moment to park his cigar in a nearby ashtray. "It did play a rather large part in the university's history."

Ralph held his ground. "To a certain extent Bob, we're all a part of Rudyard's history. Anyone who sets foot on this campus, on some level, contributes to its story. However, nothing is permanent. Students graduate, the professors go on to teach at other universities and one day, my administration is going to be replaced by another. You certainly wouldn't keep me on as President if, one day, it appeared as if some of the decisions I was making were holding the university back."

"I can only speak for myself Ralph, but if it ever came to that, I would do so with great reluctance."

Garibaldi held up a hand. "Of course you would Bob, and I appreciate it. But that's not what I'm getting at. My point is that while we all play some role in Rudyard's History, nothing, be it a teacher, a student, the President of the University, or the campus' *oldest building*, should be allowed to stand in the way of progress."

"That's a *very* interesting point of view."

"I'm simply being practical. The building, for its size, takes up far too much room. Right in the middle of campus." Ralph made his way over to the stained-brown bookcase behind his desk. "A building we can't use because of its age. And I wouldn't recommend a renovation. That would only be postponing the inevitable."

"I guess we couldn't move it."

"I thought of that myself." Ralph returned with a thin red binder. "So I had a firm do a feasibility study." He handed it to Falconbruder. "But the engineer says it's out of the question. The building wouldn't make the trip. The size of the hall, its age and the inferior construction make it impractical." Ralph leaned both hands on the table. "Besides, the cost would be astronomical. We would need to set up a committee and organize a fund drive to help with the expenses. And even then, I'm not sure what the Board would say."

Falconbruder held the report at arm's length and flipped through the first couple of pages. "I know what Kit Grayson would say."

"And what's that?"

Falconbruder stopped reading. "That you're up to your old tricks again."

Ralph looked at the campus. "I'm not quite sure what you mean Bob."

"Ralph…" Falconbruder placed the report down on the table. "….need I remind you that just a couple of months ago, you assured the Board that the Rudyard identity was safe? That you wouldn't 'dismantle the campus brick by brick,' is I think how you

160

put it, until Rudyard looked like any other large, urban college campus? Because if I don't, I'm sure Kit Grayson, and several other Board Members as well, will."

"Biddle Hall is not part of the Rudyard University identity." Ralph set the small building closer to the edge. "At least, it hasn't been for a decade or so."

"Ralph, you know how long a memory the Board has. You're going to have an uphill battle on your hands with this one."

Ralph stared at the campus. "At first. But I think they'll eventually come round to my way of thinking. Once they see what the next phase is."

"Well let's hear it."

Ralph took a deep breath. "Bob, I don't want to tear Biddle Hall down any more than you do. However, we need to free up the land it's standing on. We need the space." He started around the table. "Now we can't build out any further on a lot that size, but we can certainly build up." He stopped on the other side of the table and his hand dropped to a console below. "And when we do, this is what we'll wind up with." Ralph pressed a button.

"*Gggggggt!*"

A tall, sleek, black skyscraper shot up from under the table where Biddle Hall had been minutes before.

Falconbruder was impressed. "Well would you look at that? That is *slick*."

"Thank you."

"How many stories *is* that?"

"As many as the City of Philadelphia will allow."

161

"Goodness." Falconbruder retrieved his drink. "And where exactly does this, this monolith come in?"

"Well Bob, let's just say this building will allow us to put all our eggs in one basket."

"Does that sound like a good idea Ralph," Falconbruder asked over the rim of his glass.

Garibaldi wasn't listening. "My plan Bob, is to consolidate as many administrative offices as we can into one large space. This way, we'll be able to eliminate a good deal of the communication problems we've experienced in the past, and streamline some of the operating systems we now have in place. Why, if this works out, during Registration, for example, a student could conceivably conduct all their business in a matter of hours."

He placed his finger halfway down the smooth tower, and as he spoke, moved it from floor to floor. "Financial Aid would be located below the Registrar's Office. And below them, the Bursar. All separated by an elevator ride, not a ten minute walk, which will make the process much more convenient for everyone."

"What about Student Traffic? During your busy times, for instance, say, during Registration, will those offices be able to handle all those students?"

"We've taken all those factors into account when deciding how much floor space we needed to dedicate to each office, and while there's no way of fixing it so the students will never have to stand in line again, it will still be a much more comfortable environment for them to wait. We'll obviously be boosting the number of staff in these offices as well."

"And what are your plans for the buildings that this move will free up?"

Ralph smiled. "Let me show you." He removed more buildings from the face of the campus. "What will happen is that we'll be able to clear five or six lots across campus."

"Five or six?!" Falconbruder asked into his glass.

"Starting with Marner Hall."

"Marner Hall?"

Ralph pointed at one of the halls in the right hand corner of the table. "That one, over there."

"You mean the tall building…?"

"No, that's Stanton Hall." Garibaldi took a step closer and put his hand directly over a squat building located next to Stanton Hall. "This one, here."

Falconbruder nodded. "Oh yes. Now I see it. It was the name that was throwing me. When I was here, it was called Grenadier Hall. I don't remember why."

"Yes." Ralph circled to the other side of the table. "It's always been a bit of a problem, figuring out what to do with it."

"That's very true," Falconbruder agreed. "It was even a bit of a white elephant back in the 50's when I was here, as I recall." He glanced down at the glass in his hand, remembering the campus as it once was, and swirled the aged brown liquid inside. "The university was constantly talking about moving certain departments and offices there. Of course, as was characteristic of that particular Administration, they never did follow through with it."

Garibaldi stared at the tiny model of Marner Hall. "Probably because there was never a time when the building was completely empty. There was always at least one department or administrative office headquartered there. But once we've moved

163

Financial Aid across campus and relocated the dance studio on the second floor—we're not quite sure where—that'll pretty much free the building up for demolition."

Falconbruder nodded. "And what would go in its place?"

"Bob, what is one of the biggest problems facing the university today?"

"Well," Falconbruder said thoughtfully. "Actually there are quite a number of them. For one thing, there's the skyrocketing cost of running a university, especially with funding down these days, thanks to the President."

Garibaldi crossed his arms. "True."

"There's the problem of what some people see as a decline in academic standards, thanks to the growing number of people enrolling each year…"

"There is that, yes."

"….and I guess there's the question of how to deal with the growing dissatisfaction among teachers, due to the rather precarious position they find themselves in nowadays, thanks to the new approaches your larger universities have taken in terms of tenure and the changes they've made to their core curriculums."

Ralph nodded. "True, true. In fact, everything you've said so far is true, but most colleges face those problems every day of the week. No Bob, what I'm talking about is something that effects our type of campus. You know, the kind that operates out of a large city. For instance, Temple and Penn have the same problem, and it seems to get worse every year. That's why my administration feels that we must deal with it now before we even consider anything else. Because if we don't, it could very well be a thorn in the side of the campus for the next fifteen years."

Falconbruder couldn't help being slightly amused by the seriousness with which Ralph had delivered this last statement. Ralph was definitely laying it on a little thick. "Okay Ralph, I'll bite." He released a puff of smoke. "What is this terrible problem nipping at the heels of the university?"

"Something that has plagued Rudyard since the mid-seventies."

"Go on."

"Bob, after carefully reviewing all the available data, we believe the ground where Marner Hall stands..." Garibaldi reached under the table and slid out a small drawer. "....would be the perfect location for..."

Falconbruder leaned forward.

"....this." He plunked something down on the table.

"I'm not quite sure what that is Ralph." Falconbruder stared at the gray block.

Garibaldi smiled proudly. "It's a four-story parking garage."

Falconbruder removed the cigar from his mouth. "You mean you want to replace Grenadier Hall, I mean Marner Hall, with a garage?" His eyes would not budge from the tiny block. "Am I to take it then that *parking* is the major problem you were talking about before?"

"Yes."

Falconbruder was incredulous. "Ralph...I...don't know what to say."

Garibaldi placed both Marner and Biddle Hall into the open drawer, and the drawer disappeared under the table. "Don't say anything. Let the idea sink in first."

165

"So you aren't planning on erecting a new hall or a dorm on this spot. Just a garage."

"Well, at one time, we were considering putting up a new dorm," Garibaldi said over his shoulder. He returned to the bookcase behind his desk. "But the studies we had done last spring—conducted by an outside consulting firm—showed that that isn't what Rudyard needs at this crucial time."

He pulled a bound copy of the firm's findings from the bookcase and brought it over to Falconbruder. "It's all here in black and white. Rudyard is going to need better parking facilities if it ever hopes to maintain its edge in the highly competitive field of higher education."

"Let's have a look," Falconbruder said as he took the report over to a large velvet chair. He sat down, and, setting his drink on the polished oak table next to it, opened the cover of the heavy volume. "And they took into account the number of transit lines that run past the campus, correct?" He balanced his cigar on the edge of the crystal ashtray at his elbow and slid a pair of glasses from his bright green jacket. "The el down the street, a trolley line and the various bus routes?"

"They did Bob." Ralph crossed his arms. "And they came to the conclusion that unless some radical changes are made to the public transit system here, the service will only get worse. So a certain segment of the campus will always prefer to drive. It's all in there."

"Uh-huh." Falconbruder skimmed over the first couple of pages, pausing whenever he came across a statistic or a chart, but as he sunk deeper into the text, he was surprised to find no real explanation as to how the firm had arrived at its rather odd conclusion.

Falconbruder suspected that Ralph had probably run into the same difficulty—if he had even read the report all the way through--but, as President of his own multimillion dollar business, he knew that it was often necessary to follow the advice of someone he had never met on matters he had never even considered before. Still, with what he knew about Rudyard, he was having trouble swallowing the firm's parking crisis evaluation, and wondered if perhaps they had somehow forwarded Ralph the wrong report.

"Well," he said dubiously, removing his glasses, "I guess if you did a study..."

"We always do a study." Ralph straightened up. "You can take that with you, if you'd like."

Falconbruder returned his glasses to his jacket and placed the book down on the table in exchange for his cigar. "No, no. That won't be necessary." He stood up. "As long as you did a study."

"Like I said Bob, we always do a study." He refilled Falconbruder's glass on the table. "We can't afford not to. You know as well as I do how many people the university has watching over its shoulder."

Falconbruder smiled. "You mean the number of people *you* have watching over your shoulder."

"I guess when you come right down to it," admitted Ralph, "it's the same thing. But it's to be expected. After all, what I'm proposing Monday is going to require a huge expenditure of time and money from the university." He adjusted his glasses. "But

167

if the numbers check out, and they will, and the Board green lights my plan, these renovations are going to make it possible for Rudyard to enter the next century ahead of the pack."

"You always did know how to spot a trend Ralph. I think that's been a big part of your success over the years."

Garibaldi loosened his tie. "That's very nice of you to say Bob."

"And that's why I'm convinced that the Board of Trustees will back your plan a hundred percent. And if they don't, they will by the time I'm through with them."

"I was hoping you would say that Bob."

Falconbruder patted him on the shoulder. "You know I only want what's best for Rudyard, Ralph."

"Of course."

"But now that you know where I stand, I'm wondering if you're going to tell me what your plans are for those lots this is going to free up."

"I'm so glad you asked." Ralph moved to the other side of the table. "Bob, with the amazing changes going on, people are going to want to get involved. Be a part of the excitement. Fortune 500 Companies no less. So what I'm going to propose on Monday is that once all this construction and demolition is finished, we open these lots up to the private sector.

"I've already put out a couple of feelers, and one or two corporations have already expressed an interest in setting up shop right here on campus. I have another study back at my desk that says the trend in the real estate market the next ten years will be towards office space. There are several office buildings going up in Center City as we speak."

Falconbruder looked into his glass. "Well if that's the way the market's going, why not save ourselves the trouble and just close down the university? We'll sell off the land to the highest bidder."

"Not a bad idea Bob." Ralph winked. "I'll have to mention that somewhere in my presentation on Monday."

"Seriously though Ralph, are you telling me you're actually going to recommend that the Board of Trustees *sell off* part of the campus?"

He shook his head. "Not sell. Lease. This way the corporations will be responsible for the cost of the buildings that go up, not the university."

"I see."

"And we wouldn't be leasing all the space."

"All right, what are you going to put on *those* lots?"

Ralph's hand disappeared under the table again. "Building blocks for the campus of the 21st Century..."

6

Richard Mead was already on his fourth bag of junk food for the day, and, while unschooled in the basic principles of modern psychology, was convinced that his increased appetite was a classic example of sublimation; but he didn't care. He was hungry.

His hand dove into the blue and white cellophane package, resurfaced and deposited a sixth pretzel in his mouth. They were small, round pretzels with a W baked in the center, and he was mechanically shoveling them in one after the other. His jaw tightened and relaxed several times, and he quickly swallowed.

He was standing in the middle of a dingy alley located in a rather broken down part of Philadelphia, and he was waiting for Turpin, Tollhausler and Mennon. They had separated back at the last turn, and the others still hadn't caught up to him yet. Richard could feel his impatience growing, and attributed it to the fact that he didn't really want to be there. To be perfectly honest, he didn't want to be anywhere at the moment.

If asked, he felt he could say, without a doubt, that he was having one of the worst days of his life—and he wasn't being overly dramatic either, in his opinion.

His morning had been atrocious, thanks to Holly and her classroom revelation, and the afternoon hadn't been much better, thanks to a surprise quiz he had taken in his afternoon Marketing class. Now, an ominous swelled curtain of dark gray clouds was steadily inching its way across the sky, and he wanted to go home.

The bag rustled around his fingers as he reached for another pretzel, and the planks to his right suddenly began to growl. He wasn't clear on what exactly it was he had done to elicit such an angry response, especially from a wooden fence, but he made a quick mental note to review the situation at a later date. He forced a smile across his face. "Nice fence," he cooed. "Good fence." He slowly backed down the alley, being careful not to make any sudden movements, and was overcome by an overwhelming desire to see Holly. He still didn't know what he was going to do about her or if there was anything he could do.

Tollhausler broke the silence. "....and it felt as if I was being tailed."

Mennon was right behind him. "Ahhh, now who would want to follow *you*?"

"How should I know? Why would anybody follow you?"

"You got me." Mennon patted his coat for something. "Although one guy *did* drive after me a whole weekend once 'cause he thought I was seeing his girlfriend."

Tollhausler removed his glasses. "Were you?"

Mennon chuckled. "Not that weekend." He drew something out of his coat. "Say you aren't seein' anybody behind their boyfriend's back, are you?"

"Are you?"

Mennon stared at his cigarettes. "I don't ask these girls if they have boyfriends."

"Why not?"

"Because they might tell me, stupid!"

Tollhausler shook his head. "No wonder my mom told me to stay away from you when I was younger."

"What are you talkin' about?" Mennon slipped a cigarette from the pack. "My mom didn't want *me* playin' with *you*."

"Come to think of it Johnny, a lot of mothers didn't want their kids playing with us. Remember how Mead's mom used to pretend there wasn't anybody home when we would come by?"

Mennon pocketed the cigarettes. "I remember."

They were expecting some sort of reaction from Mead, but Rich didn't seem to be listening.

Tollhausler gestured at him. "He's been awfully quiet today."

Mennon nodded. "Since this morning."

He returned to the matter at hand. "Hey, I know. Maybe you owe somebody money, and they want to keep an eye on you."

"Now who would do something like that?"

Mennon reached into his other pocket. "*I would*."

"I don't owe money to any loan sharks." Tollhausler stared at Mennon. "Do I?"

Johnny shook his head. "Too many people know me."

"So there you are. The only people I owe money to are the government and several banks, and the last I heard, they don't go after you until you're out of school."

"Maybe they heard something about you dropping out."

"I *have* mentioned it to a lot of people."

Mennon's lighter sparked as he thumbed the small wheel. "Then I don't know who it could have been." He cupped a hand over the flame and lit his cigarette. "It's a crazy world out there, you know? It could have been anybody." He snapped the lighter shut. "A mugger. Or maybe it was some woman who found you irresistible, but was too shy to say."

"Well, like you say," Tollhausler said, laughing, "it's a crazy world."

"It could happen." Mennon pocketed the lighter. "You know, lots of women chase after me."

"You borrowed money from them too hunh?"

"No, not 'cause I owe them money Tol. It's because I'm cute."

"Well, I guess you wouldn't lie about a thing like that."

"It was nice, for a while, but you don't want some woman runnin' after you." He blew a smoke ring. "There's no challenge. Wouldn't you miss the thrill of the chase?"

"Who cares about the chase? I just want the thrill."

"All right, suit yourself, but I think you're makin' a *big* mistake."

Tollhausler walked up to Mead and took a pretzel. "Why didn't Holly come along today?"

Rich swallowed. "She had a paper to write."

"That's too bad." Mennon also helped himself to a pretzel. "I kinda' like having her around. She's real nice."

"Yep," Tollhausler agreed.

"You better treat her right," Mennon warned. "Girls like her don't come along often."

Rich practically shattered a tooth as he clamped down on the next pretzel. "She is great," he declared, "but it's not like I'm going to marry her, you know?"

"Sure, sure," Mennon agreed. "You're having fun."

"I sure am," he lied.

"'Course, if you ever want to dump her, let me know. I'd love to go out with her."

Mead almost bit off a finger eating the last pretzel.

He realized he hadn't tasted anything since breakfast, and crushed the bag into a crumpled ball. He didn't relish the idea of losing Holly, and hoped he could still talk things over with her. He had seen a pay phone down at the corner, but, even though he desperately wanted to talk to her, knew he didn't have time for a phone call.

Tollhausler was studying the crumbling fence to his right. "By the way, this is a really nice neighborhood." He appraised the swastika painted on it. "But why would anybody want to live here if they didn't have to?"

Mead nodded in an aggravated manner. "I know, I know, not the nicest of places, but let's go inside before we make up our minds. It could be nice." He tossed the pretzel bag aside. "Besides, I bet we could get this place cheap."

"How much do haunted houses go for these days?"

Mennon shrugged. "Depends on how many ghosts the house comes with."

Mead ignored them. "Where's Ernie?"

Mennon pulled his cap lower. "He'll be along. He stopped to write out his last will and testament."

"Oh *commmme onnnn*," Mead complained. "The neighborhood isn't *that* bad."

Tollhausler nodded. "He does have a point Johnny. Why, they tear down a couple more houses around here, and there'll be nothing but fields as far as the eye can see."

Mead stuffed his hands in his pockets. He had only been apartment hunting since the second week of September, and already felt as if he had set foot in every available space in the city. He had crossed glass-enclosed walkways, climbed colorful flights of sound-proofed stairs and rode in elevators that were nicer than some of the apartments he had seen, but he still wasn't any closer to renting a place. Good apartments, like reliable used cars, were apparently scarce, and even when he did track one down that fit most of his requirements, it was either too expensive or to small.

His luck hadn't been much better with houses. Mennon, Turpin and Tollhausler had traveled with him from one end of the city to the other, as well as into New Jersey, and looked at row homes, duplexes, bungalows and even a warehouse, and all they had come away with was the helpful tip, screamed at them from a screen door, that one doesn't park "just anywhere" in a cul-de-sac.

It was pretty frustrating; especially since Rich occasionally got the impression that the boys didn't appreciate all his hard work. They were constantly criticizing the apartments or houses he chose, and would insult him about the way he spoke to landlords. Ingrates. They weren't much help either. Tollhausler and Mennon would frequently offend prospective landlords with their comments and Turpin was always breaking things.

To be fair, Mead knew their antics weren't the only things holding them back. Some landlords lost interest in them the moment they discovered Mead and the others were in college. Others seemed to take an instant dislike to them before anything was even said. That was usually when Turpin would find something to break. It had crossed Rich's mind from time to time to act as their agent and seek out living quarters in their absence, but he knew, sooner or later, someone would meet the boys and register a complaint. That was why he had been forced to contact his uncle, Stan Carson.

Stan appeared, as if he had been conjured up on the spot by Rich simply thinking his name, and counted the gates to his right with a short, pudgy finger. "Hi Rich."

Rich still couldn't believe he had called his uncle for help. "Hi."

Ernie followed Stan down the alley with a crow bar and several flashlights in his arms, and Stan's index finger leveled at an aged door over Rich's shoulder. "This is it." He tugged at the blunt purple nose in the middle of his crimson face, and wiped the palm of his hand down the side of his gray raincoat. He took the crowbar from Ernie, and jabbed it into the side of the gate; the line of fences shuddered down the entire length of the alleyway.

The gate, as well as the fence it was attached to, was covered in a rainbow of colors. A thousand people had spray-painted a thousand names across the uneven boards in an attempt to leave their mark on the world. Unfortunately, the many nicknames, phrases and curses had simply blurred together over the years, and all that was left were the colors.

Five minutes later, Stan was still struggling with the unyielding door, his chins jiggling as his round body twisted with each motion, and he would occasionally stop to pull at the wide collar of his black shirt in order to catch his breath. Then the door finally creaked as if it were about to give. "Whew," Stan puffed. "There it goes." There was a loud crack, Stan collided with the fence and the gate swung free. "There," he said, still out of breath, "now let's take a look at your new home."

On the other side of the rocking fence, a sea of fallen leaves had flooded the length of the L-shaped yard, and it clung to their legs as they crunched towards the back of the house. Like a lot of abandoned properties, the building had that flat, gray, forgotten look about it, and they crept towards it as if it were a wounded lion. The disrepair was painfully obvious, even from the outside, and a broken TV antenna jutted over the roof at a thirty-degree angle. The windows were hidden behind sheets of tin, and a huge padlock hung from the back door. Stan pulled out a set of keys, and searched for the one that opened the heavy lock.

Turpin grinned. "It leans to the left."

"What," Stan asked over his shoulder.

"The house. It leans to the left."

Stan popped the lock and removed it from the latch. "No it doesn't."

The other three stared in disbelief for a couple of seconds, and then the house's angle was suddenly quite apparent.

Mennon laughed. "It does."

"Don't be silly son. That's an optical illusion. It's just the way the houses sit together on the block. It's the ground that's uneven, not the house. Trust me." Stan went inside.

"Ohhh, that's beautiful," Mennon said. "We can call it Pisa West."

Tollhausler took a step back. "If it's the ground that's uneven, then why do all the other houses on the block seem to be standing straight?"

"You got it all wrong, Toll," Mennon announced. "Those other houses are tilting to the *right*, making this one *look* like it's leaning to the left. That's why it's such a good buy."

Rich sighed. This was exactly what he had been afraid of. "All right guys, that's enough. Now let's find out which way the floors tip inside."

7

"*Gggggggggggt!*"

"*Gggggggggggt!*"

"*Gggggggggggt!*"

"*Gggggggggggt!*"

Four more skyscrapers rose from underneath the wide table and formed an ominous, jagged line across the center of the tiny campus. They were duplicates of the building Ralph wanted to replace Biddle Hall with in every way, and towered over the campus like dominoes over the hotels on a Monopoly board.

"And this is where I lost him," President Garibaldi declared. He proceeded to take a bite out of a turkey sandwich. He had already removed his jacket and unbuttoned his shirt collar. "The same place," he continued, chewing, "I always lose them."

Doug Shellington, the head of Ralph's staff, looked up from the black buildings. "We always knew this part of the presentation was going to be difficult. It *is* rather formidable."

Sarah Mitchell, Ralph's secretary for the last three years, shook her head. "I don't care what you say. I still think those buildings make the campus look like a moon base."

Andrea Golden, Doug's second, chuckled. "Yes. One of those fifties' drawings you see on paperback books."

"They always make me think of missiles," Don Gretz admitted from the other side of the room. He was standing with a phone in his hand. Someone over in the Finance Department had put him on hold. "Especially the way they come sliding out of the ground."

"True, true." Shellington shook the ice around in the red and white cup he was holding. "That's because it was always *supposed* to look like something out of a science fiction movie. The idea was to grab people's imaginations the same way those 'City of the Future' pictures used to. Instead, it's putting people off."

Andrea Golden set down a small container of chicken noodle soup in the quad next to Pfaehler Library. "Maybe we should do what Dwight originally suggested. Use a picture of the buildings for the presentation instead of models."

"Sketches done in pastels or colored pencils," Dwight Stevenson elucidated from the very same chair Bob Falconbruder had sat in hours before. "To give them a softer edge."

"That way they won't seem so...so intimidating." Don Gretz nodded.

"That might work. I've always thought there was something very sterile about the whole model thing."

Ralph considered this. "And we can get those sketches done by Monday."

"That shouldn't be a problem," Doug Shellington said. Then he gave Dwight the nod, and Stevenson took a deep breath. "Or maybe we should just leave those four out of the presentation altogether."

Ralph turned. He had been hearing this argument from various people ever since the first numbers had come in on what the project would eventually cost. "We've had this discussion before Dwight, and you know how I feel. I think the Board needs to know about every phase of the project up front to avoid any misunderstandings down the road. I don't want anyone on the Board coming back to me in a couple of months saying I hid anything from them."

Shellington leaned against the table with both hands. "It's just that this part makes the plan look really big. *Too big.* Hence the negative reaction you've gotten from everyone so far."

"I know." Ralph walked over to his desk. "Falconbruder said this part makes it look like we're more interested in Real Estate than in Education." He tossed his sandwich down. "So I guess it's time we considered Plan B."

Shellington was relieved. "Plan B. Leave this phase out of the presentation, cut the cost from the budget and get the first building up. Then, once the ground is clear, we go back to the Board and ask them to approve the money to erect four more buildings."

"That might make the most sense." Don Gretz was still on hold with Finance. "The Board might not go for it any other way."

"All right." Ralph walked over to the window behind his desk." All right. Whatever we need to do to get this project funded and off the ground, let's do it." Surrounded by only the most trusted people on his staff, Ralph finally allowed himself to vent his frustration. "But those fools on the Board are going to have to face up to some harsh realities the next couple of years." He stared down at the campus. "What do they think? That this place is always going to stay the same? That it's always going to look like those pictures they took back in the twenties?! A university isn't a collection of buildings any more than an education is a collection of facts. Of course what I'm proposing is radical. But it has to be. Education is changing too fast. We have to be ready." He turned around. "We all know there's going to come a time when students won't even have to travel to campus to take a class. What are we going to do with all these dilapidated buildings and halls then?! We have to be ready to make the jump, and the only way we're going to be able to do that is if we're already up and running."

The office was quiet for a moment. No one on Ralph's staff ever knew what to say after one of his little tirades. They would usually wait a couple of seconds after he had, as Don Gretz put it, "spouted off like a character in an Ayn Rand novel," allowing Ralph to settle down, and then go on as if nothing had happened.

"Maybe we could get some outside parties involved," Andrea Golden suggested around a mouthful of noodles. She swallowed. "Do a survey. Trot it out for some people and see what they think. Maybe the Board would be a little more willing to listen if they knew a certain percentage of people out there thought this was the right direction for the university to go."

Dwight Stevenson looked up from a red and green binder. "We should get a wider sampling of students as well. Not just talk to the usual groups who go along with everything we do."

"'Go along with everything we--?!'" Ralph frowned. "Why wouldn't every student out there go along with this? Think of the opportunities they'll have. The students're going to love this. Sure, it might not be exactly what they were expecting, but in the end, they're going to thank us. It's the best thing Rudyard has ever done for them."

8

Fifteen minutes later, Ernie Turpin was carefully pushing leaves into a large pile in the center of the narrow yard, and he paused when he heard Stan's voice.

It sounded like Rich's uncle was concluding some sort of sales pitch, and Ernie giggled. He thought Stan was one of the funniest people alive, probably because he didn't believe a word the man said. He certainly didn't take Stan's house seriously, which is why he didn't even bother going in. He knew they weren't going to take it.

Ernie counted off ten paces, stopping once or twice to gage the distance separating him and the leaves, turned and leaped into the air. He disappeared under a swell of brittle leaves.

Stan exited the house. "….and because the house isn't in the best shape, I'm willing to give you guys a break." He brushed a leaf from his lapel. "It also helps that you're my nephew."

"I *knew* you were gonna' hold that against us," Mennon commented from inside.

Mead blinked as he came out into the light.

"How does two hundred dollars a month sound?"

Tollhausler stopped in the doorway. "Is that all? I thought you'd be able to pay us a lot more than that."

Stan couldn't believe his ears. "You mean you don't *like* this place?!"

"Oh, it's not your fault." Tollhausler came down the steps and brushed a foot long cobweb off his sleeve. "It's mine. I'm too demanding. There are certain luxuries I expect when it comes to housing. You know, walls, a ceiling, a sewer line. All the things I think that make a house a home, and the outdoors indoors."

"You mean you aren't interested in turning this place into something you can call home?"

"I'm not even interested in turning it into something the city can call condemned."

Mead moved between his uncle and his friend. "What Tollhausler means is, it looks like it'd be a lot of work, and between our classes and our jobs, I'm not sure we could do it."

"Come on Rich," Stan said, glowering at Tollhausler, "you don't get offers like this every day. This is one of my best properties, and you're telling me you're going to pass on it because you don't like the idea of getting your hands a little dirty?! You guys had better grow up."

Turpin, Mennon and Tollhausler just stared at Stan, and Rich spoke fast. "The thing is, we've got one more place to look at today."

"Really, where?"

Tollhausler smiled. "There's a burnt out factory over on Twelfth Street. From the description, it sounds downright *cozy*."

"Actually, it's a place out in West Philly," Mead corrected. "We already called the people, and they're expecting us. After that, we'll decide."

Stan nodded. "All right, but I bet you won't find a deal like this anywhere else."

"Yeah," Mennon agreed. "You'd certainly have to search high and low for a place like this."

"You're darn right." Stan winked at Mennon. "So call me, and let me know what you guys are going to do."

"Sure Uncle Stan. I'll call as soon as I know. And thanks for your help today."

"No problem." Stan shook Rich's hand. "And tell your mother I said hello."

"I will."

They emerged from the alleyway exhausted, and walked down the street in silence. They stopped beside a green car, and Mennon drummed on Rich's hood. "Hey, remember to tell your

183

mother Stan said hello." He snapped his fingers. "Oh yeah, then I want you to tell her what a monumental scumbag he is."

"I'll do it," Tollhausler volunteered.

"No you won't." Mead pulled out a key ring. "He means well, but unfortunately, he treats everyone the same way when it comes to business." He opened the door. "I think he *was* trying to help, but—"

"You mean he wants us to help him." Johnny looked at Turpin and Tollhausler. "We fix the place up, pay low rent the first year, and then one day he raises the rent and we have to move out."

"I don't know about that," Mead said. He was determined to give his uncle the benefit of the doubt. "He looks at things a little differently, that's all. But I don't want to take this place either. So I'll call him tomorrow, and tell him we're going to pass on it. That'll be the end of it."

9

The car shook as the other three doors slammed shut, and Mead placed his key in the ignition.

"I don't think I want to move out anymore."

Mead and Mennon turned around in the front seat, and Turpin gaped across the backseat at Tollhausler. They could tell from his tone he wasn't joking.

Mead placed a hand on the steering wheel. "What?"

"I said I don't want to move out. Okay?"

Rich glanced at Johnny. "Why?"

184

Tollhausler leaned forward. "Because I don't know what I'm going to do next. I'm thinking of dropping out of school again."

Mead looked back. "Your classes haven't gotten any better?"

"Not really." Tollhausler sat back. "I don't know whether it's Rudyard's fault or mine, but somebody isn't doing their job."

"So you think leaving is the answer."

"I don't know." Tollhausler peered out the window. "I guess I was hoping for a miracle or something. You know something would click, and I'd suddenly know what I should do. But it hasn't happened. Nothing's changed. My teachers are still boring, and I haven't learned a thing."

"Hey, I wanted to drop out of school the first day," Ernie complained. "But you guys talked me out of it."

Tollhausler and Mennon stared at Turpin, then laughed. "Sucker," Tollhausler proclaimed.

Mennon shook his head. "You guys and school. You wouldn't have this trouble if you didn't go to class so much."

Mead started the engine. "So what are you going to do after you drop out?"

"I guess I'll finally take a shot at writing."

"Why drop out? Why not change majors?"

"Rich, man, I've already done that already. It didn't make any difference."

Mead put the car in drive. "You should still move out."

"Yeah, but I don't think I could leave home, work and write at the same time. Not right now." Tollhausler stared out the window again. "I want to write full time. I don't want to have to worry about keeping a job and making rent each week."

Mennon smirked. "Ohhhhhh right. You don't want to have to get another job."

"That's not true. I like having a job."

"Uh-hunh," Mead said skeptically. He made a left on the next street.

"No, really I do. It isn't my fault they fired me today." Tollhausler smirked. "All I did was ask a teacher to explain my dream. Is that so bad?"

Mead knew better. "There's got to be more to it than that."

"There is, but I can't remember all the clever things I said, so I'd rather not talk about it." He watched a motorcycle pass. "The main thing is I'm out of the Psychology Department, and that's good. There was something very strange going on there."

"Like what," Mennon asked.

"Take last week," Tollhausler began. "One minute they were telling me they were giving me a bonus, and the next, they were asking if I would mind hanging upside down with a hundred and fifty electrodes attached to my body."

Mennon grimaced. "What'd you say?"

"Not much. I crawled out a window and climbed down a tree."

"Was that part of the experiment?"

"It is now."

"Tollhausler, there are other jobs."

"I know Rich. One way or another, they're going to get me. They get everybody in the end. The bastards." He sighed. "But I'm not beaten yet."

"So you're going to drop out of school," Mead restated.

"I might. We'll see how I feel after midterms." He leaned against the armrest. "I was also thinking about finishing the semester, and not returning in the Spring. That way, if the writing doesn't go anywhere, I can return to college with six full semesters behind me."

"That's a good idea," Mennon conceded. "Would you move out if you stayed at Rudyard then?"

"No."

Mead frowned. "Why?"

"Because I still wouldn't get any work done."

"You don't know that," Mead grumbled.

"I can't be a hundred percent sure, but think about it. Say we move out, okay? So there we are in our new place in a new neighborhood. Do you think any of us is going to get any school work done that semester?"

Mead framed his answer very carefully. "*Well-*"

"No way," Mennon replied.

"Nope," Turpin agreed.

Mead considered crashing the car into a pole. "That's not the point. Don't you want to be on your own?" Mead caught a glimpse of Tollhausler in the mirror. "Don't you want to be independent?"

"Not really."

Mead wasn't giving up. "Don't you know how important living on your own can be? It'd certainly change the way you see the world and live your life."

"Well if I knew *all that* was gonna' happen, I'd have said no back in September."

Rich clicked his tongue. "Come onnn, it'd be good for you."

"That's another reason I shouldn't do it."

"Jon, man, for once in your life, be serious," Mead demanded. "This is important. You can't avoid growing up forever."

Tollhausler was confused as to when exactly Mead had cornered the market on maturity. "Rich," he exclaimed, "why do you equate living in an apartment with growing up?"

"It forces you to be responsible."

"But I *am* responsible. I wake myself up in the morning, shower and even remember to brush my teeth most days. You mature because of your experiences, not because of where you live."

"But if you stay home you aren't going to have as many experiences."

"I could say the same thing about living on your own. When you're not in school, you're going to be working, or doing laundry or homework, and I don't see how you're going to find much time for anything else."

"I'll find it," Mead vowed. "We all will."

"I hope you do," Tollhausler said. "But for me, I'd rather take things a little slower. I don't think I could handle moving out right now."

"But it'd be *good* for you."

Tollhausler sneered. "Why? Because everyone else says it is? They told us that about college too, and see where it got us. Maybe they were wrong about a lot of things."

"They were right about one thing," Mennon declared.

"What's that?"

Turpin grinned. "*Sex.*"

Tollhausler rolled his eyes. "Hey, I'm trying to be bitter here, and you guys aren't helping at all. How am I ever gonna' be a true artist?"

"If you moved out with us you could be a starving one," Mead promised. He turned the car on to another street.

"Well, when you put it like that," Tollhausler mused.

Mead looked in the mirror again. "So you'll move out?"

"No, but thinking about going hungry has added new depth to my soul hitherto thought impossible."

They rode in silence for a couple of minutes. Rich was disappointed, while Mennon and Turpin accepted Tollhausler's decision. It was obvious he wasn't ready to move out yet.

Mennon leaned over in the seat. "You call Seth?"

"Before we left Rudyard," Turpin reported.

"And?"

"He's still fighting with Chuck."

"Wonderful."

"But he said we don't have to worry about picking up his stuff. He's going to catch a ride with his girlfriend. He'll meet us at the frat."

Mennon relaxed. "Beautiful. I didn't feel like traveling with him in the same car tonight anyway." He looked at Rich. "You guys are still coming, right?"

"Probably."

Tollhausler brushed some dirt off his pant leg. "Unless of course Rich and me find something better to do. Like maybe Holly could introduce me to one of her cute friends, and we could go on a double date instead."

Mead changed lanes. "We'll be there Johnny. Just make sure we can get in."

Mennon smiled. "I'll see what I can do, but I can't promise you anything. They're a very discriminating bunch of Greeks."

"Then why are they letting you in?" Tollhausler snapped.

They rode in silence some more.

10

After Rich had dropped off the others—and cleared his trunk of Mennon's equipment--he headed directly to his house, and, once he was safe in the privacy of his own room, dialed Holly's number. He knew he couldn't leave things the way they were with her, and hoped he could talk her into accepting a truce.

Unfortunately, she wasn't home--or so he was told. He stiffly thanked Holly's mother, hung up and began pacing. The success of his plan had rather depended a good deal on her being there anxiously waiting for his call, but he realized he had made a slight miscalculation. It was obviously going to take more than a phone call to get her back.

He stared out the window into the night, and tried not to think too hard about where Holly could have been. After all, he told himself, it's none of my business. Holly could go wherever she wanted and with whomever. He didn't care.

It was at this point that the urge arose to chuck the telephone out the window, but it soon passed. He knew meaningless destruction wasn't going to solve anything, and he would need the phone in the event that Holly actually called him back.

"What am I getting so upset about anyway," he asked. "There are plenty of other women in the world. I don't need her."

Still, he was somewhat relieved when he felt the phone ring in his hand. He answered it.

"Hey Rich."

He was less than thrilled to find that it was Tollhausler. "Changed your mind about moving out?"

"No. Have you?"

"No, I still think you should move out."

Tollhausler laughed. "That's all right. You'll come to your senses soon enough."

"Well while we're waiting, what can I do for you?"

"I was just checking about tonight."

"Why?"

"You know why. I figured the program was subject to change depending on what Holly's plans were tonight."

Mead tried not to think about it. "Well don't worry your pretty little head. I'll still be over about eight o'clock."

"All right then. I'll be ready at eight-thirty."

"Great."

Richard sat on his bed, and set the phone down on the floor. "Holly, where the hell are you?" The suspense was killing him, and Rich suspected that if he didn't discuss his predicament with someone soon, he was going to lose his mind. Which is why he was so grateful when Tollhausler asked about Holly later that night.

"We're fighting again," he divulged, and Tollhausler didn't seem at all surprised. "Is it something she did to you or you did to her?"

"Ohhhh, we did it to each other," Mead declared with a great deal of authority.

"That's too bad."

"Yeah."

They started across the front lawn of the Lambda Sigma Delta House, and Tollhausler watched Richard out of the corner of his eye. "Is she seeing someone else?"

Rich kept moving straight ahead. "Of course."

"Did you see them together?"

"No, she told me about him in class."

Tollhausler was stunned. "She told you?"

"Well first I had to guess."

He grimaced. "You had to…what is it, a game?"

"Look…" Mead stopped walking. "….unless I put her on the spot, and let her know I knew something was up, she wasn't going to come right out and tell me. You know?"

"Sure. But it still sounds like a game."

"That's because when you come right down to it." He started walking. "It is."

192

Tollhausler watched a trio of young women enter the building. "So what are you going to do?"

"I don't know." Rich stepped over a crack in the sidewalk. "I know we can't continue like this, but I can't walk away either."

Since Tollhausler had never been in a relationship, a question came to mind that, no matter how relevant, still betrayed his ignorance on the subject. "Why do people always want to go out with someone who doesn't want to go out with them?"

"Tollhausler," Rich sighed, "if I could answer that, I'd be the richest, happiest, wisest, most sought after person in the world."

"Ohhh." Tollhausler held the door for him. "I guess it's better if you don't try to figure it out then."

They fell in behind the women who had entered before them. Standing in such close proximity, Tollhausler could now smell the interplay of various perfumes; then, he detected the scent of spearmint gum in the mix, and was suddenly transported back to his high school days. The familiar blend always had this effect, reminding him of the many house parties and dances he had gone to, and with it, came a tingle of excitement.

Four Fraternity Brothers, sporting their finest Lambda Sigma Delta sweatshirts, were seated at a long table blocking the hall, and each had a stack of papers at their elbows. To the far left, a rather stern fellow was coolly regarding those present, and when Tollhausler moved up the line, he stared right through him.

"Name?"

Tollhausler considered for an instant giving the name Amerigo Vespucci, but knew that displaying such frivolity here in the sanctity of the Frat House would not be tolerated.

He told the gentleman his name, and the gentleman took his good sweet time tracking it down in the pages of a large notebook. His index finger eventually came to rest on the line, presumably, where Tollhausler's name had been recorded, and he slid a green paper from under his elbow, stamped it with the date, and reversed it towards him.

"Okay, sign here."

Tollhausler leaned over and skimmed the document.

The paper was, surprisingly, knee-deep in legalese, the gist of which was that the undersigned was indeed who they identified themselves as, and that if it were determined, at a later date, they were in fact lying, any suits filed against Lambda Sigma Delta, herein known as The Fraternity, would be null and void owing to the claimant's misrepresentation of said person. In addition, The Fraternity would not be responsible for any personal items or articles of clothing lost or damaged on the premises.

Tollhausler signed, handed it over, and was then handed a red piece of paper by the mild-mannered frat brother seated next to the stern one.

"Just initial it."

This one basically stated that the undersigned was aware of the fact that there was indeed alcohol on the premises and that he/she was of legal age to consume said alcohol. In the event of an accident, especially one involving a minor, the Fraternity could not be deemed negligent without proof The Fraternity knowingly allowed said minor to misrepresent themselves by signing the proffered contract.

Tollhausler had barely finished signing his initials when the paper was whisked away, checked and filed away with the green one.

The third gentleman was sipping coffee from a mug emblazoned with the fraternity's logo, and he handed Tollhausler a blue page. This one warned the undersigned that they were wholly responsible for any furniture or objects d'art destroyed or defaced by him/her accidentally or with malice aforethought for the duration of their attendance in the house, and that damages could be levied upon those responsible at any given time.

The signed paper was stamped and notarized before Jonathan could ask anybody why a fraternity felt the need to have a notary public on duty in the first place. The last guy handed Tollhausler a yellow sheet. He signed it.

Tollhausler joined Mead. "I didn't fill out that many forms to get into college."

Mead laughed. "Ahhh, the wacky goings-on at the Frat Party."

They stepped out of the short foyer into another hall, and the sounds of music and conversation grew louder. Tollhausler couldn't help feeling the thrill of anticipation as he and Mead hung up their coats. It was his first Frat Party, and he hoped he was ready. Over the years, he had heard a good deal of stories detailing the outrageous pranks perpetrated by fun-loving fraternities, as well as screened a variety of movies celebrating such wacky high-jinks, so he wasn't quite sure what to expect.

However, as they traveled from room to room, Tollhausler's excitement dwindled, and was soon replaced by disappointment. There wasn't really all that much going on out of the ordinary here, as far as he could tell, except for the usual horseplay that ensues when men, women and alcohol are brought together under one roof without supervision. All the drunken flirtations, anachronistic machismo and old jokes were there, but those were the type of things one could find anywhere.

"Is this it?"

Rich understood almost immediately. "Pretty much. Why?"

"I don't know. I guess I was expecting something else."

"It's a little different when you're just a guest," Mead explained.

"Mmmmmm."

"And it's a lot better when you're drunk," he added.

"You mean it all seems a lot less meaningless with a little beer."

"Or a lot. It's free you know."

"I see." Tollhausler appeared skeptical. "So after a belt or two, the people won't seem as insipid, the music won't seem so harsh and I won't be as bored."

"Yep."

"Well you know what I have to say to that, don't you?"

"What?"

"Let's get a drink."

11

The Lambda Sigma Delta House, being no stranger to the beer party, had cunningly situated all the booze its members had corralled that particular afternoon in its recently renovated basement, and two lines of people were impatiently waiting side by side on the stairs, the left side, leading up, smugly spilling beer on the empty-handed people to their right.

Tollhausler and Mead took their place in line, and it took them about ten minutes before they were halfway down the stairs.

"Great system," Richard observed.

Tollhausler nodded. "You can certainly tell it's a Rudyard Fraternity."

"Oh yeah."

Tollhausler noticed that the other line wasn't moving much faster, and was surprised when his line descended three more steps. He leaned against the banister, glanced to his left and his glazed eyes suddenly cleared. He stood up straight. "Diane?"

She went through pretty much the same motions. "J.R.R. Tollhausler?"

They both stepped forward and exchanged silly grins.

"I didn't think I'd ever see you again," Tollhausler blurted out.

Recalling how she had felt earlier that day, she nodded. "I know the feeling. How have you been?"

"Great." He tried to relax. "Had any trouble finding Brady Hall lately?"

Diane smirked. "No, the last couple of weeks it's been right where I've left it."

"What a relief."

Their conversation exhausted, they reverted back to regarding one another with goofy smiles, and eventually remembered they were not alone.

Diane put a hand to her head. "I'm sorry. This is Gus Wills."

"Don't be sorry. I'm sure he's-"

"Gus, this is J.R.R. Tollhausler."

Gus couldn't have cared less. "Hi."

"Please, please," Tollhausler said, a little embarrassed—why had he revealed his pen name to her back in September? "J.R.R. is so formal..."

"And quite a mouthful," she added.

Tollhausler took a breath, grateful that he was in mid-sentence. "....call me Jonathan."

"Okay."

Mead nudged Tollhausler, who promptly winced. "And this jerk trying to cave in my ribs is Richard Mead. Rich, this is Diane Curzewski."

"You remembered my last name," Diane said, impressed.

"Well, it's only fair. You remembered mine."

Gus did not like the way Diane was acting, and decided he had better take a closer look. "Say, aren't you in Hathaway's speech class?"

Mead twisted his mouth. "Noooo."

"He was talking to me," Tollhausler said.

"Are you sure?"

"Well I could be wrong." Tollhausler smiled at Gus. "You were talking to me, weren't you soldier?"

Gus wasn't quite sure they really needed to go over this. "Yes."

"Because I am in a Speech Class taught by a woman named Hathaway," Tollhausler reminded Mead. "And of course, as you have said, you are not."

"He could have been talking to me anyway. I look a lot like other people."

"As do I," Tollhausler returned, "but as I am in the class, I can tell you that there isn't anyone there who even mildly resembles you. So we can safely assume that he was talking to me."

"I sure wish this line would move a little faster," Gus muttered. He took a sip of beer from a blue cup, and tried to see what was going on at the top of the stairs.

"So to answer your question Gus, yes, I am enrolled in Hathaway's Speech Class."

Gus already knew that. "He's that guy who's always making those crazy speeches," he told Diane, and she smiled. "Really? You?"

"Shocking, isn't it?" Tollhausler stared at Gus' camouflage uniform. "And you're that fellow who's always trying to get people to enlist in the Army."

"Yeah, I've given a couple of recruiting speeches this semester," Gus said with pride.

Diane looked from Gus to Tollhausler. "Gus' ROTC Class climbed down Roberts Hall today."

Gus immediately came to life. "You guys come out and watch?"

"I was on the other side of campus," Mead lied.

199

Tollhausler thought that sounded good. "Me too."

"You guys missed a great drill."

Mead decided there was no polite response to a statement like that, and immediately bit his tongue. He had always considered college to be the very antithesis of the Armed Forces, and consequently, had never really understood what the Army was doing there on the Rudyard Campus in the first place. He was equally disturbed by the fact that so many of his classmates were involved with it. How they could stand to be impersonally ordered about by people they didn't know was beyond him.

Of course, after hearing his friends' doubts about the necessity of college, as well as wrestling with his own, he could see how liberating it might be to turn his life over to someone else for a couple of years. After all, a stint in the Army wouldn't last forever, and it would allow him to concentrate on the more important things in life. Like what he was going to do with himself once his hitch was finally up.

"You guys shouldn't feel too bad," Gus continued. "A *lot* of people missed the demonstration this afternoon." He raised an eyebrow at Diane.

"Gus, I told you before, I was in class the *whole time*." Then she looked at Tollhausler and blushed.

"Uh-huh." Gus looked back at the head of the stairs.

Both lines had started moving again.

Diane smiled. "It was good seeing you again."

Tollhausler beamed back. "Same here."

"Wait." She grabbed Tollhausler's arm, and they both stepped out of line. She leaned close, and Tollhausler breathed in her perfume. "Did you *really* dream that you were wearing a red bra?"

Tollhausler was too busy memorizing her face. "What?"

"I mean, you said you dreamt—"

He had to think for a moment, but then he shook his head. "Oh that. No."

"I knew it."

"It was striped."

"Come on," she implored, "did you?"

"I really did. It was red and white. Why?"

Gus called to Diane.

"I'll be *right there*." She looked at Tollhausler, her eyes screaming to be rescued. "I've got to go."

"Well why don't we talk about my dreams some time on campus?"

"That'd be great," Diane said hopefully, and Tollhausler smiled. "I'm, always in the cafeteria. Stop by some time, and I'll tell you anything you want to know."

Diane had been expecting something a little more definite than that, but realized the circumstance, as well as the presence of her boyfriend, didn't allow for much else. She looked in his eyes. "Sure."

They were soon at opposite ends of the staircase, but it was obvious from their backward glances that their thoughts were still very much on each other.

Mead laughed. "Tollhausler, I have *never* seen you that way before in my life."

"Hmm?" Tollhausler's mind was still on Diane.

"Soooo smoooooth. I mean, you didn't insult her once, and you didn't even jump on that straight line she gave you." He snickered. "About J.R.R. Tollhausler being 'quite a mouthful.'"

"Fortunately, I was already talking when she said that. If not, I might have said something I would have regretted."

"Might have?!"

"Okay, okay, I would have *definitely* said something I would have regretted."

Mead was very proud. "I can not believe it. Such restraint. And you were *so nice.*"

Tollhausler blushed. "Look, I don't even know her, okay?"

"Yeah, but you'd like to."

"Welllll…"

Mead laughed. "Jon, man, go after her. She seems great."

"Yeah Rich, except that thing standing next to her wasn't a tree. It was her boyfriend."

"So?"

"What do you mean so? She's not gonna' dump him just like that."

"Jon, did you see the way she was looking at you when she left? If you had asked, I bet she would have dumped him right there on the spot."

"Then he would have dropped me right there on the stairs."

"I bet she'd go out with you if you asked."

"If she comes looking for me in the cafeteria, I will."

"You mean you don't even have her phone number?!"

"Real <u>Seventeen</u> magazine, huh?"

202

"Haven't you learned anything from Mennon and me?"

"Just how to cheat at cards."

"Toll, I don't know if you noticed, but that girl really, really likes you."

"Really?" Tollhausler smiled. He had suspected as much, but, knowing how people tended to delude themselves, he needed the additional confirmation. "Well there isn't much I can do about it right now. I'll just have to hope I run into her again. Then I'll know it was meant to be."

Mead shook his head. "It doesn't work that way Tollhausler. You've got to go after what you want."

"Is that what you're going to do with Holly?"

Mead's enthusiasm quickly dissipated. "That's different. Getting into a relationship is a lot more fun than being in one."

"Oh man." Tollhausler laughed. "Forget about that Business degree. You should be a marriage counselor!"

12

Upon reaching the Lambda Sigma Delta basement, Tollhausler and Mead were greeted by the rumor that some of the Frat Brothers serving as bartenders were randomly dumping pharmaceuticals and psychedelics into the drinks of those people not associated with the fraternity. A story they were inclined to believe since a number of men and women were staggering about the place confused, and some were even laid out on a sofa unconscious. Richard and Jonathan returned to the first floor immediately.

"These frat guys are idiots," Tollhausler announced.

"Keep it down."

"Why? Is it supposed to be a secret?"

"Some people call us idiots Tollhausler."

"Yeah, but these guys are organized. We're not." He looked around. "I get the feeling they're doing half this stuff because they think they have to."

"So?"

"So they might as well be in the Army with Gus."

Mead was about to disagree when something caught his eye across the room. "It's Holly," he announced. "She's here."

Tollhausler tried to spot her through the crowd. "Is she with anybody?"

"I can't tell from here," were Mead's final words as he started after her through the dense forest of swaying party-goers.

"Good luck," Tollhausler called, and a woman stared back at him as if he had two heads. "And good luck to you too Ma'am."

She scowled back. "Leave me alone."

"Ohhhhh-kay," Tollhausler replied. "Gosh, I am having *so much fun*."

He walked off, and, having nothing better to do, planned on spending the rest of the evening watching the band contest. He wasn't exactly in the mood to sit through two or three hours of substandard music, but at least it would give him something to do while waiting for Mennon and Turpin's band.

However, as he worked his way through the thick cordons of deafened, comatose men and women crowding the fraternity's makeshift concert hall, he realized the room had been filled to capacity twenty minutes earlier. Covering his ears from the music blaring overhead, he struggled back out.

Someone scratched his arm.

"Kelly."

She put her hand on his shoulder, and placed her lips to his ear. "Jonathan, I didn't expect to find you here."

"Where *did* you expect to find me?"

"Not here." She smiled. "You don't strike me as the frat party type." She shook her silky brown hair from side to side. "Are you here with anybody?"

Tollhausler didn't think Rich counted. "Not really."

"That's too bad," Kelly purred, but Tollhausler could tell she didn't mean it. She put her hand on his arm. "I was wondering. Would you mind walking me up to the second floor? I have to get something out of my coat—if I can even find it—and I don't like traveling around the place by myself."

Tollhausler figured it would be all right. "Lead the way."

Kelly Mitchell and Tollhausler were both in the same film theory class, and over the last couple of weeks, had worked together on several papers. He was glad to see a friendly face, and happier to get away from all the noise. He rummaged through his many thoughts for the appropriate small talk, and shook something loose.

"Did you start that chapter for Benson yet?"

Kelly's eyes brightened. "I didn't read the last one."

He reached into his pocket for some gum. "Who would have thought a film course could be so dull?"

"I didn't. Benson just has this way of making film boring." She giggled. "It's a gift you know."

205

"Ohhhhh." He flashed her the green pack of chewing gum. "Would you like some?"

"No thank you." She stepped on to the landing. "You wouldn't happen to have any floss, would you?"

"I'm sorry. I gave away my last strand downstairs."

"Awww."

He chewed his gum, and she led him into a dimly lit alcove. She sat down on a windowsill. "Have a seat." He did, and she laid a hand on his knee. "You know Jonathan, I've got to be honest with you. I've brought you here under false pretenses."

"You mean this isn't the second floor?"

"No." She took a deep breath. "You see, there's something very important I'd like to discuss with you."

Tollhausler's head dropped. "Look, you don't have to be so formal. I admit it. I copied a couple sentences from your Eisenstein essay last week, but that was all. I'm sorry. I won't do it again."

"No, no, silly. Nothing like that." Kelly hesitated. "You see, I've wanted to tell you something for some time now."

"Oh? Really?"

13

Unbeknownst to Tollhausler, as the Tide of Fate drew him heedlessly onward, at that very moment, Richard Mead was washing up on its rocky shores.

He was cold, sweating and his clothes were practically falling off his back. Holly lay beside him, in the same condition, and she had an arm slung over his shoulder. He pulled at the gray blanket drawn about his waist, and arranged it across her naked back.

"Thank you," she said, and kissed him.

"Your welcome."

If nothing else, they always tried to be civil to one another. However, in the middle of their frank discussion about their relationship, things had suddenly gotten very confused, and before either one knew it, they were heatedly pressing their nude bodies together in an unbridled display of passion. At least, that was the way Rich was going to tell the story.

Holly was at rest, listening to the light drizzle of rain as it popped and clicked along the car, and her mind was starting to sift through the various questions she hadn't bothered asking before. Had she done the right thing? Did Richard reciprocate her feelings or did he just want her one last time?

She breathed in the scent of his naked body, and realized it didn't matter. The sex had been incredible, and she felt great. She had been distressed by the prospect of their breaking up, and it was pretty obvious that he had been as well.

Still, she was concerned about what he was going to do now that they had made love. He had said a good many things she had wanted to hear, but that was no guarantee he was going to stand by them now. What if he had only said them in order to enjoy her one last time? She stared at him in the dim, angled light, and wondered what he was thinking. Would he renege on everything he had said or stay with her?

She couldn't believe she had put herself in such a vulnerable spot, and became angry--but mostly with herself. "This is crazy."

"Hm?" Mead gently stirred.

Holly pushed herself up. "I said this is crazy."

He smiled. "Yeah."

"Not like that." She kneeled on the seat, and the blanket fell away. "I mean what we're doing. What we just did."

He quickly whistled for his thoughts to return from wherever it was they had perched, and sat up. "What do you mean?"

"What'd we do?"

He was stunned. "Don't you remember?"

"That's the problem. I do." She reached down, and grabbed her bra off the floor. "But shouldn't we have at least talked a little more or tried to work some things out before we did?"

Mead was in no shape to dissect the many emotions and intricacies of what had gone before--he barely understood them himself--and tried to martial his thoughts for the argument he now found himself in the middle of. "Um...I didn't think it was necessary."

"Why?" Holly slid into her bra and hooked it in back. "Doesn't it feel like we're going in a bit of a circle? One minute we're talking about breaking up, the next, we're all over each other."

"Well I'll admit it's a bit unusual, but it isn't *that* unusual either."

"So what was the point?"

Rich pulled a safety belt from under his hip. "The point is that I really care for you and don't want you out of my life."

Holly took great comfort in that, and ran a finger along his thigh. "You did say a lot of sweet things."

"I was pretty worried back there."

"You didn't look it."

Rich frowned. "Well I was. I just didn't show it."

"What if," Holly hypothesized, annoyed, "I decided to go ahead and dump you because of the way you took the news?"

"I would have done what any self-respecting guy does when a cool exterior doesn't work."

"What's that?"

"I would have gotten pathetic and begged you to give me a second chance."

She set her jaw. "What if it was too late by then? What if your stoical acceptance made me think you didn't care? Then what?"

He rearranged the blanket. "Then I would have learned a very valuable lesson."

"See?" Holly retrieved her panties and rolled to her side. "It's that kind of attitude that worries me about you. About us."

"Us?" Rich noticed how fogged up the car windows had gotten. "Come on Holly, neither of us even knew there was an us until about half an hour ago."

"I just have to know that you're going to be serious about this."

"Of course I am." He took her by the hand. "I've been chasing after you haven't I? I called you three times today, right? What else can I do?"

"I don't know." Holly sat upright. "And I know how I must sound, like all your other silly girlfriends, I'm sure, but if we're going to be together, I need to know you're going to work at it. I don't like clichés any more than you do, but I'll be damned if I'm going to waste my time with another hopeless relationship. I've got to know you're going to try."

Unsure of what Holly wanted from him, Rich guessed, and raised his right hand into the air. "I promise that I will date you exclusively, be a good boyfriend and always be there for you."

It in no way approached what she was looking for, but she knew it was a step in the right direction. "I hope so."

He laughed. "I don't seem to recall you being an angel here."

"I didn't think you cared."

"I didn't think *you* cared."

Holly sat back and put an arm behind her head. "I know, but…"

"I mean, you're the one who's been seeing someone else the last couple of weeks, right?"

She thought about it for a second. "Because I didn't see us having anything more than a casual relationship. You don't strike me as the faithful type."

"So you thought you should cheat on me first."

She smiled at him. "Something like that."

"Well do you think we should at least try to make this work? For a little while anyway?"

"Sure, we'll do it on a trial basis. And if one of us gets bored or wants out, we'll end it."

Mead snickered. "It sounds so simple."

Holly laughed. "Doesn't it though?"

14

There was a quick series of knocks, and a green towel fell from a small orange basketball hoop hanging from the middle of the door. Then a red towel slid off the blue backboard as the door slowly opened.

Tollhausler poked his head inside. "Hello?"

"Is it empty," Kelly asked over his shoulder.

"I wish." Tollhausler entered. "This place is a mess."

"I don't think anyone saw us come up here," Kelly reported. She shut the door and locked it. "It's dark in here."

The only light in the room was coming from a partially closed door to their left, and Tollhausler carefully padded over to it. He pushed the door open with his fingertips, and it swung in on a narrow bathroom. "And look it's got all the basic amenities: running water *and* electricity. We'll never have to leave."

"Great." Kelly examined the bed located between her and the bathroom and started clearing it. "I hope nobody minds us using their room."

"I do."

Kelly cleared away more laundry, and Tollhausler walked over to her. She put her arms around him, and they kissed.

"That was very nice Jonathan."

"Thanks."

"And you say you haven't kissed many women before?"

211

"Wellll, a couple of aunts, but they don't count. We weren't dating or anything."

"I'm glad." Kelly sat down. "Come here."

He jumped on the bed, and Kelly hugged him.

"Jonathan, would you do *anything* for me?"

He noticed she had an amazing neck. "You name it."

"Would you fight for me?"

"Of course." He noticed her hair smelled great.

"Would you even…die for me?"

He chortled. "You're not *that* pretty."

Kelly leaned away. "*Jonathan.*"

"I'm sorry." He pulled her back. "I didn't know what I was saying. Why, I must be drunk with love."

She rested her head on his shoulder. "Oh Jonathan, you do care if I live or die."

"Of course. What would I do with the body?"

She looked up. "What?"

"Nothing. Nothing my love." He kissed her forehead. "Ohhh, can't you feel that extra something in the air? Can you feel the electricity?"

"Yes." She bit his neck. "I can."

"You can?" he asked in surprise, and squeezed her tighter. "Ohhh Kelly. Make the world go away." He kissed her shoulder. "Or better yet, we'll go away. That'll make it easier on everyone."

"Oh Jonathan," Kelly whispered passionately, "you're not like the other men I've known."

"Ohhhh yes I am."

"Jonathan. Kiss me."

"All right, but remember, it was your idea."

It was a heated embrace. Kelly moaned. "Oh Jonathan. Take me."

Now, Tollhausler was relatively certain he knew exactly what Kelly meant. However, while he had envisioned this scenario many times before, he was still at a loss as to how he should proceed. He toyed with the idea of throwing off his clothes, and then he thought perhaps it would be better if he started off by removing hers, but as he weighed the pros and cons of each option, he found himself distracted by something he kept trying to ignore there at the back of his mind: his virginity.

Kelly slid her tongue into Tollhausler's ear and he moaned. It occurred to him that he should probably let her in on his little secret, but like a lot of nineteen-year olds, he was slightly embarrassed by it. He was also worried about how Kelly would take the news once she heard it. Would she politely excuse herself, never to be seen again, or would she graciously remain at his side?

Kelly threw a leg over his and started to unbutton his shirt. Swallowing, he decided this was no time for true confessions, and told himself that everything would be fine. He would catch on as they went along.

After all, he reasoned, I have a general idea of the basic mechanics involved, and can still remember most of the instructional material they gave us back in high school. Unfortunately, his frantic rationalizations didn't bring him much comfort. He had told himself the very same things the day he failed his driver's test.

Kelly kissed his chest. "Jonathan, did you ever think of me the way I've thought of you?"

"Of course."

"Did you ever want to kiss me?"

Tollhausler lowered his eyes. "I've wanted to kiss a lot of women."

"Was I one of them?"

"Welllll..." He looked up at the ceiling, as if he were trying to work out the square root of a hundred and seventy-nine in his head. "....now give me a second."

"No." She pushed him down on the bed and kissed him.

Tollhausler rolled her off, and he was suddenly on top of her. "*Kelly*."

She placed her hand on his cheek. "Jonathan..."

"Yes?"

"....be gentle."

"All right," Tollhausler said. "But it isn't going to be any fun *that* way."

15

Seconds later, there was a loud knock on the door, and both Kelly and Jonathan sat up on the bed.

"Oh my God," Kelly whispered. Somebody tried the doorknob, and she jumped to her feet. "I hope it isn't my boyfriend."

Tollhausler frowned. "Boyfriend? You didn't mention anything about a boyfriend."

She sat down on the bed. "Yes I did."

"Well you didn't say anything about him being here."

"I didn't think it was important."

"Up until now I probably would have agreed with you."

Another knock shook the entire door, and an avalanche of shirts and towels slid along the floor. Kelly stood up, and so did Tollhausler.

"How do you know that's his knock?"

"I don't."

"Then what are you getting so upset about?"

"Because with my luck, it's probably him."

Tollhausler frowned. "Well this night is turning into one big farce, isn't it?"

Somebody yelled something in the hall outside, and Kelly started pacing. "This is dreadful."

Tollhausler sat back down on the bed. "You're telling me. Here I thought I was finally going to lose my virginity, and *this* has to happen."

"You're a virgin?!"

"Yep."

Kelly struggled to get a hold of herself. "But you don't act like one."

Tollhausler snickered. "I know. I don't dress like one either. My whole life has been one big lie."

"I didn't mean it like that," she assured him. "It's just a bit of a surprise, that's all. I've never been with a virgin before."

Tollhausler found that interesting. "Really?"

"Yes, but the idea kind of appeals to me. It would have been nice being your first."

Tollhausler ran to the door. "Could you come back in fifteen minutes?"

"No, no!" Kelly's knees buckled. "That's no good. You've got to hide. He'll be drunk, and when he's that way he gets violent."

"I'm not afraid of him," Tollhausler said defiantly. "He can come in here and act anyway he wants." He walked over to a door to his left and opened it. "I'll be hiding in here." He stepped inside, and Kelly swung the door shut. "Wait," Tollhausler said, opening the door, "what are you going to do?"

Kelly looked flustered. "I'm going to run down the fire escape."

"What fire escape?"

"The one that runs down the side of the building."

"That's where I'd put it."

Kelly tried to close the door again, but Tollhausler stopped her. Her face was flushed. "What?!"

"Why don't I run down the fire escape with you?" Kelly expelled an exasperated sigh. "Because if we both run down, he'll follow us, and if you go by yourself, he'll still chase you. This way if I go down alone, he'll come after me, and you'll be able to walk right out of here."

"When will I see you again?"

Someone began pounding on the door, and a hanger clanked across the headboard of the bed.

"In Benson's class." She ran to the window.

"I mean outside of school."

"Oh." She lifted the bottom of the window as high as possible. "Um, well…" She clambered over the windowsill and turned. "….why don't we let things settle for a little while." She started lowering the window from the outside. "That'll give me a

216

chance to clear things up with Pierre, and then we'll take things from there."

Tollhausler was crushed. "I hope it was as good for you as it was for me."

"I'll call you, I promise," she stated as she closed the window.

"But you don't even have my number…"

16

He secreted himself in a bank of empty shirts. He couldn't help feeling somewhat violated, and wondered what had happened. One minute Kelly was telling him about the huge crush she had had on him since the beginning of the semester, punctuating her words with passionate kisses, and the next, she was scrambling out the window as if she had just found out there was a bomb in the room.

It was a very disappointing turn of events.

The sound of knocking grew louder, stopped and then there was a loud crash. Tollhausler took a deep breath, and tried to remain completely still.

"Who the hell is in my room," someone bellowed.

Angry footsteps thumped back and forth across the floor, and the closet door was ripped open. Flashing eyes took a cursory inventory, and the door was violently thrust shut.

Tollhausler pushed into the shirts a little further and exhaled.

"There's somebody on the fire escape," somebody yelled.

"You guys go after them, and I'll see if there's anything missing."

"Right."

A tense silence followed, and Tollhausler could hear someone going through the bureau in the next room. A pinstripe suit shifted to Tollhausler's right.

"Pssst. You're standin' on my foot."

Tollhausler's face fell. "Mennon?!"

"Yeah, and you're still on my foot."

"Sorry." He took a step in the opposite direction. "I didn't expect to run into anybody here."

"Neither did I."

"I bet." Tollhausler was glad to see Mennon, until, of course, he remembered what he had been up to before entering the closet. "Sayyyyyyy, how long have you been in here anyway?"

"Long enough," Mennon said cryptically.

Tollhausler was aghast. "Yes, but you couldn't hear anything in here, right?"

"Don't you worry. With the door closed, I couldn't tell what was goin' on out there."

"Then how do you know there *was* anything going on?"

"Well," Mennon said with a chuckle, "you must have been up to somethin' or you wouldn't be in here hiding right now, would you?"

"Uh-huh." Tollhausler remained unconvinced. "Because that would be a little weird, you being in here and all, while I was out there..." He mumbled something.

"What?"

"I said I don't think I'm ready for an audience yet."

"Tollhausler, what are you talking about?"

His voice went up an octave. "Nothing. Nothing at all."

"Uh-hunh."

It was suddenly very quiet on the other side of the door, and Tollhausler could no longer feel his heart pounding in his ears. Then Mennon snickered. "I can't believe you told her you were a virgin."

Tollhausler scrunched up his face. "Ohhhhhh, well isn't that *just great*."

"Don't you know anything? You never tell the girl you're a virgin. Or you always will be." Mennon sat down on the floor. "Of course, it's okay to tell them that if you aren't."

Perplexed, Tollhausler slowly said, "Tell them I'm a virgin if I'm not."

"Sure. Some girls like virgins."

"I don't think Kelly was one of them."

"Yeah, most girls don't like virgins. They've got enough to worry about without having to worry about *that*."

"Well it isn't like I'm going to stop periodically and take notes." He shrugged. "Not that many anyway."

Mennon grinned. "All in the name of science, right?"

"Sure Science. And I think some other women might benefit from my research as well."

"Well we'll never know, will we? Thanks to you and that big mouth of yours."

Footsteps clunked passed the door, and Tollhausler peeked through the keyhole. "It just slipped out. Besides, isn't it better that she knew?"

"Why?"

"Because then she knew the truth."

"The truth?" Mennon made a noise as he exhaled. "How many times do I gotta' tell you…"

"Shhh."

Mennon started again in a lower voice. "How many times do I gotta' tell you, sex and honesty do *not* go together."

"Is that what you tell all your girlfriends," Tollhausler asked over his shoulder.

"Not in so many words."

"Uh-huh."

"But it's implied."

"That you're lying."

"Hey, they gotta' learn not to trust men some time."

Tollhausler rolled his eyes. "You know, with you and Mead advising me on women, I truly pity the first woman I have a serious relationship with."

"Serious re—" Mennon sputtered. "What the heck do you want with one of *those*?!"

"I couldn't imagine." Tollhausler listened at the door. "All right Johnny, now that we both know what I'm doing here, why don't you tell me what brings you here. You know, so I'll be able to give the therapist as many details about this incident as possible."

"Well that should be obvious." Mennon extended his leg. "I'm hiding."

"Really? Why I thought you were in here picking out an outfit for this evening's performance."

"Nahh." Mennon leaned on a ski boot to his right. "See, there're a couple of guys from Lambda's entertainment committee lookin' for me, and I'd rather not speak with them right now."

"Why?"

"Because they're going to want to know where my band is."

"What's wrong with that?"

"Nothing, except I don't know."

"What?"

"None of them showed."

"Even Ernie?"

"Oh, he showed, sure, but I had to send him out to look for the other guys."

"What do you think happened?"

"Well Toll, my theory is they were abducted by aliens."

Having known more than a little about Mennon's checkered history with bands, he had some trouble accepting this explanation. "Johnny, did it ever occur to you that this is their subtle way of telling you they quit?"

"Yeah," Mennon agreed. "But I just can't believe they'd do something like this."

"Why? You think they were that dedicated?"

"No. I owe them money."

"Oh, well, maybe they're just on strike."

"Either way, they aren't coming." He kicked the wall. "And of all nights for them to do it too. I mean, Toll, we had this contest locked."

"The rest of the bands are that bad?"

"Nooo." Mennon didn't bother complaining about how Tollhausler had phrased the question. "Actually, there are some good ones here tonight."

"But you still thought you could win."

"Sure."

"You mean the contest's fixed."

"Oh yeah."

"Johnny, Johnny, Johnny. I know it might be silly of me to ask, but what are you doing entered in a fixed contest?"

Mennon rubbed his eyes. "Couple of days ago, I got a call from some of the guys I know on Lambda's entertainment committee."

"The guys who you're avoiding right now."

"Yeah, and they asked me if I wanted to make some fast cash."

"And what'd you say?"

Mennon laughed. "What do you think?"

"Oh I know, but I thought you might surprise me."

"Anyway, they told me they wanted me and my band to stop by tonight and play a set."

"And why would they want you to do that?"

"It's a little complicated."

Outside, more feet came stomping into the room, and another angry barrage was unleashed at the fraternity's disrespectful guests.

"Well Johnny," Tollhausler whispered, "it looks like I've got plenty of time."

"Okay." Mennon waved him closer.

And then he told him the whole sordid tale.

Boy did he tell him.

And Tollhausler was suddenly getting to his feet.

"You've got to get out of here."

"How can I? They got all my equipment in a room behind the stage."

"You mean you didn't lose it all in a poker game?"

"Hey, come on. I haven't done that in years. Besides, most of the equipment's borrowed."

"Borrowed?"

"Okay, so some of it was stolen too."

Tollhausler was confused. "What happened to *your* equipment?"

"It blew up."

"What?!"

Mennon stood up. "Tollhausler, do you really want to hear about that right now?"

"No. One disaster at a time." He pressed his ear to the door. "Say, where's your date? Lose her in a crap game?"

"Yeah, I lost her in a crap game." He pushed a shirt from his shoulder. "She didn't come."

"Good, there isn't enough room for three people in here."

"Yeah, she cancelled on me at the last minute. Said she didn't like the way I kept forgetting her name."

"Go figure." Tollhausler put an ear to the door. "What do you think will upset the guys from the Fraternity more: Your band not coming or you're not having their money?"

"Beats me. Which is probably what they'll do the moment they find out."

"I guess they will." Tollhausler adjusted his glasses. "And what have we learned?"

Mennon frowned. "Plenty. And the next time I play a rigged contest, I'm gong to make sure the band knows about it."

"Ah, I'm so proud."

Mennon took off his hat. "Yeah, but I still have to figure a way of getting my equipment out of here."

"Do you really have to leave with the equipment you came with? I mean, it isn't really yours."

"I can avoid these fraternity clowns for a while, but I can't dodge the people I got the equipment from."

"Well," Tollhausler began reluctantly, "maybe me and Mead could smuggle it out before anyone notices."

"That's a great idea." Johnny replaced his cap. "'Course, you guys don't look much like musicians."

"We will with a couple of guitars in our hands."

Johnny grinned. "So you do know something about the music business."

17

Tollhausler still couldn't hear anything on the other side of the door. "You think they're going to come back?"

"I don't know. Why don't you go out and take a look around?"

Tollhausler frowned. "Why don't you?"

"You're closer to the door."

"Not in spirit."

"All right, let's flip for it." Mennon's body arched as he reached into his pocket and pulled out a coin. "Call it." He shot the silver coin into the air.

"Heads," Tollhausler guessed.

The quarter hit the low ceiling, pinged off the shelf above and dropped into one of the shoes lining the closet.

"I win," Mennon announced.

"What do you mean? You don't even know which side of the coin landed up."

"Sure I do. It's a trick quarter."

Tollhausler crossed his arms. "Then it doesn't count."

"Yes it does."

"No it doesn't."

"Why?"

"Because you're trying to pull a fast one."

"But you wouldn't have known that if I hadn't told you."

"So?"

"So you should let me win because I was honest about cheating."

Tollhausler shoved Mennon out into the room.

Johnny knocked on the door and Tollhausler popped into view. "Yeah?"

"What if Kelly's boyfriend thinks I was the one who was in here with her?"

Tollhausler clapped a hand to Johnny's shoulder. "I'll know in my heart it's a dirty lie." He disappeared.

"That guy," Mennon grumbled, "I ought to leave him in there the rest of the night." He pushed his cap to the back of his head, and examined the place. "It sure looks clear to me."

Suddenly, there was a quick succession of knocks, the door opened and Mennon dove under the bed. Four feet entered the room.

"Is there anybody in here?" a woman's voice asked, and Mennon wondered if he should answer.

"Todd, lock the door."

"Yes Jane." There was a series of clicks, and Todd sighed in exasperation. "The lock doesn't work. The door's busted."

"Oh well," Jane's voice responded. "We'll just have to hope nobody comes in."

The bed springs quivered over Mennon's head, and he tried to imagine how the night could possibly get any worse.

"Oh Jane, I've waited so long for this."

"It's been too long Todd."

A pair of empty red shoes tumbled to the floor, and Mennon decided that, despite his growing curiosity, it was time for him to leave. His right shoulder dipped as he extended his left hand, and he slid along the dusty rug on his stomach.

That was when a resounding boom shook the door to its hinges. Bare feet and a single sneaker swung into view about an inch away from Mennon's nose, and he carefully backed up.

"You don't think," Todd began breathlessly.

"Yes I do. He probably had that creep Jack watching me."

"I've got to hide."

"Right," Jane said, and she pressed her way back into her red heels. "Quick, under the bed."

Mennon didn't think that was such a good idea, and fortunately, neither did Todd.

"That's the first place he'll look."

Another thud vibrated from the center of the door.

"The bathroom! Quick!"

Todd's sneakers circled the bed and were soon out of sight behind the bathroom door.

The other door opened up, and Mennon stared helplessly as a pair of cowboy boots entered the room.

"Jane," someone said.

"Stack," she replied, "what are you doing here?"

"Looking for you. What are *you* doing in here?"

"I had to get away from that loud music for a while. It was giving me a headache."

"My friend Jack said he thought he saw you come up here with a guy."

"What?"

The boots sauntered over the carpet. "Yep, he said you met some guy in a red sweater by the kitchen, and the two of you came up here."

"Well he was mistaken. I'm alone."

"You weren't with someone."

"No," she answered. "And even if I was, do you think I'd be doing anything in here with the door unlocked?"

"I guess not. But I did hear voices."

"I don't see how," she said testily. "I'm in here by myself."

"I see that."

The polished cowboy boots carefully made their way to the other side of the bed, and Mennon realized he was holding his breath. Who he was holding it for, Todd or himself, he couldn't say.

Then, Stack dropped to the floor

"Stack, what are you—"

"Well look at what we got here."

"What?" The bedsprings squeaked, and tresses of flaming red hair swung past Stack. Jane's face tightened as her blue eyes settled on Mennon. "What is this?! Do you have more than one person spying on me?"

Stunned by her reaction, Stack started to shake his head.

She hopped off the bed. "Because I don't think you have the right to be doing any such thing. How sick can you get?"

Stack got to his feet. "Jane, I don't have anybody following you. I don't even know this guy." He knelt beside the bed. "*What* were you doing under there buddy?"

"Not a whole heck of a lot," Mennon said. "There isn't much you can do under a bed by yourself."

Stack's ears flushed red, and he reached for Mennon. "Get out of there." Mennon sprang in the opposite direction, and Stack grabbed one of his ankles. "Come here!" He caught hold of Mennon's other ankle and pulled.

Mennon rolled to his back, and latched on to the underside of the bed with both hands. "Oh no, I'm stayin' right where I am." The bed slid across the floor.

"Oh my God," Jane said.

Tollhausler guessed that if he was going to get out of there, there probably wasn't going to be a better time, and slithered out of the closet. He started across the carpet on all fours.

"Come on you idiot," Stack said through gritted teeth.

228

Mennon shook his head. "You don't scare me."

"Then come out from under there."

"Okay, so maybe I'm a little afraid."

Jane didn't know what to do.

"Grrr." Stack yanked Mennon's legs again, and the bed slid along the floor a little further. He could now see Tollhausler, and he released Mennon's ankles. "Who the hell are you?!"

Jane gaped at Tollhausler, who was now about five feet from the door.

He smiled. "Hi."

Jane gazed uncertainly about the room. "How many people are in here?"

Stack bolted on to the bed and landed between Tollhausler and the door. "I didn't hear you come in."

Tollhausler was already on his feet. "That's all right, I'll make a lot more noise on the way out." He tried to walk past Stack.

Stack spun him around. "You aren't going anywhere until after I punch your lights out."

Tollhausler's eyebrows went up. "Is that a threat?"

"No. More like a promise."

"You don't have to promise him anything," Mennon said from the floor. "He trusts you."

"Shut up." Stack glared at Tollhausler. "But I am gonna' show you how you shouldn't be playing around with other people's girls."

Jane ran over to Stack. "But he wasn't in here with me."

"Sure," Stack said skeptically.

"He wasn't."

"Well he is now," Stack answered.

"Wait a minute Stack." Tollhausler didn't bother stopping to wonder if that was the guy's first or last name. "Would it make you feel better if I told you that she didn't enjoy one minute of it?"

"No."

Tollhausler shrugged. "Well I guess there's no point in me lying then."

Stack's ears flattened against his skull. "Why you—" His left arm became rigid, holding Jonathan at arm's length and he pulled his right arm back to swing.

Tollhausler tossed his glasses to Mennon and Jane cringed.

However, before Stack could throw his punch, the door to the room was suddenly flung wide, and clipped Tollhausler on the back of the head.

18

The next thing Tollhausler knew, two ROTC Cadets were carrying him by the arms and legs across the roof of Roberts Hall. They didn't seem too concerned about his comfort, and, reaching the edge, they bundled him over the side.

A human ladder, comprised of other ROTC Cadets, was waiting there for him, and, being handed from one cadet to the other, he traveled from the top of the multi-limbed ladder to the bottom in seemingly one motion.

He wasn't overcome by panic, however, until after he had heard Diane Curzewski call his name from above. She had also been lowered over the side of the building, only she was stalled halfway.

The cadet there apparently refused to send her down the line. It was only after Tollhausler started shouting that he was able to identify the cadet: it was Gus.

19

He sat up.

Unfortunately, he did this without knowing where he was or what was around, and smashed his head into a cymbal. The odd crash immediately drew the attention of everyone, Frat Brothers and musicians alike, who had heard it, so they were watching a second later when the cymbal and its stand toppled over like a felled tree.

Tollhausler put a hand on top of his head. "Owww."

"Hi Toll. How's everything?"

He opened his eyes. "Can't complain Rich. How's about yourself?"

"Ohhhh, you know." He returned Tollhausler's glasses.

"Good. Good." He slid them on and noticed someone standing next to Rich. "Hi Holly."

She appeared to be very concerned. "Are you all right?"

Mead smiled. "It'll take more than a couple of blows to the head to hurt him."

Tollhausler gently fingered a lump on the back of his head. "It's a pretty good start though."

In the next room, two guitars, a saxophone and the usual complement of drums awkwardly launched into what some people would have categorized, in the most general sense of the word, a song.

Tollhausler held his throbbing head and closed his eyes. "Where am I?"

"In a room next to the stage."

That's what it sounded like to him. "How did I get here?"

"A couple of guys from the frat brought you down."

"Oh." Jonathan considered that for a couple of seconds, but something didn't seem quite right. "Why would they bring me here? To the band room?"

"That's a very good question. To which I actually have the answer." Mead sat next to him on the floor. "Because Johnny told them you were in his band."

Tollhausler's eyes widened. "What?"

"Yeah, and they want everyone from Johnny's band to stay in this room. We're apparently about to go on."

"We're--?"

"Oh yeah. Didn't you know? I'm in the band too."

"Mennon told them you were...too?"

"Yeah. He told me you'd be able to explain why." He stood up. "Imagine my surprise when we came back and found you unconscious."

"Mmm—yes. Help me up."

Rich pulled Tollhausler to his feet. "How's the head?"

"It feels like a soccer ball does after a goal."

"All right. Now, why are we here?"

Tollhausler brushed himself off. "You remember when Mennon promised us he wasn't going to get us involved in any more of his schemes?"

"Yes."

"Well he lied."

Mead rolled his eyes. "Toll, I already figured that out. What is it this time?"

Tollhausler scanned the surrounding area, and dropped his voice. "The contest's a fake."

"Ohhh."

Holly didn't understand. It looked genuine enough to her.

"Yep. All the sound and fury's for nothing. Mennon's taking home the prize tonight whether he deserves it or not. The fix's in."

"And he's introducing us to everybody as his band…?"

"Because his band hasn't arrived yet."

"Are they going to?"

"Sure. They should be showing up right about the same time that pigs fly."

Mead groaned. "Something tells me I should have kept up with those piano lessons."

Holly was shocked. "You mean he would actually get you guys involved with something like this?"

"Him or Tollhausler," Mead said in disgust. "It's a wonder I've lived this long knowing both of them."

"Hey," Tollhausler protested. "I didn't have anything to do with this."

"That's what you said the night we got caught in that street brawl in Juniata."

"How many times do I have to tell you? I had nothing to do with that!"

"No, nothing at all." Mead looked at Holly. "One minute, it was a nice, quiet party with everyone sitting around talking and drinking, the next, it was a free-for-all in the street. But he didn't have anything to do with it."

"What did you do?" Holly asked in horror.

Tollhausler shrugged. "Nothing. All I did was proposition some woman. How was I supposed to know she was some tough guy's girlfriend?"

Mead exhaled. "Because she'd been telling you about him all night." He suddenly wondered if Mennon was even still in the building and took Holly by the hand. "You've got to get out of here."

"No. I want to stay. I'm not going to abandon you at a time like this."

"Thanks." He gave her a peck on the cheek.

"And what instrument do you play Holly?"

"Shut up Tollhausler."

"That's it Rich. You're out of the band."

"Heyyyyy," Mennon called from across the room. "You can't do that. Only the leader can say who's in or out."

"No, no, no," Mead sang. "I know when I'm not wanted."

"Oh noooo. You aren't getting' away that easily." Mennon smiled at Tollhausler. "How was your nap?"

"I'll let you know as soon as I wake up."

234

"Hi Holly."

"Hi."

Turpin walked over with a guitar case in each hand, and Mead nodded. "How are you Ernie?"

He scowled. "What?! Are you kidding me?" He set the cases down.

"I don't think I am," Mead told Tollhausler.

"You don't sound very sure."

"I'm not. I know what a rascal I can be."

Ernie handed Tollhausler a bass. "Take this."

A tall, burly fellow in a green sweatshirt with a wide black L stitched across the front walked right up to Mennon. "Johnny," he said, scowling, "You better be ready to go on. This band's set is just about over."

"Great Art." He studied the jumble of equipment he had managed to collect that afternoon, and wondered if it would even all work together. "Do you have somebody helping the bands get their equipment on stage?"

"Didn't you hear? Oh that's right, you were *missing*. It was taking too much time for each band to set up and break it all down again, so we asked one of the bands if the rest of the contestants could use their equipment. Everyone's been using the same sound system for the last couple hours now. All your band's gonna' need to do is go up there and plug in."

Mennon was motionless for a moment, and then a smile slowly spread across his face. "Great news. We'll be right out."

Art cracked his knuckles. "You'd better be."

Tollhausler, Turpin and Mead instinctively circled round and waited. Holly joined them.

"You guys get on stage," Mennon said from a far off place.

"And what are you going to be doing?"

Mennon wandered off as if in a dream. "Sorry Rich, I ain't got time to talk. I gotta' remember something someone showed me last night. Fast."

20

Feeling a little like Louis XVI, right before the guillotine separated him from church and state, Tollhausler did his best to ignore the barrage of jeers and catcalls being hurled his way as he started across the stage. He was surprised to feel the boards dip beneath his feet. Broken glass crunched under his shoes, and he could now see the audience.

The menacing hordes were in various states of inebriation, and quite a few of them looked angry. What had put them in this surly mood was a mystery to him, but Tollhausler got the feeling they were ready to take it out on him anyway.

Turpin adjusted the microphone for him, and plugged a cord into the bass. "Ready my son?"

Tollhausler looked a little pale, and Turpin patted him on the shoulder. "Don't worry. They're more afraid of you than you are of them."

"Oh shut up."

"Okay, okay. Let's have a look at you." Turpin studied him. "Say, could you at least put that on and act like you're going to play it?"

"Why?" Tollhausler lifted the strap over his head and hung the bass on his left shoulder. "I'm not."

"They don't know that."

"Ohhh, right. So what should I do?"

Ernie's eyebrows dipped. "Come on. You've watched us set up a hundred times. Fake it."

Tollhausler gave it some thought and nodded. "Right." He tapped the microphone. "One, two," he said in a mechanical voice. "One, two."

Ernie was perplexed. "Is that all we do when we set up?"

"That's what it looks like to me."

"Never mind." Turpin was insulted. "You'll do fine."

He strolled back to the drums, and advised Mead along similar lines.

Mennon appeared from behind a huge column of speakers with his keyboard, waved at some Frat Brothers in the audience, and moved across stage.

Tollhausler turned. "Where were you?"

"Just making a couple of adjustments to the sound board." Mennon set his case down and kneeled beside it. He jumped up. "Ugh. What is that, beer?"

"You'd better hope so."

"I can't believe they're encouraging people to throw bottles at the stage between bands."

"Wait'll they hear us play. They'll be throwing everything they can get their hands on."

Mennon plugged a cord into his keyboard. "What are you talking about? You know how to play the guitar."

"This is a bass."

237

"Then it should be even simpler. It's got less strings." Mennon set his keyboard stand up a little behind Tollhausler. "Look, when I count four, just make sure you hit the bottom string, all right?"

"Johnny—"

"Then run." He laid his keyboard on the stand. "But before you do, make sure you grab some equipment."

"You've got a plan."

"Of course I've got a plan." He slapped Tollhausler on the back. "I've always got a plan, don't I?"

"No."

"Well I do tonight." He sat down. "We set?"

Ernie looked up from his guitar and gave him a thumb's up.

The entire stage began to bounce up and down, and a tall, good-looking fellow came charging to the front of the stage. "Excuse me," he said to Tollhausler, and slid the microphone out from under his nose. He grinned at the audience. "And how is *everyone doing*?!" he yelled. The various replies merged into one, loud, indecipherable growl.

"Great!!!" He jumped to the other side of the stage. "For those of you who may have just joined us or just sobered up. Or are coming down--you know who you are--I'm Rock Pitchikowski, and I'm your M.C. for tonight. By the way, I just want you all to know how lucky you are to have me here. I should be over in the library writing a paper, but with midterms right around the corner and a certain sorority girl backstage, I knew there was only one thing I could do." He leaned over the crowd. "Party!!!"

Everyone in the audience started thrashing about. "Yeahhhhhhh!!!"

Rock blew a kiss. "I love you people! And does Lambda Sigma Delta know how to throw a party or *what?!!!*"

Tollhausler frowned at Mennon. "Is this guy for real?"

"Hey be nice. He's workin' the crowd for us. He's gonna' give us a great introduction."

Seeing that everyone in Mennon's band was in place, Pitchikowski began to wrap it up. "As you can plainly see, we're ready for the next band, and the Lambda House has got a real treat for you. Heyyyy mister, put that bottle down! House rules say you aren't allowed to throw anything at the band until *after* they've played their first song. Then *chuck at will!!*"

The crowd howled in merriment, and Tollhausler toyed with the idea of kicking Rock off the stage.

"I guarantee you've never heard anything like this band before, and once you do, you're not gonna' want to hear anyone else. So get ready for a head-on collision with rock and roll! Get ready for a hit and run beat! Get ready to be totaled by a kick ass band!" He shoved the microphone back into its stand. "Ladies and gentlemen, freaks and animals, Lambda Sigma Delta proudly presents..." he extended his arm. "....Beat Poets."

Rock dashed off.

"All right you guys," Mennon said confidently. He had taken the precaution of praying during the final part of their intro. "On four. A one-a and a two-a. One two three *four!*"

Tollhausler, Turpin and Mennon simultaneously hit their instruments, and a horribly loud, unpleasant mix of ear-shattering feedback and what could only be described as a humming, electronic belch vibrated through the entire house shaking it to its very foundation.

Then the stage collapsed.

21

After what had seemed like an eternity, somebody pulled a large, shattered plank from over Tollhausler's face, and Johnny Mennon smiled down through a cloud of smoke.

"Ah, he looks fine."

Tollhausler took a wheezing breath and coughed out a splinter. "Why didn't you tell us you were going to blow up the stage?"

"What're you talkin' about? I did no such thing." He winked. "Not directly anyway."

Turpin, Mennon and Mead cleared away a few more boards, and Tollhausler looked around the room. It had been cleared except for one or two people. "Hi Holly."

Once again, Holly looked upon the prostrate Tollhausler with a very worried expression on her face. "Hi."

Mennon slid the bass from Tollhausler's chest. "Oh hooo Tollhausler, am I ever glad you're okay."

"That flashlight's right in my eyes."

"Oh. Sorry." Mennon giggled.

"You're pretty cheerful for someone who's about to get their fingers broke."

"These guys ain't gonna' break nothin' . They love me."

Tollhausler slowly curled himself into a sitting position. "How's that?"

"We delivered exactly what they wanted."

Mead laughed. "What he's trying to say is, we won the contest."

It took a moment for Mead's words to register, but when they did, all Tollhausler could do was shake his head. "Of course we did. The contest was fixed."

Mead offered Tollhausler a hand. "Yeah, but the audience was in complete agreement. They loved us."

Tollhausler took Mead's hand. "How?"

"Who cares?" Mennon grabbed Tollhausler's other arm. "We won."

"But…"

They got him to his feet.

"….we didn't play a single song."

Mennon laughed. "Don't trouble yourself, Toll. See, the first bunch of bands were all playin' songs and stuff, you know covers and original songs with melodies and lyrics and such, but after a while, these kids, well they're kinda' drunk, and they got bored with all that. They were lookin' for somethin' a little more interesting. You know, a show. So when we went up there, and hit that loud, atrocious-sounding, heart-punching chord and the stage disintegrated, it got their attention."

"Along with the falling debris."

"Sure, but when it came down to it, our sound was so…so…" Mennon searched for just the right word.

"Obnoxious," Turpin suggested.

"Yeah, it was so obnoxious, the judges knew they could make us the winner and no one in any of the other bands or the audience would kick about it."

Tollhausler shook his head. "Mennon, how the hell do you do it?"

Johnny laughed. "It's a crazy business." He chuckled. "A couple of these kids even asked if we have a recording of that sound."

"Really?"

"Yeah, they think we're some kind of ground-breaking punk band."

"Stage-breaking."

"That too."

Tollhausler noticed his shirt was torn. "So when do we go on tour?"

Mennon leaned closer. "As soon as the guys who own this equipment find out it's trashed."

NOVEMBER 2,
1983:
MIDTERMS

POP QUIZ : MIDTERMS

INSTRUCTIONS: Please read the following questions very carefully, and on the lines provided, please write the letter of the statement that you think best answers each one.

The answers follow on page 386.

(1) In Chapter 7 of the previous section, Tollhausler told Mennon, Turpin and Mead that he would decide whether or not he would stay at Rudyard after midterms. Knowing that, how do you think he prepared for his first exam?

———————

(a) Being up to date on the assigned readings, all Tollhausler really had to do was go over his notes; brush up on the chronology of certain historical events and make sure he understood their ramifications. He turned in early.

(b) Tollhausler locked himself in a room with his History of Broadcasting textbook, and after catching up on those chapters he hadn't already read, he carefully reviewed his notes. Then he made sure he got a good night's sleep to ensure that he would be nice and fresh for the next day's challenge.

(c) Woefully behind on the chapters he was supposed to have read, Tollhausler spent the night before desperately skimming through the narrow print of his wide textbook, and about 3:30 AM, he started racing through his notes. He dropped off about 4:15.

(d) Tollhausler would have liked nothing better than to have spent the evening before buried under the poorly-written, fact-clogged pages of his History of Broadcasting textbook, however, on the way to his room, armed only with a cup of coffee and 3 oatmeal-raisin cookies, he noticed that one of his favorite movies, *Casablanca*, was playing on TV. Making a mental note to begin his studies as soon as the credits rolled, he joined his father and watched the movie.

(e) None of the above.

(2) Tollhausler was dismayed as soon as Professor Von Steimetz' midterm hit his desk. Why? _____

    (a) He could tell at a glance that it was going to be a very challenging test, despite his careful preparation.

    (b) He didn't think his classmates were ready for the many in-depth questions.

    (c) Sadly, it landed on his pet spider Maximilian, and brought an abrupt end to the young arachnid's life.

    (d) Because for some insane reason, he had spent more time watching *Casablanca* the previous night than studying.

    (e) None of the above.

(3) 40 grueling minutes later, it became painfully obvious to Tollhausler that he had completed all the exam questions he was going to that morning. Unfortunately, it was equally clear that there were still more questions left unanswered on the page than had been answered. What do you think he did next? _____

    (a) Like any good student would in this situation, he reread the questions to see if perhaps he could recall more of the information he had painstakingly reviewed the night before.

    (b) Admitting defeat, he simply handed in his incomplete test, and promised himself that he would study much harder for the course's final.

(c) He performed one of the dirtiest tricks known to academia. Erasing his name at the top of his computer sheet, he handed it in at the exact moment that one of his classmates was handing in theirs, and acted as if he was going to leave. However, on the way out, he went up to his teacher, Professor Hermione Von Steimetz, and explained to her how he had just remembered an answer. He asked, no, begged, her if he could have his test back, and, moved by Tollhausler's heartfelt plea, the trusting Von Steimetz said it would be all right. He then made his move. Sliding another student's answer sheet from the pile, he went over to a desk and, fighting back his loud, maniacal laughter, erased the name at the top, as well as the social security number. He then filled in his own name and number.

(d) What else could he do? Tollhausler didn't want to have to take the course a 2nd time, and he would have done pretty much anything, short of cutting off a finger, to pass Von Steimetz' exam. He cheated.

(e) None of the above.

(4) Rudyard University's policy on students caught cheating during a major exam clearly states that those students will receive a failing grade for the semester and repeat the course at a later date. If Tollhausler got caught cheating, what do you think he would do? _____

(a) Tollhausler would never get caught cheating.

(b) He would admit his mistake, and accept whatever punishment such a violation warranted.

(c) With his back up against it, Tollhausler would probably do something drastic, like leap up from his desk, drop to one knee and propose to his teacher, Professor Hermione Von Steimetz, hoping she wouldn't have the heart to flunk her own fiancée.

(d) Tollhausler would beg and whine, and make a general nuisance of himself until his teacher had no other choice but to forgive him for this terrible breach of student ethics. He would then resume the test.

(e) None of the above.

(5) Earlier that semester, it had been decided by the Economics Department, in conjunction with the Rudyard Administration, in association with Professors Buckles, O'Hanrahan & Scher, that it would make more sense if all the Economics 251 classes took their midterms at the same time. There were nine sections in all, and even though they fit rather snugly in the curved, carpeted rows lining Ziegler Theater, a wide, football field of an auditorium situated at the back of Tyson Hall, there were still complaints. Some people claimed that it was a flagrant attempt to cut corners at the expense of the students. However, the university maintained that they were not doing it to save money. Why did they do it then? _____

(a) The university did it in order to maximize the amount of time available to students for particularly difficult exams.

(b) Some departments, like the Economics Department, administered standardized tests at the middle of the semester and at the end, and to curtail incidents of cheating, i.e. stolen exams, they

249

were forced to schedule as many sections together as possible.

(c) To save money.

(d) To get the college's name into the <u>Guinness Book of World Records</u> for bringing together so many students in one place for an exam.

(e) None of the above.

(6) The Economics 251 examination was much more challenging than anyone could have possibly imagined that morning. How did the assembled students display their feelings of frustration? _____

(a) Some students' hands shook while they read over the exam.

(b) Many students drummed their fingers on their desks or tapped their feet on the floor.

(c) A select few threw things at the Graduate Assistants proctoring the exam.

(d) Almost 1 out of every 5 students snapped their pencils in two either in their hands or with their teeth.

(e) All of the above.

(7) As Richard Mead fought his way through the obstacle course of questions crowding the pages of his Economics 251 midterm, a quiet argument broke out between 2 classmates seated behind him about the correct formula for determining something called the Price Elasticity of Supply or Demand. Why did he find it so disturbing? _____

(a) He didn't think it was right for them to be having a discussion like this during a major exam.

(b) It appeared that a lot of people were perplexed by the many intricate questions on the test.

(c) At first, he didn't know it was his classmates who were speaking, and he always found it disturbing when he thought he heard voices in his head.

(d) Because Rich needed the formula just as much as they did, but couldn't decide which of them was right.

(e) None of the above.

(8) Which one of the following is the correct formula for determining price elasticity of supply or demand?

————————

(a)

$$E = \frac{\text{Percentage change in price before quantity shift}}{\text{Percentage change in price after quantity shift}}$$

(b)

$$E = \frac{\text{Percentage change in price \& quantity before}}{\text{Percentage change in price \& quantity after}}$$

(c)

$$E = \frac{\text{Percentage change in price before \& after}}{\text{Percentage change in quantity before \& after}}$$

(d)

$$E = \frac{\text{Percentage change in quantity before \& after}}{\text{Percentage change in price before \& after}}$$

(e)

None of the above

(9) Richard Mead became quite upset when he heard that one of his classmates was planning on slipping across the aisle in order to copy off of another student's paper. Why? _____

(a) He was greatly distressed by the idea that one of his classmates would cheat on the test.

(b) He was faced with the dilemma of whether or not he should turn the misguided young woman in.

(c) Because his classmate needed someone to create a diversion to occupy the 6 Grad Students monitoring the exam, and Holly had volunteered Rich for the job.

(d) Because he wanted to go and get the answers himself.

(e) None of the above.

(10) Since the onset of the semester, Ernie Turpin had been frequently warned about the exams his teacher, Roger Van Vandehorne, gave to his Survey of European Art 195 classes. When do you think he began preparing for Van Vandehorne's exam? _____

(a) Working from a schedule of his own devising, Ernie began his preparations over 3 weeks in advance: poring over the course's 4 textbooks, reviewing the copious amount of notes he had

taken on his teacher's verbose lectures and
organizing study groups on the weekends with his
classmates.

(b) He began his studies days ahead of time, and
comfortably finished his review the night before
the exam.

(c) Ernie began the previous afternoon, and after
ingesting 3 pots of coffee, 2 dozen donuts, a half-
cooked hamburger, 12 cold French fries, a small
pickle, 4 chocolate chip cookies, a glass of milk and
a stalk of celery—not in that order—he felt certain
that he would be too ill to take Van Vandehorne's
exam.

(d) Like Tollhausler, Ernie had left everything until
the last minute, but he wasn't going to let a little
thing like his not studying affect his grade. Writing
frantically, he transferred all the necessary
information on to a dozen slips of lined paper, and
taped them to his body the following morning.

(e) None of the above.

(11) As Ernie sat there with Van Vandehorne's 7-page,
leather-bound midterm in his hands, he couldn't help
feeling somewhat upset. Why was he in such a state?
————————

(a) It had started raining earlier, and he'd left his
house without an umbrella.

(b) The rain that morning had slowed him down, and
he had to chase his bus for 2 blocks.

(c) Due to the weather, the bus Ernie was on had
progressively fallen further and further behind

schedule, and he had wound up arriving 15 minutes late for Van Vandehorne's exam.

(d) Because after reaching for one of the cheat sheets he had affixed to his body, he was surprised to find that the ink he had used was smeared across the page. A quick inventory of the other sheets showed that the rain had destroyed them as well.

(e) All of the above.

(12) Obviously, Ernie felt that he was in a rather bad spot. What do you think he would do next? _____

(a) He would vow to begin his preparations for Van Vandehorne's Final much earlier.

(b) He would slyly open his guitar case and, when no one was looking, climb in.

(c) Close his eyes and form a psychic link with one of the class' brightest students, Rosemary Kentner. He would then proceed to copy her answers down as she wrote them on the page.

(d) Ernie would run out of the room while the proctor's back was turned.

(e) None of the above.

(13) If Ernie would have actually left the room, which route do you think he would have taken? (Please choose one of the diagrams on the following pages.) _____

254

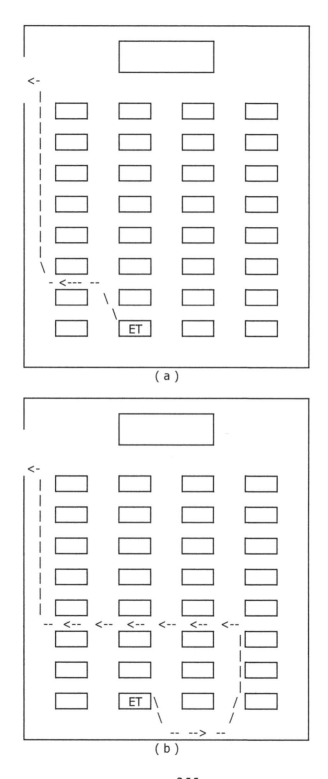

(a)

(b)

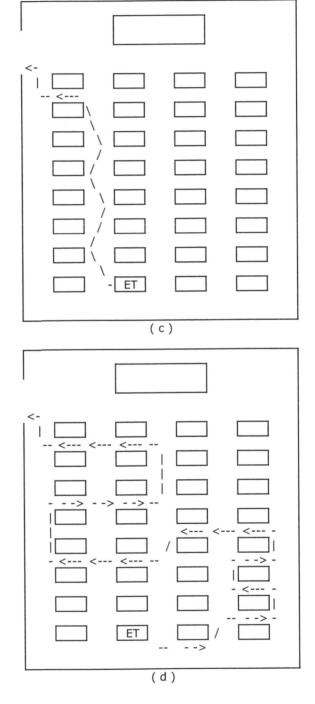

(c)

(d)

(14) Tollhausler had 2 midterms that morning, and the 2nd was for his Speech 101 class. Like his classmates, he was expected to give a 6-minute presentation on the topic of his choice, and when he was called upon, he walked to the front of the room and began. However, as Tollhausler proceeded, he did so in a very erratic manner. Why?

_____

(a) He was still a little nervous about talking to a roomful of people.

(b) The topic he had chosen was very interesting, and he was having trouble concealing his excitement about it.

(c) As he continued, it became quite apparent that except for the introduction, he was repeating most of the Gettysburg Address.

(d) Because in between watching *Casablanca* and worrying about his History of Broadcasting exam, he had completely forgot about this exam and was making his presentation up, all 6 minutes of it, as he went along.

(e) None of the above.

(15) Halfway through Tollhausler's speech, he found it necessary to pause for a brief instant. Why? _____

(a) His mouth had gone dry, and he needed to take a second or two to regain his voice.

(b) Much to his chagrin, he had lost his train of thought and had to quickly backtrack in order to locate the theme of his speech.

(c)   In an eerie twist, Tollhausler had suddenly become dizzy, and there, materializing at the back of the classroom, he saw the Four Horsemen of the Apocalypse. But they were not alone. They stood shoulder to shoulder with their terrifying cousins: The Seven Dentists of Armageddon--and their Dry Cleaners.

(d)   Because Ernie Turpin had come bursting into the room, and asked him who the father of the Impressionist Revolution was.

(e)   None of the above.

(16) Sitting down at his desk, Tollhausler felt relatively certain that his presentation had gone quite well. There was only one thing he wished he hadn't done during the course of his speech. What was it? _____

(a)   He didn't substantiate the crux of his argument with enough numbers.

(b)   He had quoted a statistic incorrectly.

(c)   He supposed it would have made more sense for him to chew the tobacco *after* his speech.

(d)   Towards the end, he had started giggling and blurted out, "I can't believe I'm going to get away with this."

(e)   None of the above.

(17) Knowing how obstinate his teacher, Lyle G. Adams, was being about what he expected from him as a student,

Johnny Mennon had decided that it would be in his best interests if he actually studied for Adams' midterm. If so, then what was it that Johnny felt he had to discuss with his teacher before the test? _____

    (a)   Obviously, Johnny wanted to talk about the ramifications of the Constitutional Union Party nominating John Bell of Tennessee for President in 1860.

    (b)   Johnny merely wished to thank his teacher for helping him see the light by making him study.

    (c)   Mennon felt it was important that he explain to his teacher why he had brought a date.

    (d)   Johnny felt compelled to explain why representatives of the FBI, CIA and the DEA were about to come crashing into the room.

    (e)   None of the above.

(18) When Johnny was finally ready for the test, Professor Adams informed him he would be taking his exam in a desk situated all the way at the front of the room. Why do you think Mennon's first reaction was one of disappointment?

_____

    (a)   Mennon was distressed to see how compromised their student-teacher relationship had become, and couldn't help feeling that he was partially to blame.

    (b)   Johnny felt he was being singled out from the rest of the class because Adams didn't like him.

    (c)   Because the day before he had spent over an hour writing answers on another desk.

(d) It didn't look like there was any place for his date to sit.

(e) None of the above.

(19) Knowing he was going to study for Adams' midterm, Johnny had made a harmless wager or two with some of his classmates about how he was going to do on the test. What kind of odds do you think he gave them?
_____

(a) 2 to 1

(b) 3 to 1

(c) 15 to 1

(d) 67 to 1

(e) None of the above.

(20) Do you think Mennon would have revealed that he intended on studying for the test? _____

(a) Of course.

(b) Certainly.

(c) Most assuredly so.

(d) Not if he quoted them odds like 67 to 1.

(e) None of the above.

(21) Earlier in the book, there was a good deal of talk about a strike being called by the teachers and maybe the guards. However, there was no talk about a strike in the previous section. How would you explain this? _____

   (a) The Rudyard Administration was able to appease both unions, and there was promise of a settlement with both as soon as the details could be ironed out.

   (b) The Rudyard Administration told the representatives from both unions some real whoppers, and successfully stalled them for a good part of the semester.

   (c) The Teachers, Guards and the Rudyard Administration were so dedicated to the Students that they couldn't bring themselves to interrupt the academic year all because of their petty squabbles, and promised each other they would hammer out an agreement over the Christmas Holidays on their own time.

   (d) This being the Author's first novel, he simply forgot about that particular subplot.

   (e) None of the above.

Answers on page 386.

November 30, 1983: "Strike!"

1

University and Teachers Close Ranks As Latest Strike News Sweeps Campus

By Scott Crowley

Rumors once again rocked the Rudyard University Campus Tuesday as word of an impending Teachers' Strike hit the streets.

Spreading like wildfire from one building to the next, nobody was really sure where the news had initially broke, all that was certain was that, by noon, everyone had heard it. The Rudyard Administration, deluged by phone calls, quickly issued a statement denying what it described as "the latest in a series of spurious gossip," and asked for the Teachers' assistance in squashing it.

"I was unaware of any animosity existing between the university and its faculty," the President of the University, Ralph Garibaldi, remarked late Tuesday afternoon. "I can't imagine why anybody would be circulating such a story."

"Neither can I," Teachers Union Representative Ron Isaacs said a couple hours later. "At this time, the union has no plans of calling a strike. However, I can see how someone might think that we would. What with the projected budget cuts the university announced back in October, and with the departure of 8 more tenured professors scheduled for the end of the year, what can the students think? The teachers are obviously unhappy, and the university doesn't seem concerned about it in the least.

"This is the same university that has allowed its contract negotiations with the security guards to drag on since the first week of September. And there's still no settlement in sight. The students, especially the graduating seniors, can't have much faith in an institution that is obviously more concerned with budgets than anything else."

This is the third time this semester that word of a Teachers' Strike has hit the campus, and follows on the heels of a rumor that circulated before Thanksgiving Break about a possible walkout by the Security Guards. It was the second time for such news.

Whether or not there's any truth to these rumors, or if the Teachers and Guards Unions had anything to do with their dissemination is still, as yet, unknown.

2

Nothing against the <u>Rudyard Chronicle</u>, but the alleged strike news actually did not reach every part of the campus the day before. In actuality, it had only made it to those places where students tended to congregate the most: the benches around Pfaehler Library, the outdoor tables in Bailey Square, the Student Center and, at this juncture in the semester, Marner Hall.

Marner Hall was a short, nondescript building which stood by itself on a patch of ground about twenty minutes walk from the center of campus, and with one or two exceptions, was generally known as one of the quietest places on campus. Its first floor housed the university's Financial Aid Department, and some time during the mid-seventies, the floor above had been converted into dance studios due to a sudden expansion of the university's dance program. It was an odd combination to be sure, seldom have art and commerce gotten along so well together under one roof, but as everyone knew, it was more a marriage of convenience than anything else.

So when it was discovered one semester that there was somebody spying on the dancers as they changed in and out of their dance clothes on the second floor, the office workers downstairs were immediately pressed into service and asked to ensure that, in future, everyone who came into the building actually belonged there. In return, the dance students and their instructors would pitch in during Pre-Registration, one of the Financial Aid Department's busiest times, and stay as far the hell away as possible.

This was one of those days.

However, unlike other semesters, the main topic of conversation that morning was not the growing column of students crowding the hallway, but the story on the front page of the Rudyard Chronicle; and the general sentiment was that the more the university and the teachers denied the possibility of a strike, the more likely it was that there was going to be one.

"Come on Greg. Why would the teachers tip their hand at this point in the semester," a woman in a Lincoln green coat demanded. "It would be foolish for them to say anything right now. It'd ruin their bargaining position."

To her right, a crabby fellow with a sleepy expression grimaced. "Not necessarily Barbara. It could also help to expedite the negotiations. The university would know exactly how far the teachers are willing to go."

"Maybe," she conceded.

"Why couldn't they have started this *after* the semester," a skinny guy hugging a large parka asked. "I don't want to have to sit around the next couple of months wondering when I'm going to take finals."

Barbara frowned. "You don't really think they'll let it drag on that long, do you?"

"Who can say? All I'm saying is they could if they wanted to."

Barbara slowly turned, removing her green coat, and positioned herself closer to the person behind. She had had her eye on him since he had first arrived, and she had been waiting for just the right moment to engage him in conversation. "What did *you* think about that article in the Rudyard Chronicle?"

"I think it was one of the best things they've ever printed," Richard Mead confidently replied. He was seated to her left in a blue and yellow lawn chair, and he was paging through the latest issue of <u>Mad Magazine</u>. "I mean, sure, other college papers have done stories on sororities, but when that reporter asked the head of the sorority if she or the girls had ever participated in a topless pillow fight, I almost cheered. I mean, *I* never would have thought to ask something like that."

She frowned. "I was talking about the article on the Teachers' Strike."

"Teachers' Strike?!" He crossed his legs. "No, I didn't read anything about a Teachers' Strike. But did you read about all that toilet paper they found in the trees outside Brisbane Hall?"

She turned away. "Idiot."

Barbara and her friends started whispering to one another, and Rich smiled. He was grateful for the silence. The last twenty minutes they had been selflessly treating everyone within earshot to a long-winded discussion on the sad state of Rudyard's labor affairs, and he didn't know how much more of it he could take. That morning, everyone and their brother—and their sister for that matter—had been talking at great length about whether or not the strike rumors were really true, and it hadn't taken very long before he had tired of the entire subject. All he cared about at the moment was making it into the Financial Aid Office before nightfall.

He looked up at the person standing behind him. "Do you know what time it is?"

"One o'clock."

"Thanks." Rich couldn't believe he had been there since twelve, and he peered down the corridor. The line hadn't moved for some time, and he wondered if everything was all right.

As if on cue, four people suddenly emerged from the office. They were laughing and playfully bickering with one another, and didn't seem to have any trouble ignoring the students there. A hail of curses filled the air almost immediately, and the people in line glared at the happy quartet as they giggled their way passed. It was obvious that they were employees of the Financial Aid Office because they were the only people smiling within a one-block radius. It was equally apparent that they were on their way out to lunch.

Rich slumped back in his chair, and stared morosely at the floor. He hated going to Financial Aid, especially during Pre-registration. That was generally when everyone would come running and try to iron out any problems they may have been notified about during the course of the semester. It was also when all activity in the office slowed down to a virtual crawl.

Earlier Rich had estimated he wouldn't be talking to anyone for an hour or so, but now, he had to guess that he wouldn't be seeing anyone until well after 2:30. The only problem was, he was supposed to meet Holly at 2:30.

They had planned a rendezvous outside Rockford Hall for the afternoon, so they could register for classes together, but now it looked as if he wasn't going to be able to make it. He sat up in his chair and rolled the magazine up in his hands. Holly wasn't going to like that. Worse, Rich suspected she would blame him, and not the Rudyard Bureaucracy, for being late, and say that he had done it, for some reason, on purpose.

Things between them hadn't been going so well the last couple of weeks, and lately it had seemed as if they were doing more arguing than anything else. He didn't know why or what exactly he had done, but it was obvious that Holly was treating him differently. Something had changed, right about the time that midterms had ended, but he couldn't put his finger on what.

He could hear it occasionally in the way she spoke, and other times in the way she acted. It bothered him no end, but he didn't know how to broach the subject with her. Every time he tried, she would act as if she didn't know what he was talking about or offer an explanation that convinced him he had misread the situation--almost.

He found the whole thing incredibly nerve-wracking, and from time to time would toy with the idea of breaking up with her. If it had been anyone else, he would have done it already. At least, that was what he kept telling himself anyway. Unfortunately, the pledge they had made to one another about making the relationship work the night of Mennon's rigged band contest was constantly on his mind, and he knew he couldn't simply walk away. He felt he owed Holly more than that.

Rich gazed at his sneaker, brooding, and jokingly told himself he could avoid all of this simply by walking to the front of the line and demanding to be next. Picturing himself doing something that outrageous immediately brought a twisted grin to his face, and it wasn't long before he was on his feet folding his lawn chair closed.

What did he have to lose?

ACT FOUR

SCENE THREE

<u>Scene:</u> The Rudyard University Financial Aid Office

It is a large office with two rows of desks, 3 on each side, running diagonally from the back of the stage, stage right, and ending about mid—stage, stage left. There is a bank of gray filing cabinets along the wall stage right, and the door to this office is located in the corner of the back wall, stage left. A long wooden bench sits beside the door, and above it hangs a large calendar/poster listing the Rudyard University football team's schedule for the year before, 1982.

There is a computer terminal on each desk, as well as one with a broken screen atop the filing cabinets. The desks have the usual accessories: staplers, pen holders, pens, baskets crammed with papers and folders, clocks, paper clip holders, name plates, pictures of family members, coffee mugs, telephones, desk calendars (Presumably for the current year), all arranged on desk blotters.

The wall stage left also runs in a diagonal along the stage, and the ancient green paint is cracked and peeling. It could be any other wall in the building, and will serve as the corridor in Act Four, Scene three. At the center of this wall is your standard barred window, which is covered on both sides with a layer of dirt. In fact, the entire room could use a good cleaning—which it will never get.

<u>AT RISE:</u> Discovered: Three drowsy-looking students seated on the bench at the back of the stage, and the one on the end, stage right, is reading James Joyce's <u>Ulysses</u>.* However, just to show him he isn't so smart, the woman on the opposite side of the bench,

---

* For the Chicago run, F. Scott Fitzgerald's <u>This Side Of Paradise</u> was used.

271

stage left, is reading a copy of Kurt Vonnegut's <u>Deadeye Dick</u>. There is a phone ringing, and it will ring several more times before someone answers it.

Comfortably seated at the front of the stage are two Financial Aid Officers: stage left is Mrs. Eva Miaskowski, a middle-aged woman with graying hair, and at stage right is Mr. Roger Webster, a rather large, muscular man in his mid-thirties who looks as if he is dangerously close to outgrowing his desk. Each is quietly speaking to a student standing on the other side of their desk, and it is Mr. Webster who finally answers the phone. He will remain on the phone until some time after Richard Mead's entrance.

(Enter Mead with his lawn chair and schoolbag in hand. Lacking a definite plan of attack, he hesitates by the three students seated on the bench.)

<u>Mrs. Miaskowski</u>: (Sits back and adjusts the bifocals teetering on the end of her nose) I'm sorry Betsy, there's nothing more we can do.

<u>Betsy Snyder</u>: (Nods forlornly and gathers up her papers) Thanks anyway.

(She turns and starts for the door, and Rich heads straight for Eva's desk. He carefully lays his belongings on the floor and crouches beside them. Eva stands and Betsy exits the office.)

<u>Mrs. Miaskowski</u>: What in the *world* do you think you're doing? Don't you see that line?

<u>Richard Mead</u>: Every semester. (He pulls a couple of papers out of his bag) But I'm not going to let a little thing like *that* get me down. (Stands up) Now I know you folks're busy. (To both Eva and Webster) But I'm in a real hurry. (He steps closer to Eva and smiles) See, I have to register for classes this afternoon, but I can't do that until after I clear up this problem with my bill.

<u>Mrs. Miaskowski</u>: (Glances at the letter in Rich's hand) I understand that, but what you have to realize is that that's why

everyone else is here as well. So you'll just have to wait in line like everyone else.

Mead: Please... (Reads the name plate on her desk) ....Mrs. Miaskowski. Eva. Do you mind if I call you by your first name?

Mrs. Miaskowski: Yes.

Mead: All right, Mrs. *Me—Ask—How—Ski*...

(She reacts unfavorably to this pronunciation)

Mead: Like I was going to say before, ordinarily, I wouldn't mind spending half the day standing in line over here—that's how I met my first wife—but I really need to get over to Rockford Hall and stand in line over there. (He straightens his papers by tapping them on her desk) I've got a date.

Mrs. Miaskowski: Well I'm sorry, but that has nothing to do with this office.

Mead: No, but the letters I keep getting from the government do. You see, Rudyard keeps sending me these bills that say I owe the university six hundred dollars. (Tries to hand her one of them) But the government says I've received enough aid to cover that. (Tries to hand her another)

Mrs. Miaskowski: (With crossed arms) I'm afraid there's nothing I can do.

Mead: Couldn't you just—

Mrs. Miaskowski: It wouldn't be fair to the other students. I'm sorry.

Mead: But this is an emergency. I've got a date.

Mrs. Miaskowski: (Unmoved) that doesn't really concern me. What does concern me is keeping this office running as smoothly as possible. So as I see it, you've got two choices: you can either stand in line or else come back another day.

Mead: Aren't you forgetting my third choice?

Mrs. Miaskowski: which is?

Mead: (Unfolds lawn chair) I can stay here and make a general nuisance out of myself until somebody helps me. (Sits and puts his feet up on Eva's desk)

(Mr. Webster, who has been trying to follow all this while still on the phone, finally hangs up.)

Mrs. Miaskowski: You *can not* sit there. I'll call security.

Mead: Go ahead. Then you won't get anything done for an hour.

Mr. Webster: (Stands) Now see here—

Mrs. Miaskowski: (Holds up a hand) Please Roger, finish up with the student you're with. I'll handle this.

Mr. Webster: (Grudgingly) All right. (He sits and talks to the student at his desk while keeping an eye on Mead)

Mrs. Miaskowski: (To Mead) And you're sure it'll only take a minute.

Mead: Yep.

Mrs. Miaskowski: (Lowers into her seat) All right, but I want you to know that I'm only doing this to get rid of you.

Mead: I wouldn't want it any other way.

Mrs. Miaskowski: And I wouldn't be so smug if I were you. I could still call security.

Mead: Come on. It isn't like everyone's rushing to the front of the line today. (To the people waiting on the bench) This'll only take a second.

Mrs. Miaskowski: Social Security Number?

Mead: (Hands her one of his letters) That's all here.

(She takes the paper, and punches the number into her computer. She squints at the screen)

Mrs. Miaskowski: And you're Richard Mead?

Mead: Yes ma'am.

Mrs. Miaskowski: (She punches a few more buttons) I'm sorry, but it says here you *do* owe the university six hundred dollars. Maybe the aid was cancelled.

Mead: (Hands her another letter) Maybe, but this says I've got enough aid coming in to cover that.

Mrs. Miaskowski: (Takes letter and skims it) I understand what you're saying, but our computer says you still have an outstanding balance. And this was coming in as a grant from the state agency?

Mead: Yes.

Mrs. Miaskowski: Maybe they sent you the wrong information.

Mead: Well they use a computer too.

Mrs. Miaskowski: That doesn't mean they can't be wrong.

(Mead sits down. Enter Johnny Mennon with a brief case and a huge grin on his face)

Johnny Mennon: (To the entire office) Heyyy excuse me, but I got this letter in the mail the other day, and--

(Both Eva and Mr. Webster stand up)

Mrs. Miaskowski: Oh this is the absolute limit!

Mr. Webster: (Points over Johnny's left shoulder) Didn't you see that line out there?

Mennon: Sure. Why do you think I barged to the front of it?

Mr. Webster: (Frowns) Look, this office is *not* going to help anyone who hasn't stood in line. So you might as well go right back outside.

Mennon: (Shaking his head) Oh no. I ain't budgin' .

(The student in front of Mr. Webster's desk taps Johnny on the shoulder)

Arthur Drexson: (Haughtily) Do you mind?

Mennon: (Shrugs) You can stand there if you want.

(Mead rolls his eyes, Eva crosses her arms and Mr. Webster escorts Mr. Drexson back to his desk)

Mrs. Miaskowski: And I suppose you're here to tell us how you're having a terrible problem with your aid, and that we have to do something about it right away.

Mennon: Nahh, I never have a problem with my financial aid. In fact... (Hands Eva a folded piece of paper) ....Monday you folks sent me a letter sayin' I had received more money than I needed for the semester.

Mead: (Astonished) Really?

Mennon: Sure. The government sent me an extra six hundred bucks. Can you believe it?

Mrs. Miaskowski: Then what are you doing here?

Mennon: What am I doin' here?! I'm here to pick up my money. (Opens his brief case) I'd like it in tens and twenties please.

Mrs. Miaskowski: (Reading the document) That letter may say you qualified for more aid then you needed, but... (Hands the correspondence back) ....any balance left over from that particular loan reverts back to the lending agency.

Mennon: (Unpleasantly surprised) What?!

Mrs. Miaskowski: This type of aid... (Struggling to simplify her answer) ....the money only exists on paper.

Mennon: Ahhh, that's what they kept saying back in my first economics class, and if I didn't believe it then, I ain't gonna' believe it now.

Mrs. Miaskowski: Well I'm sorry, but that's the way it works. Besides, even if you did have a refund coming, it would be issued in the form of a check. And you probably wouldn't receive it until after the semester ends.

Mennon: (Moves hat to the back of his head) And I thought Christmas had come a little early this year. (Taps the letter on his other hand) Tell you what. Why don't you give me the six hundred dollars anyway, keep this letter as collateral, and I promise I'll bring the money back as soon as I'm done with it.

Mrs. Miaskowski: (Mystified) I—

Mennon: You can even keep the brief case. (Hands it to her)

Mead: (Leaves his chair and taps Mennon on the shoulder) Pardon me Johnny, but did you say six hundred dollars?

Mennon: (Frowns at Eva) Uh-huh.

Mead: You know, you're not going to believe this, but it just so happens that's the exact amount I owe the university.

Mennon: Well you better pay them. You know how Rudyard gets when you owe it money.

Mead: (To Miaskowski) Is there any way he could give that money to me?

Mennon: (Shrugs) It's okay by me.

Mrs. Miaskowski: No, I'm afraid the system doesn't work that way.

Mead: But you just said they're going to send back the money he doesn't use anyway.

Mrs. Miaskowski: But it's not transferable. That money belongs to the student who applies him or herself the most.

Mennon: (Nodding) 'Strue. I have applied for every loan and grant I could get the papers for.

Mrs. Miaskowski: No, no. I mean that money is for the student who utilizes his or her scholastic opportunities to the fullest. (Looks at Mead) Maybe he's a better student than you are.

Mead: Him?!

Mennon: (Humbly) I'm not one to brag, but whenever I ask, my teachers do say that my grades couldn't possibly get any higher-- unless of course, I studied.

Mead: *Wait a minute!*

BLACKOUT AND EVENTUALLY THE LIGHTS COME UP ON THE WALL STAGE LEFT

ACT FOUR

SCENE FOUR

Scene: In the Hall

A line of tired-looking students is now stretched across the wall, and, standing in various positions (Some leaning against the wall with an arm or on a leg or with their backs etc.), they are weighed down by their coats and schoolbags. They would seem to be in a trance, except for two students standing in front of the window. The one on the left, "Roach" Landis, is agitated and displays this by repeatedly stroking his goatee while peering up and down the hall. The one on the right, Jerry Bernstein, seems a little calmer, and is paging through that day's Rudyard Chronicle (The headline "University and Teachers Close Ranks As Latest Strike

278

News Sweeps Campus" can be easily read by the audience). Suddenly, Roach steps out of line and peers down the hall.

Roach Landis: I don't know what's going on here Jerry, but it isn't right that those guys went in there ahead of us. We've been here since noon.

Jerry Bernstein: (Doesn't look up from paper) Maybe they work there.

Roach: *Those* guys? They didn't look like office workers to me.

Jerry: Well maybe they were stopping by to say hello to someone.

Roach: Right. And maybe they were just impatient jerks. (Starts pacing) You know the type. People who can't bear the thought of having to wait in line any longer than they feel they have to. They're too good for that. They're always willing to butt their way to the front of any line, even if it's for poison, because they don't think they should have to wait.

Jerry: Could be. I couldn't say. (Turns page of the paper) All I know is, if they aren't out of there soon, I'm going to go inside and throw a major fit. (He grins menacingly at Roach)

(The woman in front turns around)

Andrea Johnson: Honey, if they aren't out of there in five minutes, I'm going with you.

(There is a loud buzz as everyone else in the hallway pledges his or her support as well, but the celebration immediately grinds to a halt when Jonathan Tollhausler appears. He charges by, and they glare at him as he disappears down the hall.)

BLACKOUT AND THE LIGHTS EVENTUALLY COME UP ON THE REST OF THE STAGE

ACT FOUR

SCENE FIVE

Scene: Still the Financial Aid Office

Mead is still asking Mrs. Miaskowski to give him Mennon's aid ("Oh please." "I can't." "Aw come on, you could if you really wanted to."), and Mennon has started to go through the drawers in Eva's desk. Mr. Webster stops him, and then Arthur Drexson starts complaining to Webster. Mead continues to implore Mrs. Miaskowski to help him out. She circles behind her desk, and picks up the phone. Tollhausler enters as she begins to dial.

Jonathan Tollhausler: (Looking incredibly irritated, he scowls at both Webster and Miaskowski) Who's in charge here?

Mrs. Miaskowski: (Puts phone down, and she and Webster exchange worried expressions) We...both are.

Tollhausler: (Sternly) Do you see that line?

Mrs. Miaskowski: (Looks at Roger) Yes.

Tollhausler: Good. (Unzips his army jacket) Than let's not waste any more time.

Mrs. Miaskowski: (Suddenly) You're a student.

Tollhausler: Now, now, you don't have to say it like that. (He glances at Mennon and Mead) These guys bothering you? Because I could run outside and get a security guard.

Mr. Webster: (Stretches to his full height and steps in front of Tollhausler) They were just leaving. And so are you. You're going to have to go wait in line like everybody else.

Tollhausler: Not on your Nelly. Even if I *did* know her. You know what's going on out there? (Loosens the red and white scarf around his neck) Sheesh. You'd think a bunch of college students could think of something else to talk about then just sports, strike rumors, and what was on TV last night.

Mrs. Miaskowski: (Sitting down) That doesn't excuse you from standing in line.

Tollhausler: What does? (Leans closer) Maybe we could work something out.

Mrs. Miaskowski: There's nothing to work out. You're going to have to leave. (Looks at Mennon and Mead) *All* of you.

Mennon: (Picks up his brief case) I'd have been gone already if you had given me my money.

Mr. Webster: (Good-naturedly) Come on now guys, you've had your fun. Why don't you take it outside?

Mrs. Miaskowski: He's right you know. Don't make us call Security.

Mennon: (Chuckles) Well I hope you don't think *we're* gonna' call them.

Mrs. Miaskowski: (Stands) Will you people *please leave*?!

Tollhausler: You know, maybe if you had asked me why I'm here or what my question is, I might—might mind you—consider standing in line, but you didn't even bother to ask.

Mrs. Miaskowski: (Shuffles through the papers on her desk) I'm sorry, but we've already wasted enough time with these two. Why, we haven't been able to help anyone for fifteen minutes.

Tollhausler: (Quips) And don't think there aren't going to be any complaints. (Inspired, he immediately begins to pace back and forth) In fact, Jammison, take a letter!

Mead: (Grabs a piece of paper and pen from Eva's desk, and sits in his lawn chair) Ready when you are Captain.

Mr. Webster: This guy's crazy.

Mennon: Ahhhh, how do you know? You haven't even heard the letter yet.

Tollhausler: To Ralph Garibaldi, the President of Rudyard University.

Mrs. Miaskowski: Now just a—

Tollhausler: Dear Sir, it pains me no end to have to write to you about the experience I had today in your Financial Aid Department.

(Eva frowns and slumps into her chair)

But seeing as I've been having rather a bad week, I feel I must take it out on someone.

(Stops pacing) And please, don't get the impression that I am merely writing in order to get someone into trouble. On the contrary, the employee to whom I am referring shall remain nameless. (Waits a beat.) I'll send her name along in a separate letter.

(Begins pacing again, and he will roam around the office as he speaks until he winds up at the front of the stage)

Oh Ralph, for shame. What is going on at my old alma mater? Whatever happened to the Rudyard I used to know? Where have all the happy-go-lucky office workers gone? Why don't the teachers sing and dance on their way to class anymore? Or the students? What has become of the college experience I knew so many years ago? What happened? Is it the times? The Economy? Miss Scarlet in the library with a dagger?

And please don't think it old fashioned of me to believe in this day and age that we still need to hold ourselves accountable to some kind of standard. One can't simply abandon them like a…well, like an old umbrella on a bus.

This will only lead to your being forced to run across campus in a rainstorm with a drenched newspaper over your head. I know of what I speak because the very same thing just happened to me the other day. And I still have the ink on my scalp to prove it.
Which brings me to my next point: You didn't happen to see my umbrella, did you Ralph?

(Mead clears his throat)

I left it around here somewhere. It was black with a brown handle. It was a gift you know, and I'd hate to think it was gone forever.

Mead: Uhhhh, pardon me Captain, but I think you may have strayed a little from the point.

Tollhausler: (Annoyed) Is that so?! Well, you didn't see this umbrella. It was a good one.

Mead: I'm sure it was—

Tollhausler: Push button and all.

Mead: But still…

Tollhausler: All right, all right, read back what you have so far.

(Mead stares down at his notes)

Mead: I can't.

Tollhausler: Why not?

Mead: I can't read my own writing.

Tollhausler: (Does slow burn) Then how, pray tell, are you going to type up what I've just said?

Mead: (Crumples up paper) I'm not. I'll do what I always do: write my own letter and have you sign it.

Tollhausler: (Frowns) No wonder no one ever answers any of my letters.

Mead: Oh, they answer them. (Tosses paper into wastebasket)

Tollhausler: Well *I've* never seen any of the responses.

Mead: Why should you? I'm the one who writes them.

Tollhausler: (Exasperated) Then why should I even bother dictating the rest of *this* one?!

Mead: Because you like hearing yourself talk?

Tollhausler: (Shocked) Humph! *How dare you*! Like hearing myself talk. Indeed!

(Walks to edge of stage, and removes portable tape recorder from his pocket. He turns it on)

Captain's Log, November 30th, 1983. Had to let my secretary go today: he's on to me. (Shuts recorder off and places it in his pocket.) I say Jammison.

Mead: Yes?

Tollhausler: (Very seriously) After much soul-searching, and a couple of sleepless nights, I've decided…I've decided…

Mead: Yes?

Tollhausler: …that I'm going to have to change my toothpaste. Oh, and you're fired.

Mead: (Stands) What?!

Tollhausler: I'm so sorry. (Shakes Mead's hand) Really, but these things happen. Can't possibly imagine how I'm ever going to get along without you. (Looks over at Mennon) Oh look, there's somebody. You. Take this down.

Mennon: (Insulted) Hey what are you talkin' about?! I'm a musician, not a secretary!

Tollhausler: Well, I guess it doesn't have to be a letter. It could always be a singing telegram.

Mrs. Miaskowski: (Slams her hands down on the desk and stands) All right! *That is it!*

(Everyone stares)

We *can not* get *anything* done with *you people* in the way!

Mennon: Oh, so now it's *our* fault.

Mrs. Miaskowski: (Picks up phone) I'm calling security.

Mead: (Runs over to Webster's desk and picks up the phone there) So am I!

Mrs. Miaskowski: What?!

Mead: That's right. I'm gonna' turn you people in as impostors. You don't care about helping anyone. All you care about are long lines, your forms and telling students there isn't anything you can do for them!.

Tollhausler: (Inspired) That's a great idea! (Goes over to the desk behind Mead, and picks up a phone as well) I've always wanted to be on the six o'clock news.

Mennon: (Tosses brief case aside) Well, I ain't gonna' be seein' that six hundred dollars today.

Mr. Webster: (Furious) *Put down those phones*!

Tollhausler: Oh hoooo, you don't want word of this getting out, do you, you desk-bound behemoth!

Mr. Webster: (Crosses over to Tollhausler) Look, I've had just about enough of you and your big mouth.

(Webster lunges for the phone in Tollhausler's hand, but Tollhausler spins around holding it out of reach)

Tollhausler: Heyyy, I didn't even get to dial yet!

(With a growl, Webster jerks Tollhausler into the air. The students on the bench jump up and back away towards the door)

Oh come on, stay. Don't you want to see how this is going to turn out?

(He drops the phone, and the students run out)

Mead: (Throws the phone down and grabs Webster's arm) Come on fella' , let him go!

(Grunting, Webster flings Tollhausler under his left arm and snatches Mead off the floor with his right)

Mrs. Miaskowski: Roger! (She hangs up the phone) Please, put them down!

Mr. Webster: I'm throwing these guys out on their ears.

Mrs. Miaskowski: (To Mennon) For heaven's sake. Don't just stand there. Do something!

Mennon: (Reaches into his pocket) Heads I do something, tails I go to lunch.

Mrs. Miaskowski: But they're your friends!

Mennon: Don't worry. If it's tails I'll be glad to bring them something back.

Mrs. Miaskowski: Uh!

(Mennon flips the coin, catches it and slaps it down on his left wrist. He raises his right hand, and Eva can't help but look to see which side of the coin is facing up)

Mennon: (Annoyed, he examines it) This isn't my trick quarter.

Mrs. Miaskowski: All right. Now do something!

Mennon: And I was hungry too. (Throws off his coat.)

(The whole time Tollhausler and Mead have been struggling to get free, but all their exertions have been unsuccessful. Then Tollhausler suddenly giggles.)

Mead: What the hell are you laughing at?

Tollhausler: I was just wondering when Turpin's going to get here.

Mead: He must be running late.

Tollhausler: (Pulls out a piece of gum and taps it on Webster's chest) Say muscles, when we're done here, do you think you could drop me over at the Bursar's Office? (He tries to unwrap the gum) Maybe they've had some luck finding my loan check.

Mr. Webster: I'll drop you all right.

(Webster takes a step, lurches to the right and Mead crashes to the floor. He will not appear again until Tollhausler delivers a line from William Shakespeare's Richard III. Mennon then launches himself at Webster)

Mennon: Jump Toll!

(Webster meets Johnny head on with his shoulder, and lifts him into the air)

Tollhausler: (Staring down) Oh no. I dropped my gum.

(Webster drops Tollhausler on the nearest desk, and squeezes Mennon closer)

Mennon: (Breathlessly) Mister, I hope you know that you're taking this all wayyy too seriously.

(Enter Ernie Turpin who walks directly up to Eva. He does this without even looking at the battle going on in the middle of the room. He tries to hand Eva a folded piece of pink paper)

Mrs. Miaskowski: (Grabbing Ernie's arm) Quick! Do something!

(Ernie seems puzzled, and then gazes over his shoulder. He reacts when he finally sees Tollhausler trying to get Mr. Webster to release Mennon, and turns back to Eva with a look of purpose on his face. He runs back to the vacated bench, lays his guitar case down and throws off his blue parka)

Mrs. Miaskowski: (Relieved) Thank goodness.

(Ernie rolls up the sleeves of his flannel shirt, as if he's about to remove somebody's burst appendix, and pops open his guitar case. He starts strumming his guitar)

Mrs. Miaskowski: *What are you doing?!*

(Enter a throng of angry students led by Jerry and Roach. They pause briefly to stare at Mr. Webster and the boys, and march right up to Eva)

Roach: Excuse me, but who's in charge?

Mrs. Miaskowski: (She glances over at Roger, and puts a hand to her head) I am.

Jerry: Well we represent the hundreds of students standing in line outside, and we'd really like to know what's going on in here.

Andrea Johnson: We feel like you people have forgotten all about us.

Roach: You know lady, some of us have been standing out there for over an hour, and we don't appreciate the fact that these guys...(He points a thumb over his shoulder)....were allowed to just stroll right in here.

Tollhausler: A horse, a horse, my kingdom for a horse.

(Mead rejoins his friends)

Mrs. Miaskowski: (Glares at the students crowded around her) What do you people think is going on here?! Are you blind? Does it look like we're giving these people preferential treatment? Do you even see what's going on here? (Gestures at the Battle Royal going on across the room) Look, Mr. Webster's trying to get these people out of here.

(The sound of Turpin's guitar grows louder, and Ernie stands up on the bench at the back of the room)

And as for that young man, I don't know *what* he's doing.

(Ernie plays louder, and the action on stage stops. Webster releases Mennon and Tollhausler. Then, everyone turns towards Ernie on the bench. He plays a little more and finishes his song. Everyone claps, and he bows)

Tollhausler: (To audience) Don't worry, this won't take very long. We had to add this number because the producers didn't think there was enough music in this part of the show.

(Ernie starts playing again. It is a very difficult, intricate flamenco piece, and he grins with pride as he plays—until about thirty seconds later when one of his strings breaks. He grimaces, and throws his guitar down. There is a loud bonk. He steps off the bench out of sight)

Tollhausler: Well, it looks like we're going to be getting out of here early tonight.

(Everyone takes his or her original place on stage before the guitar solo.)

Mrs. Miaskowski: So as you can see, what this office needs right now is a little cooperation from you people. Can't you see what we're up against?

(Mead and Tollhausler climb up on a desk to pry Johnny loose from Mr. Webster's grip.)

Roach: That doesn't really concern us.

Mrs. Miaskowski: What?!

(Suddenly, Mennon pops free, and Mr. Webster falls into someone who slams into someone else. This sets off a chain reaction and everyone yells as they fall about the room like dominoes. Everyone except Tollhausler, Mennon, Turpin, and Mead. It is so quiet you can hear a pin drop—or a large truck passing on the street outside the theater. Eva--who landed atop her desk--slowly pushes herself up, and, right then, a battery of security guards comes bursting into the room. She sees them.)

Thank goodness.

(She swoons)

END OF SCENE

CURTAIN

6

The campus that afternoon seemed very...different, and Holly Rake, occasionally distracted by the sub-arctic winds that had been buffeting the region for the last three days, was having trouble putting her finger on what exactly it was about the place that had actually changed. It certainly wasn't anything obvious. The hallowed halls and ivy-covered buildings were all still where they were supposed to be, as were the many food trucks and stands which, over the years, had taken up permanent residence to the front and side of them.

Nevertheless, Holly couldn't get it out of her head that there was something very...odd going on, especially for a Wednesday. She crossed the street, confused as to how exactly she had gotten into this particular frame of mind, and it was while she was pondering this that a five-foot guy with a three-foot backpack stumbled on to her foot.

"Guh—" he exclaimed with a great deal of sincerity. "Are you all right?"

Holly's boot was already off the ground. "Oof." She wiggled her toes. "I guess."

"I'm really sorry," the fellow with the bulging backpack announced, "but this..." He motioned over his shoulder. "....well, *somebody* almost ran into me with a slice of pizza."

"It's okay," she reaffirmed and lowered her foot.

"So you're all right?"

"Yes."

"Great." He looked at his watch. "I'm going to miss my bus." He hurried off. "I'm really sorry," he called over his shoulder one more time.

"Me too," Holly mumbled, and limped over to the railing separating Bailey Square from the rest of the sidewalk. She rested her weight against it with a gloved hand and painfully flexed her injured foot.

"That was entirely my fault," someone enunciated around a mouthful of food, and Holly looked up at a security guard who was also leaning against the railing. He had a half-eaten piece of pizza in his right hand.

In his left, he was holding a napkin that, at the moment, he was wiping his mouth with. He lowered it to reveal one of the largest moustaches Holly had ever seen in her life. It had been painstakingly trimmed in the shape of a horseshoe, and she couldn't help staring as the fuzzy ends slid up and down its owners chin. He swallowed. "I guess I wasn't watching where I was going."

"That's all right," she said, reminding herself it was impolite to stare, and forced her attention to the smudge marking the top of her boot. "I'll be fine."

"You were limping."

"I'm okay. He just got a couple of my toes." She lowered her foot to the ground. "I can walk on it."

"I've got to learn to be more careful," he said around another mouthful of pizza.

"Really, it's no big deal." She couldn't understand why he was going on like this. "People are bumping into each other here all the time. Because of the trucks."

292

"Is there anything I can do? You know, take you over to the infirmary or something?"

"That won't be necessary." She lifted the bag of books from her shoulder, and unconsciously held it in front of the leg that had been trampled. "I'll be all right."

"Well that's a relief." He smiled. "I'm Glenn Bettinger."

A spark suddenly glided across a network of synapses located on the left side of Holly's brain, and seconds later, a red light flashed in the foreground of her mind. "Er, hi."

Holly suspected that Glenn-boy was only seconds away from asking her for a date, her phone number or both. She immediately took evasive action, and hobbled away, as if she were trying to calculate the tenderness of her stomped toes.

Sergeant Bettinger followed her. "What's your name?"

Holly stopped. She was beginning to hate Wednesdays. "Lisa."

"Well Lisa. I know you don't know me, but I was wondering if you could do me a favor."

"And what's that?"

"Do you think you could pretend that I was the one who stepped on your foot just now?"

Holly could see it coming a mile away. "And why would I do that?"

"So I can make it up to you. You know, buy you dinner or something."

Another blip of electricity rushed across the circuitry board located on the left side of Holly's brain, congratulating her on the accuracy of her previous guess, while also commanding her facial muscles to contort her features into a sneer.

"I've got a better idea," she replied. "Why don't *you* pretend that I fell for your pitiful little line and go somewhere nice tonight and *pretend* I'm there with you. This way I won't have to waste my evening *pretending* I'm having a good time."

7

Holly looked back and frowned. "Stupid, pathetic rent-a-cop." Then her mouth snapped shut and she twisted her head to the right to avoid making eye contact with the security guard who had suddenly appeared before her. She didn't know whether or not he had actually heard her last comment, and, quite frankly, she didn't want to know. She walked around him.

Seconds later, she passed another security guard waiting in line outside Zorba's Gyros. There were three more standing at the next food truck, The Hunan Kitchen, and it suddenly dawned on her what was different about the campus that chilly Wednesday afternoon: the security guards.

There were hundreds of them in the streets, and Holly couldn't remember ever having seen this many members of Guards Local 258 assembled in one place before. The phrase "Guards Local 258" resonated in her mind, and she suddenly thought she knew why they were there: the guards were finally going to go on strike. However, she dismissed this theory as she watched them move about the sidewalk. She didn't really get the impression they were standing around waiting for word to come down about the strike. Quite the opposite: they appeared to be very much on duty.

Whether standing in line or munching away at their lunches, the guards, except for Officer Bettinger, seemed to be very interested in the movements of everyone in the immediate vicinity. She assumed that there must have been something big going on to require this many guards, but she didn't know what it could be.

Halfway down the next block, she thought she had stumbled upon the answer. The sidewalk in front of Pfaehler Library was overrun with students, and she could hear someone shouting something. Probably some kind of an arrest, she told herself, but drawing nearer, she realized she was mistaken. The students weren't gawking at the final, tense stages of an unfolding police drama. They were focused on a lone woman standing atop one of the wooden benches outside the library.

"....but you can see how frightened the university must be," the woman was saying in an angry voice. "After all, what are all these guards doing here?" She snickered. "I didn't even know Rudyard *had* this many guards." The crowd laughed, and she shook her head. "When three guys with knives tried to rob the bus stop I was waiting at last September—there were a bunch of us there—you know how many guards security sent over? Two." Somebody in front chuckled, and she looked at him. "Really. Two guards. And a van. The guards must have mentioned that stupid van a dozen times. Like we were special because security had gone out of its way to send over a van and not a patrol car. Anyway, I asked why only two guards had been dispatched, and the one told me we were lucky they didn't just transfer the call to the transit police.

"And you know what? I wish they had. Because at least the transit cops would have caught those guys." She brushed her short black hair back. "I guess the only way security can show us how effective it is by taking on the easy jobs. You know, like arresting students who have a legitimate right to protest."

The men and women cheered, and Holly turned to the person beside her. "What's going on?"

The gentleman she had spoken to frowned, as if she had just asked him one of the dumbest questions he had ever heard in his life, and he promptly turned his attention back to the front of the crowd. "Didn't you hear," he said with a slight southern drawl. "There was a demonstration in Marner Hall today, and, apparently before the guards went in, they lobbed a bunch of tear gas into the building. They arrested everyone in the place."

Holly was stunned. "Oh my God. And who's that on the bench?"

"Why that's Audrey Thomas."

"Was she one of the people who was there?"

"No. She heard about the whole thing from a janitor over in the Student Center."

"Ohhh." Holly stared back.

Ordinarily, upon hearing something like this, Holly's first reaction would have been to smile, the obvious response to an absurd statement such as that, much to its speaker's delight, but there was something in this gentleman's tone, as well as in his eyes, that told her he was deadly serious.

"Well is there anyone here who was actually in Marner Hall when it happened?"

"Course not," the man replied. "Didn't you hear what I just said?! The guards arrested everybody."

"Oh."

"....and we *can not* allow the university, *or its armed flunkies*, to tell us what we can and can not do here. We have a right to speak out, and if our complaints go unheeded, it is our *duty* to demonstrate. This is our university. Not theirs!"

8

The crowd erupted, giving an awfully good impersonation of an angry mob, alternately shouting for justice and hurling abuse at anyone in the university's employ who had been perceived as having done them some wrong over the last couple of months; all Holly could do was watch.

She couldn't believe they were allowing this story to affect them this way, and since Audrey hadn't even been in Marner Hall, that's all it was, a story. No reflection on the janitor who had passed it along, but Holly suspected he had, unavoidably, gotten some of his facts wrong.

She excused herself past the people gathered behind her, and continued down the street. She could only attribute her classmates' rather extreme reaction to Audrey's speech to the time of year. It was right before finals, and that point in the semester when Rudyard Students were most susceptible to the power of suggestion. In their fragile state, she knew, the little dears would pretty much believe anything they heard. Hence the endless theorizing that day about what the article on the front page of the Rudyard Chronicle *really* meant.

This was also why she hadn't gotten too upset when Rich had asked her if she wanted to break up. It was plain to see that he wasn't acting on his own. Someone—Mennon or Tollhausler, she couldn't be sure which—had obviously planted the idea in his head, and he wouldn't be able to shake it until after the craziness of finals was over.

Admittedly, Holly *did* want to break up with him, but didn't, for a second, believe that he could know that. She had been much too careful concealing her true feelings from him the last couple of weeks, and done everything in her power to convince him she was very happy.

Of course, she *wasn't*, but Holly wasn't quite prepared to discuss that with him right now. First, they had to make it through Finals. Second, she had to make sure that her feelings for Nick Bianco were genuine, and not the fleeting type one experiences while under the influence of that most dreaded of afflictions, the Mid-semester Crush.

Near as Holly could figure, her feelings for Nick had changed, much to her surprise, some time at the beginning of November, on a rainy Monday, about an hour after she and Richard had had a fight. (To be completely accurate, Holly's feelings didn't change that afternoon so much as surface. Seated there, while her teacher, Assistant Professor Joe Corcoran, went on and on about James Madison and the Bill of Rights, as he would occasionally do, Holly had innocently smiled at Nick, and her classmate had done what anyone else would have done in that situation: he had innocently smiled back. It was at that precise

298

moment, as Holly fought back the urge to leap across the aisle and throw her arms around him when it became abundantly clear to her that what she was feeling for Nick was something a little more complicated than simple camaraderie.) She had gone to her Poli-Sci 202 class that afternoon expecting nothing more than to take some notes on Professor Corcoran's lecture and ask him several questions about their term paper, but all she had managed to do, after only filling in half a page of her notebook, was to allow Richard to slip completely from her thoughts.

To borrow a cliché, it wasn't anything she had planned. Nor had Nick for that matter. It had simply happened. And to be quite frank, Holly wasn't at all pleased about it. It was so…so high school, and reminded her of the kinds of dilemmas she used to hear about from her girlfriends between classes on Monday mornings back in the tenth grade. It was crazy. One minute she was telling Andy Condello that she couldn't see him any more—as per her agreement with Richard—and the next, she was obsessing over whether or not Nick regarded her as anything more than a friend.

Coincidentally, Nick's real name was Richard as well, but he always made it a point to tell people, even his professors on the first day of classes, that he much rather preferred being called Nick than Richard or any of its various permutations. He was smart, funny and he wasn't as close-minded as Richard seemed to be. Holly could talk to Nick, about anything, which is something she didn't feel absolutely comfortable doing with Rich. Which is why she was starting to suspect that her relationship with him had gone about as far as it was going to go. Richard didn't seem to be as willing to listen to her as he used to, whereas Nick was generally all ears.

That was why she enjoyed spending so much time with him. Nick genuinely seemed interested in what she had to say. Besides, there was no pressure involved when they were together. They talked about things, some important and some not, laughed and Nick would occasionally give her a ride home on his motorcycle. She found it all very exciting, and never got the feeling that there were any strings attached. She didn't have to worry about talking to Nick each night or planning her Friday or Saturday nights around him or his friends or his friends' band. They never forced themselves on each other, and neither appeared to worry about what the other was doing when they weren't together. Of course, Holly knew that that would change if they actually started dating, but she also knew that Nick could handle it. He was very mature.

Rich, on the other hand, could be quite infuriating at times.

Holly scowled at a guard on the pavement ahead of her. It was quite apparent, with or without Nick's presence in her life, she and Rich weren't going to make it. Then she told herself, as she often did, that deep down she had already known this. Unfortunately, knowing this didn't make things any easier for her, especially since Richard would occasionally do something that would remind her of how much fun he could be. The things they had done together back in September and October were still fresh in her mind, and she didn't think she would forget them any time soon.

Two women clutching paper bags hurried up the steps of Rockford Hall, and Holly held the door for them.

"Thanks," they said almost simultaneously, and went into the building.

Holly followed.

"So do you think it really happened?"

"No, I'm sorry, I do not." The woman on the left glanced over her shoulder, "I do not believe," she continued in a low voice, "the guards marched in and, after spraying the students with mace, beat them with their clubs."

Holly heard this. It was quiet in the hall, and she tried to keep up with the two women.

"I mean, come on Betty, do you really think the guards would do something like that? They're not..." She paused as they both walked around a student seated on a trio of marble steps, and entered the building's main corridor. "....they're not animals. They know the difference between right and wrong for gosh sakes. Besides, the university would never stand for anything like that. Do you know what kind of a law suit that would open them up to?"

"Well Jim Dunnigan in Payroll says that's exactly what happened. And Myra, he dates one of the dance teachers over there."

Myra shook her head. "I might believe there was a riot today, but Security would have never responded like that." She looked both ways, past Holly. "Darling, you *know* how they are. If something isn't written in their contract, they won't do it. It's like Arthur says, they wouldn't carry their mother out of a burning building unless someone from Local 258 hadn't first worked out how much of a bonus they were going to get for doing it."

Betty wanted to disagree, but she couldn't deny that there *was* a certain logic to what Myra was saying. "Well that's what Jim Dunnigan told me."

"As if *he* ever had a clue. Have you ever met that...that *child* he goes out with?"

"Now Myra. Don't be like that..."

They started up a wide set of carpeted stairs to the right of the hall, and Holly unbuttoned her coat. She wished she could have accompanied them a little further, but it was obvious that she didn't have any business to transact in the offices headquartered above and it wouldn't have taken Betty and Myra very long to figure out why she was still with them. Even so, Holly would have liked to know what happened in Marner Hall that afternoon.

However, she knew she didn't have time for that at the moment. She slid the green scarf from around her neck and walked back down the hall to a line of students that she knew led downstairs to the Registrar's Office.

"Tell me you're not waiting to see the Registrar," she said, and the person at the end of the line smiled. "On no, not at all. This is the line to see Santy Claus."

"Great."

The last thing she felt like doing was waiting around a couple of hours to Pre-register for classes.

Then Richard Mead came running by.

9

"Richard?!" Holly called from the back of the line, and he turned—along with everyone else in the corridor named Richard—and ran back. "Thank God."

He grabbed her by the arm. "I thought I was going to have to search all over for you. Quick." He dragged her away. "There's an elevator around the corner."

"What are you talking about?"

Somebody stepped into Rich's path. "Holly?"

Rich stopped, and Holly bumped into him.

"Rich," she exclaimed, throwing an arm around him for support, "what are you doing?"

"Holly?"

She peeked over Rich's right shoulder. "Nick?"

Rich turned his head. "Who?"

"Nick," she replied. "Nick Bianco."

The name didn't register with Richard at first, mainly because he had a good deal of other things on his mind at the moment, and Holly stared at him as if he should have recognized the name immediately.

"The guy in my Poli-Sci 202 class?"

"Ohhh," Rich said. "*That* Nick."

"Yes."

He leaned forward and extended a hand. "I'm Richard Mead."

"Hi."

Rich shook Nick's hand as forcefully as he could, and Nick squeezed back.

"I feel as if I already know you Rich. Holly mentions you all the time."

"She talks a lot about you too."

"Really?"

Rich released Nick's hand. "All the time." Rich cast a baleful expression over his shoulder, but Holly didn't notice. Her full attention was on Nick.

Now he knew why Holly had spoken about Nick so often, at least once in every conversation, and why he had almost always experienced a pang of jealousy when she did. Of course, since Rich had never laid eyes on his girlfriend's oft-mentioned classmate, it was hard for him to gauge how much of a threat Nick actually posed, so he had simply dismissed his reaction as the irrational byproduct of a jealous mind. Seeing how right he had been the entire time, however, Rich promised himself that he would listen a little more closely to his feelings next time.

Nick inspected Holly with concern. "Is everything all right?"

"Oh, um, sure," she said. "He was just…" She wondered why she felt it was important to explain Rich's actions to Nick. "….I mean, we were on our way…" It suddenly struck her that she didn't have the faintest idea why Rich had plucked her out of line the way he had. She straightened her coat. "….to register for classes."

"Oh."

She changed the subject. "I didn't expect to see you here."

Of that, Rich was sure.

Nick nodded. "I know. I thought I was cool yesterday, bragging to everyone how I wasn't going to have to come to school today, but when I got home last night…"

Holly tensed up. She thought he might let it slip that he had given her a ride home after school.

"….I found a letter from Rudyard at my house. One of my classes got washed out." He glanced at Mead. "Bad news when you have a double major like I do. My schedule's so tight that if I lose a single credit, it can throw everything off. Not good, what with my internship coming up next semester…"

Rich studied Nick while he blathered on further about himself, and, whether it was the way they had been introduced or an irregularity in the fluorescent lighting overhead, Rich found himself taking an instant dislike to the guy. Rich felt certain that he was not the first person to respond to Nick this way, especially in this particular situation, nor would he be the last.

"….I just hope I can get into a different class. I'm graduating on time no matter what."

"Yeah, well," Rich said with disinterest. "Good for you." He put a hand on Holly's arm. "I really need to speak with you about something." He glowered at Nick. "Alone."

"Oh, hey, I didn't mean to interrupt."

"You're not interrupting," Holly assured him.

"But when I saw you pull her out of line like that, I didn't know what was going on. It didn't look like she wanted to go with you."

"Well Mick—"

"*Nick.*"

"I guess you just don't know Holly as well as you think."

305

Nick frowned. "Really."

Holly acted fast. "Come on guys, don't be that way. How we got together isn't half as important as the fact that we're here together now."

Rich fixed his eyes on Holly. She sounded like a Sunday School teacher.

"Which means we can all wait in line together. Time'll pass a lot faster this way."

Nick smiled. "I guess you're right."

Rich's expression soured. "Do you two want to be alone?"

"*Rich*," Holly muttered.

"*Holly*."

"Shhh," she replied.

It was obvious to Nick, as well as to everyone else in the hallway, that this was one of those awkward boy/girl moments that generally occur at a point in a relationship when the people in question are either considering breaking up or getting engaged.

Nick looked away. "Maybe I'd better leave you two alone."

"Don't be silly. We'll—"

"Holly," Rich said forcefully. "I really need to talk to you about something."

She tilted her head back and scowled at the ceiling. "All right, all right." She lowered her head. "Nick, why don't you get in line, and we'll be over in a minute."

"Are you sure," he asked in a fatherly tone, and she smiled. "It'll be all right."

"Okay."

Holly waited until Nick was out of earshot before she spoke. "All right, what *is* it?"

Rich's jaw tightened. Holly had obviously overlooked the fact he had managed to arrive that afternoon on time.

"Well?!"

A sneer sprouted above his chin, while his mind was busy bouncing back and forth among the events of the past month like a ball in play in a pinball machine. Like it or not, Holly had just answered every one of the questions Rich had been struggling with over the past couple of weeks, and there was no denying it now. Holly definitely *did not* want to go out with him any more. He took the news rather well, cushioned by the cocktail of adrenaline and testosterone coursing through his veins at the moment, but he could still feel a piece of himself break off and retreat somewhere at the back of his mind. It promised to return just as soon as everyone else had left.

"Okay, if you want to do this right here..." He peered up and down the corridor. "....I've got a little time."

"What are you talking about?"

"Let me put it this way. I didn't run all the way over here to register for classes."

Holly's eyebrows collided. "What? You mean you're not going to register today?!" She quickly got a hold of herself, convinced that her previous question had come out entirely too loud. "Why didn't you tell me?! I would've come in earlier if I'd've known that. I only came here this late because we were supposed to *register together*."

Rich was pleased with her response, it was much better than anything he had been expecting, and, fully aware of what he

307

was going to say next, he tried to contain his growing excitement. "Holly, I'm dropping out."

Taken completely off guard, all Holly could do was gawk back at him. "What?"

Concerned by Holly's shaken expression, Nick joined them once again. "Holly, are you all right?" He glared at Mead.

Rich stared back. "I'm pregnant."

Nick stiffened. "That is *not* funny."

"Nick, please." Holly was still stunned. She looked at Rich. "You're dropping out."

"I'm dropping out."

The news did not have quite the same effect on Nick that it had had on Holly. In fact, Nick didn't react at all. "Oh?"

That didn't fool Holly or Rich, and they promptly ignored him.

"I decided about twenty minutes ago."

Holly wasn't sure what she found more unsettling: Richard's news or the fact that she was actually upset by it. After all, hadn't she already convinced herself that the best thing she could possibly do was to break up with him? And wouldn't his dropping out make the transition for her even easier?

"But shouldn't you at least think about it for a little while before you actually do it?"

"I have been thinking about it. Since the beginning of the semester."

Nick started to shake his head. "Man, I know *exactly* what you're going through—"

"Nick, please," interrupted Holly. "Have you talked to anyone else about this? Mennon or Tollhausler?"

"Not yet. But we're supposed to rendezvous behind the library a little later."

"Rendezvous?!" She frowned. That was a strange word to use. "Why are you going to—"

"Hey!" A guard suddenly shouted from down the hall. "He's here!"

Nobody in the hall moved, except Mead.

Holly looked at him. "Richard. Where are you—"

He was about a yard away. "They think I started the riot in Marner Hall."

Flummoxed, Holly's mouth fell open. "*You?! You* started the riot?"

He laughed. "You know, it wasn't half as difficult as you might think." He darted over to the stairs and turned. "By the way, I was going to tell you this later, you know, in a more appropriate setting, but seeing as you're so busy…"

Seven guards charged down the hall.

Rich ran up the stairs two at a time, but midway, he turned. "Holly," he said, a little out of breath, "I don't think we should see each other any more." He sprinted up the remaining steps to the landing and disappeared.

"What?!"

Nick put a hand on Holly's shoulder. "Are you all right? This is pretty crazy."

She wasn't listening. "I *did not* say I was too busy. I just wanted him to get on with whatever it was he had to say."

Five more guards appeared, and everyone watched as they dashed up the stairs.

Holly took a step in their direction. "Nick, could you excuse me for a minute?"

He noticed the far off look in her eyes. "Sure."

"Thanks." Holly started down the hall and stopped. She glanced over her shoulder at Nick and tried to smile.

She hurried up the steps.

10

Two blocks over, as the crow flies—a sober crow mind you, not one of those drunken ones that keep cawing incessantly at Lord knows what--Ernie Turpin was standing, alone.

He didn't know how or when it had happened, but at some point, during all the running and jumping around, he had somehow managed to lose the security guards who had been chasing after him. Dejected, he lowered his guitar case to the ground and hugged it to his side.

He had been having such a good time too.

Ernie still didn't know how he had done it. He hadn't been running half as fast as he could have been, and using his guitar case as a handicap, he had periodically held it over his head so his pursuers wouldn't lose him on Rudyard's busier byways and thoroughfares. Ernie didn't know what he could have done to make their job any easier for them, except maybe to have stood completely still, but he knew he wasn't going to do that. That would have been cheating.

Turpin exhaled, leaning an elbow on his case, and began to pout. He didn't know what he was going to do now. Where was he going to find more security guards on such short notice?

A split second later, the answer to this question fortuitously presented itself when Sergeants Quimby and Buck tumbled into view, the former dodging around a short woman in a long purple coat, the latter hopping over a stray dog.

Turpin's face brightened instantly. He started off in the opposite direction, and to allow the guards time to catch up, he did it on one foot.

"Look at that," Sergeant Buck growled. "He thinks this is one big joke."

"He won't much longer."

Both guards were sure they had him now.

And they did too.

Until of course, Ernie spotted Lloyd Hall.

11

For reasons which had never been made completely clear—especially to the people footing the bill—a rather imposing fifteen foot high wall (Decorated with an uneven line of three foot wide circular indentations) had been erected around the perimeter of Lloyd Hall sometime after the building's completion in the summer of 1971; and while the seemingly endless bank of dull concrete was unquestionably a classic example of the type of thing architects were turning out in the late sixties and early seventies, it was equally apparent that, barring a surprise attack by Huns, it served no real practical purpose whatsoever. At least, none discernible to anyone who had not been present at any of the initial planning meetings, and up until that day, the wall had pretty much gone unnoticed since the building's ribbon-cutting ceremony at the start of 1972.

The blur of pocked gray caught Ernie's eye, and he headed straight for it.

"Now what's he up to?" Buck asked.

The first thing Ernie did was to stretch himself to his full height of five foot seven inches, and in one go, tossed his guitar case on top of the gray, gouged wall.

"Oh damn," Quimby muttered.

Using the sunken circles as footholds, Ernie climbed the wall in a matter of seconds, and with one jump, landed astride the wide barrier like a cowboy leaping onto a horse. He smiled, impressed with the view, leaned back and enthusiastically waved the guards on.

"Stop right there!" Buck yelled.

Ernie laughed, then threw a leg into the air, spun sideways and grabbed the handle of his guitar case. He dropped out of sight.

Quimby and Buck came to a halt, and stared up at the empty space where Ernie had just been seconds before.

The wall didn't say a word.

Sergeant Quimby bent over, holding his sides and painfully breathed in and out. "Damn it."

Buck patted him on the shoulder. "No no. This is good. The gate's all the way on the other side of the hall. We've got him."

"Yeah?" Quimby stood up, intrigued.

"Sure. I can outrun this guy. I'll head him off at the gate."

"What should I do?"

"Go over after him, and chase him towards the gate."

"Will do." Quimby aimed his foot at the nearest circular indentation and mounted the wall. "See you in a few."

"Right," Sergeant Buck yelled over his shoulder.

He tore down the street. Sergeant Quimby leaned his left forearm on top of the wall, and, throwing his other arm over for support, hurled himself to the other side.

There was a loud yelp, followed by the clumsy, staccato sounds of a struggle, and this brief interlude was soon brought to an unceremonious end with a loud bonk. The noise, which is usually produced when an acoustic guitar collides with something of equal or greater proportion to itself, eventually subsided, and then Ernie's scuffed, black guitar case reappeared at the top of the wall.

He pulled himself up beside it, his tongue unconsciously extended in heavy concentration, and he sat down. He carefully lowered his case, gripping it with his legs before he let it drop to the ground, and, stepping on the lip of one of the circles, he followed after it.

He had a pair of trousers slung over his left shoulder, and they slid off when he touched down. He didn't know why he had removed the guard's pants, it wasn't anything he had planned, but then, he hadn't been planning on conking the poor guy on the head either. To be fair, the guard *had* tried to club him into submission first, but Ernie didn't think that would make much of a difference to the guard. Experiencing a sudden pang of guilt—a vestige leftover from a religion class he had attended in the fourth grade—Ernie suspected that he might have gone too far this time, and told himself that he should probably give the guard back his pants. It was cold out there.

He looked up and down the street, making sure the coast was clear, and held the blue, striped trousers by the waistband. Using a circle for a step, Ernie flipped the pants into the air and draped them over the wall.

Backing away, he snickered.

Perfect, he thought, and, retrieving his guitar, he ran back down the street.

12

In the meantime, a team of harried-looking security guards had rumbled their way into the belly of Rockford Hall. They had been dispatched ostensibly to assist the first group with their search of the premises for Mead, but in reality, they had been rushed to the scene in order to avoid an unpleasant incident similar to the one that had occurred in Marner Hall. They had been told in no uncertain terms to make it clear to the students amassed for Pre-Registration that the campus police were still very much in the picture and therefore still very much in charge. Unfortunately, despite their presence, the mood in the building had not dramatically changed much since Mead had made his rather noisy escape, and the surrounding tension only seemed to have grown worse.

Four floors above, Myra Yasner was on the phone with her friend Betty McAdams. "....Evie Cohen said they were chasing the guy up and down the stairs."

"Barbara told me about that too," Betty confirmed from an office two floors below. "I'm just sorry we missed it."

"I'm not. I wouldn't know what to think if I saw something like that. What is going on around here?"

"I don't know. But just imagine what must have been going through the minds of those kids downstairs when they saw all those guards chasing one student."

Myra shook her head. "It's like something out of a movie."

"Well it isn't over yet. While I was out, Jean Fisher called and told Barbara that members of the Student Council are trying to organize the students for some kind of a rally outside the Student Center. They want to meet with the administration and get an honest account of what went on in Marner Hall."

Myra frowned.

"So do you still think that everything I told you was an exaggeration?"

"Well..." Myra stared at the top of her desk. "....I still don't believe the guards did everything you say they did, but—"

"Myra," Betty said in a strange voice, "could you hold for a second?"

"Sure." The phone clicked in Myra's ear and the sound of Betty's office was replaced with a dull electric hum. Myra assumed Betty had another call. A minute later, there was another click.

"Myra?"

"I'm here."

"Myra, you aren't going to believe this, but three guards just came into my office and asked if Barbara or I had seen a student in a gray hat."

"You mean that kid's still in the building?"

"They say he is. He apparently made the mistake of going up in the fire tower instead of down, towards the exit." She took a breath. "And get this, they say he's definitely one of the kids who started all that trouble over in Financial Aid."

"*Did* you see anyone?"

"Come on Myra. You know I haven't seen anyone under the age of forty on this floor since last year's Christmas Party."

Someone coughed.

"Sorry Barbara," Betty replied.

Myra stood up and walked out from behind her desk. "Are they sure he's somewhere in the building?"

"How should I know?" Betty snickered. "Knowing our guards, the kid's probably halfway across campus by now."

"You think?" Myra had gone to the door of her office and was looking up and down the hall. She was relieved to find it completely empty, and looked like it always did: to her left, under the window at the end of the corridor, sat an old beige sofa, a short table that had been transferred there from an office up on the tenth floor the year before, and a white trash can with a dome and a dark stain streaking its side, the sum of which was supposed to serve as an employees lounge but which nobody used, and in the corner to her right hung a bright, red fire extinguisher.

"I hope for his sake he is. Those guards looked pretty mad."

"Oh come on Betty. Don't talk like that."

"Myra, you didn't see these guards. They were furious."

"Well…" She retreated a couple of steps, and pushed the door closed with her foot. "….you know how much they hate exercise."

Betty laughed. "Myra."

"They don't," she said with a smirk. "I'm surprised they haven't shot anybody yet to save themselves the trouble of having to run after them."

"Myra, you are wicked."

She leaned against her desk with an outstretched arm. "It wouldn't be so farfetched after some of the things you've told me today."

"I'm just telling you what I heard…"

The door to Myra's office suddenly clicked open, and Johnny Mennon carefully backed into the room.

Myra turned. "Well, as much as I'd like to continue with this…"

"Don't tell me Donald's back already."

Myra circled to the other side of her desk. "He isn't."

"Myra," Betty gasped. "Don't tell me your boss actually has an appointment with someone today."

Myra looked at Mennon. "Maybe, maybe not." She couldn't help noticing that Johnny was also holding the fire extinguisher from out in the hall. "I'm not quite sure what he's up to."

Mennon yanked the safety ring from the top of the red tank and threw it over his shoulder.

"Well Myra, you'd better hope it's an appointment. I hear the university might have to take Donald's office away if he doesn't start scheduling at least one there a semester."

"Yes Betty."

"Uh oh, you've got that I've-got-to-get-off-the-phone-right-now tone in your voice."

"I do have to go."

Mennon tugged the black hose from the side of the tank and held it at the ready as he listened at the door.

"All right, but if I hear any more news, I'll call."

Myra nodded. "Same here." She hung up. "Can I help you?"

Johnny looked away from the door. "What?"

"I said, 'Can I help you?'"

"And what did I say?"

"Well…" Myra pursed her lips. "….you said 'What?'"

He smiled. "Hey, what do you know? That *does* sound like something I would say."

He took in his surroundings. He had not backed into the first door he had seen, like he had thought, the one that looked like a janitor's closet, but he had somehow slipped into the office next to it, the realization of which brightened his spirits immeasurably. Janitor's closets are seldom heated, and frequently contain buckets that smell as if someone had just emptied the contents of a bottle of disinfectant on a litter of wet puppies. *

---

* Now the reader should in no way deduce from this particular passage that Johnny Mennon had spent an inordinate amount of his youth hiding out in musty closets and poorly lit stairwells. Hardly. However, the occasion had definitely arisen often enough that he had been forced to develop some sort of routine for executing such maneuvers, and along the way, he had even managed to form a guideline or two.

"I guess you're wondering what I'm doing here," he said with a little more volume than was absolutely necessary, and Myra's eyebrows dipped. "I'd rather you explained why you're holding that fire extinguisher."

"Oh." He looked down. "I thought I smelled smoke."

"In here?" She sniffed at the air. "I don't smell anything."

"Well that's a relief." Mennon set the extinguisher down on the floor. "I was pretty scared there for a minute."

"Uh-huh."

"Anyway, the reason I'm here..."

"Yes?"

"....is because..." His eyes shot to the door located five feet behind Myra's desk, and, while he only skimmed it, the middle initial ensured that it did not open on a closet. "....because I'm here to see your boss." Johnny removed his cap and unbuttoned his coat. "Is he in?"

Myra frowned. "I'm afraid he isn't."

"Good, I don't feel like talking to him right now anyway. I'm beat." Mennon tossed his cap on to the green divan across from Myra's desk and immediately installed himself on the cushion beside it.

Myra gracefully slid a small desk calendar from the computer terminal to her left. "And you say that Mr. Crenchshaw is expecting you?"

"If this is his office, he is."

For instance, while Mennon knew that ducking into a nice warm office was a hundred times better than lurking in a dusty, dank closet (See the above description.), he would frequently choose the latter simply because office workers generally spend more time at their desks than a janitor does in his closet. Consequently, Johnny's tenure there would depend entirely on his ability to manufacture, on the spot, a credible reason why he was there. Which wasn't always easy depending on the office or his mood.

"Oh." Myra still couldn't understand how she had managed to miss one of Donald's appointments, and paged through her calendar. "Is this something I might be able to help you with?"

"Well it might," Johnny said, "but I'd rather your boss took care of it. It's kind of personal."

That didn't sound right.

"And you say that Donald Crenchshaw, *the Sub-treasurer to the Treasurer* is expecting you?"

"Oh sure," he lied, "we got lots of important business to talk over." He threw a leg up on the sofa.

"I see," she said, and sat down behind her desk.

Johnny made himself even more comfortable, and his hand disappeared into his right coat pocket. "Boy, some day, huh?" He produced a pack of cigarettes and shook one loose.

"There's no smoking in here."

"Oh, I'm sorry." Johnny leaned forward and offered her one.

"No thank you. I don't smoke."

"Ohhh, you mean there really *isn't* any smoking in here." He returned the cigarette to the pack, and the pack to his pocket.

"And you're sure there isn't anything I can do for you right now? Maybe call someone else?"

Johnny lowered his leg from the couch. "Maybe there is."

Myra set her hands flat on the desk. "I was hoping I could be of some help."

"Okay." Mennon flipped open a red notebook. "What do you think is more romantic? A full moon or a sunrise?"

Myra's thoughts suddenly found themselves circling each other in a holding pattern behind her eyes. She stared at Mennon. "What?"

He brought a pen out of his other pocket. "I'm workin' on this love song see, and I'm tryin' to figure out what the girls in the audience'll think is more romantic."

Myra smiled. "I see, you're a Music Major."

"*Music Major*?!" Johnny snickered. "Yeah, like *they* know anything about music."

"Well I...thought—"

"Never mind about that." He scribbled a word out in his notebook. "So which is it?"

"Which is what?"

"What makes your little heart go pitty-pat? A full moon or a sunrise?"

"Oh, well," she said, adjusting her left earring, "I guess I'd have to say that they're both equally romantic."

"Sure, there's nothing like staring at the moon from the backseat of a car." He placed the pen to his lips. "But there's something to be said about watching the sun rise from there as well." He tapped the pen against his jaw. "And I thought this was going to be easy. See, this song is for the last set of the evening, and while my band's playin' , it has to make every girl in the bar want to go home with every guy there." He grinned. "Of course, it wouldn't hurt if they wanted to go home with one or two of the guys in the band either."

Myra looked up. "Well what do you think is more romantic?"

"What do I care? I've already got a girlfriend."

"Well what does she think is more romantic?"

"The usual stuff: flowers, birthday cards, little presents. But I figure as long as her boyfriend gives her those things, why should I?"

"Oh…"

"She's spoiled enough as it is."

"….I…what?"

Fortunately for Myra, at that moment, she was saved from having to untwist the knots of Johnny's tangled logic when the hall outside thundered with the footsteps of three or four people. A loud discussion immediately erupted on the other side of the door as to who exactly was in charge, and therefore the one most qualified to choose who would go into the office first.

Relatively certain he knew to whom these voices belonged, Johnny promptly stashed his cap under the sofa cushion to his left. He jumped up. "So, um, let me get this straight. You're sayin' that you don't know when your boss…" He threw off his coat. "….Mr. Coleslaw—"

"Crenchshaw."

"Sorry." He stuffed the coat under the sofa "When Mr. Crenchshaw is going to get back. Right?"

"Yes."

"Well then…" Johnny hurried over to Crenchshaw's office. "….why don't I just get out of your way and wait for him in his office?"

"What?"

Johnny opened the door. "Buzz me when he gets back."

Myra stood up. "Wait a—"

13

A guard came swinging into the room on the door, nightstick in hand, and Myra fell back in her chair. "Oh!"

Another guard hastily took up a position behind him in the doorway.

"Sorry to scare you ma'am," the first guard said. "But has anyone come in here the last couple of minutes?"

"Um…" Myra sat up while her eyes held momentarily on the club in the guard's hand. It looked incredibly dangerous.

"A guy wearing a gray hat and a blue coat?"

It was at that precise moment when everything that had transpired the last ten minutes finally fell into place for her, and all Myra could think of was how relieved she was that she *hadn't* made a mistake and forgotten about one of Donald's appointments.

"Well actually…" she began, fully intending on telling the guard where Mennon was, when the guard impatiently slapped his club into the palm of his left hand. The clipped sound of wood striking flesh instantly filled her with dread, what with Betty's vivid, blood-soaked horror stories of overreacting guards still fresh in her mind, and Myra immediately feared for the safety of whoever was hiding in the next room. "….no."

"That's funny. We definitely thought he was somewhere on this floor." The guard's smoldering brown eyes made a quick circuit of the file cabinets and shelves lining the walls and then lighted on Myra. "Did you maybe see someone who matches that description in the hall?"

She shook her head. "No, I'm afraid I didn't see anyone. The door was closed."

The guard's eyes slowly drifted to the door across the room. "Are you the only one here?"

"Y-es," she stammered.

"And how long have you been here?"

"A little under an hour, I'd say."

He walked around her desk. "Sorry. It's just that your office is the only one on this floor that's open right now, and we were sure he was up here. We were right behind him." He took a step towards Crenchshaw's office, and Myra gripped the arm of her chair. "What did this person do anyway?"

The guard turned. "He's one of the guys who started the riot in Marner Hall."

"And you want to arrest him for that?"

"Ohhhh," the officer drawled, absently tapping his club against the top of his thigh. "I'd like to do more to him than just that."

Myra's stomach fell as if she were on an elevator. "Oh my."

"But the administration wants to have a little talk with him first." The guard sauntered over to her desk. "I don't know what they expect to find out."

"I see."

"Is there anything you want to tell us about?"

Myra felt a little dizzy. "Anything--?"

The guard reached down for something. "Had a little trouble here?"

"Trouble?"

He raised the fire extinguisher to her desk.

Relieved that it wasn't one of Mennon's outer garments, Myra stood up. "Oh, that." She suddenly remembered something that had actually happened the month before. "The secretary down the hall was smoking in her office and accidentally set her trash can on fire."

He stared back menacingly. "She shouldn't be smoking in her office."

"That's what I told her—"

There was more noise out in the hallway, more discussion, and another guard, who looked equally homicidal, came bursting into the room. "Del."

The guard standing next to Myra continued staring at her. "Yeah?"

"Brophy says that he saw somebody in the other tower. Maybe our boy *isn't* on this floor."

"So he might have gone up to the roof?"

"It's possible."

Del nodded. "Then let's get going." He turned on the ball of his foot, carefully sliding his club into a ring at the back of his belt, and followed the other guard to the door. "Sorry to have disturbed you like this Ma'am."

Myra leaned against her desk. "That's perfectly all right."

He stopped. "It certainly was a lot to throw at someone who sits at a desk all week. I hope we didn't shake you up too much. Do you maybe want me to leave a guard in the hall? You know, until we catch this guy?"

"Oh no, no. That won't be necessary. Mr. Crenchshaw will be back soon."

Officer Del's eyes held on Crenchshaw's office. He still thought he should have seen what was on the other side of the door. "All right." His heavy shoes clunked in the silence. "But if you should see or hear anything out of the ordinary, please give us a call."

Myra smiled. "Oh, I will."

"Thanks." He closed the door.

14

Mennon stomped into the room. "Heyyyy, who does your boss think he is? If he thinks I'm gonna' sit around here waitin' for him all day, he's nuts!"

"That's right, they're gone."

He grinned. "Thanks lady. I really appreciate what you did." He started towards the sofa. "I'll just get my stuff."

Somebody threw open the door of the office.

Johnny tried stopping, his heels digging parallel grooves into the deep pile carpet, and Myra knocked her chair into the wall. "Oh!"

"Johnny," Holly Rake said, quickly shutting the door behind her, "thank God. When I saw those guards, I thought for sure…" Holly continued talking, fast, but it was a good thirty seconds before Johnny and Myra could even understand what it was she was saying. Their hearts had stopped the moment she had ripped open the door. "….then they ran into the fire tower, and I had to see if he was still maybe hiding in here."

The blood began flowing to Myra's brain first, and she slowly exhaled. "Oh thank goodness. She knows you." She sat down. "I thought that angry guard had come back to check the other office."

"Have you seen Richard?"

Johnny went straight to the sofa and pulled his coat out from underneath. "Not since Marner Hall."

"Damn it," Holly muttered. "Where is he?" She went back to the door and slowly opened it again. "It's still clear."

He yanked his cap out from between the sofa cushions. "Great. I could use a smoke." Mennon slid his coat on. "What are you chasin' around after him for anyway? You want to slow him down?"

She glared over her shoulder. "Is he really dropping out?"

He put on his hat. "Those guys have been talkin' about doin' that all semester. Today he's droppin' out. Tomorrow..." He picked up his red notebook and jammed it in his pocket. "Who knows? You can never really tell what those guys are gonna' do until after they've done it."

"Oh."

Johnny smiled. "Hey, don't worry. It'll be okay."

The frown on Holly's face didn't budge. "It's just that I've never seen Richard this way before."

"Yeah. It was pretty wild back there."

"Did he really start the riot in Marner Hall?"

"One person couldn't have done all that. It was more a group effort."

"So what really happened?"

"Nothing that's going to match all the stories you're going to be hearing the next couple of days." He walked around Holly to the door. "Thanks again lady." He winked at Myra, and Patted Holly on the shoulder. "See you around Slim." He went into the hall.

Holly couldn't believe it. There was something very different about him. She looked at Myra. "What *did* happen in Marner Hall?!"

15

Certainly Holly was not the first person that afternoon to pose this particular question, and even though several hours had now passed since Tollhausler, Turpin, Mennon and Mead had dropped by Financial Aid, it was still the one uppermost on many people's minds.

The climate at Rudyard had not improved much in the interim, despite repeated attempts by the university to diffuse the situation, and a good deal of the Student Body, still unsure of what to make of the endless supply of war stories and inflammatory rhetoric filling the air, seemed at a genuine loss as to what they should do or who they should believe. Flustered, they had simply taken to mooning about campus, and, when they weren't glaring at passing security guards, they would complain to one another about how little the university obviously cared.

Diane Curzewski happened to be standing among one of these groups, called over by some people from Professor Melange's class, and she was listening with great interest to the latest tide of rumors that had rolled in.

They ranged from the pedestrian (The Guards were confiscating beer from anyone openly carrying it on campus.) to the fantastical (A team of concussed guards had hung an innocent Grad. Student from a tree over by Oxbow Hall.), and upon hearing the last of these infamies, a student, whose revolutionary antics the last two years had earned him the sobriquet Bob the Radical, punched one hand into the other and hissed, "*The die is cast!*"

Diane's stomach responded to this, as it only could, with a growl. It was as if it too had something to say about the present state of affairs, but, in actuality, was simply hungry—not unlike Bob the Radical. She dug through her purse for something to quiet it down with, and, moving a black compact aside, came up with a bent pack of cigarettes—she had stopped hiding them ever since the first day of school. She shook one, slightly crooked, loose, and placed the pack back into her bag. Her hand came out holding a square of matches. Two seconds later, she took a deep, deep drag—a kind of reversed sigh—from the end of the sloped cigarette, and, sure it was lit, she slowly waved out the match.

She still didn't know what she was going to do. Should she go home? Or should she stay? There was talk of some kind of rally being held at the Student Center later on in the afternoon, but it was her understanding that it was being held solely because of the riot in Marner Hall, not because of the latest strike news.

The article from that morning's <u>Rudyard Chronicle</u> once again reared its ugly headline, the black and white column towering over her purple-tinged thoughts, and Diane was helpless to stop it from muscling everything else out of the way. She knew she should have been a little more concerned about what had happened in Marner Hall, but she was worried more about what a Teachers' Strike would do to the campus.

It was at this point that the campus in question dropped from underneath, leaving her suspended in midair—her body's way of registering with Diane the fact that bombarding it with nicotine was no real substitute for actual food—and she was relieved several seconds later when she felt her feet once again on solid ground.

Stepping on her cigarette, she told one of her friends she would be right back, and walked off in search of the nearest food cart.

Diane obsessed while she walked.

Will it be a long strike? How long can a strike like this go on? What if the university and the teachers *never* come to an agreement and there's another strike next semester? Or the one after that? *Or the one after that?!* Should I even bother staying at Rudyard? Or should I transfer to another, more stable college where I'll be able to graduate on time?

Diane probably would have gone on like this for another twenty minutes had she not arrived at the intersection of Allen and Leopard several seconds later. This was where Bernie's New York Deli Dog Cart had been parked since the Fall Semester of 1971, but, more importantly, where she was greeted by the unmistakable aroma of boiled hot dogs.

Any other day, Diane wouldn't even have noticed it, her mind focused on her next class, but on this day, her empty stomach wouldn't allow her to think of anything else. It immediately seized control, directing her over to the curb, and before she knew it, she was shoving money through the fogged window at Bernie. She knew exactly what she wanted too: two soft pretzels with mustard. Diane hated hot dogs.

She broke off a piece (The rounded end), being careful not to get any of the spicy brown mustard on her black and silver gloves, and, after taking a bite, she sighed. The dough was still warm, its golden-brown, oven-baked shell crisp, and there was just the right amount of salt on it. It was delicious.

She had forgotten how truly hungry she had been, and after finishing this piece of pretzel, separated another, bigger chunk...took a bite...then another...and then another. She hoped she wasn't making a spectacle of herself devouring the pretzels this way, but she couldn't help it. They were so good.

They were also gone in under five minutes, whereupon Diane signaled an end to her lunch by wiping her mouth with one of Bernie's 3 X 4 white paper napkins. She dutifully dropped it in a nearby trashcan, briefly checking her appearance in the side of Bernie's polished metal cart, and, satisfied with what she saw, she started walking.

She could already feel herself growing sleepy, the blood rushing from her head to her stomach as her body set to work absorbing the simple components of this doughy repast, and the campus began to take on a distant, dreamlike quality.

16

She stumbled out from underneath this gluten-induced torpor—as well as over a schoolbag someone had left in the middle of the sidewalk—upon her return to Sheldrake Hall.

The scene had undergone considerable change in her absence, and where there had been nothing but students lining the steps and pavement around the building before, there were now only security guards.

The students huddled behind the long yellow barriers in front of Sheldrake Hall appeared very unhappy about this latest development, and Diane cast about the crowd for her friends.

The tension in the air suddenly flared as someone came out of the building.

Diane's hand went up to her head.

"Jonathan?"

17

"What'd you say?"

"I said 'That must be him.'"

"Him?"

"Yeah, the one they've been waiting for."

"Isn't that the guy in your Economics 215 class?"

"You know, now that I look at him…"

"I wonder what he did."

"I don't know, but whatever it was, it got him an appointment with twenty-four security guards."

"Whoa, you're telling me all this fuss is over one guy?"

"I guess the guards're tired of having everybody they go after get away. Hand me another beer."

"He must be *some* desperado."

"There's no telling what he might be carrying around in that briefcase."

"Look at them. They want to hit him."

"You think they will?"

"Not with that news crew standing over there, they won't."

"Man, they better not hit him."

"Oh my God! That's *that* guy!"

"Who?"

"From my speech class."

"Really?"

"It sure looks like him."

"You're right, he is kind of cute."

"I wonder what he did."

"Meg, look at all this. He must have had some kind of run in with the guards."

"Ohhhh."

"Look, there're two more guards coming out behind him."

"For Christ's sake, he doesn't have a chance."

"Run, run!"

"He's got nowhere to run now."

"Haw, haw. Look at him run."

"Ohhh, they got him."

"Jonathan!"

"Aw, why don't you leave him alone?"

"Rogers, Hawkins, keep those students back!"

"What are we all standing around for? Let's do something!"

"Man, did you see that? Pitiful. I tell you this, if that had been me, I would've socked a couple of those guards before they took me down. Hand me another beer."

"Who *is* that?"

"Jonathan."

18

It just so happened that Bob Falconbruder was on campus that afternoon. He and President Garibaldi had a meeting scheduled to discuss the progress of Ralph's plans for the campus, but at the moment, he doubted that Ralph would be able to make it.

Seconds before, a bulletin, interrupting that afternoon's regularly scheduled programming, had come over the TV, announcing, of all things, that there was trouble on the Rudyard University campus. The words of this lead-in had barely left the anchor's mouth before the picture cut from the studio to the campus outside. That was where a woman in a green coat, the name on the screen identifying her as one Lindsay Foster Nolan-Greco, was standing in front of Sheldrake Hall.

"Yes Wade, I'm here live at Rudyard University where a confrontation between students and Campus Security has erupted in violence..."

Behind the reporter, dozens and dozens of students could be seen hurtling along the pavement in the direction of anyone wearing a blue uniform, while the men and women in those uniforms fought desperately to get the hell out of the way.

"My God Donald, look at them go."

The waiter, having just returned holding a dish with a small roll on it, shook his head. "I wouldn't have believed it if I wasn't seeing it with my own eyes, sir." He carefully leaned over Falconbruder's left shoulder and gracefully set the plate down on the round table at the nine o'clock position. "And right here on campus. In this day and age."

"….while previous altercations between students and guards started with little to no provocation, it's clear this one started after an arrest was made in front of Sheldrake Hall almost twenty minutes ago. Action News was there…"

The picture changed as a replay was run of the aforementioned arrest, and as expected, the guards, executing a classic pincer movement, grabbed the student with little to no fuss at the top of the steps. Nolan-Greco was suddenly there again on the screen.

"We've been told that the person who was arrested was part of the small group that started the demonstration earlier today in The Financial Aid Office, but as yet, we have had no confirmation on this."

Snarling, a woman brandishing a field hockey stick lunged into view and swung at the nearest officer.

"As you can see Wade, emotions are running pretty high."

With a twist of her torso, the woman brought the taped stick down on the guard's head.

"But campus security would seem to be taking this into account, and have been responding with considerable restraint…"

Another guard grabbed the woman with the stick, wresting it from her hands, but was immediately pushed off by

335

Bob the Radical, who in turn was knocked to the ground by another guard; then there were suddenly six more people pushing and pulling at the edge of the fray.

"….which may be making their job more difficult. Even with reinforcements--" Nolan-Greco hopped forward as a student flipped a security guard to the ground behind. "Even with reinforcements Wade, the guards have been unable to keep the riot contained. It didn't help that the street was so populated with students at the time of the arrest. But I'm told—"

Lindsay Foster Nolan-Greco abruptly pitched left out of shot ("Oh!"), leaving the viewer an unobstructed view of the scene beyond, the guards struggling to form a line across the pavement and the students, determined to sock at least one of them before the day was through, bumping and tripping over one another.

Then the very ground upon which this homage to Sixties' Radicalism was being performed began to shake.

A single, blurred second later, the cameraman and his crew—an intern from Rudyard named Scott Crowley—had joined Nolan-Greco there on the ground, and anyone tuning in at that particular moment would have been treated to an unexpected view of the reporter—sideways—as she struggled to free herself from under a pile of swearing students.

Somewhere across town, in an overheated control room, a button was pushed. It had become evident to the director, after three more people came crashing down, that Nolan-Greco would not be continuing her broadcast any time soon, and he had returned, without warning, to the studio. The anchor, Wade Humphrey, genuinely concerned by what he had seen, leveled his basset hound eyes straight at the camera.

"If you're just tuning in, Action News correspondent Lindsay Foster Nolan-Greco is live on the scene at Rudyard University where a full blown riot is underway."

"*Full blown?*" Falconbruder reached for his gin and tonic. "What does *that* even mean?"

Donald frowned. "Ratings, sir."

"It has been a day fraught with confrontations and high emotions, and as so often happens, misunderstanding has led to violence." Humphrey briefly paused so the word would register with his viewers. "As of this time, there have been no serious injuries reported, but we're told the university and the Philadelphia Police are in constant contact should there be any change."

A montage (Assembled from file footage of Rudyard) of the university replaced the anchorman on the screen.

"Wednesday morning started out like any other day for Rudyard University," Humphrey began. "The Fall Semester winding down, the only thing on anyone's mind, be they teacher, student or a member of the administration, preparing for the end of the semester and the start of the Christmas Break…"

Falconbruder sipped at his drink as the room gradually slipped off into the distance.

Ralph, as Falconbruder's youngest child Frankie would have said, was now in *big* trouble. There were no precedents Falconbruder could sight, no extenuating circumstances he could mention, that would prevent the Board of Trustees from once again discussing what they were going to do about, as they had recently begun to call it, the "Garibaldi Situation."

Falconbruder cut into his lamb chop—his usual entrée when visiting the Rudyard Alumni Club—weighing the pros and cons of coming to Ralph's aid, yet again, and raised the polished silver fork to his lips. He absently deposited the lamb and began to chew.

First, he made a list of those members on the Board who were loyal to the President of the University, and therefore going to support him through this latest crisis, and then mentally checked off the ones who, it was a safe bet, would not. That left those members who fell somewhere in between.

He now regretted having bullied some of those people, Kip Richardson and Tip Joyce in particular, the previous March when Ralph's budget for the 1984 fiscal year came up for a vote. He imagined that he and Ralph were going to need all the friends they could get the next couple of weeks, especially after the motion was put before the Board to demand from Ralph his resignation.

He knew it would be happening soon.

Falconbruder firmly believed the idea of removing Ralph would have never come up had the Board and him been on better terms. Unfortunately, things between them were about as bad as they could get, so much so that certain members, Kit Grayson generally leading the charge, made it a point, every other meeting, to emphasize how easy it would be to replace him.

There was the Pfaehler Library Fund incident (Half the Board had wanted Ralph fired over that), the Carpaccio Episode (They never did find out what had happened to the original draft of the independent auditor's report), Coach Tremble's open letter to the city's largest newspapers (Where *had* he gotten his hands on the Finance Department's projections for the fourth quarter?) and

338

finally, there was the little matter of those missing minutes from Garibaldi's meeting in 1980 with then President-Elect Ronald Reagan.

It had just been Ralph's good fortune that the Board could never decide what the public would make of these charges. They didn't want anyone outside the university to get the idea that Ralph, for whatever reasons, had been forced out. It would have created quite the controversy—that is, what passes for controversy in the academic world—and the consensus around the boardroom was that this really wasn't the time to have a scandal associated with the Rudyard University name. Not with the latest enrollment figures in and guidance counselors everywhere starting to mention the university's name in the same breath with Temple and Penn.

And it was all thanks, in no small part, to the tireless efforts of Rudyard's own Ralph Dimitri Garibaldi. That was why the Board Members felt they had to be careful with his termination. No doubt the public would disapprove of his firing under most circumstances, but if word got out that Ralph had been treated anything less than fair, it could have set the university back years.

Garibaldi was a very popular figure: with the state (After all, he had made it a point to be on a first name basis with any politician who might have been able to do him and the university some good.), with the city (Rudyard was one of the few businesses still flourishing in this part of town.) and within the local community itself (Ralph sat in on no less than four neighborhood committees a month.); and everybody was going to want to know what happened.

Which meant that several teams of reporters would be dispatched to the Rudyard campus that would also want to know. These reporters would in turn start interviewing anyone and everyone who crossed their paths, and, once the opportunistic teachers, mercurial students and embittered guards had had their say, there was no doubt in the Board Members' minds how sullied Rudyard's reputation would become in the public mind.

They had been hoping for something a little less complicated to rid Rudyard of Ralph for some time now, and it appeared, to Falconbruder anyway, that their wish had finally come true. He suspected that several Student Demonstrations and a "full blown" riot was just the sort of thing the Board had been waiting for.

He drained his glass.

And once Ralph's replacement—Falconbruder had interviewed the likely candidate, along with the rest of the Board, the previous July—had taken office, everyone was confident that, under the right circumstances, Ralph's departure, handled properly, would appear as a natural development to the outside world. After all, Ralph couldn't be expected to stay at Rudyard forever. His passing would then seem inevitable--as inevitable as the tuition hike that would be announced the following spring.

It would all be very slick, and, as some of the Board Members saw it, necessary if the university hoped to continue with its evolution. Nevertheless, it didn't make Falconbruder feel any better.

He truly believed that Ralph still had a couple of good years left in him. He liked Ralph, admired how far he had taken the university in such a short period of time, and, somewhere at the back of his mind, knew they would work together again. Falconbruder hadn't told many people, but, in his humble opinion, he thought Ralph would make a great governor. And after that, who knew how far Ralph could go?

"….then, without warning, a riot outside Sheldrake Hall."

A series of shouts and gasps poured from the TV, and the walls of the RAC Room steadily crept up and surrounded Falconbruder again.

The story on Rudyard was just about over. He knew this because he recognized the noises issuing from the TV, a replay of the footage from the riot broadcast earlier, Lindsay Foster Nolan–Greco back on her feet, the woman with the field hockey stick still swinging away, but, in the time it had taken the newscaster to recap the day, the video had been chopped up and reassembled into a very compelling seven seconds. The confrontation looked a lot more violent now with the awkward pauses removed, and Falconbruder guessed that anyone watching would find it very disturbing. Then he spotted Donald out of the corner of his eye.

The waiter was carrying a telephone.

"Mr. Falconbruder."

"Looks like somebody wants to speak to me."

"Yes sir."

Donald set the telephone down on the table and crouched down to plug it in. "Kit Grayson on the line sir." He stood up. "Mr. Grayson said he thought he might find you here."

"Well, wasn't that clever of him." He stared up at the TV and sighed. "I'll have another Donald."

"Very good sir." He silently swept the cut crystal glass from the table, and carried it towards the bar.

Falconbruder picked up the phone, but paused for an instant. Someone had just entered the room, and he found it difficult to look away. In this day and age, one didn't ordinarily see people who traveled about in topcoat and cape—tweed, no less— and the deerstalker cap above seemed more at home in a Sherlock Holmes movie than on a college campus.

19

Any further explanation was made unnecessary by the sudden arrival of six rather unhappy security guards. Their irritation radiated from their red, perspiring faces in waves across the paneled room, and the restaurant was suddenly very quiet— even the volume on the TV seemed to drop.

The guy in the Sherlock Holmes getup glided along the front of the bar, past Donald, past the bar stools—Falconbruder noticed he was wearing roller skates—and the guards spread out among the tables.

"Okay," the lead guard said in a low, even tone, "let's go."

Mr. Holmes spun around and shook his head.

"There's only one way this can turn out," the guard predicted. He was stalling, waiting for one of the other guards to take up a position behind the great detective.

Then Holmes reached for something under his cape, sending the hand of every guard in the room to their side arms.

The RAC Room's other patrons remained in their seats, but Falconbruder, dropping the phone, stood up. "Now hold on just a—"

Holmes threw a handful of powder into a candle to his right, and the air above crackled. There was a blinding flash, and he was suddenly standing beside Falconbruder.

The redoubtable Holmes placed a hand on Falconbruder's shoulder; his other hand weighed down by a guitar case, he rolled behind him.

"That's Robert Falconbruder," Donald nervously announced, and the guards paused for a moment wondering who *that* was.

"Everybody back off," the lead guard ordered, just in case Falconbruder *was* somebody, and the circle of guards widened. "All right, now, let him go," the guard demanded.

Sherlock did—long enough to release another cascade of flash powder. The air ignited, the powder flaring in the dark room, and Falconbruder was suddenly looking back at the guards.

He realized now, as he was being dragged to the door by a student in a Sherlock Holmes costume, pursued by six security guards with murder in their eyes, how out of hand things had gotten. He needed to speak to Ralph. Quick.

20

"Guards!"

While Holly Rake hadn't had much time to consider what it was she was actually doing, she was still convinced it was the only thing left for her to do.

"Guards!" She threw her arms around Richard Mead. "Over here!"

She had found him right where Mennon had said he would be: behind Pfaehler Library.

"Here!" she shouted. "The guy who started the riot in Marner Hall!"

She hadn't seen him at first, there were quite a lot of students milling about the back entrance, but on her second pass, she had spotted him standing at the rear of one of these groups with his head down. He was the only one wearing sunglasses.

Rich pulled away. "Holly, what the hell are you doing?!"

He hadn't seen her at first, he explained, because he had been too busy worrying that one of the hundreds of guards marching passed would suddenly spot him, and, in a matter of seconds, he would be caught.

What Rich couldn't know—or Holly for that matter--was that the seemingly endless parade of guards rolling past the library hadn't been sent there to hunt him down, but to stand ready in the Quad next door should anything untoward happen during the rally. The moment a bunch of students rushed the stage or a fight broke out or, worse, a question not cleared by one of President Garibaldi's staff was asked during the question and answer period, these officers could be instantly mobilized and sent to the Student Center—a mere block and a half away—to provide assistance.

Holly jumped up on Rich's back. "Here! The guy who started the riot in Marner Hall!!"

"For Christ's sake, Holly—"

"He's bragging about how he kicked your asses! Over here! Over here!"

21

Right about the time that Ms. Rake was coming to terms with her rather complicated feelings for Mr. Mead outside Pfaehler Library—her and two hundred security guards--Jonathan Tollhausler was, coincidentally, doing the very same thing inside. However, it was not his relationship with Richard Mead that was in question—as far as he knew things between them were solid-- but rather his on again, off again romance with Groucho Marx.

Standing in the library's fiction section, oblivious of the brouhaha unfolding four stories below, Tollhausler, his hands filled with two, bulging plastic trash bags, was wondering if perhaps he shouldn't stop on the way out and grab a copy of the Groucho Letters.

As in any relationship, he and Groucho had had their ups and downs, Tollhausler would be the first to admit that, but in the end, he had always found himself returning to the dead comedian. Was it the epigrams? Groucho's amazing delivery? Mr. Marx's disdain for all things pretentious? The greasepaint moustache? Jonathan couldn't say, but, and it wasn't the first time, he certainly wouldn't have minded being Captain Spaulding—at least for a day.

And, despite repeated warnings from the United States Postal Service and the Federal Bureau of Investigation to the contrary, how better to get to know a person than to read their mail?

That settled, Jonathan didn't waste another second. He promptly kicked open the door to the stairs.

He wasn't leaving until he had a copy of the <u>Groucho Letters</u> in his possession, and, pausing only long enough to draw breath, launched into a song Groucho had made famous in the movie <u>At The Circus</u>:

> "Oh Lydia, Oh Lydia,
> Now have you met Lydia…"

He was halfway down the steps when someone ran on to landing below.

> "Oh Lydia the taaa-ttooed lady—"

"Jonathan?!"

Tollhausler grinned. "Diane!"

She rushed over to the tempered glass enclosing the stairwell. "You shouldn't be here."

He gently rested his bags on the metal floor. "Aw shucks. I'm glad to see you too."

"I'm sorry. It's just—" She continued looking down at something. "What are you doing here, anyway?"

"Stealing books. It's my way of saying thanks to the university for having such a great collection." He couldn't help noticing Diane was in a bit of a state. "And what are you doing here?"

She pushed away from the glass. "Trying to help you."

"All right, this bag on the right isn't too heavy."

"No no no. Don't you understand?! There are guards downstairs."

He snorted. "Well I don't think *they're* going to want to help."

She shuddered. "*This is no time for jokes.*"

This effectively stopped Tollhausler in mid-Groucho. For a split second, he had even considered responding with one of the three stock responses he had reserved for this particular rebuke, but he suddenly realized Diane, despite her behavior, was not Margaret Dumont and this was not a movie.

And if he were going to win Diane's heart, he knew he could not be Groucho. Something he had been constantly reminding himself the last couple of months. So Tollhausler did something he didn't ordinarily like to do--but had been doing ever since he had met Diane--he shut up.

"Don't you understand?" She was very upset. "They'll find you."

He didn't know where he found the nerve, but he reached out and took Diane in his arms. "Who?"

"The guards," she sighed, and relaxed a little as she leaned against him.

"Ahhh," he said, pulling her close, "they'll never take me alive."

They stood together for a moment.

"How do you know they're after me anyway?"

Diane smoothed his red and white scarf. "It's a long story."

"Does it have a happy ending?"

Diane suddenly remembered where they were and why. "Oh Jonathan, why did you have to come here?"

"I just stopped by to pick up a couple of things." He glanced over at the trash bags. "But the selection here is so good, I wound up stealing *much* more than I intended."

"I thought I bought you the time you needed to get away."

"And I got something for you as well!" he chirped, and started rummaging through the bag to his left.

Diane was astonished. "Jonathan, don't you understand?! *The guards're right downstairs.*"

"Don't worry." He continued sorting. "If I know my Rudyard Guards, and I must since I've been going here for over twenty years now, they won't make a move until after they've finished their coffee."

"How did you know they were drinking coffee?"

He chuckled. "They're *always* drinking coffee."

"Jonathan, I don't think you know what's really going on here. Those guards are furious. I've been chased around by some of them. They mean business."

"Well," Tollhausler began, unable to ignore a set-up like that, "they certainly don't mean security."

Diane's eyes shut, her reaction to his joke, and she took a deep breath. "Have you even considered how you're going to get off campus?"

"The usual way." Tollhausler pulled out a blue book and studied its binding. "Turn left at the Student Center and head for the el."

She sighed. "Jonathan, that'll never work."

"Oh really?!" He had unknowingly reverted back to Groucho. "Well I'll have you know I've made it home plenty of times before that way. Just ask my parents."

"*No no no.*" She put a hand to her head. "I mean it isn't going to work today. Every guard on campus is looking for you." She closed her eyes again. "Why did you do it, anyway?"

"Do what?"

"Hold a protest in Financial Aid."

"Hold a protest?" Tollhausler snickered. "What are you talking about? There wasn't any protest. I was just trying to find my loan check."

Her eyes snapped open. "You mean you went into the Financial Aid Office and started all this...this *trouble*, shutting down the entire university, simply because they *couldn't find your loan check*?!"

He laughed. "You should have seen what I did the semester they misplaced the paperwork to my grant."

22

The sound of their conversation had been steadily tumbling down the three flights of steps to the ground floor of Pfaehler Library since Tollhausler had first called out Diane's name, and while the guards stationed there had been perfectly willing to ignore their presence—all students had been ordered out of the building over a half an hour ago—they were distressed by the turn in tone the discussion had now taken.

"Ah, see," observed the guard on the left, "now they're fighting."

The other guard looked back. "Why can't they just take it off the stairs? It would be a lot easier to forget they were there."

"College students, Officer Knox, college students." The guard on the left drained his cup. "They're always in such a hurry. He sang to her, probably hugged and kissed her, but now he's done something he shouldn't have. Moving a little too fast is my guess. Why do you think this place is such a mess? None of these kids knows how to wait."

His partner also downed his coffee. "Well I'm going up there and throw them out. That'll solve everyone's problem."

However, it was immediately after they had disposed of their coffee cups that the doors to the rear exit banged open and a troop of guards came rushing in with Richard Mead and Holly Rake.

23

The resulting din thundered from floor to floor of the empty library, flushing out the gentleman whose arrest earlier had sparked the riot outside Sheldrake Hall.

"Diane, what's going on?" he whispered. "What's all that noise?"

She and Tollhausler turned.

Seeing Tollhausler, he stumbled on to the landing. "It's you!"

Tollhausler didn't miss a beat. "Gesundheit."

Having both Tollhausler and Phil Tendon (For that was indeed who it was) in such close proximity, Diane could see how easy it had been for her—and the guards—to have gotten the two confused: they were practically twins.

Phil stood in the center of the landing. "Up until now it's been a minor inconvenience being mistaken for you, but this, this is too much."

"Is it?" With Tollhausler's thoughts focused, understandably, wholly on Diane, he had absolutely no idea what Phil was talking about, but he could see that Phil was definitely sincere.

"Having angry people periodically confront me about something you did or said is bad enough, but today...today...this is too much. You've turned my life upside down. Why now I'm nothing more than a common criminal. A...a *fugitive from the law.*"

Tollhausler reached into one of his bags. "Here, have a book."

Phil stared down at a copy of <u>A Tale of Two Cities.</u> "Do you *actually think* this...this *book*, is going to make up for everything you've put me through today?!"

"No," Tollhausler said, pushing his glasses back, "but I thought it might shut you up for a couple of minutes."

Phil threw the book aside and grabbed Tollhausler by the coat. *"I'll shut you up!"*

"How dare you," Tollhausler shouted. "I *did not* break your new rattle."

Diane and Phil followed Tollhausler in off the landing.

"Who do you think you are anyway," Tollhausler demanded. He deposited his trash bags next to a table. "Blaming

351

this all on me. Just because we happen to share a slight resemblance. Why I'll have you know I showed up here years before you did looking like me and I didn't have a lick of trouble."

Phil opened his mouth to speak, but Tollhausler kept talking.

"Which, I must admit, was a bit of a disappointment. A man in his twenties is always on the lookout for the opportunity to get licked." He walked over to a shelf of books. "Pfff. You don't even look all that much like me anyway."

Phil threw his coat off on to a chair. "I don't *want* to look like you."

"Well neither do I, but you've gotta' look like somebody in this world. It's either that or just blend in."

Phil corrected himself. "I mean, I *don't* look like you."

Tollhausler reappeared. "You know why? Because you're always frowning. Am I always frowning? Some days. But other days, I manage to crack a smile or even laugh out loud. You, you always look miserable. And why? Because you think being serious means you have to walk around campus all day looking like you have a toothache."

"I do not always walk around looking like I have a toothache."

"That's true. Sometimes you look like you've just swallowed a bug."

"Oh shut up."

"Phil, please…" Diane laid her coat on the edge of the table. "….it isn't his fault. I'm the one you should be mad at. You're mixed up in this because I thought you were him at first."

"Outside Sheldrake Hall?"

"Yes."

"I don't understand. I thought you helped me because you knew I wasn't him." Feeling very confused now—and slightly dizzy—Phil slumped into a chair beside the table. "Because you know him and could see the guards were arresting the wrong person."

She leaned on the back of the chair. "No, I wanted to rescue him, but I realized after we'd escaped that you weren't who I thought you were. I was a little out of it and...I'm sorry."

"You should be." Tollhausler was skimming the M's. "He doesn't look anything like me."

"Jonathan."

Phil removed his glasses and squeezed the bridge of his nose. "Then why did you keep leading me away? I probably could have cleared this up on the spot."

Tollhausler slid a copy of the Groucho Letters off the shelf. "Because then the guards would have kept looking for me instead of chasing after you, and I wouldn't have gotten away."

Phil replaced his glasses. "What?"

Diane wished Tollhausler didn't always have such a big mouth. "Phil, I'm sorry."

He threw up his hands and slapped them against his thighs. "Oh great, you're sorry. But that doesn't change the fact that there are still two thousand security guards out there searching for me. Because they think I'm *that* idiot."

Tollhausler tossed the book into one of his bags. "If the university doesn't hold my SAT scores against me, I see no reason why you should."

Phil stood up and yanked his coat off the chair. "Idiot."

"That's idiot savant to you."

"So you're going." Diane felt terrible about what she had done.

"Yes." Phil punched his arm into the sleeve of his coat. "So I can try to explain this to the guards. Hopefully I'll get the chance before they beat me up."

"Of course they'll give you the chance," Tollhausler said. "This is America, darn it. The police always let you say a few words before they beat you up."

"Good bye."

He stomped off, and Diane followed.

"Phil, wait. Maybe there's a better way."

"Then him getting beat up? I hope not."

"*Jonathan.*"

Tollhausler shrugged. "He seems to have his heart set on it."

"He's the one who should have to go out there." Phil thrust his arm into his other sleeve. "I was going to be on the Dean's List this semester too."

"So you'll get the coupon next semester."

Phil glared at Tollhausler. "The what?!"

"The coupon. For the free slice of pizza and a soda." He looked at Diane. "Mead told me that's what you get when you make the Dean's List."

"Jonathan, you don't get a coupon."

"What do you get?"

"The university sends you a letter and your name's recorded on a list."

"That's it?" He was disappointed. "Not even a t-shirt?"

She shook her head. "Not even a t-shirt."

"Then what's the big deal?"

Phil grimaced. "You must be some student." He walked off.

"Phil wait." Diane put a hand on Tollhausler's shoulder. "We can't let him leave."

Tollhausler grinned. "You mean we'll have to *kill* him?!"

"*Jonathan.*"

Phil paused at the door. "And don't worry. I won't tell the guards where you are. I don't know why. It'd certainly make things easier for me. But I won't."

"Maybe we can do something to help, so you won't have to deal with the guards at all."

"Like what?"

Diane looked at Tollhausler. "What's the best way to get out of here unnoticed?"

"Catapult?"

"Come on. Think. How were you planning to get out of here with all those books?"

Tollhausler shrugged. "Like I said, I was going to head for the nearest exit and run."

"That's not much of a plan. You'd get caught."

"I know. But I've been expecting to get caught all afternoon and haven't.."

This infuriated Phil no end. "Of all the people I could look like on this campus, it had to be a nut job like you." He headed for the landing.

"No, wait." Diane put a hand on Tollhausler's arm. "There must be something we can do."

"I could always go downstairs and turn myself in."

Diane brightened. "Or you could go downstairs and *lead the guards away.*"

Phil stopped with a hand on the door. "I like his idea better."

"Then he can escape in the confusion." Diane realized this would put Jonathan back on the run. "What do you think your chances are?"

"Great."

Her mood lightened. "Really? You think you'll be able to get away from the guards a second time?"

"Who cares?!" He grinned. "I was talking about my chances with you."

She threw her arms around him. "Jonathan, it's a pretty big thing you're doing."

"Why? Rudyard can't do anything to me. I'm dropping out."

Diane released him. "What?!"

"*Oh no.*" Phil crossed his arms. "A responsible student like you?"

Tollhausler could see he had taken Diane completely by surprise. "I was going to tell you."

She stared at the trash bags. "That's why you're stealing all those books."

"I realized today that I just can't do it anymore. I'm tired of jumping through the same hoops every couple of months."

Phil sneered. "Maybe if you had shown up here with more of a plan than 'I will go to college until I graduate,' you wouldn't feel that way."

"How did you know what my plan was?"

"It's a lot of people's plans."

"But Jonathan—"

"You're stunned."

She looked away. "Yes."

"But you've said it yourself: I don't belong here."

"Yes, I know, but…what are you going to do?"

"I'm not sure." He crossed his arms. "I'm considering taking a correspondence course in sheep herding. Or maybe I'll start my own religion." He put a hand to his chin. "Or figure a way of combining the two."

Diane stared into his eyes. "You're going to write, aren't you?"

"Ohhh, he's a writer, is he? That explains it. Going to write the Great American Novel, are we?"

Tollhausler shrugged. "Or the suckiest American novel. Book critics can't always beat up on Philip Roth and Stephen King you know. They don't turn out books every year."

Diane looked even more concerned now. "Are you sure you want to take such a big step?"

Tollhausler took her by the hand. "After hearing what you did for me outside Sheldrake Hall, I was going to ask you the same thing."

Diane smiled. "After much deliberation, I can truthfully say yes."

"Look, fascinated as I am by whatever the hell it is you two are talking about," Phil said from the doorway, "I'd really like to get out of here."

Tollhausler squeezed Diane's hand. "I look forward to talking to you about it later."

"Later?" Diane hurried back to the table. "I'm coming with." She collected her coat.

"What? And jeopardize your coupon for a free slice of pizza too?"

"I have to." She flapped into her coat. "They'll be looking for a man and a woman."

He followed after her. "Which one should I be?"

"You decide."

Tollhausler grinned. "You be the woman. You look so much better in boots than I do."

"Right."

They rushed on to the landing, and Phil thought it best to remind them he was still there. "So I'll give you about ten minutes. Do you think that'll be enough time?"

"Plenty," Tollhausler said as they disappeared down the steps.

"Ugh." Phil let the door close. He couldn't believe he was leaving his fate up to that...that... "Idiot," he grumbled, and glanced down at Tollhausler's trash bags. He suddenly thought of the brief case he had had to abandon outside Sheldrake Hall. "Because of *him*." He fished out a copy of <u>Les Miserables</u>.

Then Officer Knox materialized six feet away and watched as Phil dropped the book back into the bag. "Getting some books together for a term paper?"

Phil jumped. "What? Me? Oh, um..." His eyes plummeted to the trash bags. "....these? Ohhhhh, right. Well, um, see, these aren't actually..." He automatically gestured over his shoulder to the bags' absent owner. "....errrr, mine."

Knowing full well what this must have looked like to the guard, and how, if the situation were reversed, he wouldn't have believed a word that was said either, Phil instantly turned red.

"Tollhausler!"

24

Diane jumped.

Tollhausler stopped. "I guess he misses me already."

Diane looked back. "We'd better keep moving."

"Let's go in here." Tollhausler pushed open a door to his right.

"I thought we were supposed to let the guards see us."

"See us. Not catch us."

"Ohh-kay." Diane went in.

She was a little out of breath and so was he.

A loud clunk stopped them in their tracks, Tollhausler bumping right into her, and they stood together, motionless, by a water fountain on the wall.

"Was that a door," Diane whispered, but Tollhausler wasn't listening. He was too distracted by the warm sensation of her body pressed against his. He breathed in the fragrance of her hair. "*Aaa-dore.*"

"Jonathan." She turned. "This is no time for—"

He pulled her close. "Oh yes it is."

25

Downstairs, Sergeant Rob Slade, tired of yelling and his patience just about run out, stepped in front of the library's card catalog, stretched to his full height of five foot six and held up two hands. "You people are going to have to keep quiet or you'll have to leave."

Despite the repeated efforts by the guards to keep as many students out of the library as they could, the first floor was rapidly becoming as crowded and noisy as the grounds outside.

Those men and women who had witnessed Holly Rake's outburst, curious to find out if what she was saying was true, would not be turned away, and the people who had watched security escort Johnny Mennon and Ernie Turpin through the front doors were equally determined. They were expecting quite a show.

The guards were not surprised.

How could they be? They had known these two were going to be trouble the moment they laid eyes on them. The fact that Mennon was dressed as a security guard didn't make things easy, and it helped even less that Turpin was, inexplicably, wrapped in the robes of the Archbishop of Canterbury—although nobody knew exactly what he was supposed to be at the time.

And kettledrums. For some reason, the Archbishop was chasing the fake guard around a pair of kettledrums with a crosier.

"Come on folks," Slade said. "Let's move it back, give us some room here."

He was worried. The body of students had grown to such proportions that it had already wrapped around itself once in the space separating the library's main information desk from the front door, and if a big enough segment decided they wanted to liberate any or all of their suspects, they would find it easy to do. His mental state was such that he practically jumped when he heard Holly raise her voice.

"Is that it?!"

Holly scowled—at as many people as she could—and the men and women five feet away fell silent.

"We've got your names," Sergeant Shirley Waters explained, "and if security goes forward with an investigation, you'll both be contacted."

Holly was incredulous. "Then why did you even bother bringing us in here?"

"You were causing quite a commotion, Miss." Sergeant Waters folded her notebook shut. "We were worried that someone might get hurt if we didn't intervene."

"But he started the riot in Marner Hall."

Waters calmly slid her pad into her pocket. "I'm sure he did, Miss."

"Don't you at least want to take him in for identification?"

"Would that show him?"

"What?"

"Not to do whatever it was he did again?"

"What are you talking about?"

"Miss, please, do you think you're the first person this afternoon who wanted to get even with someone and reported they had something to do with the riot?"

"But he really did," Holly whined.

"I'm sure after you two make up, you're going to remember he was with you the entire time."

"No I'm not. I'll sign a statement to that effect if you want."

"Miss, I don't know what your boyfriend here did, but in a couple of hours, it isn't going to seem bad enough to have him hauled away."

Holly looked at Rich for help. "I am *not* making this up."

"She's right," Rich confirmed, shrugging and nodding at the same time, "I did...start the riot in Marner Hall."

Waters felt vindicated. "See Miss? He's already trying to make it up to you." She zipped her pocket closed. "He doesn't want you to get into trouble. So why don't you two go somewhere and see if maybe you can't work this out on your own? It'll make everyone's life a lot easier."

Holly was astonished. Even with her tip and Rich's confession, the guards seemed reluctant to do much of anything except let him go.

Out of her life.

Suddenly overcome, Holly looked at Waters and the rest of the guards. "Fine! Let him go. Lord knows you've done everything you could to get to the bottom of this." She could feel herself about to cry. "Have a nice life Rich," she managed to get out, choking up, and stomped off. The wall of people opened to allow her through.

"Geez, what's wrong with her?" Mennon called from across the room, and Mead gestured over his shoulder with a thumb. "We just broke up."

"Again?"

362

Mead moved towards Mennon. "Again."

"Aren't you going after her," Waters asked.

He looked back. "Me? No. I couldn't." Rich gazed in the direction Holly had gone. "I mean, I just broke up with her. It wouldn't be right."

"She's pretty upset about it."

"Oh, so am I." However, Rich appeared more relieved at the moment than anything else. "Maybe I should have been a gentleman and let her break up with me."

"What?"

"I said 'Maybe I should have been a gentleman and let her break up with me.'"

Mennon excused himself through the people separating him and Rich. "Well how long were you gonna' wait? Christmas is right around the corner, you know. If you waited too long, you might have wound up on New Year's Eve without a date."

"I'm sure she was waiting to see what I got her for Christmas. That always helps a woman make up her mind."

"That's why I always break up with them before Christmas. When you see as many girls as I do, that can run into some real money."

"You two know each other," Waters observed, and Rich looked away. "In truth, I do confess to share a common history with the man."

"Very interesting."

"Will you people please move back?" Sergeant Slade stomped over to Mennon. "What do you think you're doing?!"

"Having a visit."

Slade looked at Waters. "They know each other?"

She nodded and, connecting the dots, Slade immediately reached for his walkie-talkie. Waters looked over at Turpin. "You know him too?"

Mennon scowled. "Yeah, I know that son-of-a-"

It was right then and there that a gloved hand shot out from behind Ernie and clamped onto his left ear.

26

"Ernie Arthur Turpin."

Ernie immediately frowned. "Who told you my middle name?"

Susan Kahn moved closer. "I tricked your mother into telling me Thanksgiving."

"How'd you do that?"

"I asked her to pass the salt, and half an hour later, I knew more about you than any woman should ever know about her boyfriend."

Ernie laughed. "Well that's your own fault. I told you there's no stopping her once she gets started."

The security guard standing in front of Ernie turned and sprang into action. He lowered his coffee. "Whoa there now miss. Stop that."

Susan shook her head. "He was about to make a break for it."

Officer Weshensky studied Ernie. "Were you?"

Grinning, Ernie vigorously shook his head and Susan's arm bounced up and down.

Weshensky hadn't been expecting the truth. "Oh. Well then, Miss, I guess I owe you a big thanks. But now that I know, could you please let him go?"

Susan relinquished Ernie's ear. "I bet you wish you could do that to all the students."

"It certainly looks effective. Now what's this all about, anyway?"

Susan crossed her arms. "I don't see where that would be any of your business."

"Oh you don't, do you?" Weshensky's entire body stiffened. "Well I don't know if you know this, but the Pope here..." He pointed at Mennon. "....and that guy in the security guard outfit over there, the one with the maraca in his holster, are in a lot of trouble. They were fighting right outside in the middle of the sidewalk."

Susan assumed her most innocent expression. "Well where are they supposed to be fighting?"

Weshensky winced. "They aren't supposed to be fighting at all."

"Ohhhhhhh." Susan looked down, then up and then down again. "Well couldn't you just..." She bit her bottom lip. "....let the padre here off with a warning?"

"It isn't that simple Miss."

Susan quickly dropped the coquette act and locked her eyes on Weshensky. "Ernie, wouldn't it be nice for a change to run into a security guard who *didn't* think the fate of the entire known world depended on their taking you in? Which they never do anyway."

"I do not think the fate of the entire known world depends on taking him in," countered Weshensky. "It's just that I'm not going to let somebody dressed like this go without first asking him a couple of questions. Especially on a day like today."

"Oh I see. All you guards are under the gun this afternoon to arrest someone, so out of all the people running around campus setting trash cans on fire and breaking windows, you figured you'd save yourself the trouble and arrest the guy in the Pope suit."

Weshensky's expression went blank. "You can read this situation anyway you'd like, Miss, but I'm still taking this guy in."

"Weshensky, Larimor," Slade barked, and Weshensky pointed at Ernie. "I'll be right back."

"Aren't you cold in that get-up," Susan asked, and Ernie glanced down. "No, it's actually—"

She punched him on the arm. "You know I've been looking all over for you."

The men and women across from them started to laugh.

Susan hit Ernie again. "And Portia Sinclair just came running up and told me she saw you and Johnny over here fighting."

Ernie straightened his miter. "Hey, go easy there. When you're punching me you're punching God you know."

"Forgive me Father for I am pissed." Susan struck Ernie a third time and pulled him close. "Where have you been? I started to get a little worried when you didn't turn up at the cafeteria at the usual time, you know, during that class you hate, but after we heard about Marner Hall, and the other guys didn't show, we figured the four of you had been carted off with everybody else."

Noticing how interested the guards standing to their left had become at the mention of the words "Marner Hall," Ernie gestured to them with his head; then he frantically shook it.

Susan frowned at Officers Mundy and Jenkins, and spun Ernie in the opposite direction. "People have been telling me," she whispered, "how you've been running around campus all afternoon. And when I heard that, I said to myself, it couldn't possibly be Ernie. Why—I kept telling myself—Ernie would have at least taken time out from his laps to stop by and at least tell me he was all right. Right?"

In a shameless attempt to change the subject, Ernie moved in for a kiss, but Susan stopped him cold by grabbing his chin. "Because don't you think it would have been pretty thoughtless of you to leave me worrying like that if it could have been avoided?"

Ernie nodded, but it wasn't very convincing. To be fair, however, Susan did have his chin gripped in her hand.

"Somebody even told me," she announced, releasing him, "they saw you roller skating around Sellars Hall earlier, but I thought, that's crazy. Ernie doesn't even own a pair of roller skates."

Ernie was suddenly glad he had removed them when he had changed out of his Sherlock Holmes costume.

"Roller skates?" Officer Mundy said, and Susan looked over her shoulder at him. She drew Ernie forward. "But now, after finding you here playing dress-up, I'm not so sure." She was about to say something else when she stopped and stared at something. "Ernie, what're those?"

He glanced over at what she was looking at. "You mean the kettledrums?"

"Yes. The kettledrums." She took a deep breath. "I was just wondering if they were yours."

"Well Susan, you know I don't own any drums."

"Which would explain why I would find it particularly interesting if a pair that large turned up in your possession."

"Oh."

"*Are* they yours?"

He smiled. "No," he confidently replied, "they are not."

Susan wasn't a hundred percent convinced. "So you don't know anything about them."

"I didn't say that."

She closed her eyes. "Where," she said in a quiet, even tone, as if one more response like that would move her to physical violence, "did they come from?"

Ernie glanced back at the guards two feet away. "The, uh, usual place."

"The usual--?" She also peered at the guards. "You mean you *stole them*?!"

27

The buzz of conversation that followed was not in response to this latest revelation—not everyone had heard it--but to the spectacle of Phil Tendon, Jonathan Tollhausler, Diane Curzewski and eight guards exiting from the stairwell.

Phil was at the head of the procession. "....understand your position. So Tollhausler, could you please tell these guards I'm not with you?"

Tollhausler chuckled. "Sure." He looked at the officer clamped to Phil's right arm. "He isn't with us."

The guard's grip, predictably, did not loosen on Phil's arm. "Uh-huh." He pushed him along.

Tollhausler giggled. "Well you can't say I didn't try."

"All right, all right." Phil stopped, as did everyone else. "Then could you at least tell them I wasn't the one stealing books? That it was you?"

Tollhausler couldn't believe how naïve Phil was, expecting him to cop to something like that; and he responded as only someone in this situation would--especially someone who knew there was no possible way the guards could connect him with the stolen books. "Stealing books?! What are you talking about? Why I would never—" Tollhausler made sure everyone could hear his outrage. "For shame Phil! Now I know what happened to the library's copy of the Story of O! You stole it! And me with only a couple of chapters left to go too. Now I'll never know if O gets dressed."

"Keep moving." The guards awkwardly dragged their charges through the crowd.

"You've gotta' believe me. I didn't have a thing to do with any of this." Phil looked at Diane. "She's the one who got me involved. To protect her boyfriend there."

"Protect her boyfriend?!" Tollhausler frowned. "What are you talking about? He isn't even here."

The guards deposited Diane, Phil and Tollhausler in the ring where Mead, Mennon, Turpin and Susan were now standing.

"Hi Diane," Rich said.

Mennon smiled. "Hey Diane."

Susan frowned. "They got you mixed up in this too?"

Ernie simply smiled and waved, and Diane tried to fathom how they could all be so casual about this.

Tollhausler didn't say anything either. He simply took in his surroundings: Mennon, Turpin, Mead, Susan, the guards, the students jamming the room, and after a very long pause, he snickered. "I thought we were supposed to meet *behind* the library."

Rich was surprised. "You didn't go there, did you?"

"I was going to, but these guards had other ideas." He smiled at Diane. "And so did she."

Diane blushed. "*Jonathan...*"

Tollhausler looked at Mennon. "Is that where they caught you and the padre?"

Mead frowned. "Of course not. Why would he show up behind the library? Just because it was his idea?"

Mennon grimaced. "I was busy."

"Stealing drums," Susan grumbled. "Why did you steal them in the first place?"

Mennon removed his cap. "We didn't steal them in the first place." He smoothed down his hair. "The first place only had a piano."

28

All conversation ceased the following second when a nicotine-cured voice boomed along the high ceiling above. "Will you people please move out of the way?"

Everyone who heard this, and there weren't many people who didn't, immediately searched the room to see where this confident, rumbling voice was coming from, and, coincidentally, that was when a path opened up before a hulking soda machine of a man.

"Lieutenant Rostropovich," the guards standing beside Tollhausler mumbled. Then they, along with the other guards in the circle, snapped to attention.

Rostropovich stopped and immediately disapproved of what he saw. "I want a line of guards running that way," he told the officer standing next to him, holding aloft a rectangle of a hand in the direction of the main information desk, "and another line running that way." The hand chopped through the air towards the front door. "We need to be a little more organized here." He glared at Slade, Weshensky and Larimor. "Stop standing around like you're waiting for someone to ask you to dance."

The guards instantly moved, and Mennon nudged Tollhausler with his elbow. "Here come the marines."

Rostropovich took one mighty step closer and rested a pair of box-like fists on his hips. He took in the line-up of suspects and his steely eyes eventually fell on Ernie. "And what do we have here?"

Tollhausler took a step forward. "What? You mean you don't know?! You've got a pretty blonde, a guy dressed like the pope, his girlfriend, the Duchess of Kircaldy, my twin, a guy masquerading as a security guard, Richard Mead, and, to top it all off, kettledrums. I'll tell you what you've got here. Either the second act of a failed Kaufman and Hart play or a chapter straight out of Lewis Carroll's trash can."

Rostropovich looked at Slade. "Good. We've got the guy with the mouth."

Tollhausler grinned. "Now if you start talking about my big blue eyes I'll positively blush."

Rostropovich stared at Phil. "And now we know how he was able to run us all over the place. Like there were two of him. There *are* two of him."

"You're lucky." Tollhausler adjusted his glasses. "There's another guy who looks like us too, but he called out sick today."

"Very funny."

Phil stomped forward. "Look, I am *not* with these drop-outs."

Mennon chuckled. "You are now."

Mead moved next to Tollhausler. "*My name?!* That's the best you could do?"

Tollhausler shrugged. "That Duchess of Kircaldy reference took a lot out of me."

"That'll teach me to wear regular clothes on dress-up day."

Rostropovich stared at them. "And what do you think you two're doing?! Get back there."

"Oh do I have to?" Tollhausler asked. "I stick out like a sore thumb standing next to that guy in the robes. Or can I run over to the theater department and pick out a costume too?"

372

"Get over there," Rostropovich repeated, and Rich crossed his arms. "I don't have to listen to you. As of a couple of hours ago, I'm no longer a student here. I dropped out."

"Ohhh." Rostropovich turned to Slade. "He dropped out." He snickered. "You think that's the first time someone told me that today? If everyone drops out who says they are, this is going to be one empty campus."

Rich smirked. "You make it sound like you're gonna' miss us."

"Like a kidney stone." Rostropovich folded his angular arms into a rectangle. "I'm just wondering how everyone's parents are going to react once they hear about it."

"Well—"

Rostropovich leaned forward, his heavy, square torso blocking out the other side of the room. "I'll tell you: They'll be none too pleased. They don't want you dropping out. They still think school is important."

"That's because a lot of them never went," noted Tollhausler.

"Or dropped out before they graduated and regret it now," Rich continued. "Either way, they have no idea what college is like today."

"Ohhh, you got it so rough." Rostropovich took a step back. "Nobody said you had to go to college."

Rich and Jonathan laughed. "What are you talking about?! *Everybody* said we had to go."

Rostropovich frowned at Mead. "Well what difference does it make now? You're dropping out. Remember? And soon you'll have the pleasure of dealing with the forty hour work week."

A guard walked up and handed Rostropovich a blue and white container. "Thanks, er…" Rostropovich struggled to come up with the right name. "….Sinclair." Rostropovich carefully removed the top of the container and examined the inky contents within. "Yeah, and after you've been doing that a while, let me know what you think of Rudyard then."

Rich rolled his eyes. "I guess us kids just don't know how good we've got it."

"You got that right." Rostropovich took a sip. "But I'm going to make a little prediction. After they see tonight's news, I'm sure most of your folks'll be sympathetic and let you sit out the rest of the week. But come Monday morning, as sure as I'm standing here, you're all going to be back in class—hoping you didn't tell too many of your friends how you were dropping out."

He pointed across the room. "Now get back over there with your drop-out friends or—"

Phil Tendon stomped his foot. "I am *not* dropping out."

Mennon lit a cigarette. "Neither am I."

"And neither am I," Tollhausler announced, prompting Diane to speak. "What?"

"That's right." He laughed. "I've decided to go on strike instead. That way, I'll still be able to hold on to my Financial Aid."

Mennon exhaled some smoke. "If they ever find it."

"If they ever find it."

"Strike?!" Rostropovich seemed to shrink a couple of inches.

"Strike!"

The word was suddenly on the lips of every student in the building; then being spoken by every student in the street.

29

Approximately one mile away, in the basement of a nondescript building located on the southeast border of the Rudyard University campus, a small green wheel in a large black cabinet completed its rotation for the day, buzzed, and the parallel rows of switches below mechanically snapped to the left. They were connected to a network of exterior lights that lit the streets and malls for miles around, and the campus was bathed in a dull glow as those lights that hadn't burnt out or malfunctioned hummed into life.

Four of these lights, mounted on the base of the only statue in Rayzberrisch Square, steadily grew brighter. They highlighted the contours and depths of the jagged, metal sculpture (An original piece by Josef Rayzberrisch, commissioned by the class of 1973, entitled "Progress Excretes.") above, as well as the woman standing below.

"Strike?" Action News correspondent Lindsay Foster Nolan-Greco repeated.

Audrey Thomas nodded. "That's right. We, the Student Body of Rudyard University, are calling a general strike. Why should the guards and teachers be the only ones allowed to go out? None of them: not the university, the teachers or the guards would be here without us. We pay their salaries, but we're constantly being taken for granted. They act as if we'll always be here, no matter what. Well guess what? Thanks to one student, our protests are finally going to be heard, once and for all."

Audrey turned, displaying her patrician profile to the bank of photographers and camera crews located to her right, and threw a hand straight up into the air. "Everyone! Listen! We don't need a university-controlled rally to speak our minds. Tell your friends! Tonight, we'll meet outside Biddle Hall. Tomorrow, we'll fill the streets with picket signs! Let's make sure Ralph Garibaldi and the Board of Directors, the entire world, knows exactly what we want! What they need to do in order to win us back!"

The assembled undergraduates started shouting. "Strike! Strike!"

"Because Rudyard University Students," Audrey intoned, "refuse to be ignored any longer! This is our school, not there's! And it's high time we took it back!"

"Strike! Strike! Strike!"

30

Lyle G. Adams was now having second thoughts.

"Jorge—"

Seated in a padded folding chair generally reserved for visiting students, he was aghast at the change his office had undergone the past hour.

"Jorge—"

There were half-eaten sandwiches and tall paper cups (Abandoned by various people who would come and go every five minutes.) lying everywhere, and Ron Isaacs had been on the phone almost nonstop since Adams had ushered him into his office.

"Jorge—"

Still, Professor Adams felt it was his duty to provide as much assistance as he could to the charismatic leader of the teachers' union.

Isaacs' frowned and held the phone directly in front of his mouth. *"Look Jorge."* He returned the phone to his ear. "For the last time, I understand there isn't much you can do right now with half your guys stationed across campus."

Lulu Fumo held up two ties for Frank Murphy to examine, and he casually pointed at the one on the left.

"Believe me, I understand."

Lulu started to loosen the yellow tie around Isaac's neck.

"All I want--" Isaacs tilted his head back. "All I want to get from you right now is your assurance that you're going to come out with us."

Lulu slid the tie from Isaacs' collar.

"Yes, every channel," he confirmed. "And they're telling me, barring anything big happening on the national front, like a nuclear blast, all three stations are going to lead with it at six o'clock."

Murphy lowered his sandwich. "It's going to be all over the papers tomorrow."

"I'm making the announcement as soon as the news crews are here." He nodded. "Downstairs in front of the statue of Emmanuel Brady." He listened to Jorge's reaction. "You know I've got to move fast Jorge, time is short. And the students don't walk out every day. Uh-hunh. That's what I'm trying to tell you. Opportunity knocks."

At first, Adams had been excited to be present at such an auspicious moment, the teachers finally voting to go on strike and all, but the feeling of triumph had not lasted. It had started to wane right after he had opened the door to his office. Once inside, a heated discussion had immediately broken out. However, it was not the result of any differing points of view about how best to proceed with the strike—Isaacs and the other union people seemed to be in complete accord about that—but about which food truck on campus made the best sandwiches. This was followed, to Adams' surprise, by a vote.

What little enthusiasm remained was soon crushed by the conversation that Isaacs and Murphy had next.

They had begun to talk, rather wistfully Adams thought, about which reporters they hoped would be assigned to the union's impromptu press conference. Not because of any admitted bias towards the teachers or due to any sympathetic coverage by these reporters in the past, but because both Isaacs and Murphy regarded certain female members of the press core comelier than others.

Adams was flabbergasted. He didn't know what exactly to make of these behind the scenes revelations, and found Isaacs' penchant to discourse at great length—and with such passion—on any topic, like meatball sandwiches or redheads, somewhat troubling. He was worried that someone from the university would know about it and keep Isaacs talking at the bargaining table, for days on end, about everything but the strike.

"The beauty Jorge is we've got them. What can Rudyard say? That both the students *and* the teachers are being unreasonable? I look forward to hearing that argument. And if security walks out too…"

Lulu carefully tightened the knot of the red tie around Isaacs' neck.

"You see my point." Isaacs stretched his neck above his collar. "The thing is, a united front is very important right now, and if we all go together, well, what can Garibaldi do?"

He strolled around Adams' desk.

"Well, between you and me, I'm a little uncomfortable throwing all my eggs in the same basket with the students anyway." He sat down in Adams' chair and instantly reacted to its worn, bent frame. "I have no control over what they're going to do." He arched his body in an attempt to get comfortable. "I'm trying to get in touch with that kid turning up all over the TV..."

"Audrey Thomas," Lulu offered.

"....Audrey Thomas, but I haven't had any luck so far. And even if I did, I don't think it'd be much help getting the students organized." Isaacs ran a finger along the inside of his collar. "And, since we are talking about Rudyard Students here, I suspect that some time tomorrow or Friday, after they've sobered up, the thrill of standing on a picket line, in these zero degree temperatures, will fall away." He nodded. "Yes, come Monday morning, the bulk of them will be back in class." He sat up. "Exactly. If you're on strike, it won't matter. The teachers and guards can stand firm."

He speared a meatball with a plastic fork and contemplated it as if it were more than just a meatball. He took a bite.

"That's right Jorge," he said, chewing, "with the campus surrounded by three different picket lines, it's going to be very difficult for the university to do any business. I doubt if anyone'll be confused about who's in charge then…"

DECEMBER 30, 1983:

"....money-grubbing, ACLU-backed lawyers..."

"With a Heavy Heart" University Closes Doors After 103 Years

By
Robert Weinberg &
Amy Sessions

Rudyard University, a 103-year-old Philadelphia institution, will officially close its doors today at 5 PM.

The university's Board of Directors made the surprising announcement back on the 12th of December, citing "financial difficulties" as the reason. At the time, the embattled university was swarming with students, teachers and guards holding picket signs. All three groups had recently gone on strike.

"It is with a heavy heart that we make this announcement," Kit Grayson, a longtime Board Member, stated at a press conference held at the Rudyard Alumni Club. "But the private consortium that owns Rudyard University has decided that, due to recent developments, it would be best if the university ceases any and all operations at the end of the month on Friday, December 30th, 1983."

He went on to explain how the university had been operating at a loss for some time, and that "thanks to Audrey Thomas and her team of money-grubbing, ACLU-backed lawyers freezing the students' tuition and Financial Aid" the university could no longer cover basic operating costs. "Regretfully, we have no other choice but to close down the school before our creditors do."

The decision to dismiss the President of the University, Ralph Garibaldi, was also made public at that time.

This news, however, was eclipsed by the announcement of the school's closing and the gargantuan task ahead of supplying its students with transcripts and the Financial Aid information needed to enroll elsewhere. The job was so big that the Rudyard Administration turned to a local Temp Agency (Johnny Friendly's Helping Hands Inc.) for assistance.

Area colleges such as Temple, Penn, St. Joe's, Penn State, Drexel and Villanova have all seen a surge in their enrollment.

The university grounds are already being divided up into parcels to be sold sometime at the beginning of 1984.

"We'll be sorry to see the university go," Eileen Matthews, a longtime neighbor of Rudyard University, said staring at the empty campus through the bay window of her modest row home. "It's been around for so long. But I guess if these old schools are losing money, they'll have to do something. It's just a pity that they're going to have to tear the whole thing down and start over. Still, most things change for the better, right?"

POP QUIZ ANSWERS

(1) D

(2) D

(3) D

(4) C

(5) C

(6) E

(7) D

(8) Who cares?

(9) C

(10) D

(11) E

(12) D

(13) A (He wasn't a complete idiot.)

(14) D

(15) D

(16) D

(17) C

(18) C

(19) D

(20) D (My, weren't there a lot of D's?!)

(21) B

CPSIA information can be obtained at www.ICGtesting.com
Printed in the USA
LVOW01s1248310813

350424LV00016B/694/P